The Do-Over

BY CONI YOVANINIZ AND RODRIGO VARGAS

CLARION BOOKS

IMPRINTS OF HARPERCOLLINS PUBLISHERS

HARPER
alley

CLARION BOOKS IS AN IMPRINT OF HARPERCOLLINS PUBLISHERS.
HARPERALLEY IS AN IMPRINT OF HARPERCOLLINS PUBLISHERS.

THE DO-OVER

 FOR INFORMATION ADDRESS HARPERCOLLINS CHILDREN'S BOOKS, A DIVISION OF HARPERCOLLINS PUBLISHERS, 195 BROADWAY, NEW YORK, NY 10007.
WWW.HARPERALLEY.COM

ISBN 978-0-35-839404-4 — ISBN 978-0-35-839405-1 (PBK.)

THE ARTIST PENCILLED WITH A 0.3 MECHANICAL PENCIL, INKED WITH ZEBRA BRUSH PENS AND UNI PIN FINELINERS, AND COLORED DIGITALLY IN ADOBE PHOTOSHOP.
LETTERING BY CINDY HARRIS
FLATTING ASSISTANCE BY DIEGO FREDES
DESIGN BY CELESTE KNUDSEN
23 24 25 26 27 GPS 10 9 8 7 6 5 4 3 2 1

FIRST EDITION

TO MAXI (THE BEST DOG IN THE WORLD), CHRISTIAN AGUILAR,
OUR FRIENDS, FAMILIES, AND ALL THE KIDS IN THE WORLD

—R.V. & C.Y.

CHAPTER 1

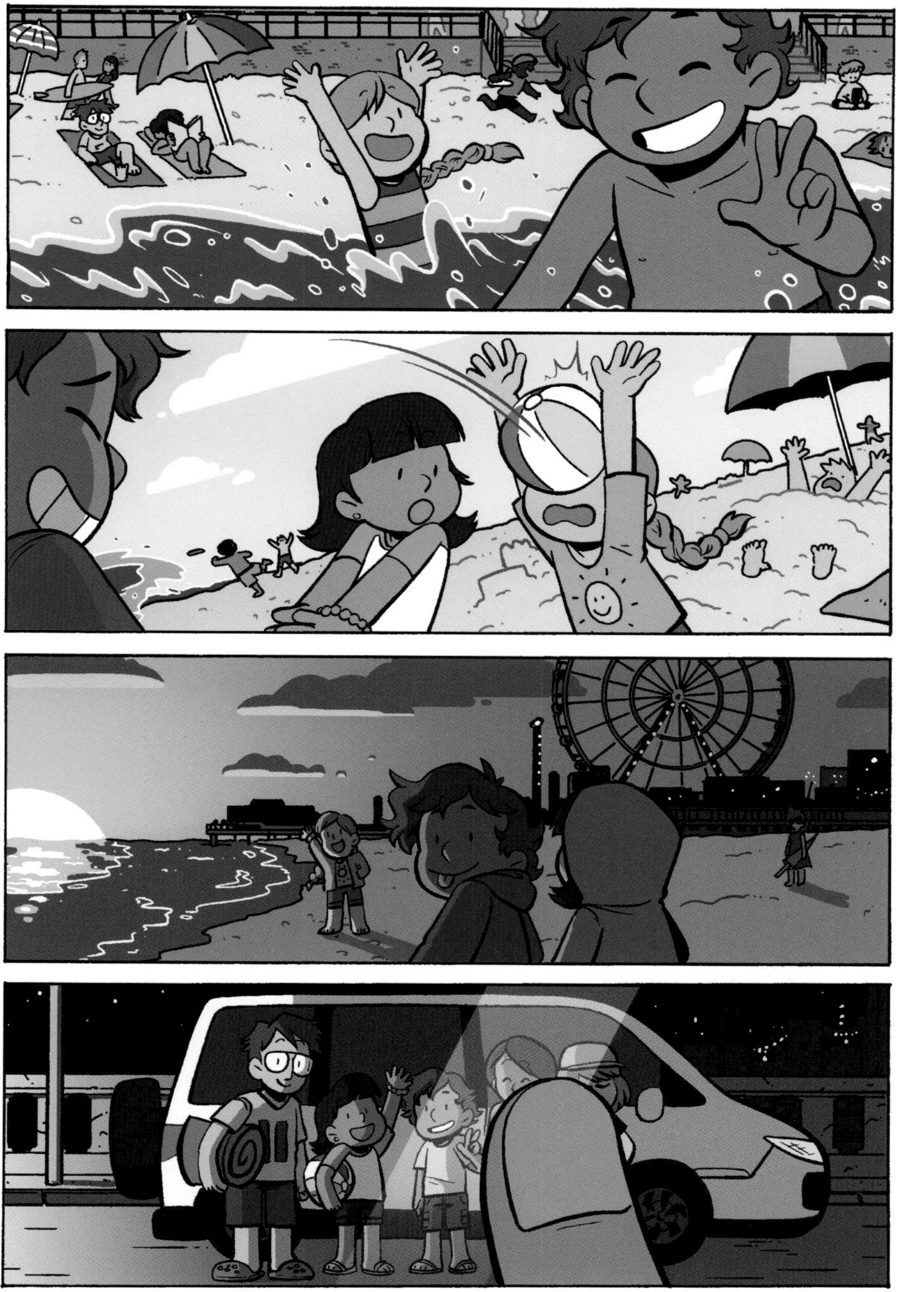

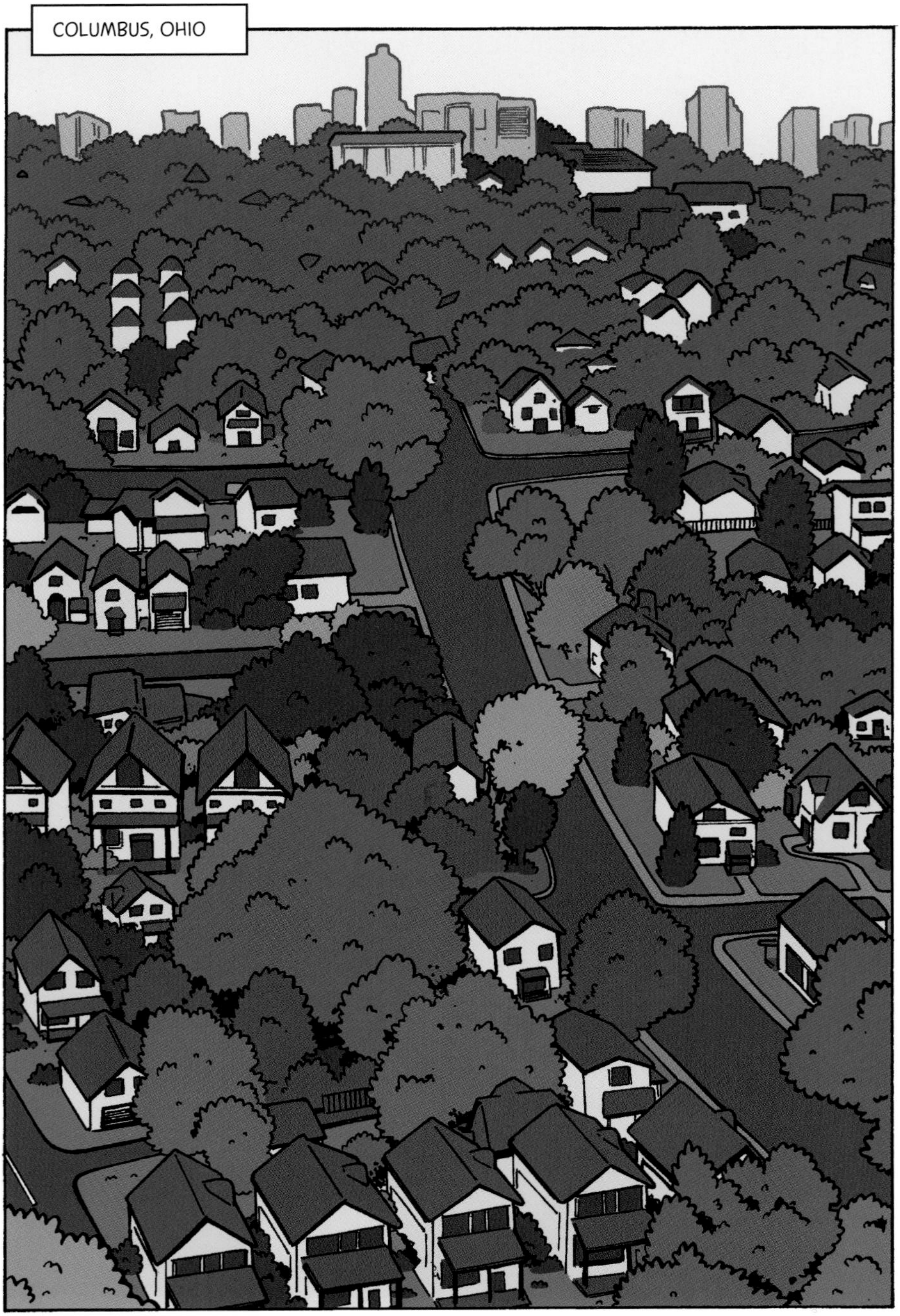
COLUMBUS, OHIO

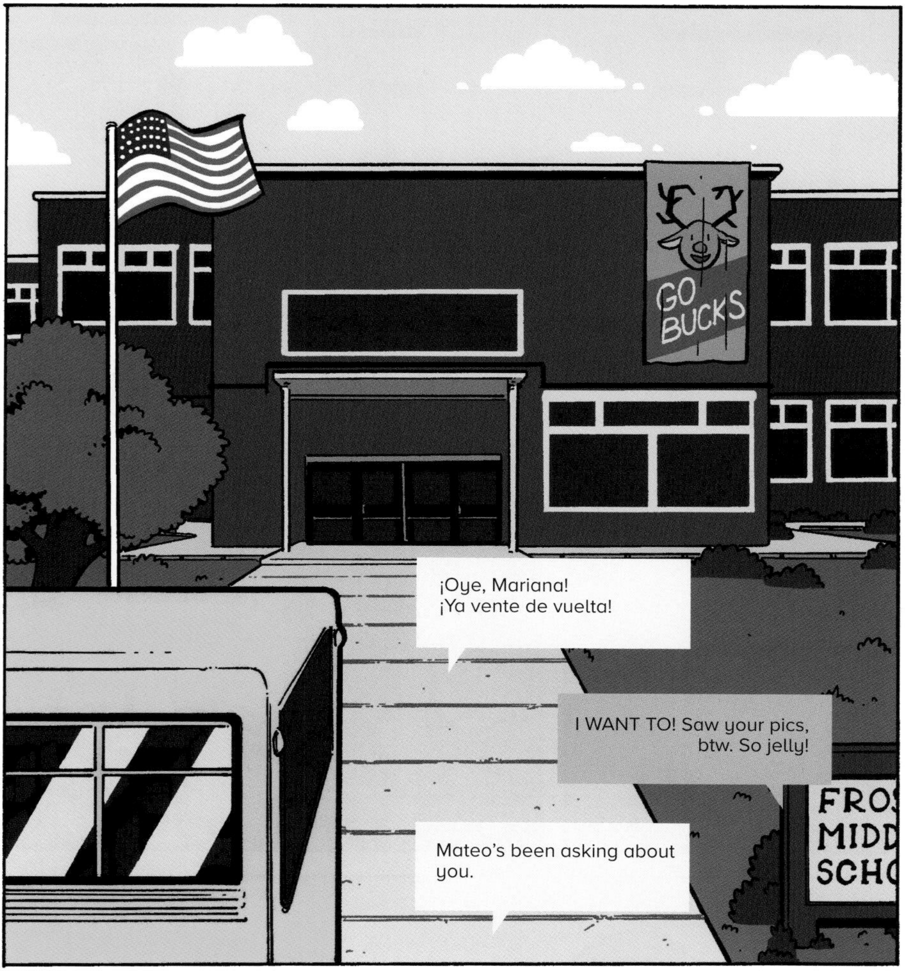
GO BUCKS
¡Oye, Mariana!
¡Ya vente de vuelta!
I WANT TO! Saw your pics, btw. So jelly!
Mateo's been asking about you.

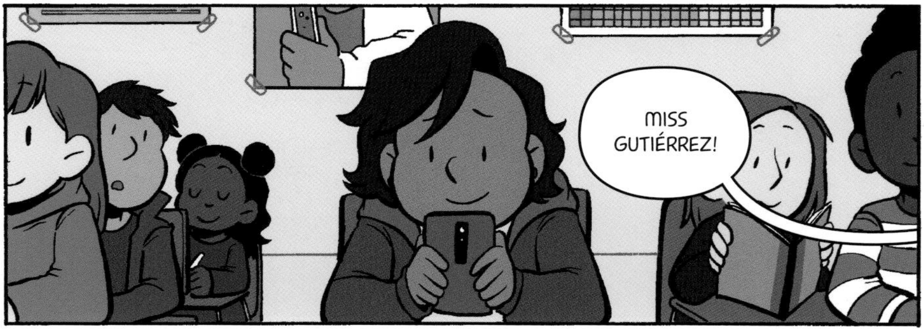
MISS GUTIÉRREZ!

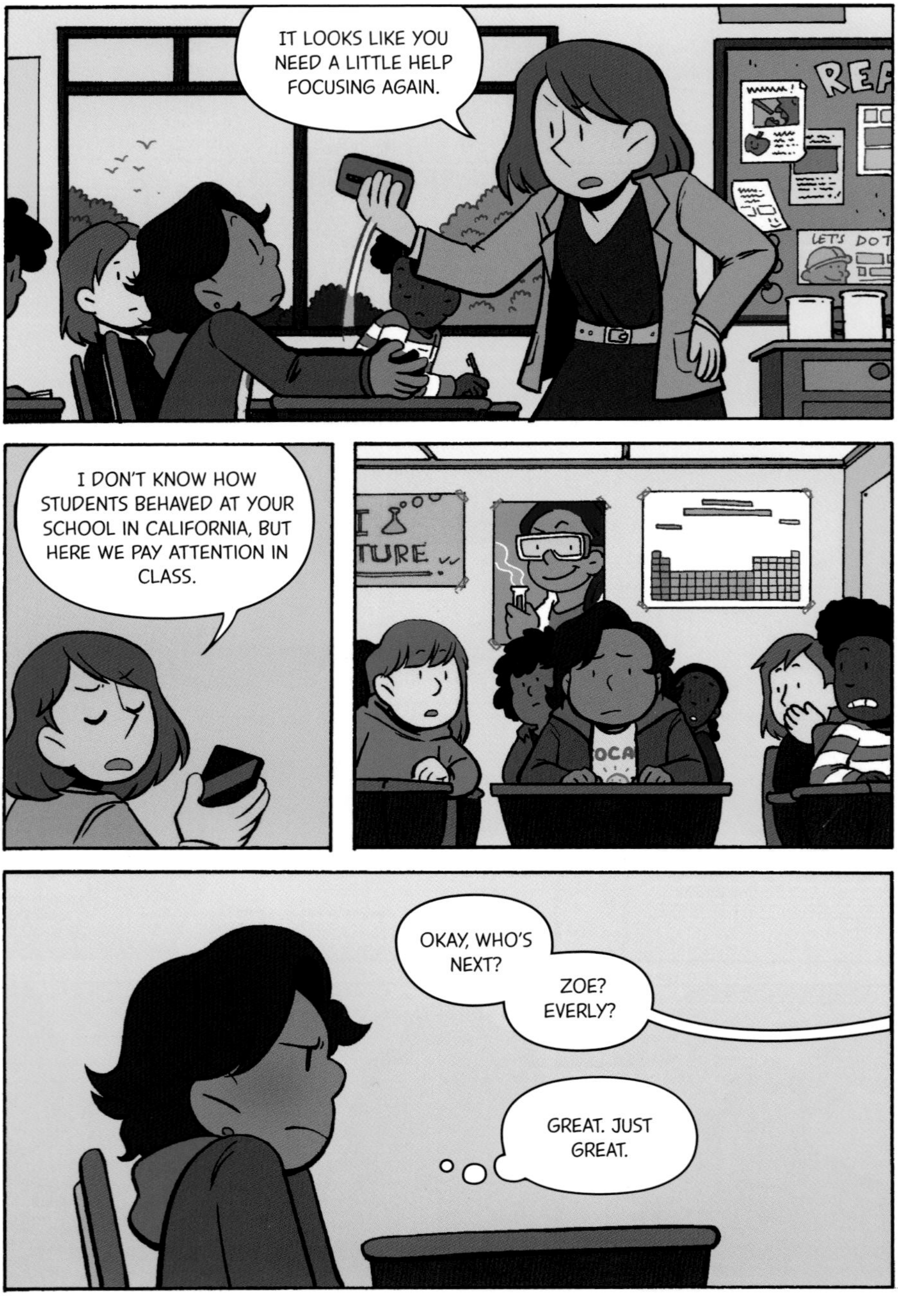
IT LOOKS LIKE YOU NEED A LITTLE HELP FOCUSING AGAIN.
I DON'T KNOW HOW STUDENTS BEHAVED AT YOUR SCHOOL IN CALIFORNIA, BUT HERE WE PAY ATTENTION IN CLASS.
OKAY, WHO'S NEXT?
ZOE? EVERLY?
GREAT. JUST GREAT.

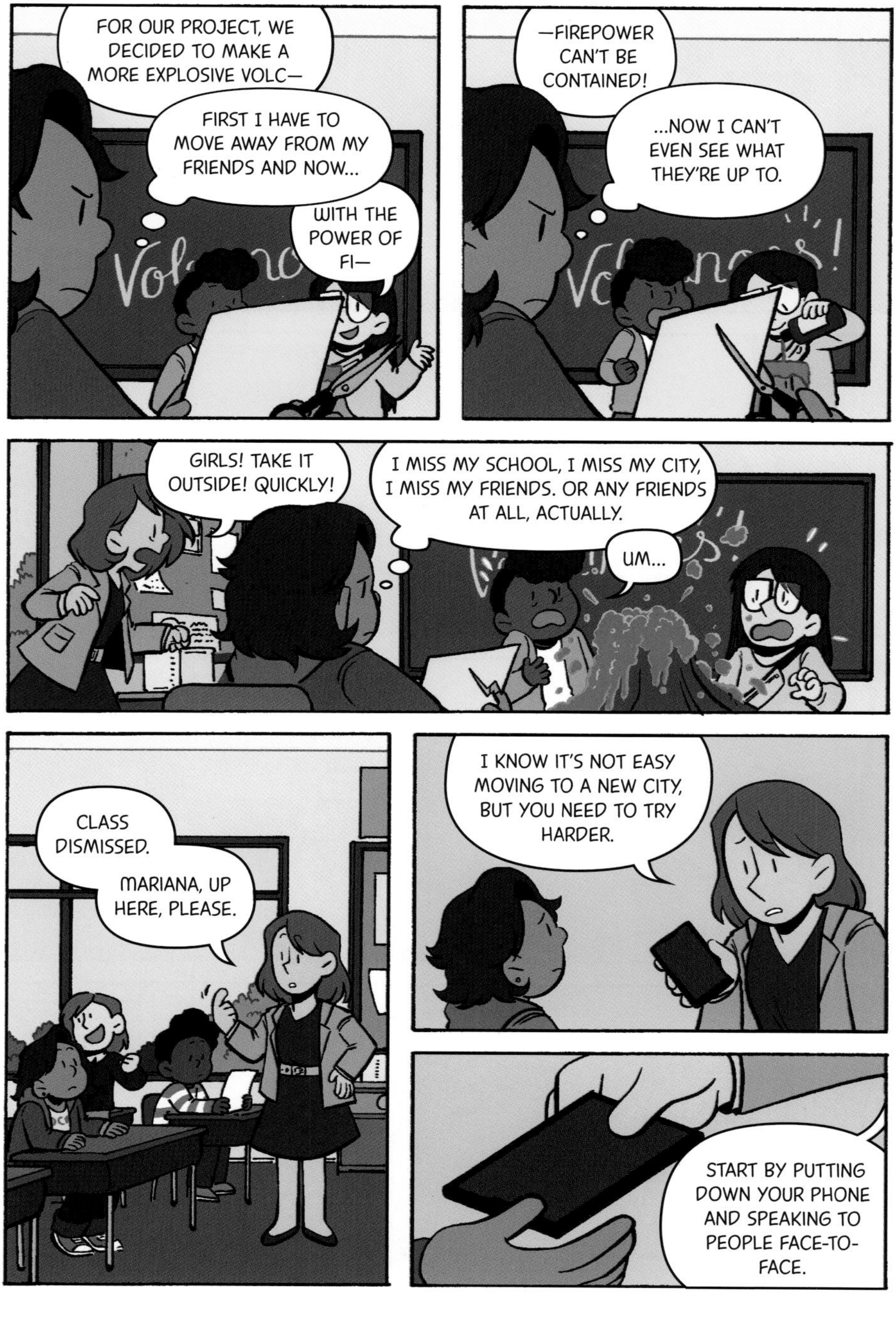
FOR OUR PROJECT, WE DECIDED TO MAKE A MORE EXPLOSIVE VOLC—
FIRST I HAVE TO MOVE AWAY FROM MY FRIENDS AND NOW...
WITH THE POWER OF FI—
—FIREPOWER CAN'T BE CONTAINED!
...NOW I CAN'T EVEN SEE WHAT THEY'RE UP TO.
GIRLS! TAKE IT OUTSIDE! QUICKLY!
I MISS MY SCHOOL, I MISS MY CITY, I MISS MY FRIENDS. OR ANY FRIENDS AT ALL, ACTUALLY.
UM...
CLASS DISMISSED.
MARIANA, UP HERE, PLEASE.
I KNOW IT'S NOT EASY MOVING TO A NEW CITY, BUT YOU NEED TO TRY HARDER.
START BY PUTTING DOWN YOUR PHONE AND SPEAKING TO PEOPLE FACE-TO-FACE.

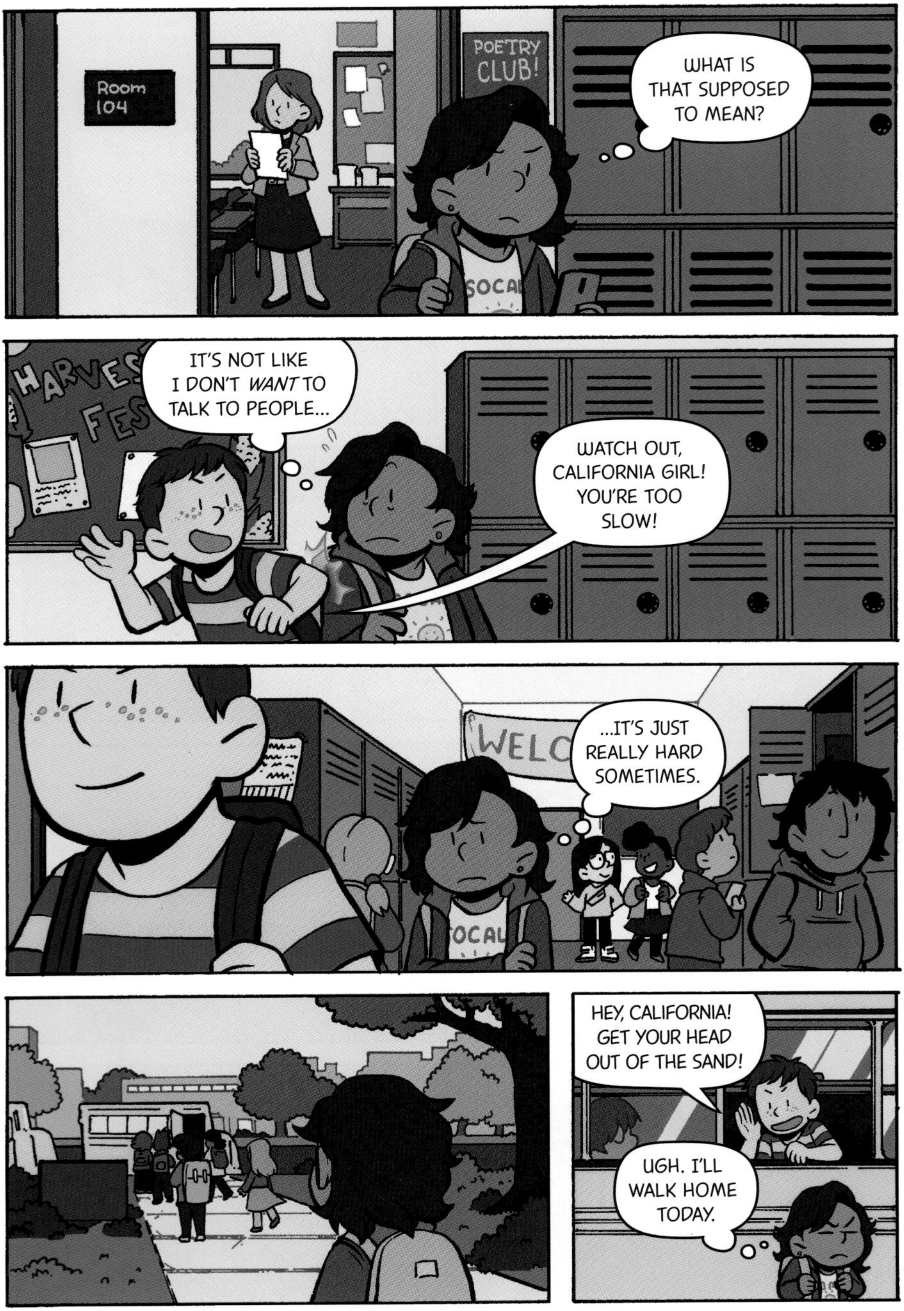
Room 104
POETRY CLUB!
WHAT IS THAT SUPPOSED TO MEAN?
HARVEST FEST
IT'S NOT LIKE I DON'T *WANT* TO TALK TO PEOPLE...
WATCH OUT, CALIFORNIA GIRL! YOU'RE TOO SLOW!
WELC
...IT'S JUST REALLY HARD SOMETIMES.
HEY, CALIFORNIA! GET YOUR HEAD OUT OF THE SAND!
UGH. I'LL WALK HOME TODAY.

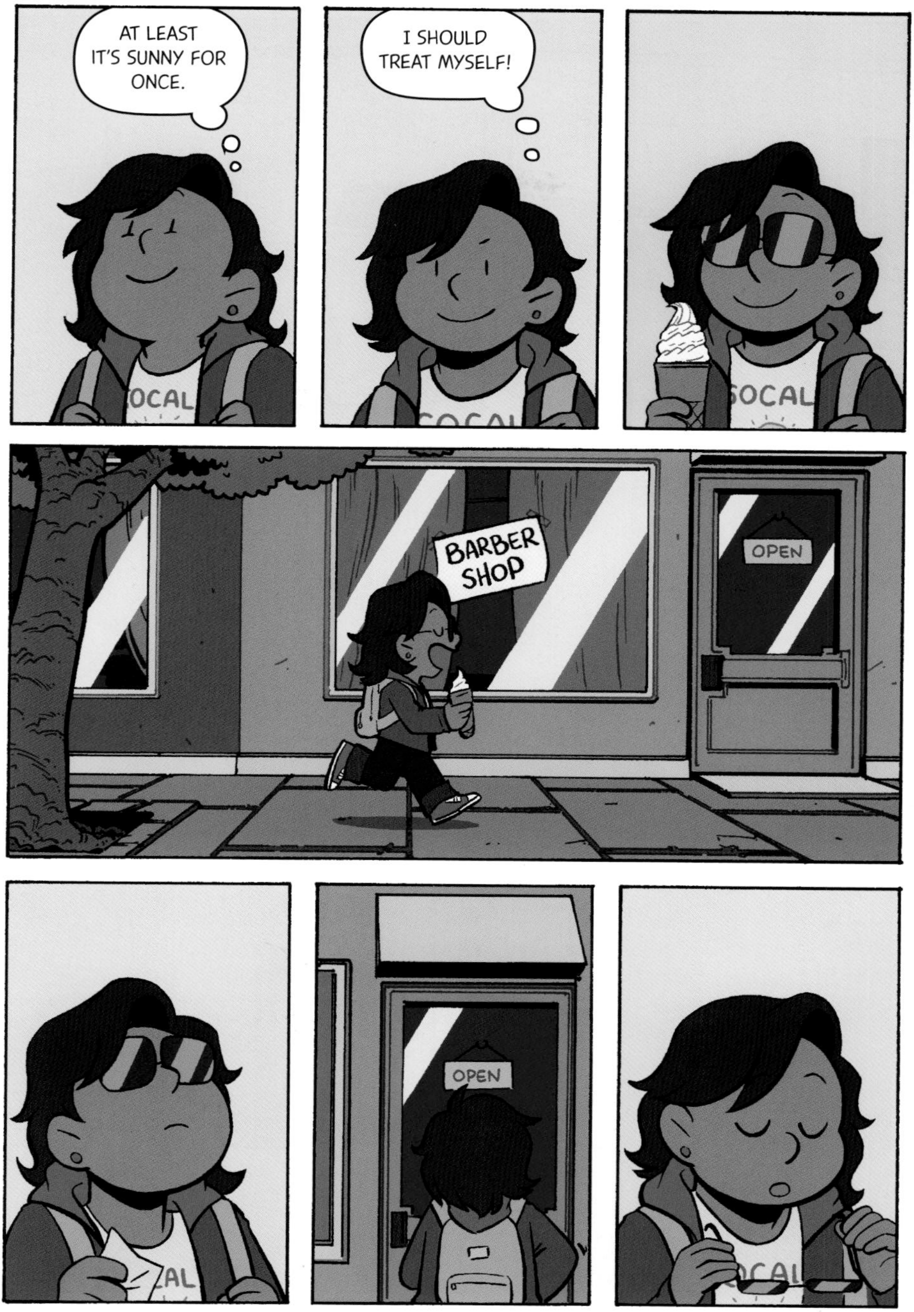
AT LEAST IT'S SUNNY FOR ONCE.
I SHOULD TREAT MYSELF!
SOCAL
BARBER SHOP
OPEN
OPEN

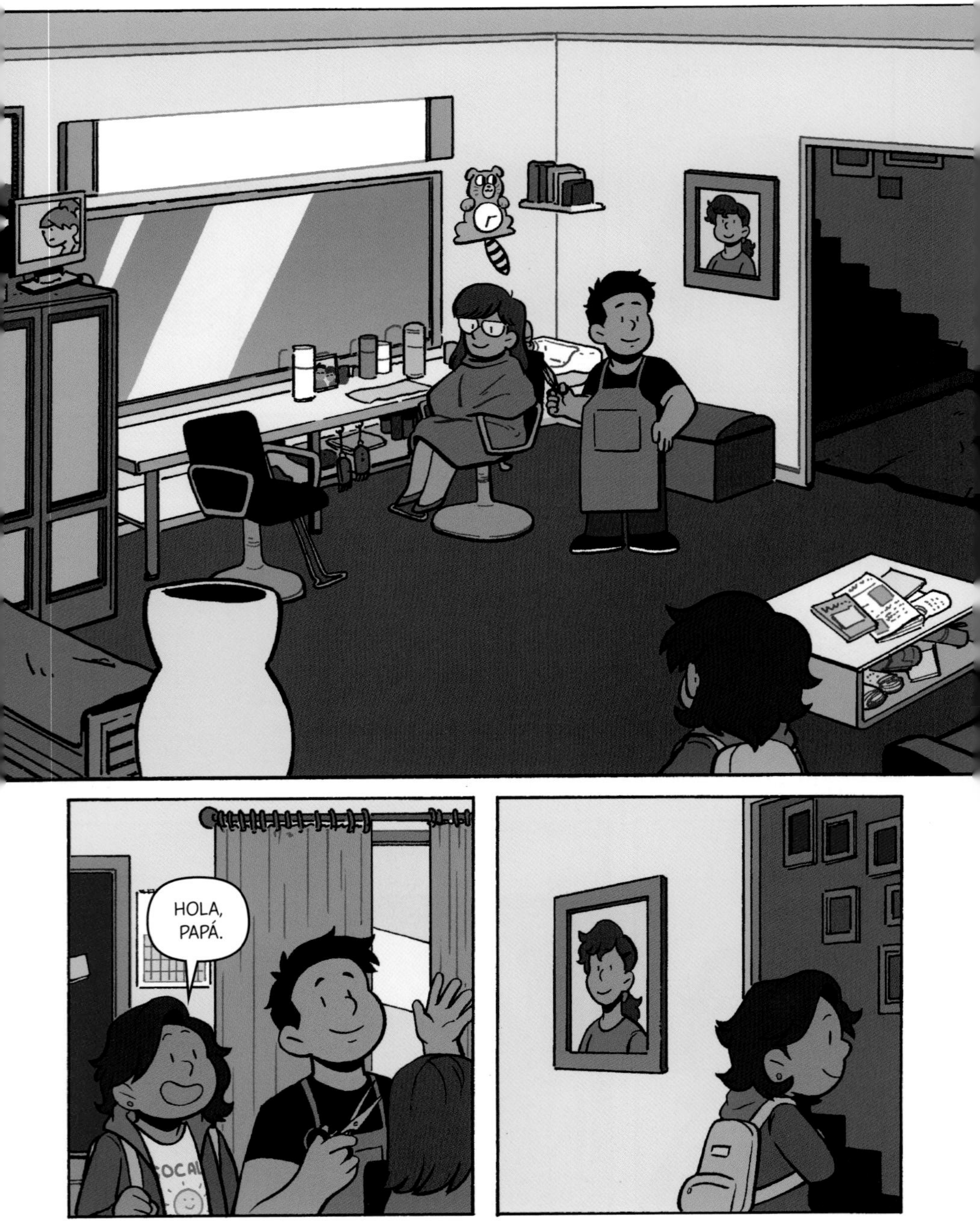
HOLA, PAPÁ.

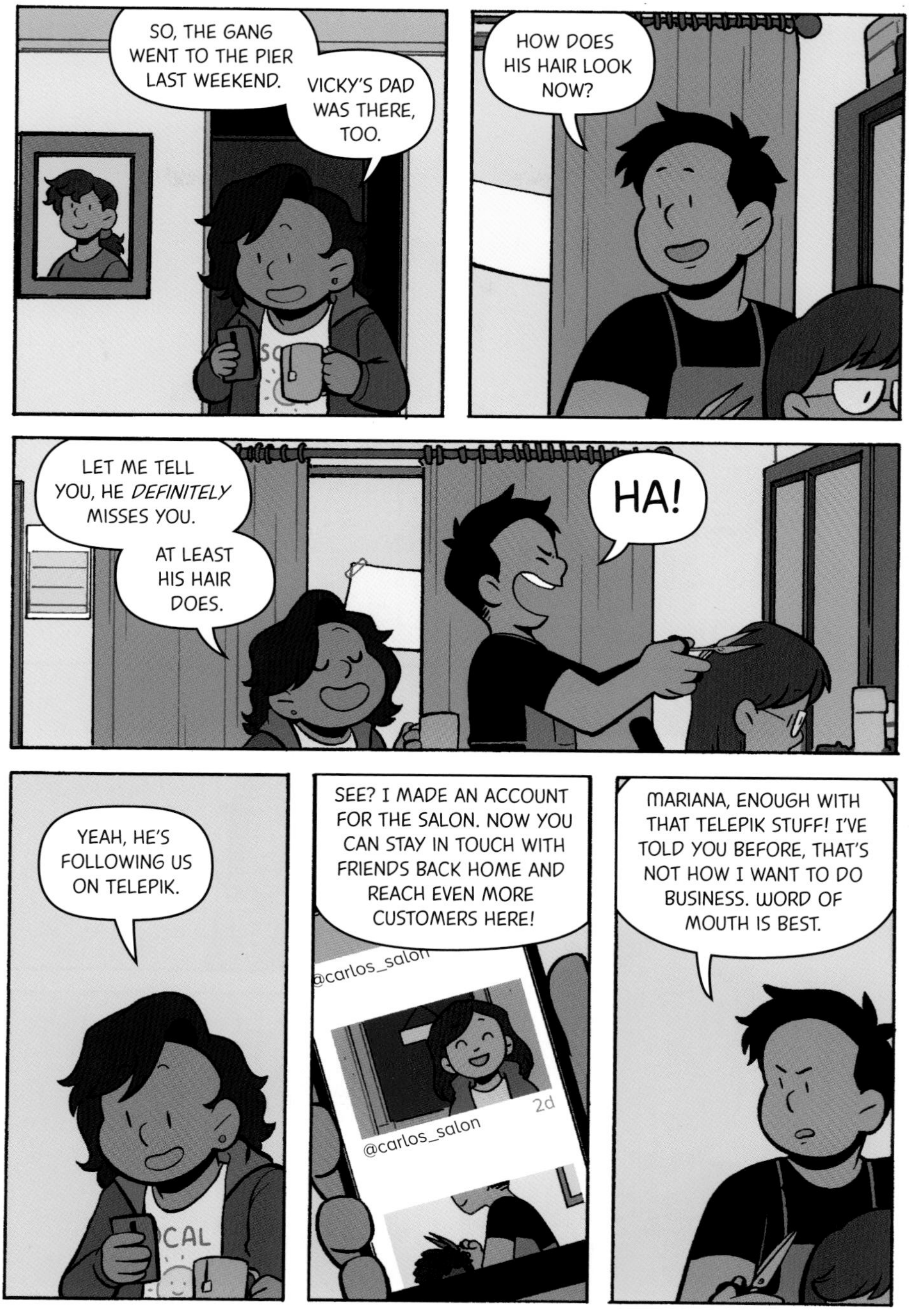
SO, THE GANG WENT TO THE PIER LAST WEEKEND.
VICKY'S DAD WAS THERE, TOO.
HOW DOES HIS HAIR LOOK NOW?
LET ME TELL YOU, HE *DEFINITELY* MISSES YOU.
AT LEAST HIS HAIR DOES.
HA!
YEAH, HE'S FOLLOWING US ON TELEPIK.
SEE? I MADE AN ACCOUNT FOR THE SALON. NOW YOU CAN STAY IN TOUCH WITH FRIENDS BACK HOME AND REACH EVEN MORE CUSTOMERS HERE!
@carlos_salon
2d
@carlos_salon
MARIANA, ENOUGH WITH THAT TELEPIK STUFF! I'VE TOLD YOU BEFORE, THAT'S NOT HOW I WANT TO DO BUSINESS. WORD OF MOUTH IS BEST.

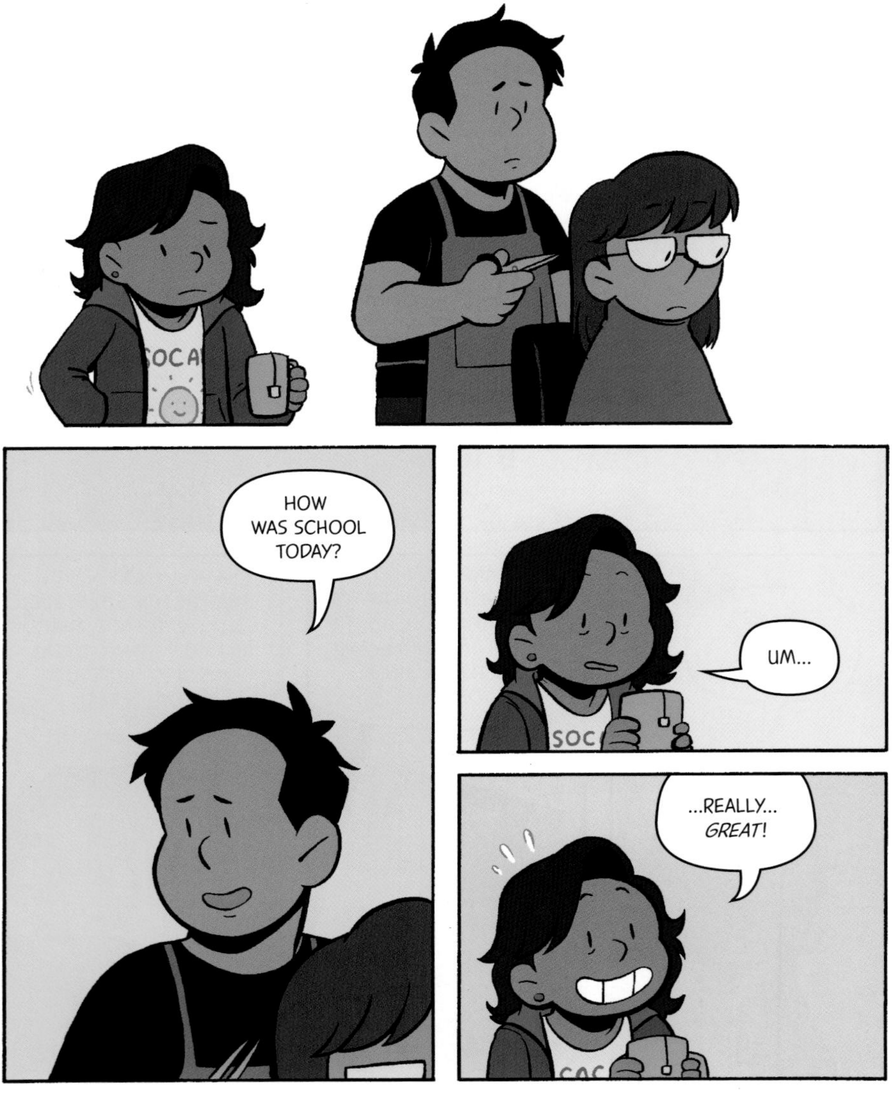

SOCA
HOW WAS SCHOOL TODAY?
UM...
...REALLY... *GREAT*!

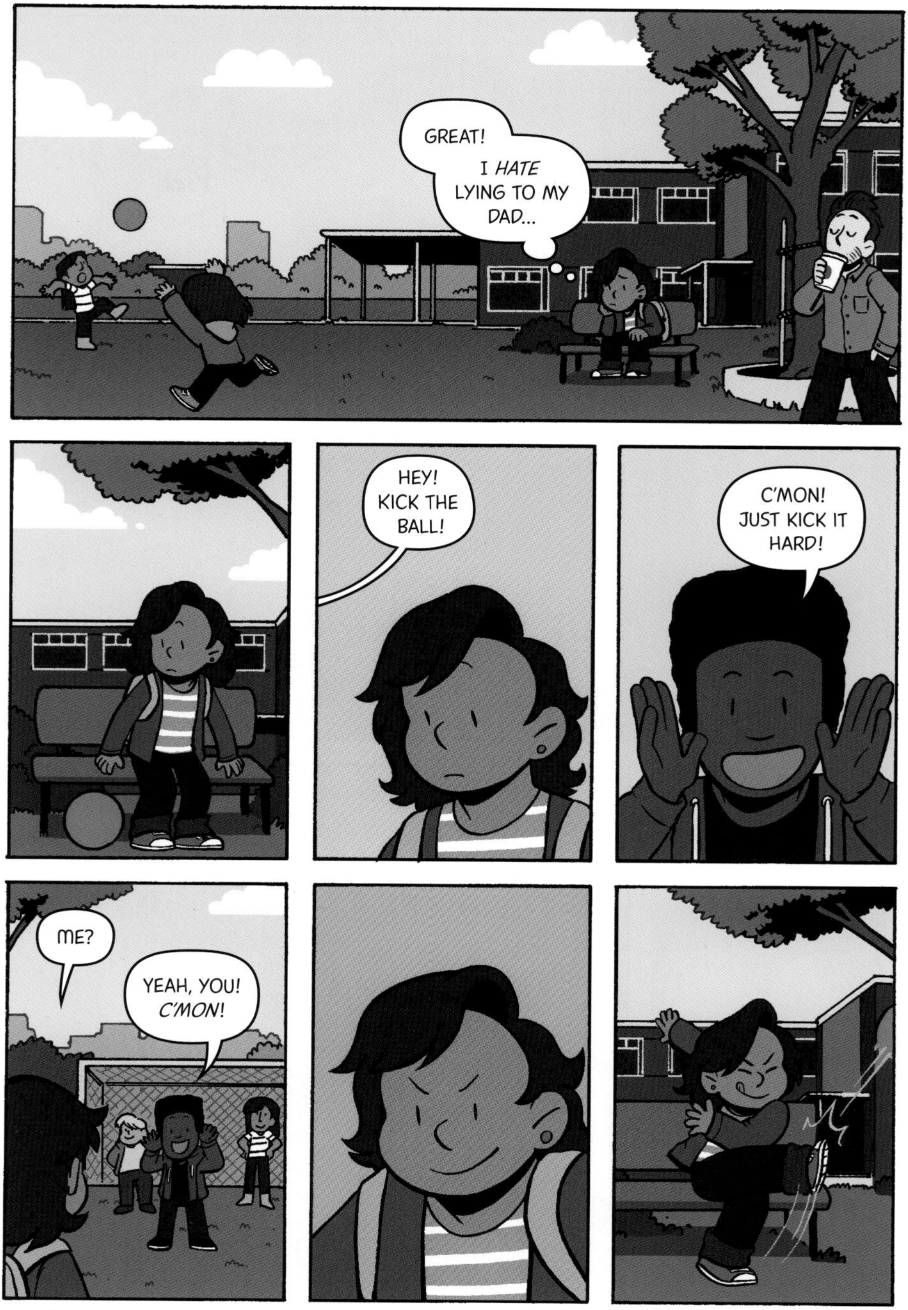
GREAT!
I *HATE* LYING TO MY DAD...
HEY! KICK THE BALL!
C'MON! JUST KICK IT HARD!
ME?
YEAH, YOU! *C'MON*!

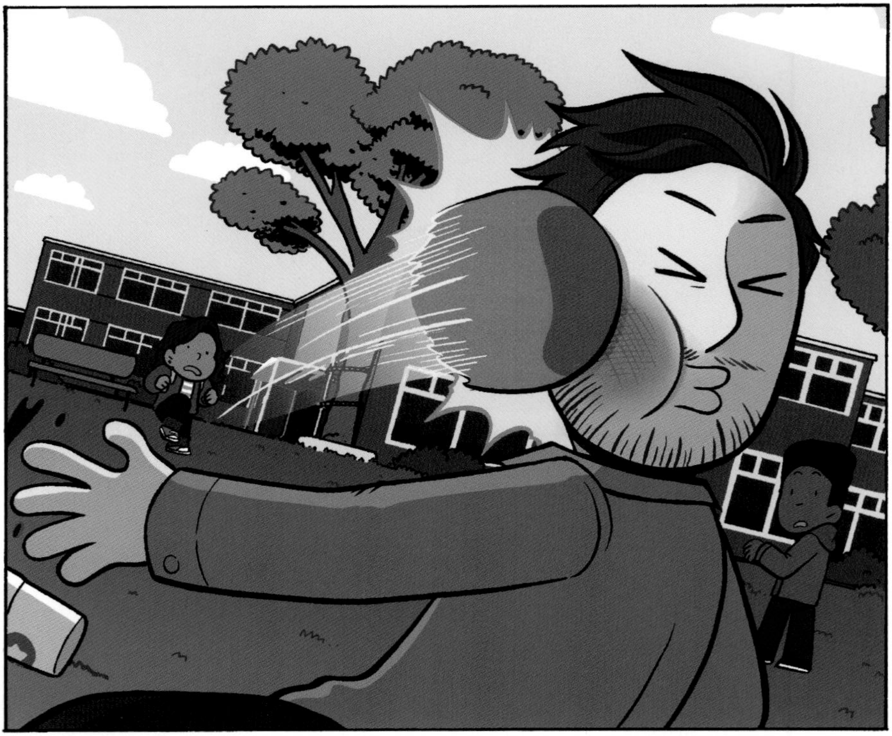

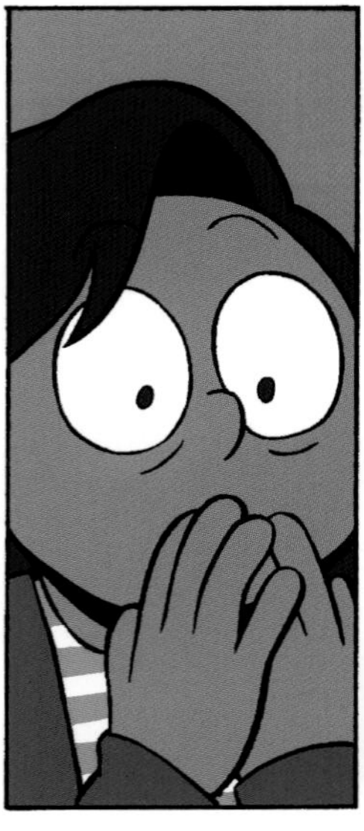

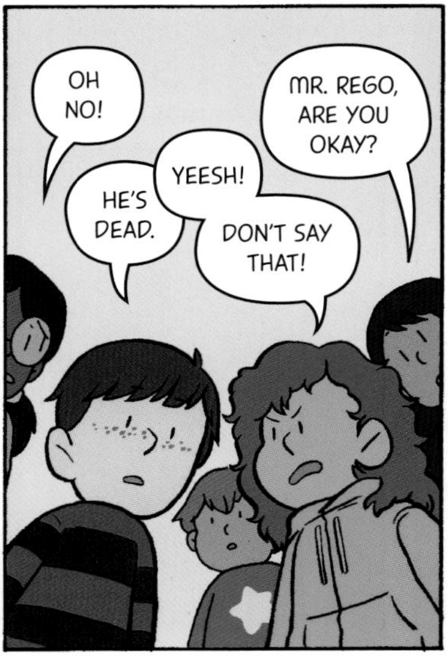
OH NO!
MR. REGO, ARE YOU OKAY?
YEESH!
HE'S DEAD.
DON'T SAY THAT!

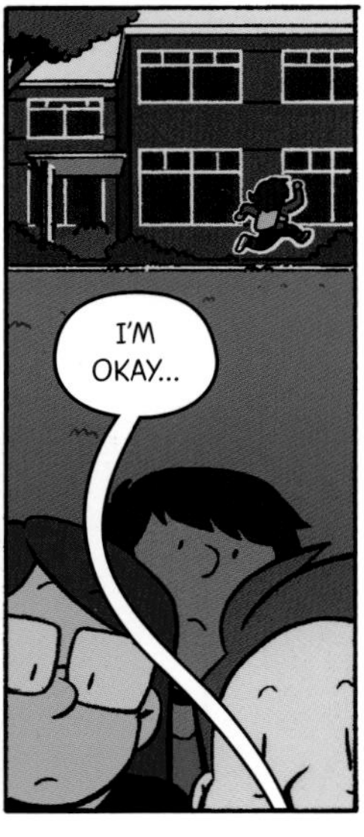
I'M OKAY...

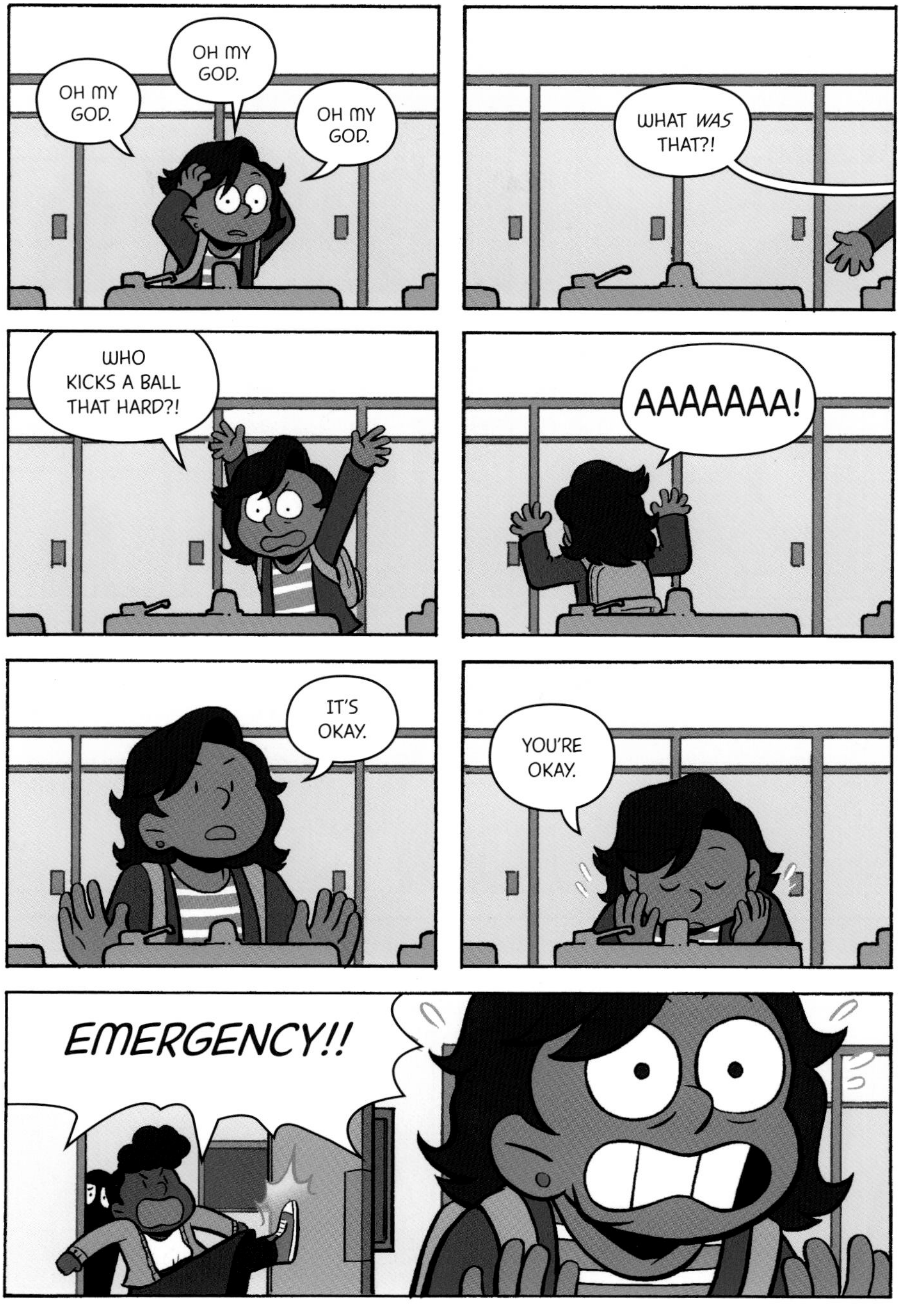
OH MY GOD.
OH MY GOD.
OH MY GOD.
WHAT WAS THAT?!
WHO KICKS A BALL THAT HARD?!
AAAAAAA!
IT'S OKAY.
YOU'RE OKAY.
EMERGENCY!!

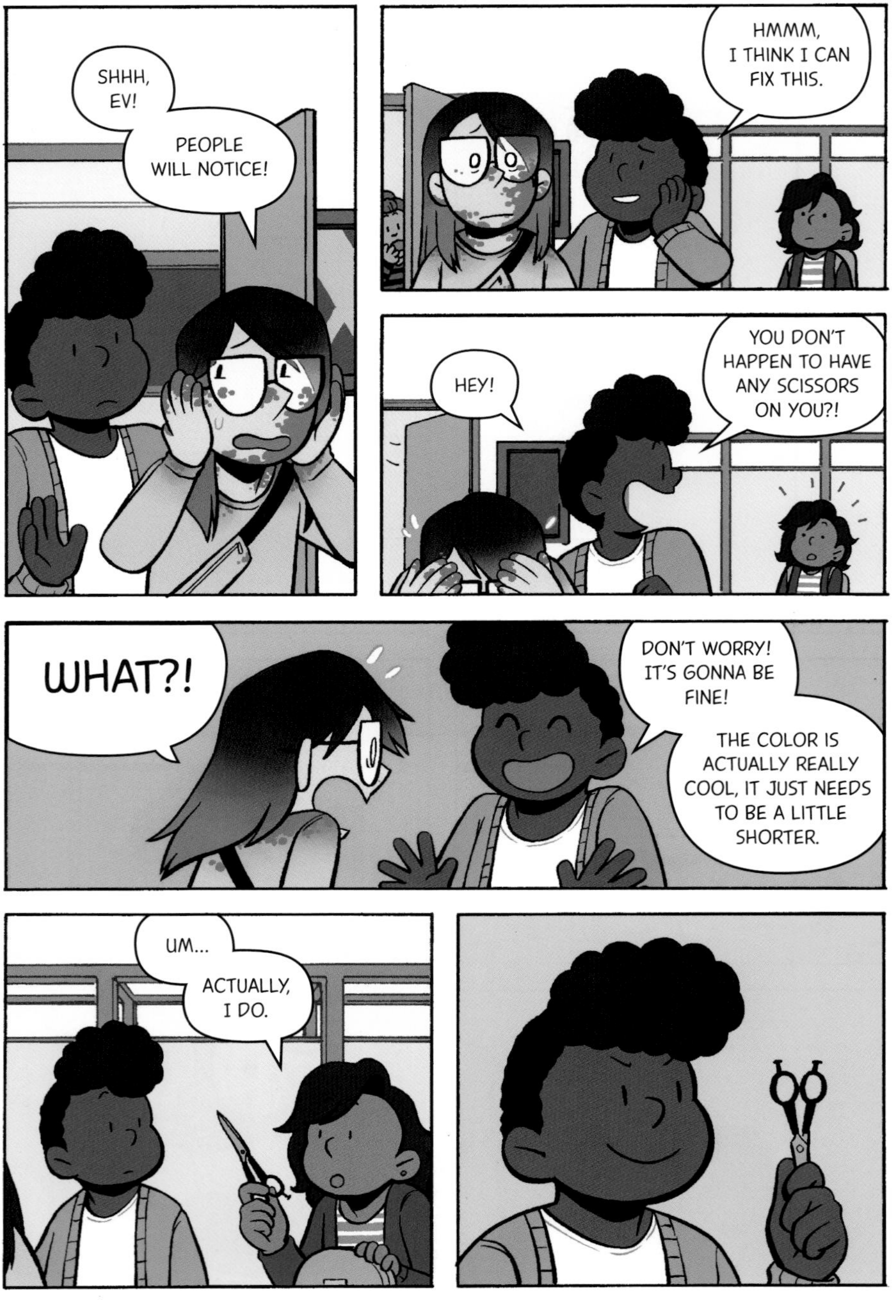
SHHH, EV!
PEOPLE WILL NOTICE!
HMMM, I THINK I CAN FIX THIS.
HEY!
YOU DON'T HAPPEN TO HAVE ANY SCISSORS ON YOU?!
WHAT?!
DON'T WORRY! IT'S GONNA BE FINE!
THE COLOR IS ACTUALLY REALLY COOL, IT JUST NEEDS TO BE A LITTLE SHORTER.
UM...
ACTUALLY, I DO.

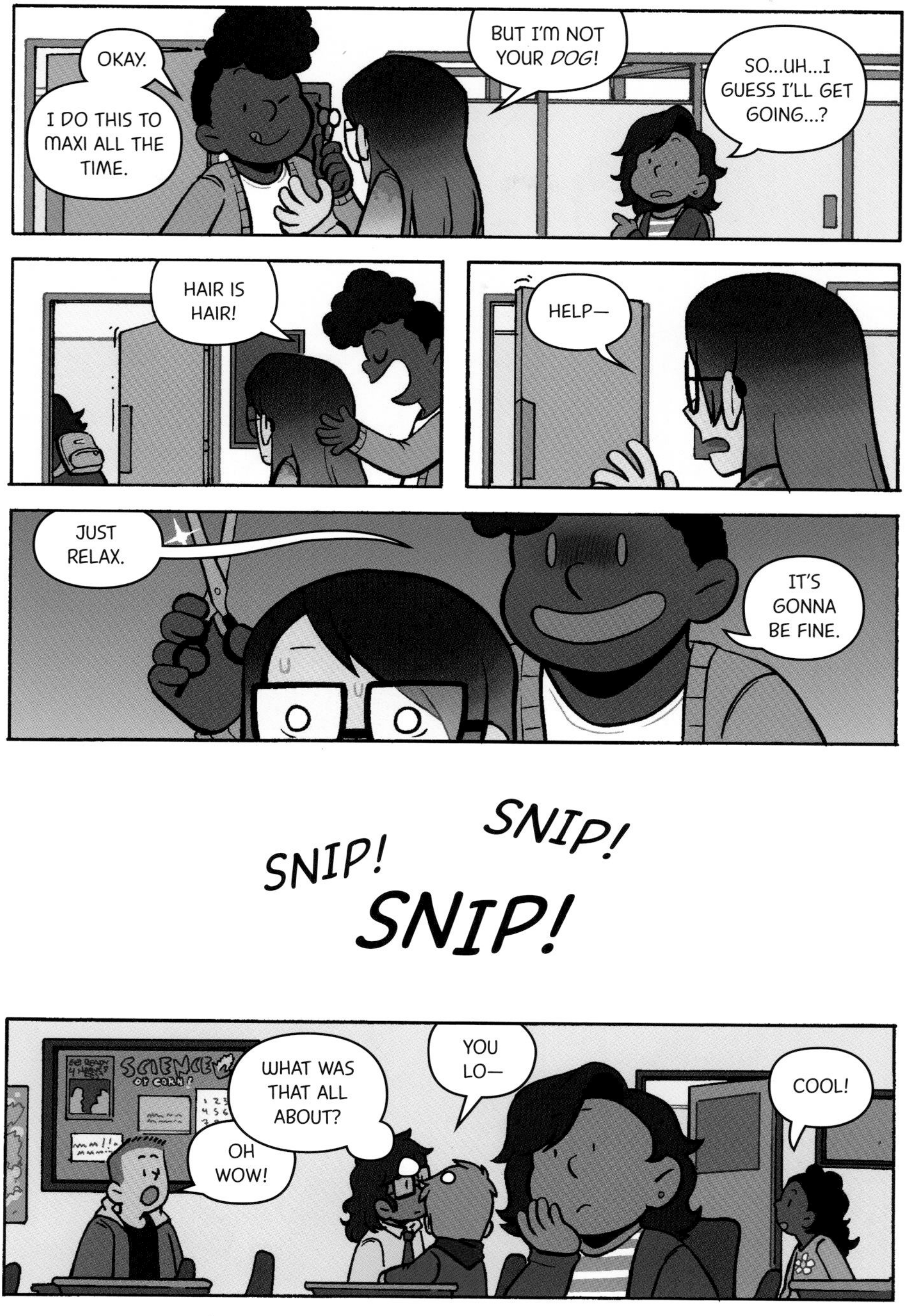
OKAY.
I DO THIS TO MAXI ALL THE TIME.
BUT I'M NOT YOUR *DOG*!
SO...UH...I GUESS I'LL GET GOING...?
HAIR IS HAIR!
HELP—
JUST RELAX.
IT'S GONNA BE FINE.
SNIP!
SNIP!
SNIP!
WHAT WAS THAT ALL ABOUT?
YOU LO—
COOL!
OH WOW!

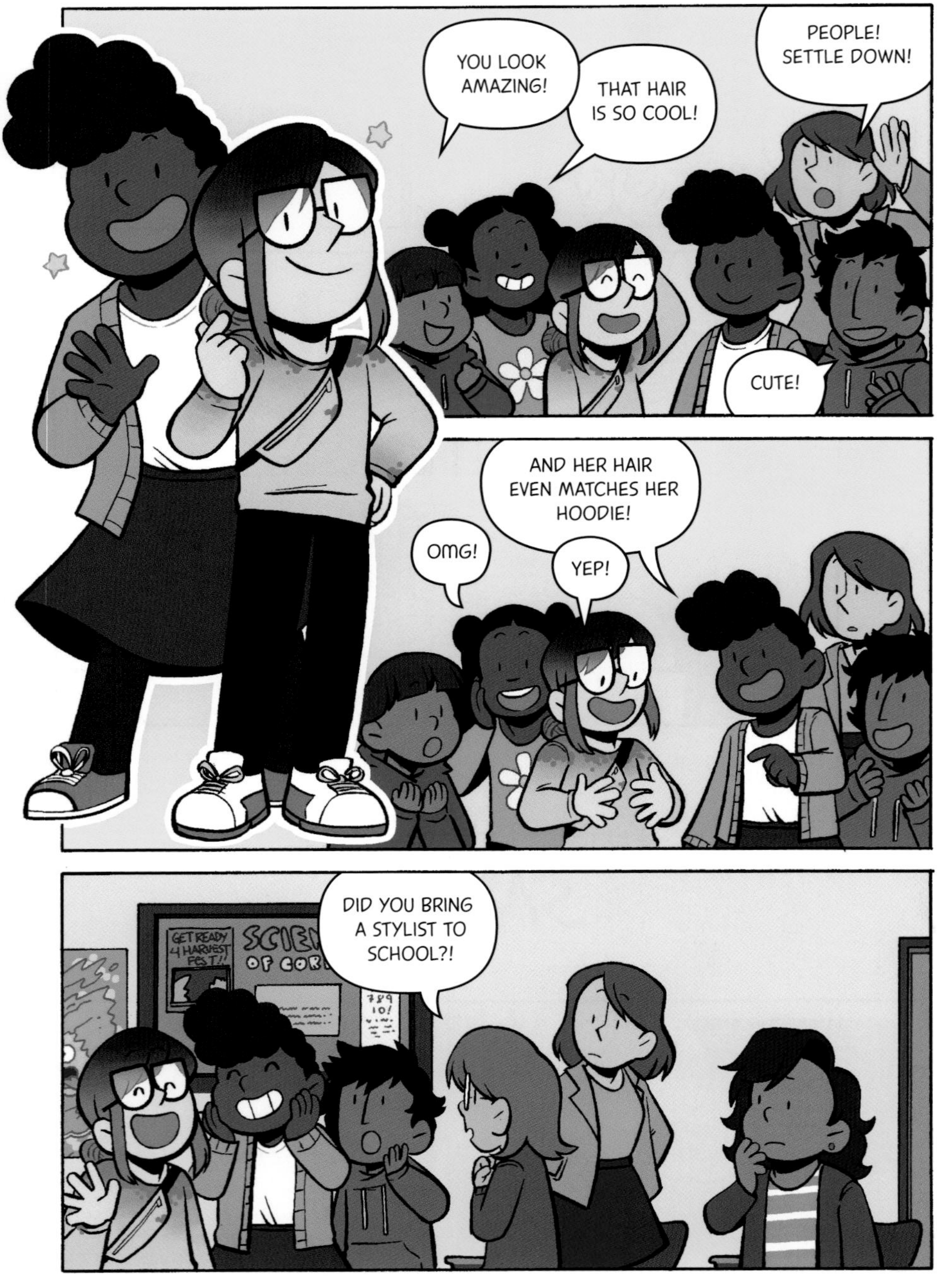
YOU LOOK AMAZING!
THAT HAIR IS SO COOL!
PEOPLE! SETTLE DOWN!
CUTE!
AND HER HAIR EVEN MATCHES HER HOODIE!
OMG!
YEP!
GET READY 4 HARVEST FEST!!
DID YOU BRING A STYLIST TO SCHOOL?!

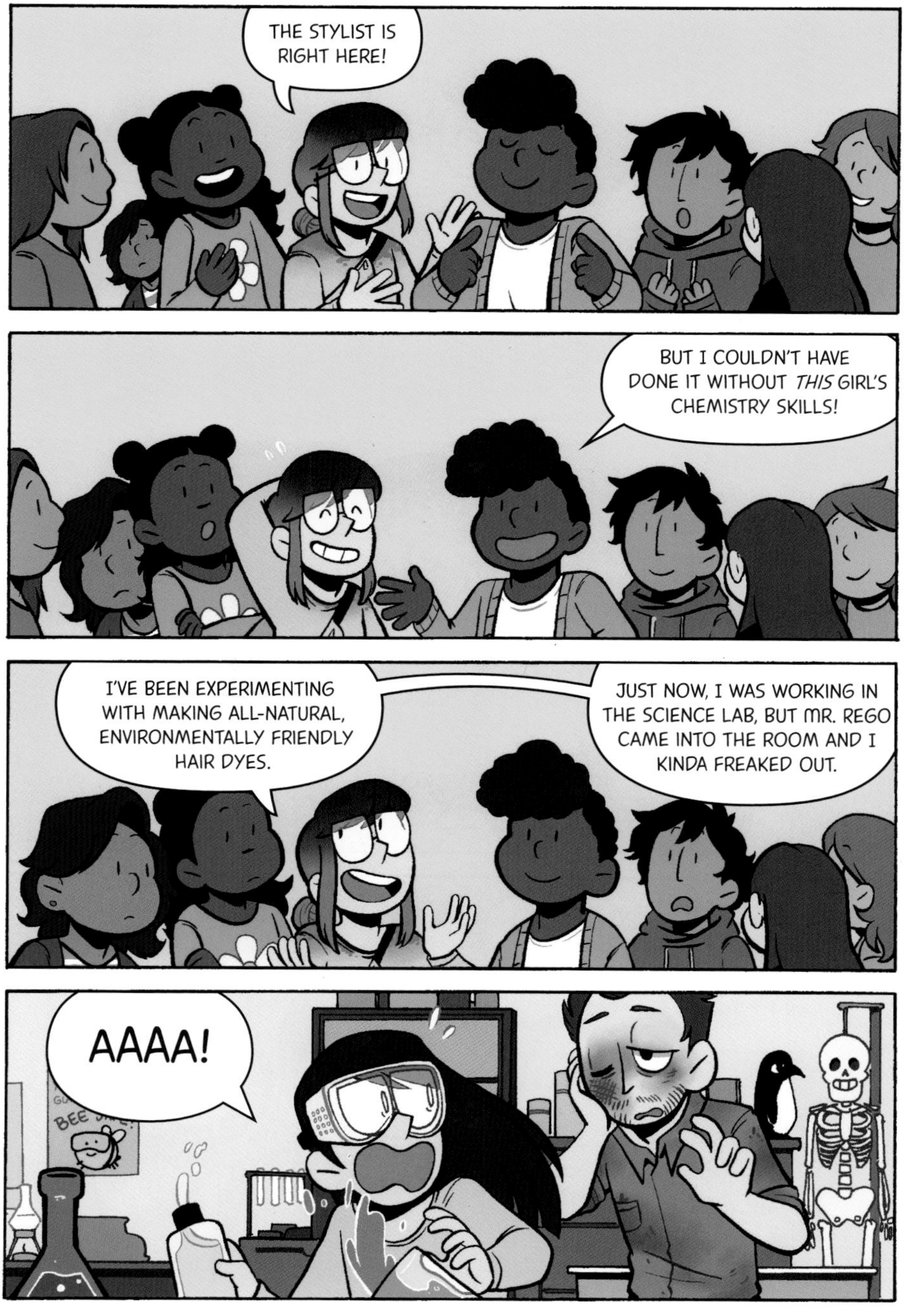
THE STYLIST IS RIGHT HERE!
BUT I COULDN'T HAVE DONE IT WITHOUT *THIS* GIRL'S CHEMISTRY SKILLS!
I'VE BEEN EXPERIMENTING WITH MAKING ALL-NATURAL, ENVIRONMENTALLY FRIENDLY HAIR DYES.
JUST NOW, I WAS WORKING IN THE SCIENCE LAB, BUT MR. REGO CAME INTO THE ROOM AND I KINDA FREAKED OUT.
AAAA!

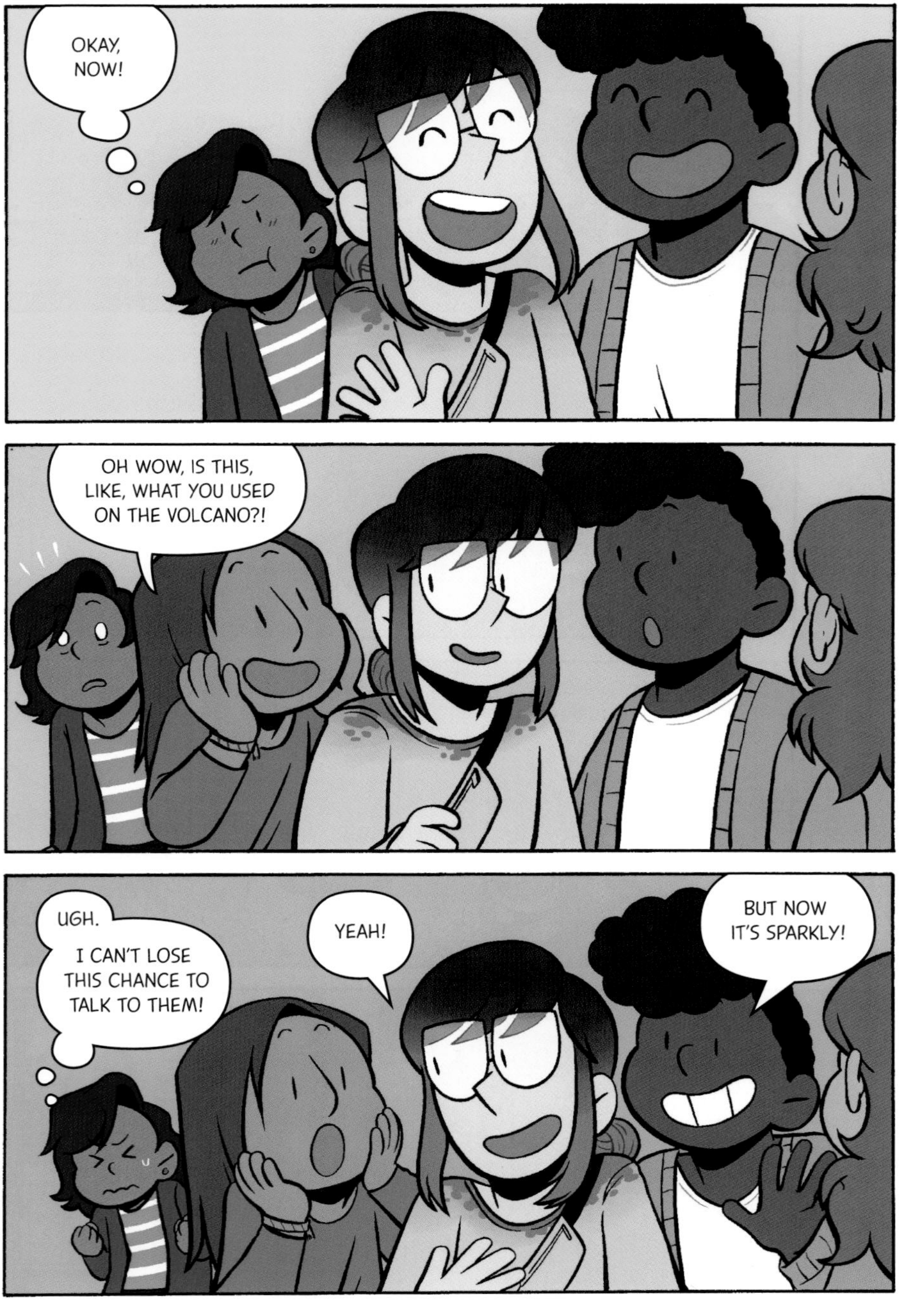
OKAY, NOW!
OH WOW, IS THIS, LIKE, WHAT YOU USED ON THE VOLCANO?!
UGH.
I CAN'T LOSE THIS CHANCE TO TALK TO THEM!
YEAH!
BUT NOW IT'S SPARKLY!

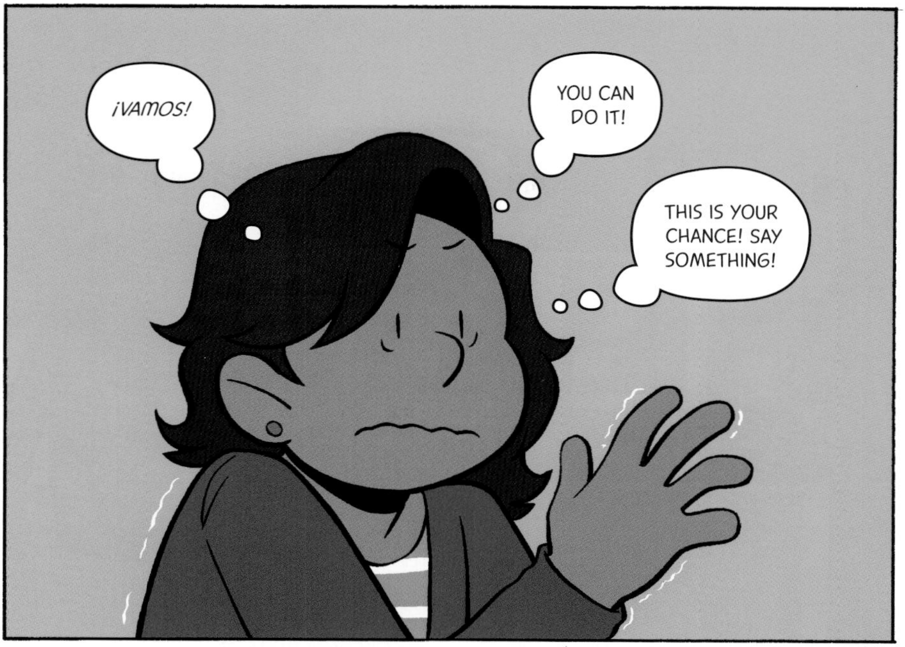
¡VAMOS!
YOU CAN DO IT!
THIS IS YOUR CHANCE! SAY SOMETHING!

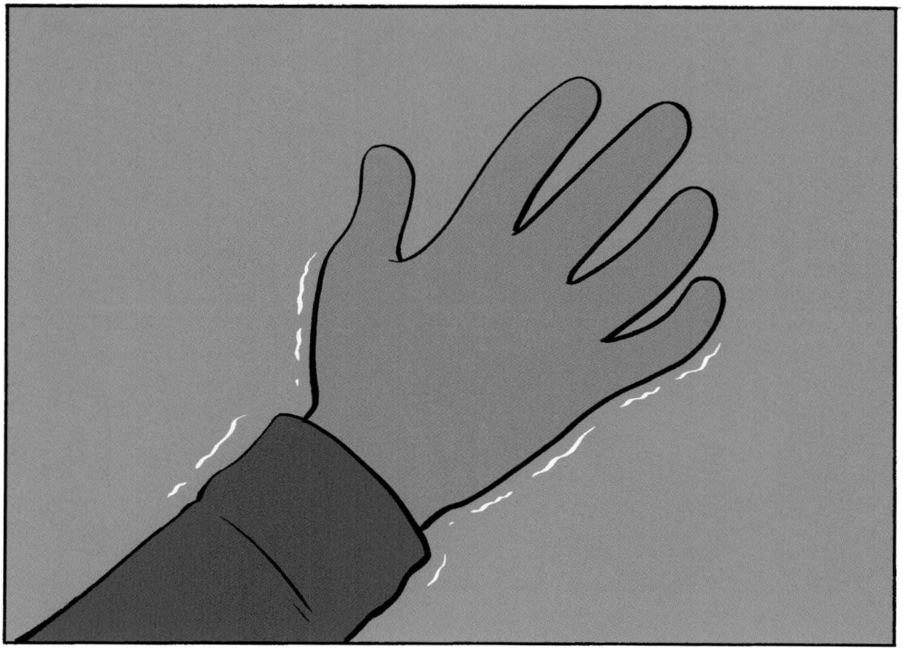

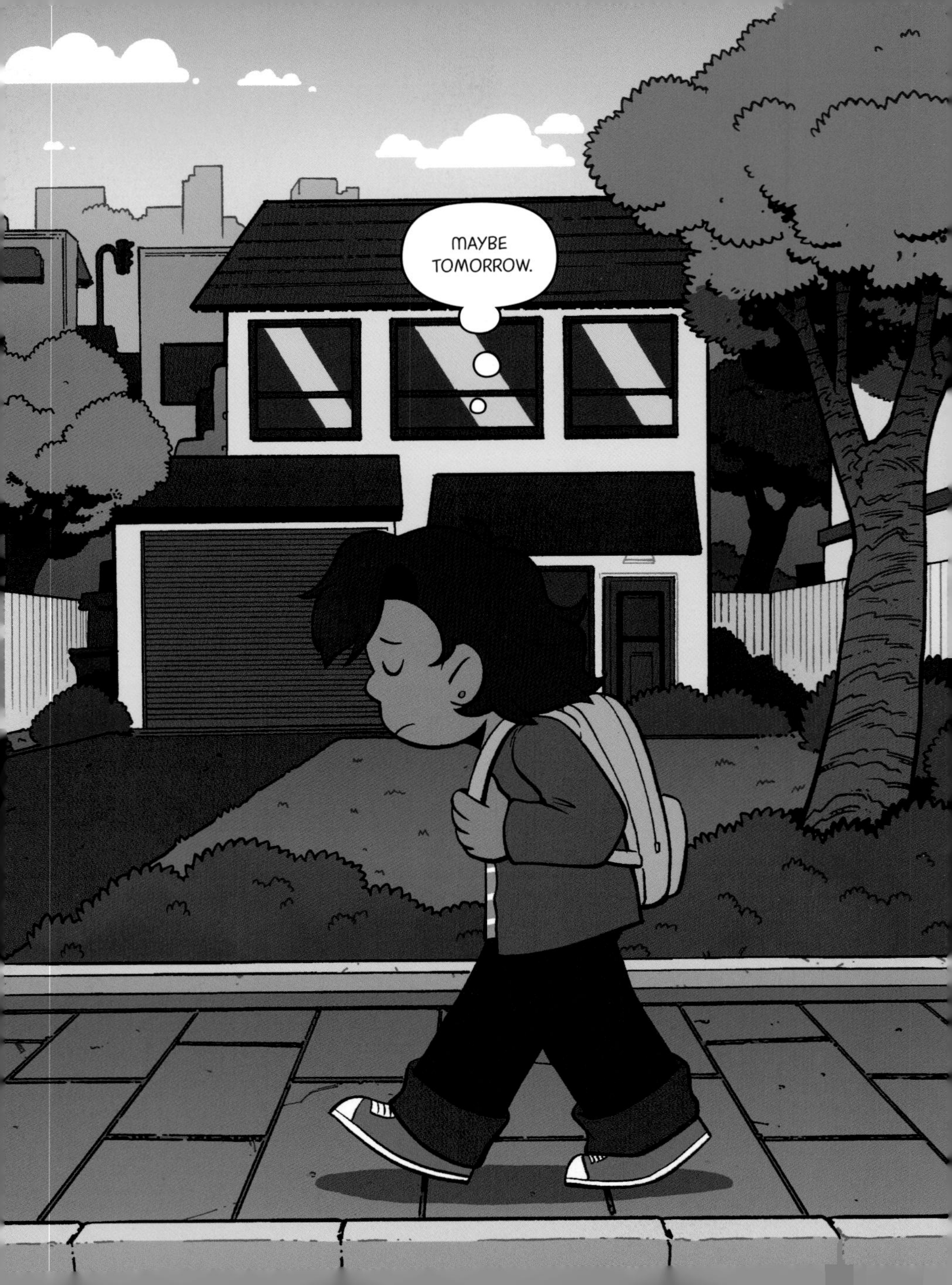
MAYBE TOMORROW.

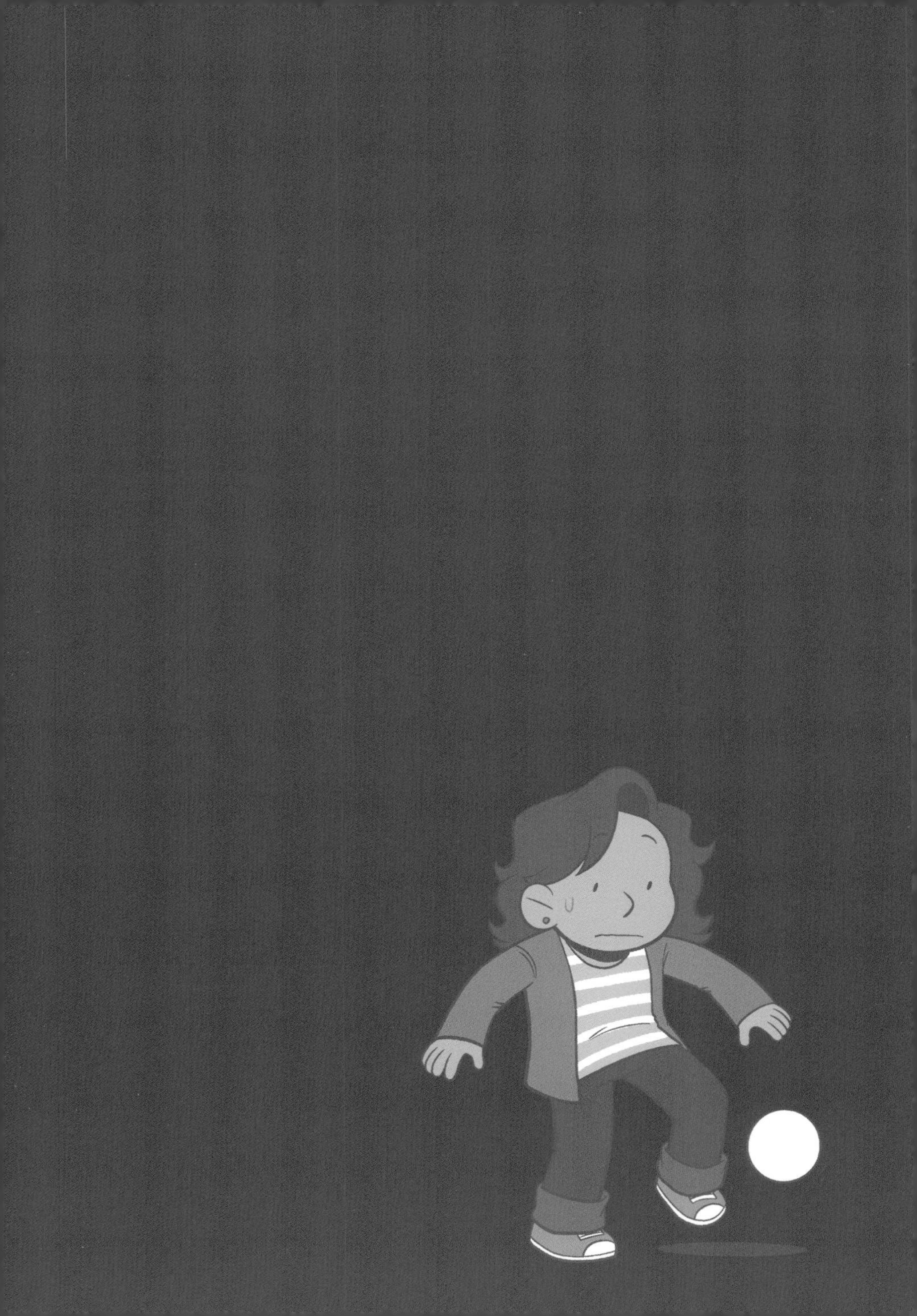

CHAPTER 2

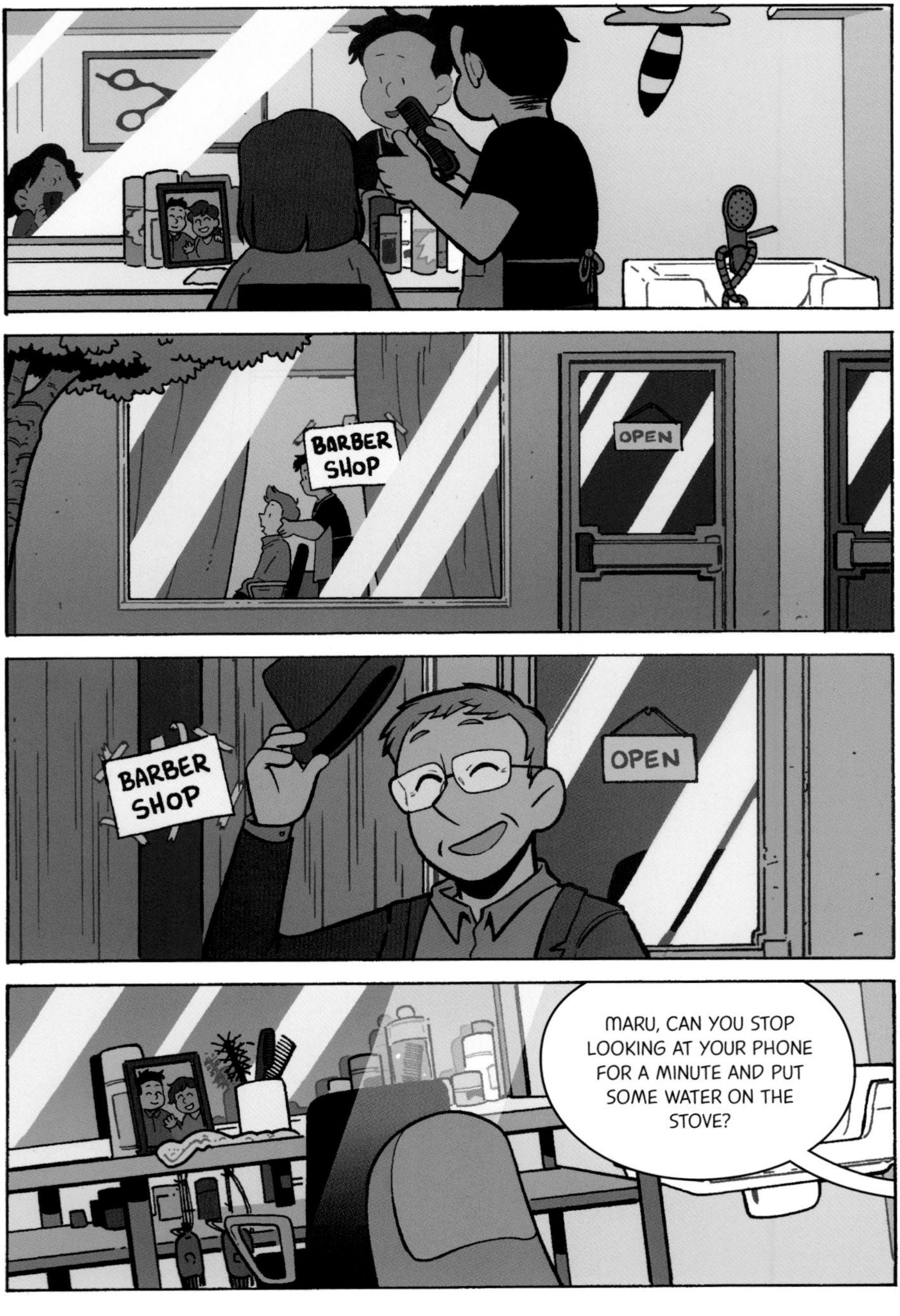
BARBER SHOP
OPEN
BARBER SHOP
OPEN
MARU, CAN YOU STOP LOOKING AT YOUR PHONE FOR A MINUTE AND PUT SOME WATER ON THE STOVE?

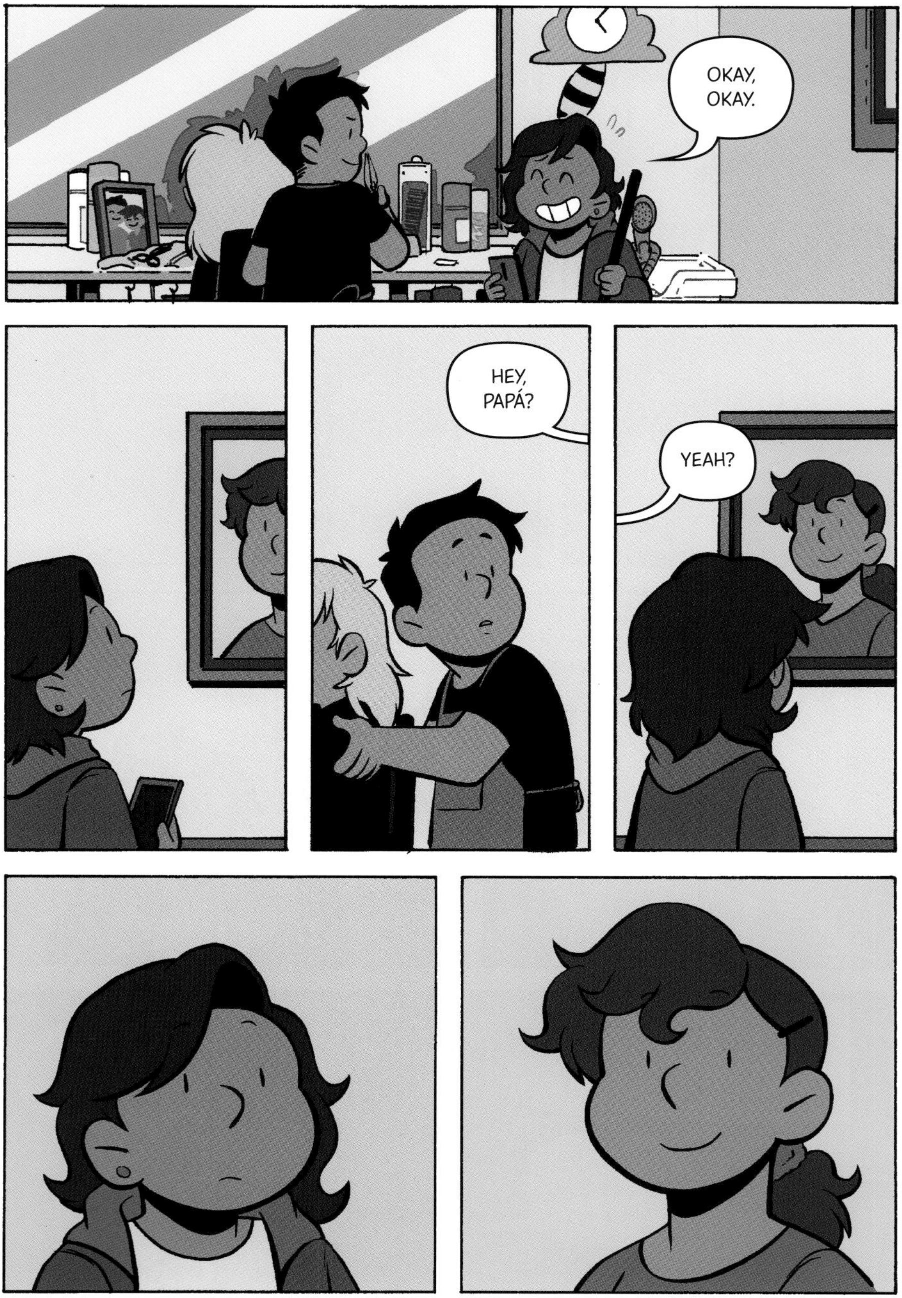
OKAY, OKAY.
HEY, PAPÁ?
YEAH?

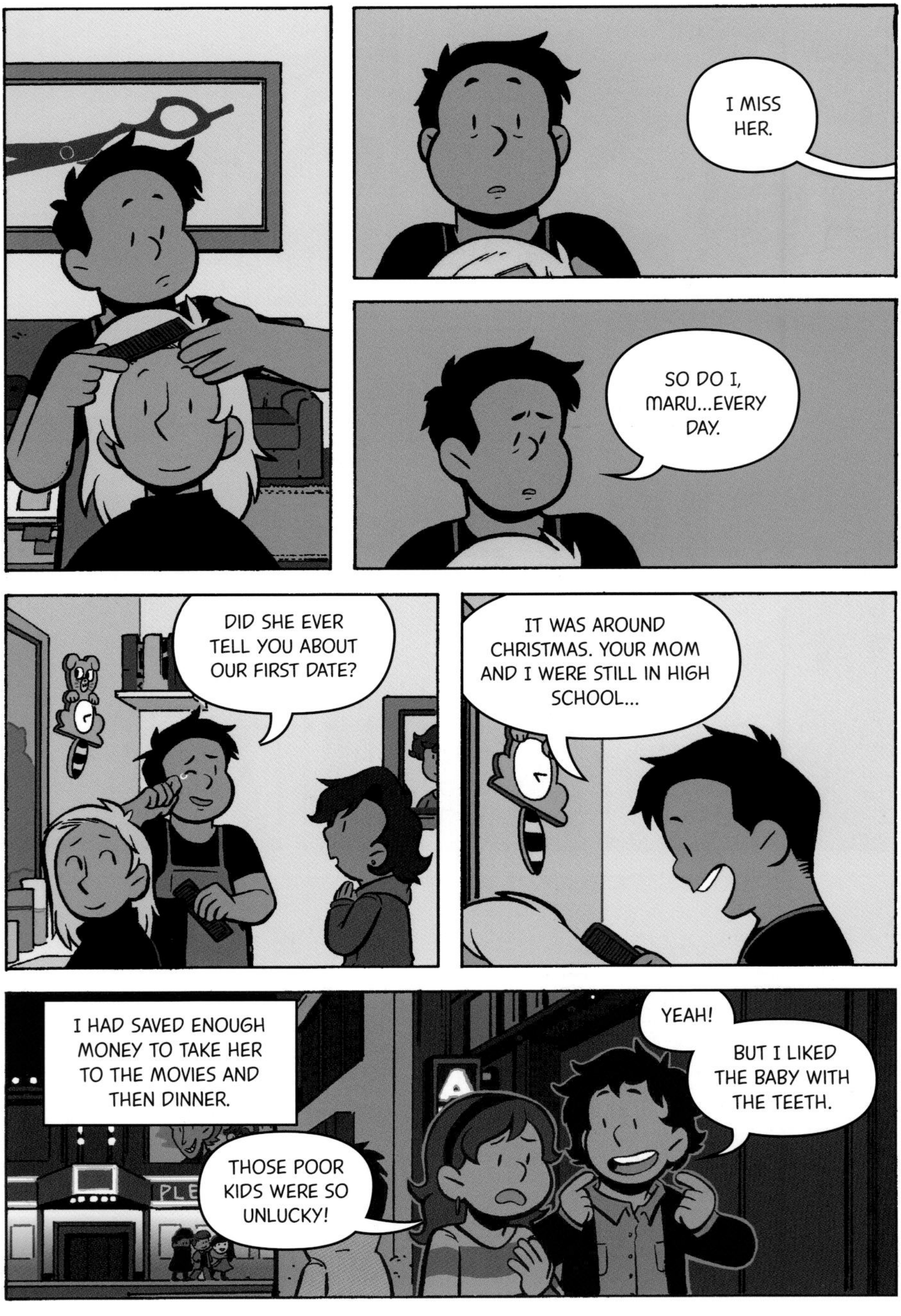
I MISS HER.
SO DO I, MARU...EVERY DAY.
DID SHE EVER TELL YOU ABOUT OUR FIRST DATE?
IT WAS AROUND CHRISTMAS. YOUR MOM AND I WERE STILL IN HIGH SCHOOL...
I HAD SAVED ENOUGH MONEY TO TAKE HER TO THE MOVIES AND THEN DINNER.
YEAH!
BUT I LIKED THE BABY WITH THE TEETH.
THOSE POOR KIDS WERE SO UNLUCKY!

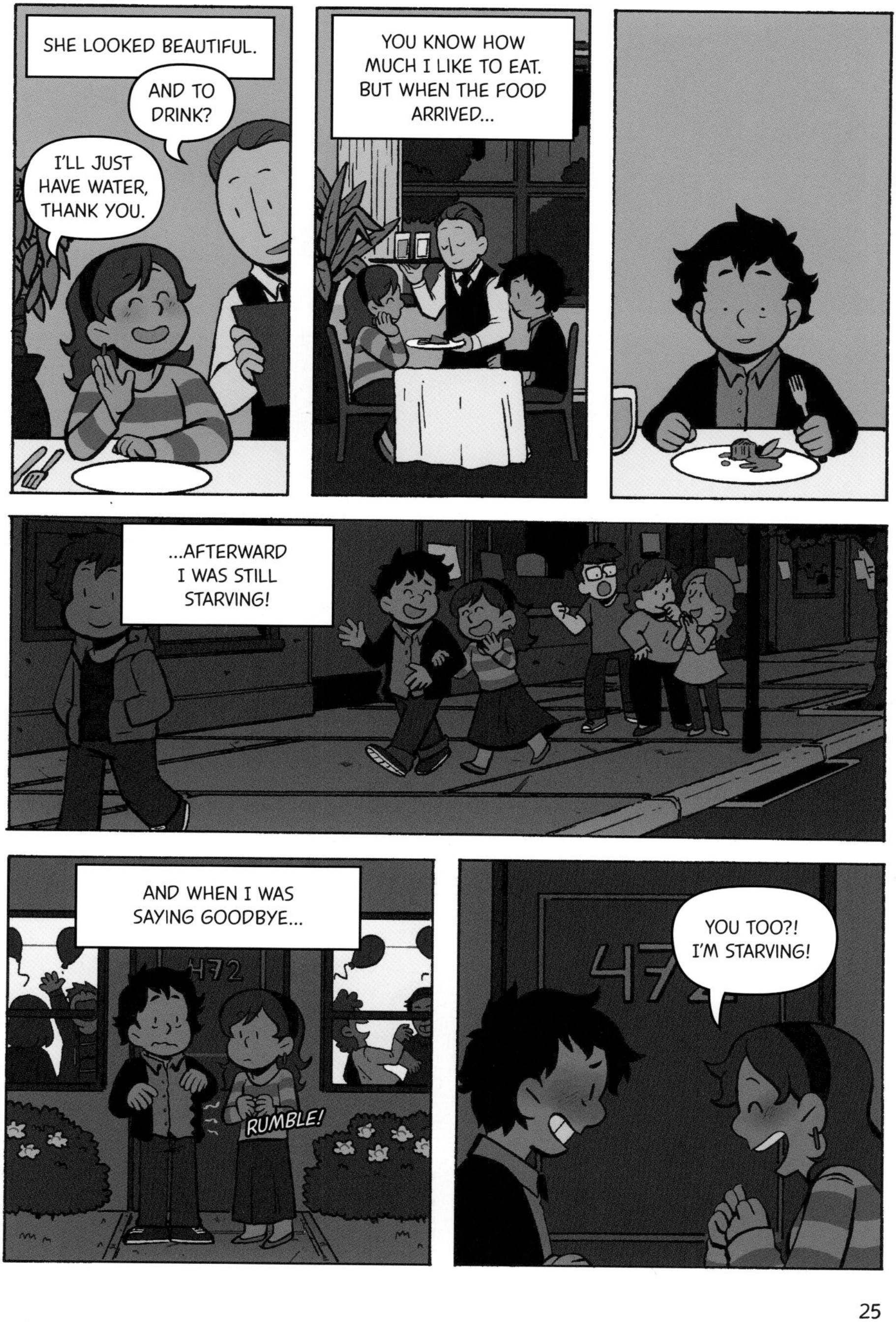
SHE LOOKED BEAUTIFUL.
AND TO DRINK?
I'LL JUST HAVE WATER, THANK YOU.
YOU KNOW HOW MUCH I LIKE TO EAT. BUT WHEN THE FOOD ARRIVED...
...AFTERWARD I WAS STILL STARVING!
AND WHEN I WAS SAYING GOODBYE...
472
RUMBLE!
YOU TOO?! I'M STARVING!

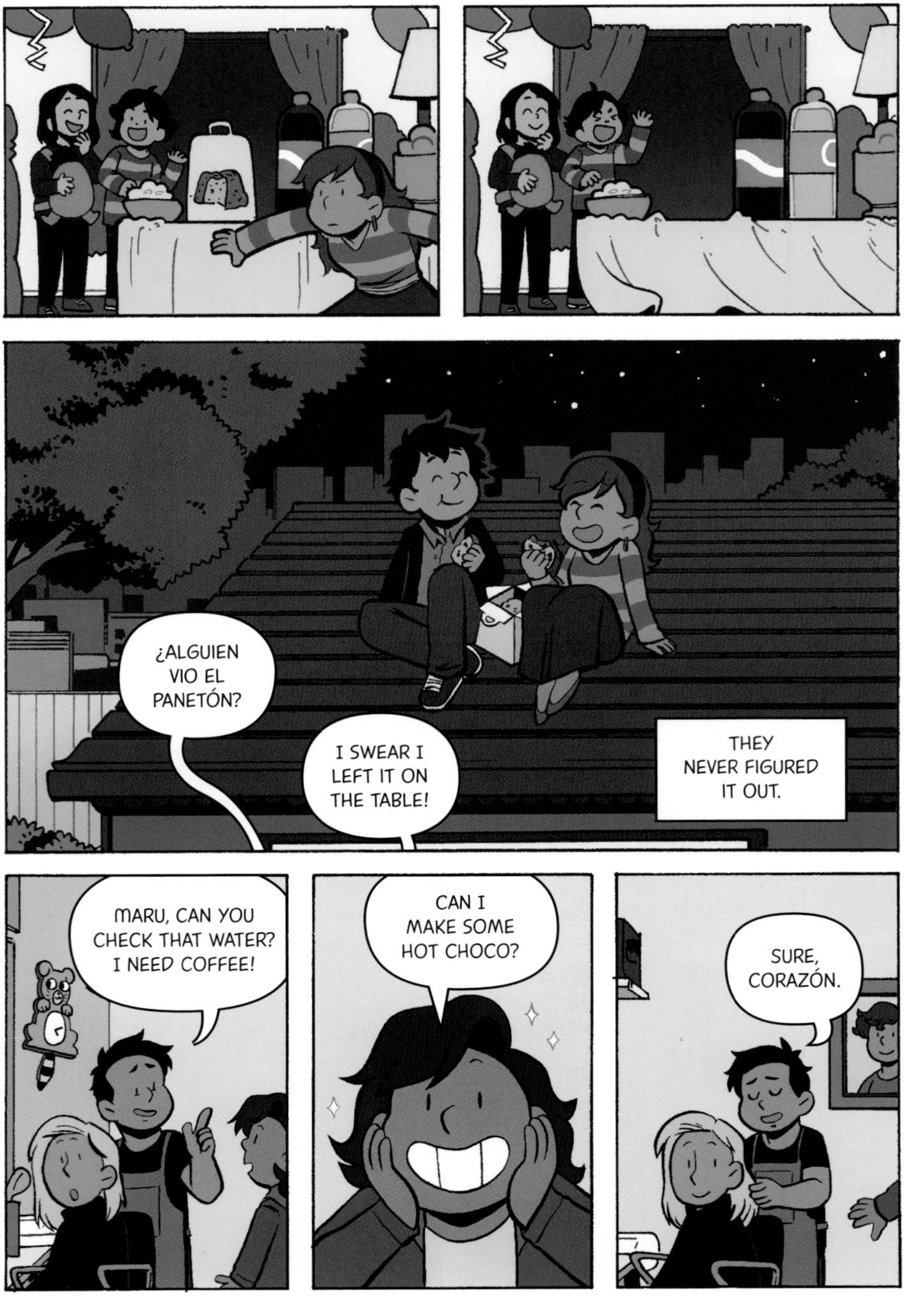
¿ALGUIEN VIO EL PANETÓN?
I SWEAR I LEFT IT ON THE TABLE!
THEY NEVER FIGURED IT OUT.
MARU, CAN YOU CHECK THAT WATER? I NEED COFFEE!
CAN I MAKE SOME HOT CHOCO?
SURE, CORAZÓN.

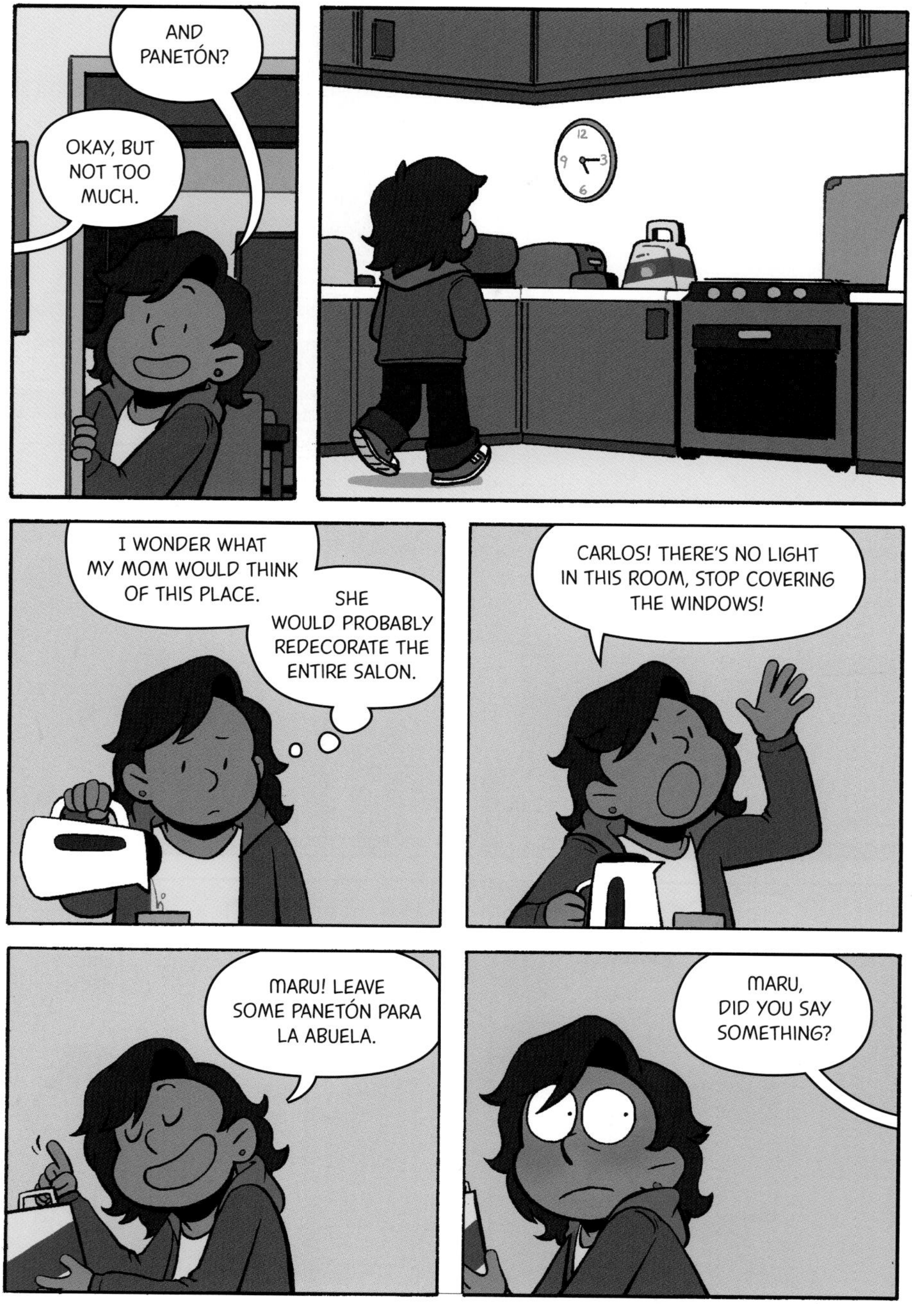
AND PANETÓN?
OKAY, BUT NOT TOO MUCH.
I WONDER WHAT MY MOM WOULD THINK OF THIS PLACE.
SHE WOULD PROBABLY REDECORATE THE ENTIRE SALON.
CARLOS! THERE'S NO LIGHT IN THIS ROOM, STOP COVERING THE WINDOWS!
MARU! LEAVE SOME PANETÓN PARA LA ABUELA.
MARU, DID YOU SAY SOMETHING?

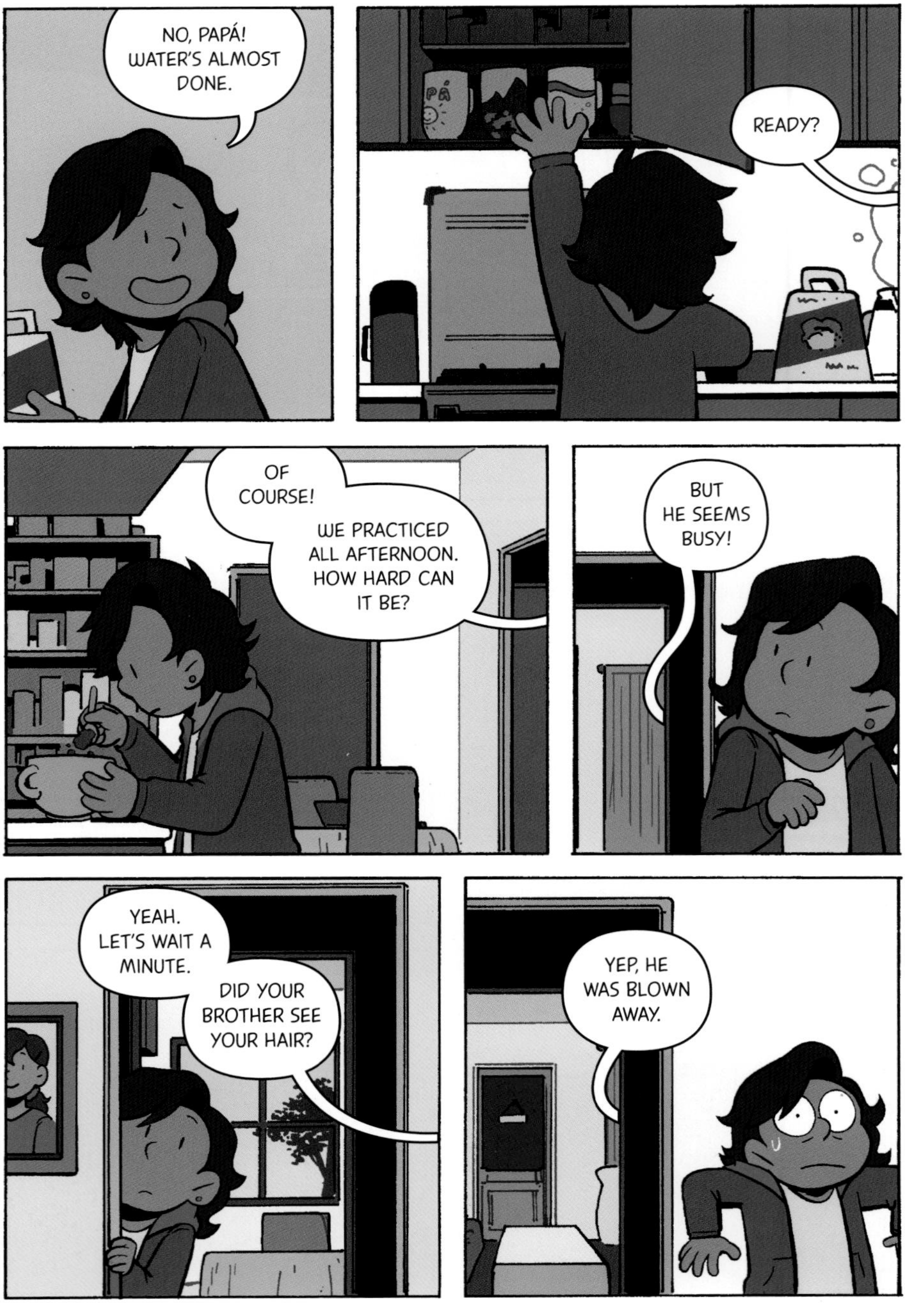
NO, PAPÁ! WATER'S ALMOST DONE.
PÁ
READY?
OF COURSE!
WE PRACTICED ALL AFTERNOON. HOW HARD CAN IT BE?
BUT HE SEEMS BUSY!
YEAH. LET'S WAIT A MINUTE.
DID YOUR BROTHER SEE YOUR HAIR?
YEP, HE WAS BLOWN AWAY.

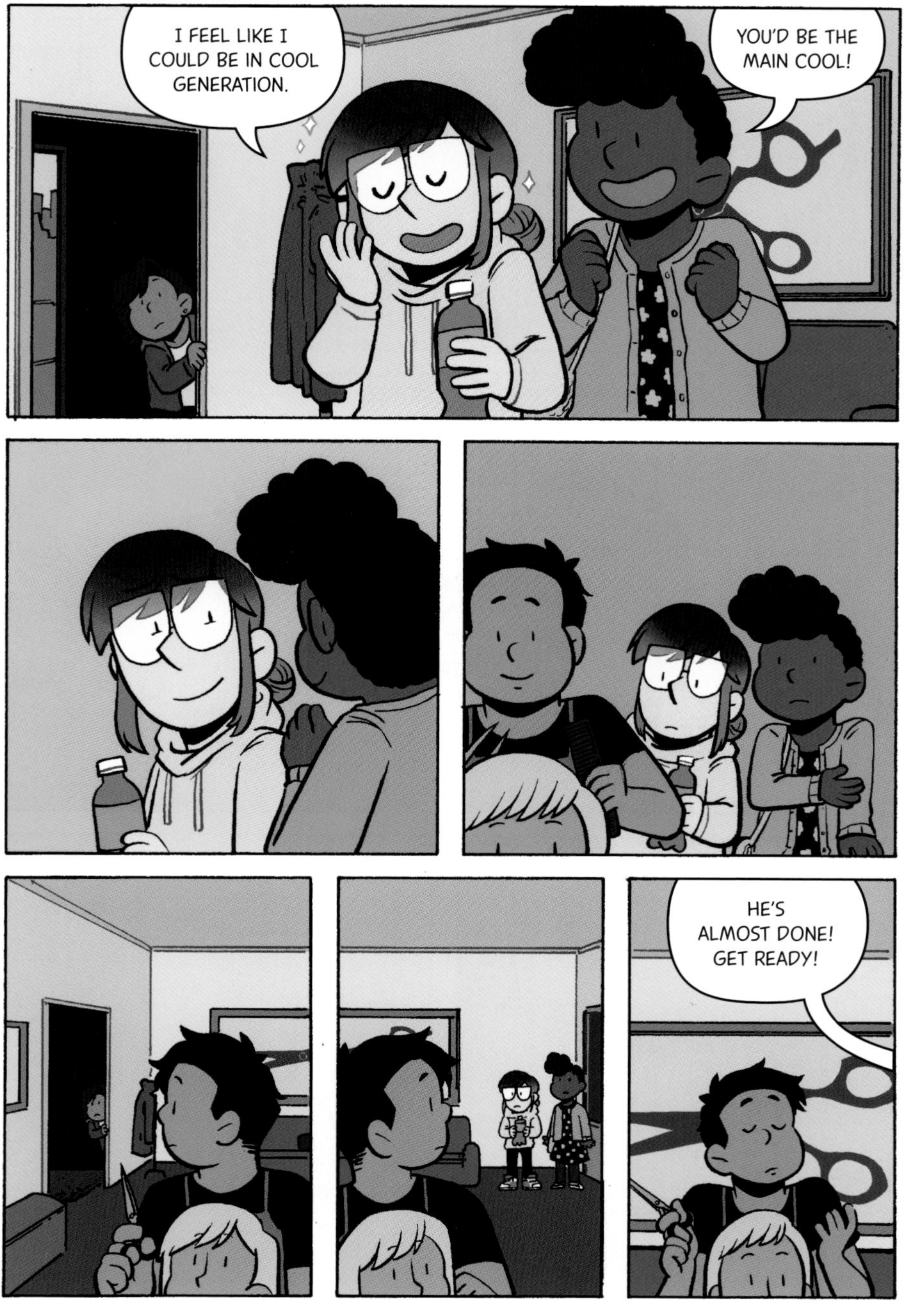
I FEEL LIKE I COULD BE IN COOL GENERATION.
YOU'D BE THE MAIN COOL!
HE'S ALMOST DONE! GET READY!

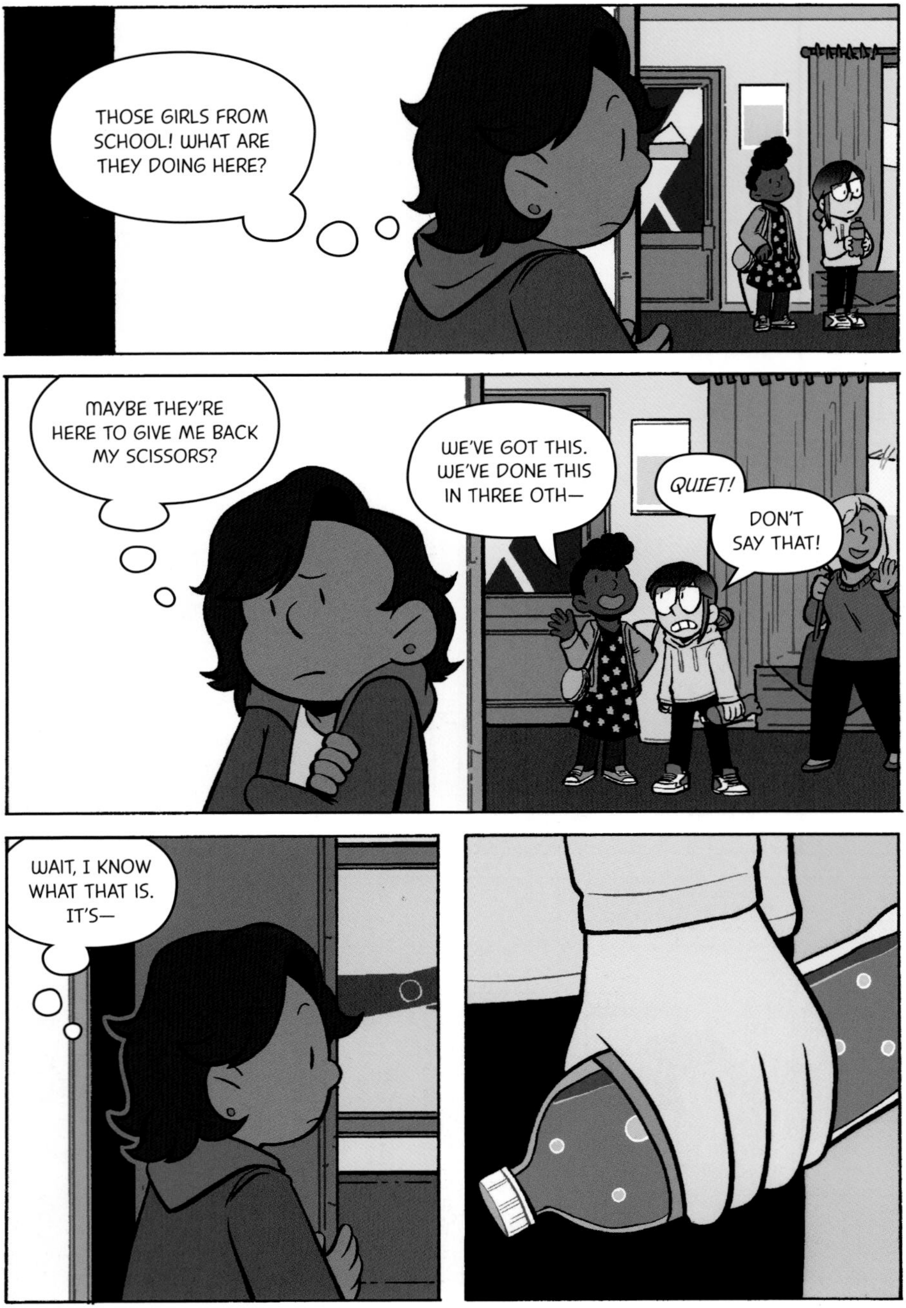
THOSE GIRLS FROM SCHOOL! WHAT ARE THEY DOING HERE?
MAYBE THEY'RE HERE TO GIVE ME BACK MY SCISSORS?
WE'VE GOT THIS. WE'VE DONE THIS IN THREE OTH—
QUIET!
DON'T SAY THAT!
WAIT, I KNOW WHAT THAT IS. IT'S—

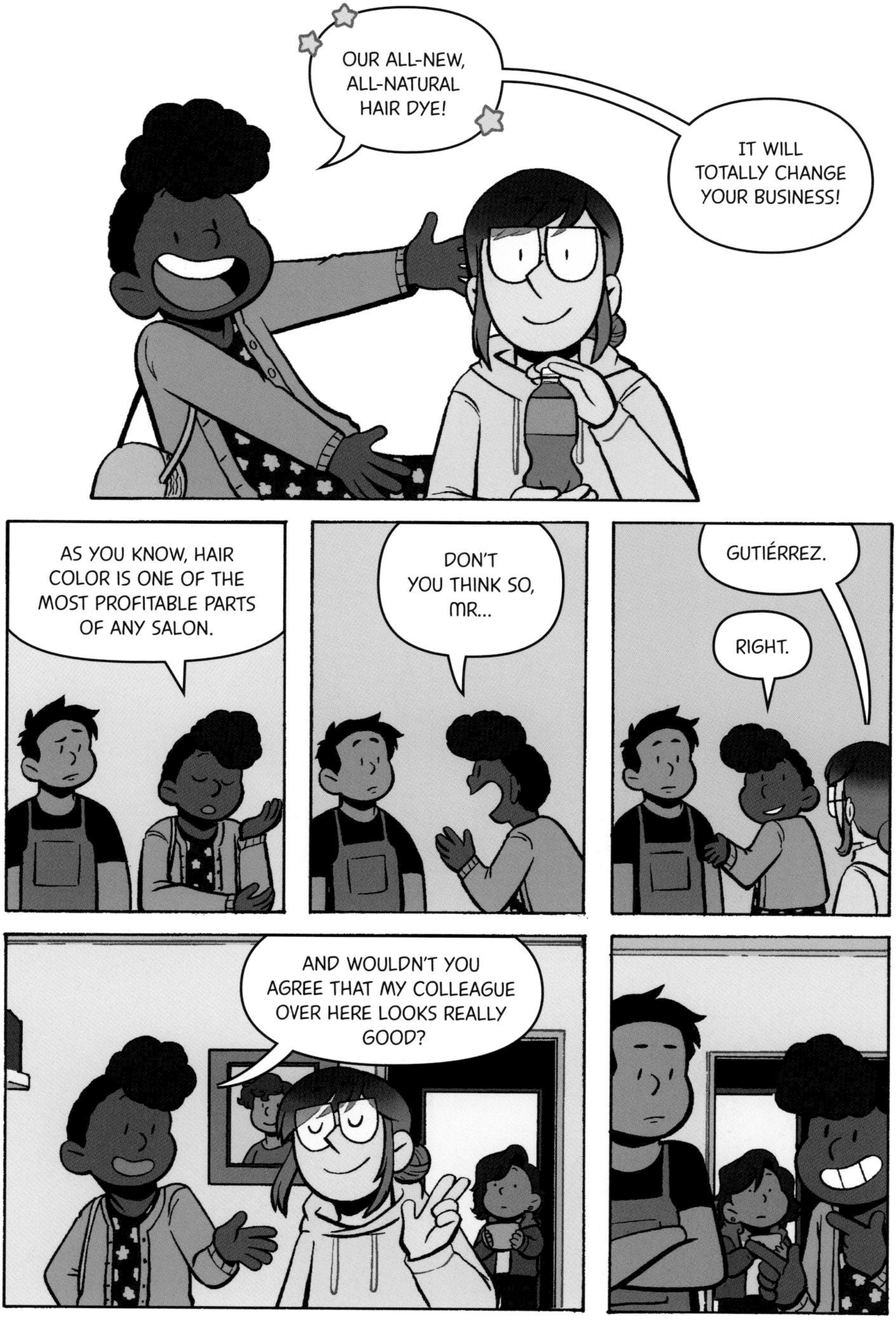
OUR ALL-NEW, ALL-NATURAL HAIR DYE!
IT WILL TOTALLY CHANGE YOUR BUSINESS!
AS YOU KNOW, HAIR COLOR IS ONE OF THE MOST PROFITABLE PARTS OF ANY SALON.
DON'T YOU THINK SO, MR...
GUTIÉRREZ.
RIGHT.
AND WOULDN'T YOU AGREE THAT MY COLLEAGUE OVER HERE LOOKS REALLY GOOD?

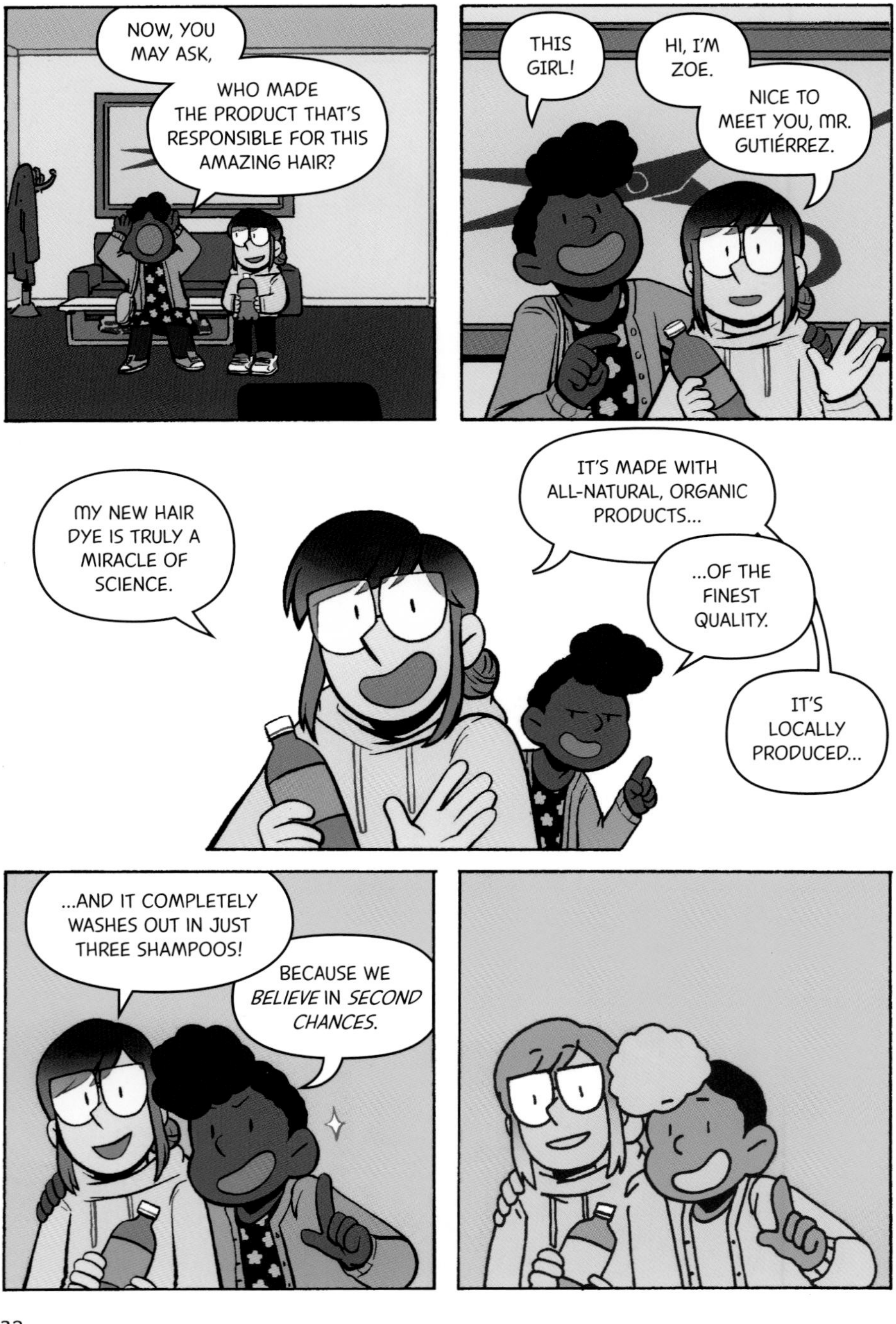
NOW, YOU MAY ASK,
WHO MADE THE PRODUCT THAT'S RESPONSIBLE FOR THIS AMAZING HAIR?
THIS GIRL!
HI, I'M ZOE.
NICE TO MEET YOU, MR. GUTIÉRREZ.
MY NEW HAIR DYE IS TRULY A MIRACLE OF SCIENCE.
IT'S MADE WITH ALL-NATURAL, ORGANIC PRODUCTS...
...OF THE FINEST QUALITY.
IT'S LOCALLY PRODUCED...
...AND IT COMPLETELY WASHES OUT IN JUST THREE SHAMPOOS!
BECAUSE WE BELIEVE IN SECOND CHANCES.

SO, MR. GUTIÉRREZ, WHAT DO YOU THINK? WANT TO BUY SOME AND TRY IT ON YOUR CLIENTS?

I'M SORRY, GIRLS.

THIS LOOKS GREAT, BUT IT JUST DOESN'T WORK WITH WHAT I DO HERE.

I'M GONNA HAVE TO SAY NO. BUT IF YOU PUT THE SAME EFFORT INTO SCHOOL AS YOU DO HAIR PRODUCTS, YOU TWO WILL GO FAR.

I HAVE TO GET BACK TO WORK NOW. NICE MEETING YOU.

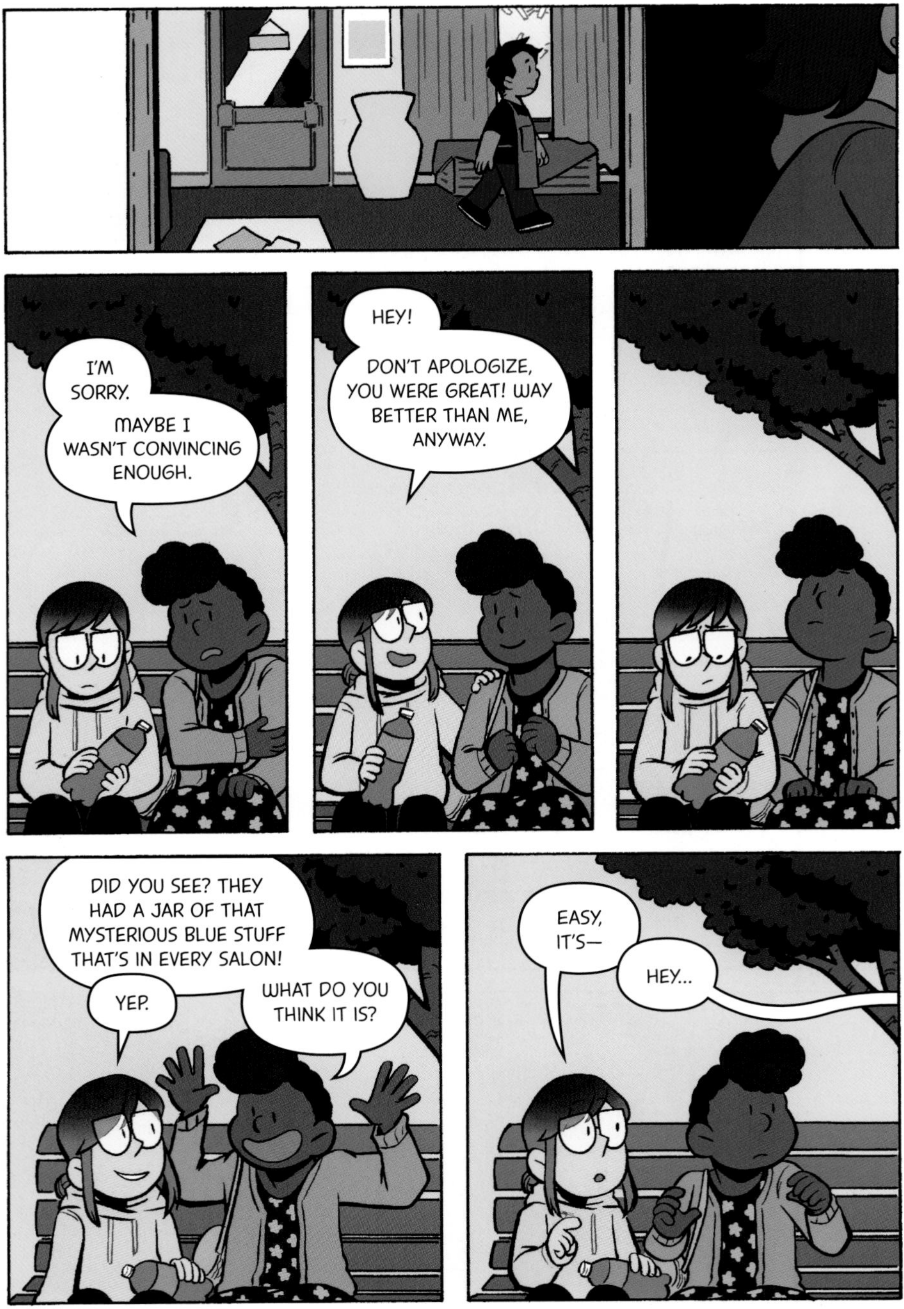
I'M SORRY.
MAYBE I WASN'T CONVINCING ENOUGH.
HEY!
DON'T APOLOGIZE, YOU WERE GREAT! WAY BETTER THAN ME, ANYWAY.
DID YOU SEE? THEY HAD A JAR OF THAT MYSTERIOUS BLUE STUFF THAT'S IN EVERY SALON!
YEP.
WHAT DO YOU THINK IT IS?
EASY, IT'S—
HEY...

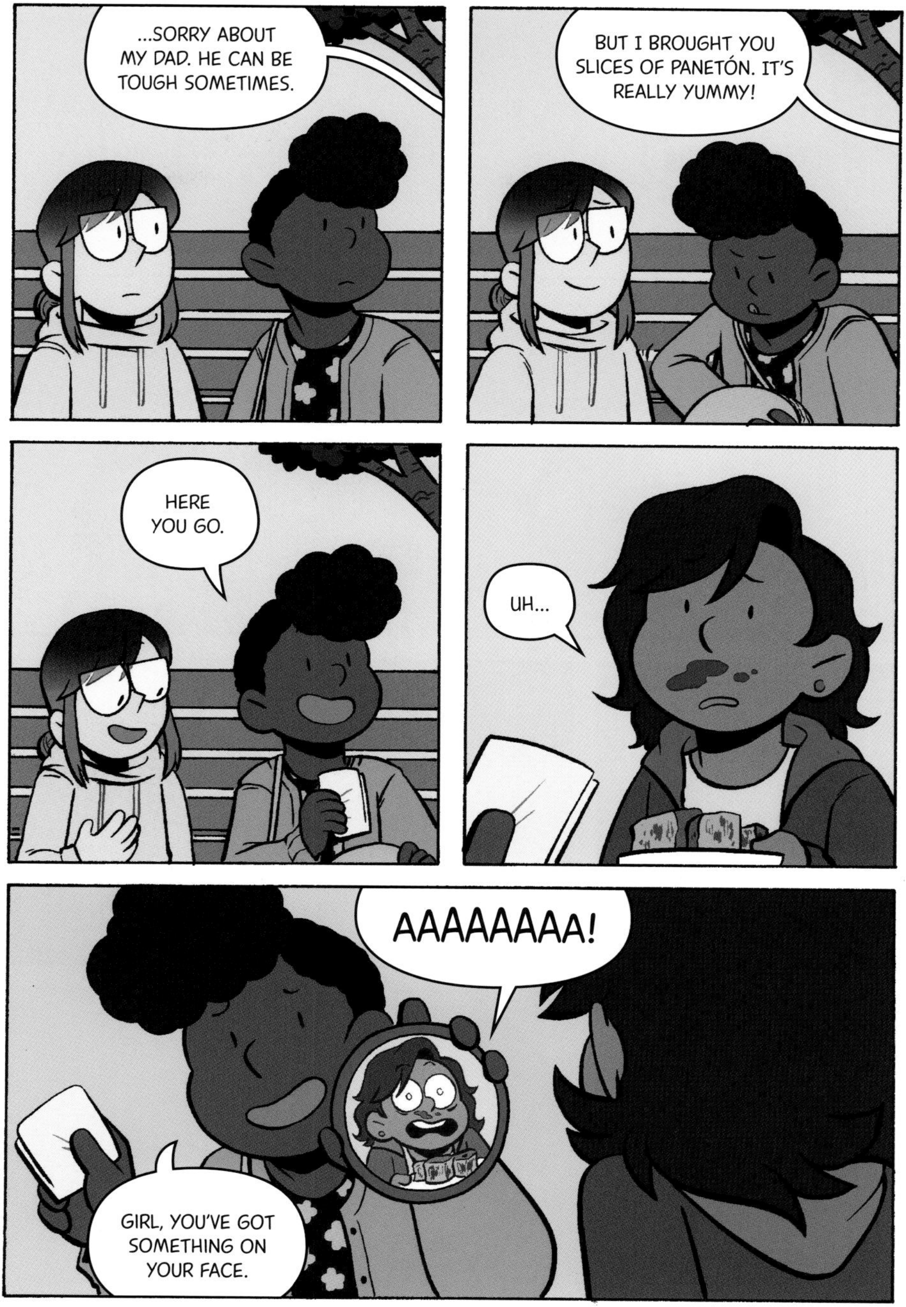
...SORRY ABOUT MY DAD. HE CAN BE TOUGH SOMETIMES.
BUT I BROUGHT YOU SLICES OF PANETÓN. IT'S REALLY YUMMY!
HERE YOU GO.
UH...
AAAAAAAA!
GIRL, YOU'VE GOT SOMETHING ON YOUR FACE.

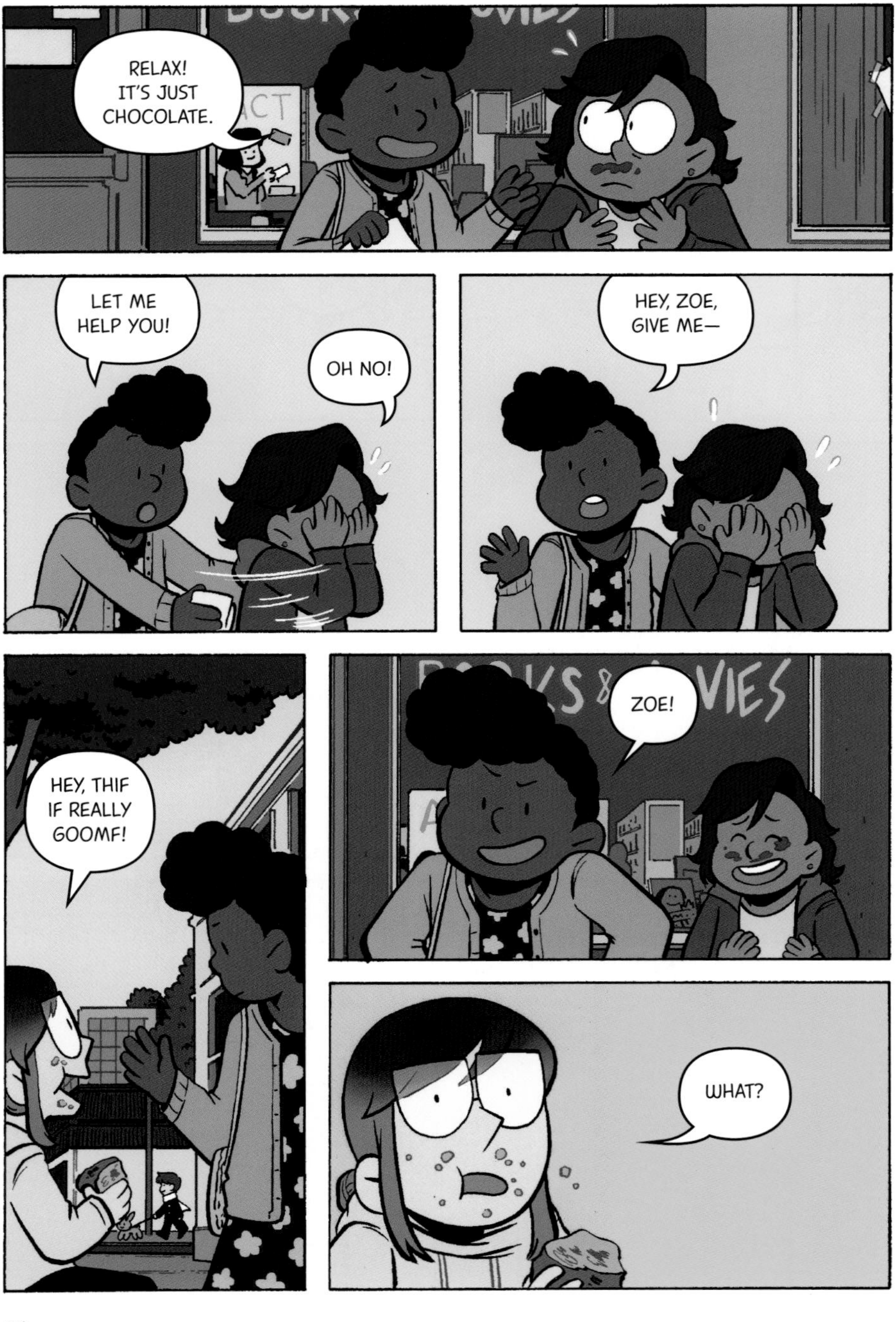
RELAX! IT'S JUST CHOCOLATE.
LET ME HELP YOU!
OH NO!
HEY, ZOE, GIVE ME—
HEY, THIF IF REALLY GOOMF!
ZOE!
WHAT?

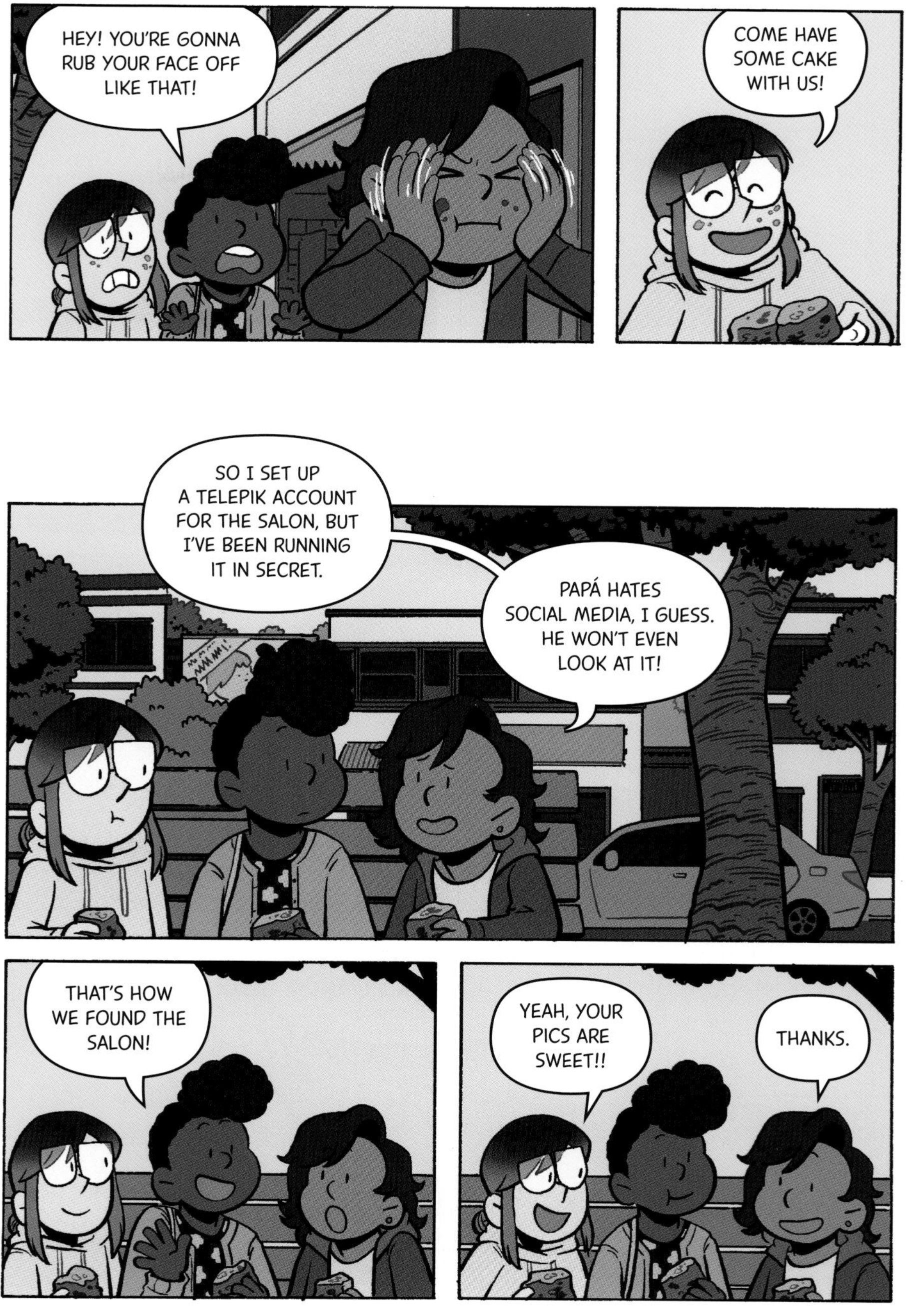
HEY! YOU'RE GONNA RUB YOUR FACE OFF LIKE THAT!
COME HAVE SOME CAKE WITH US!
SO I SET UP A TELEPIK ACCOUNT FOR THE SALON, BUT I'VE BEEN RUNNING IT IN SECRET.
PAPÁ HATES SOCIAL MEDIA, I GUESS. HE WON'T EVEN LOOK AT IT!
THAT'S HOW WE FOUND THE SALON!
YEAH, YOUR PICS ARE SWEET!!
THANKS.

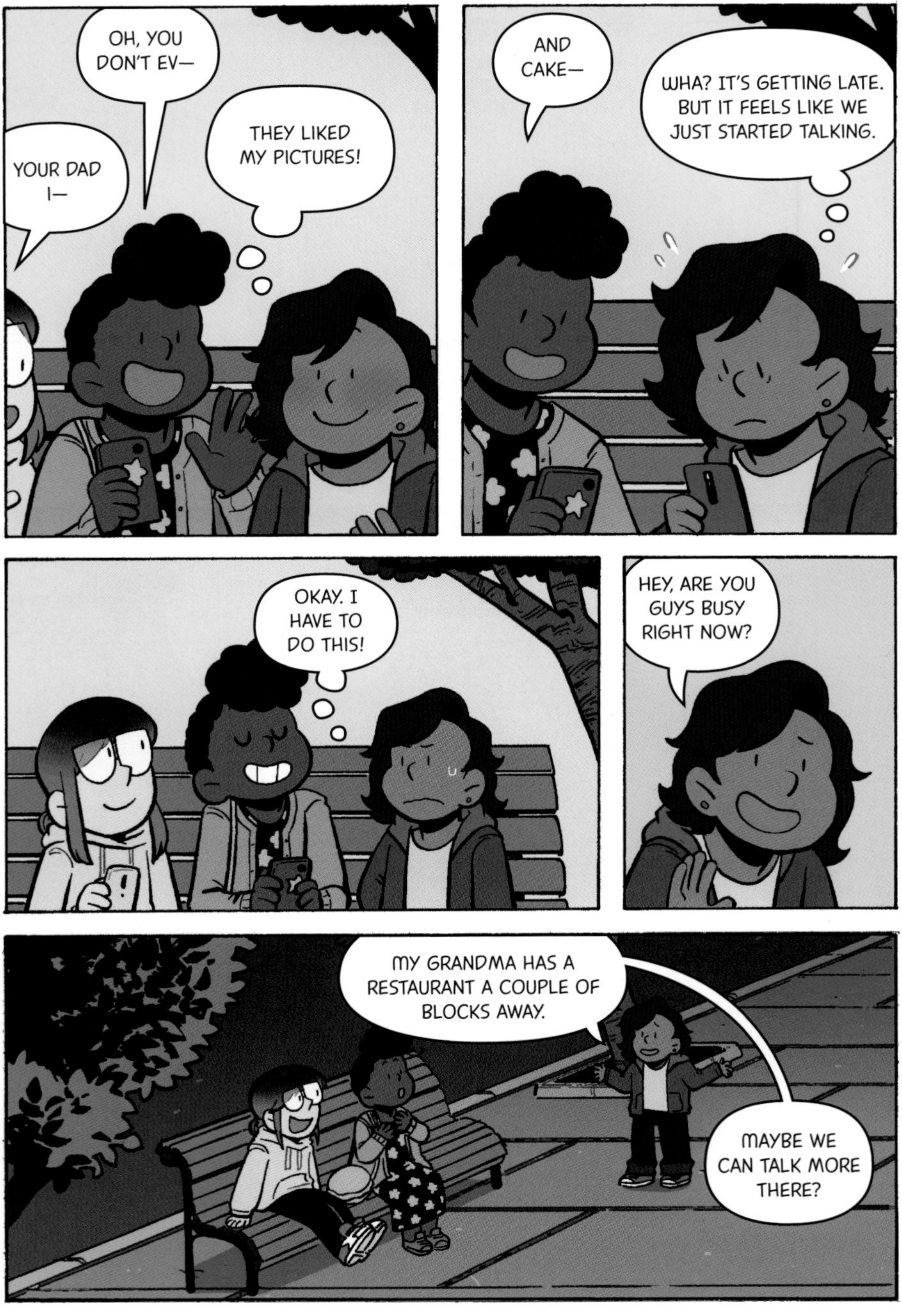
OH, YOU DON'T EV—
YOUR DAD I—
THEY LIKED MY PICTURES!
AND CAKE—
WHA? IT'S GETTING LATE. BUT IT FEELS LIKE WE JUST STARTED TALKING.
OKAY. I HAVE TO DO THIS!
HEY, ARE YOU GUYS BUSY RIGHT NOW?
MY GRANDMA HAS A RESTAURANT A COUPLE OF BLOCKS AWAY.
MAYBE WE CAN TALK MORE THERE?

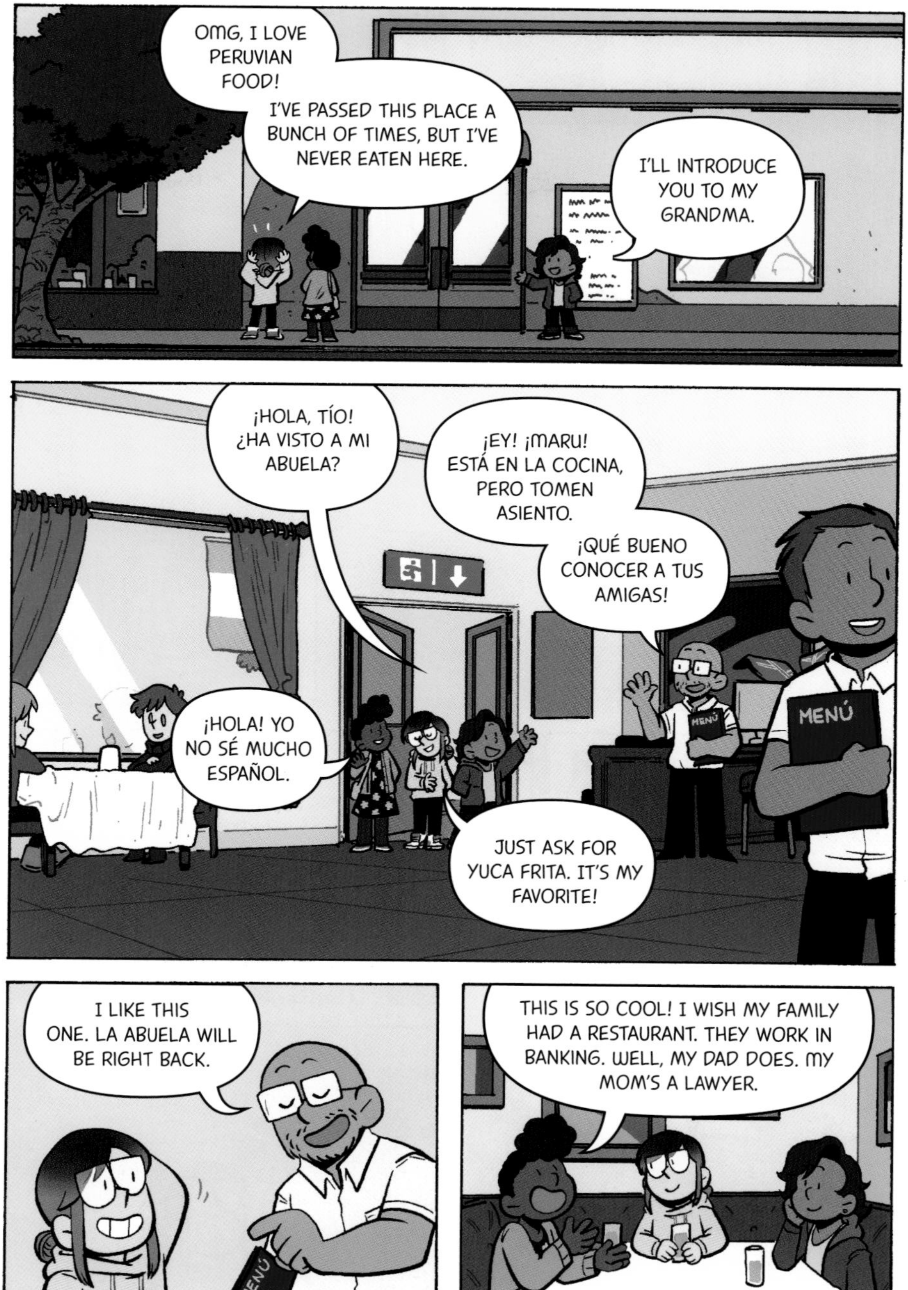
OMG, I LOVE PERUVIAN FOOD!
I'VE PASSED THIS PLACE A BUNCH OF TIMES, BUT I'VE NEVER EATEN HERE.
I'LL INTRODUCE YOU TO MY GRANDMA.
¡HOLA, TÍO! ¿HA VISTO A MI ABUELA?
¡EY! ¡MARU! ESTÁ EN LA COCINA, PERO TOMEN ASIENTO.
¡QUÉ BUENO CONOCER A TUS AMIGAS!
MENÚ
MENÚ
¡HOLA! YO NO SÉ MUCHO ESPAÑOL.
JUST ASK FOR YUCA FRITA. IT'S MY FAVORITE!
I LIKE THIS ONE. LA ABUELA WILL BE RIGHT BACK.
MENÚ
THIS IS SO COOL! I WISH MY FAMILY HAD A RESTAURANT. THEY WORK IN BANKING. WELL, MY DAD DOES. MY MOM'S A LAWYER.

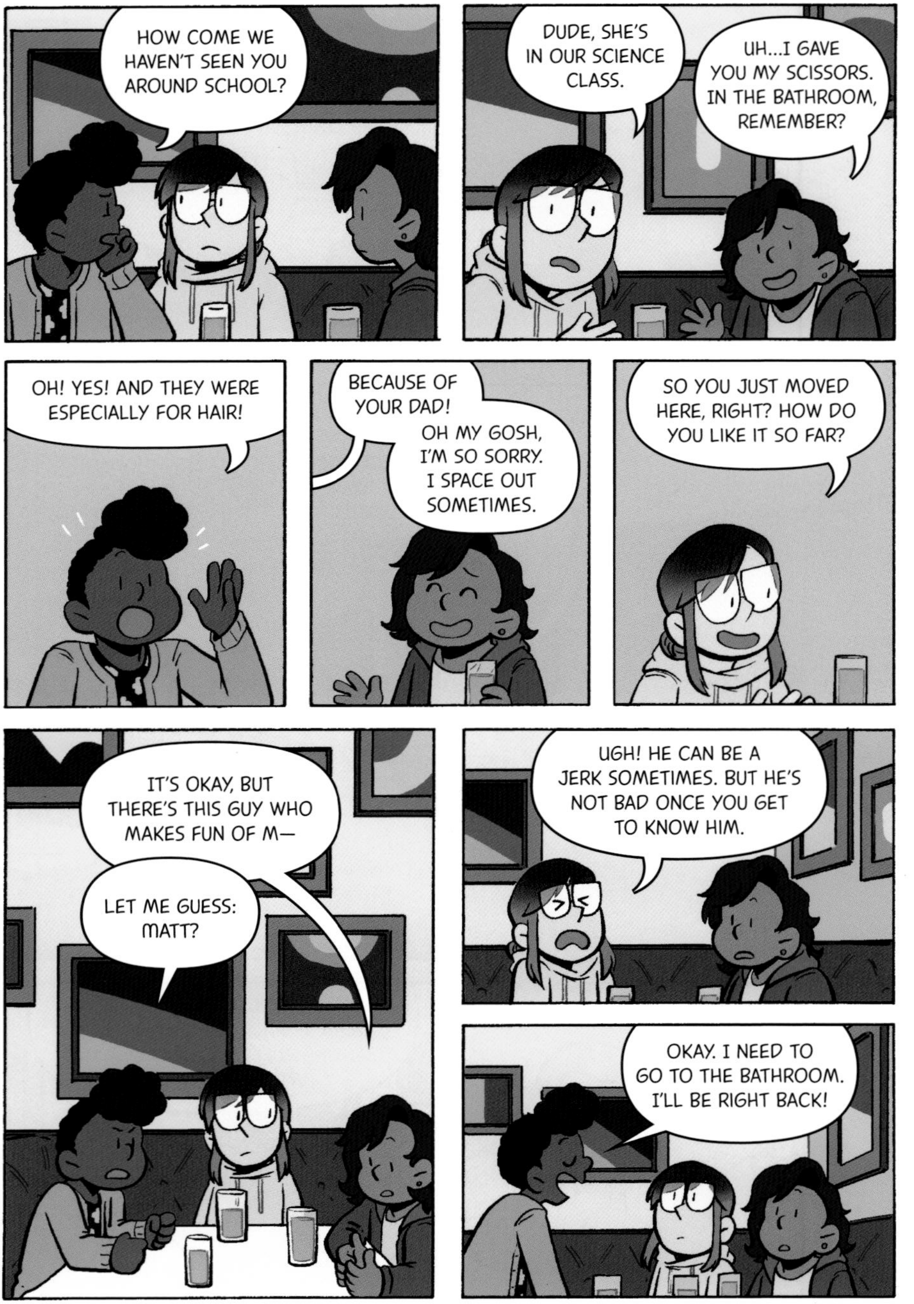
HOW COME WE HAVEN'T SEEN YOU AROUND SCHOOL?
DUDE, SHE'S IN OUR SCIENCE CLASS.
UH...I GAVE YOU MY SCISSORS. IN THE BATHROOM, REMEMBER?
OH! YES! AND THEY WERE ESPECIALLY FOR HAIR!
BECAUSE OF YOUR DAD!
OH MY GOSH, I'M SO SORRY. I SPACE OUT SOMETIMES.
SO YOU JUST MOVED HERE, RIGHT? HOW DO YOU LIKE IT SO FAR?
IT'S OKAY, BUT THERE'S THIS GUY WHO MAKES FUN OF M—
LET ME GUESS: MATT?
UGH! HE CAN BE A JERK SOMETIMES. BUT HE'S NOT BAD ONCE YOU GET TO KNOW HIM.
OKAY. I NEED TO GO TO THE BATHROOM. I'LL BE RIGHT BACK!

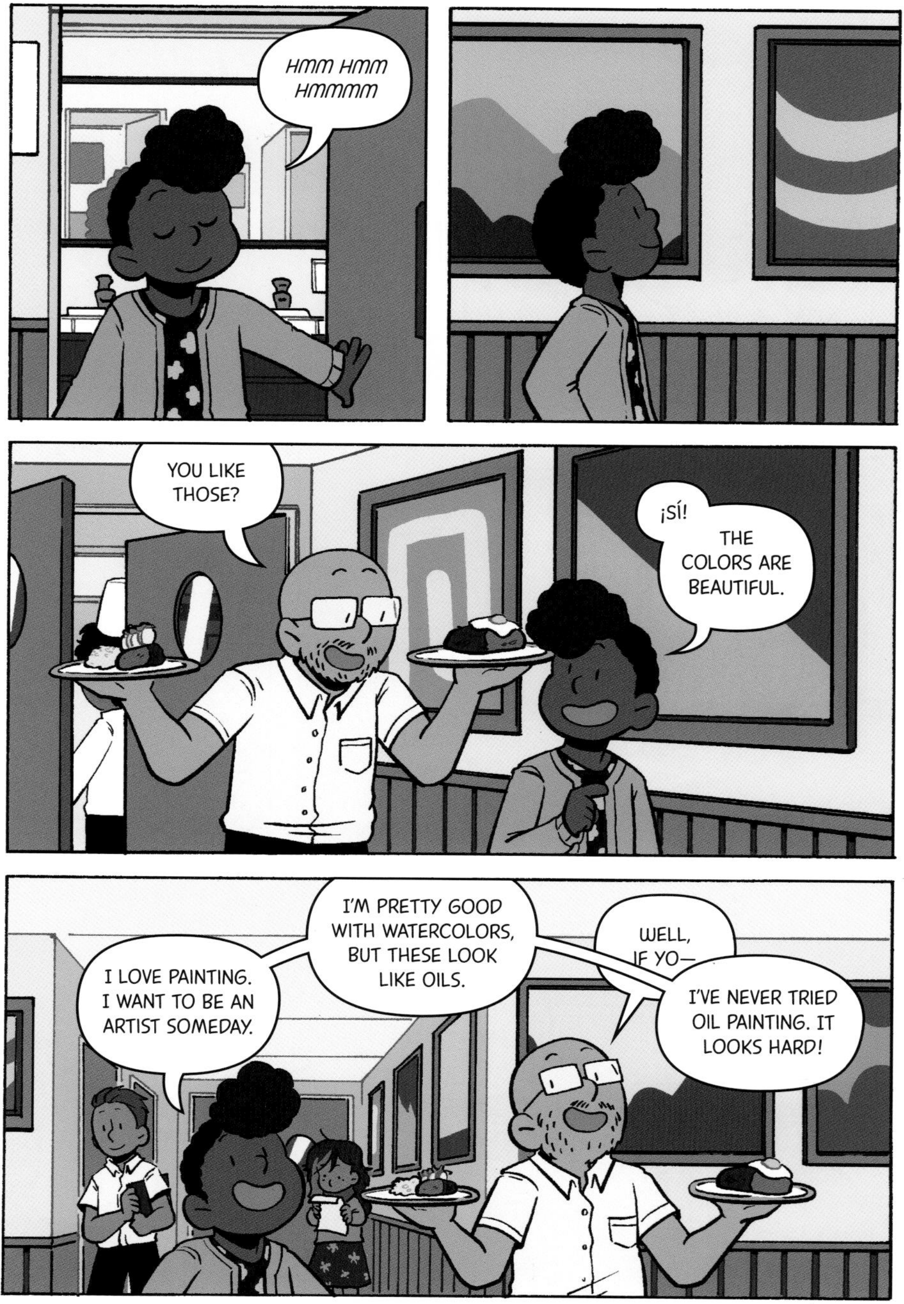
HMM HMM HMMMM
YOU LIKE THOSE?
¡SÍ!
THE COLORS ARE BEAUTIFUL.
I LOVE PAINTING. I WANT TO BE AN ARTIST SOMEDAY.
I'M PRETTY GOOD WITH WATERCOLORS, BUT THESE LOOK LIKE OILS.
WELL, IF YO—
I'VE NEVER TRIED OIL PAINTING. IT LOOKS HARD!

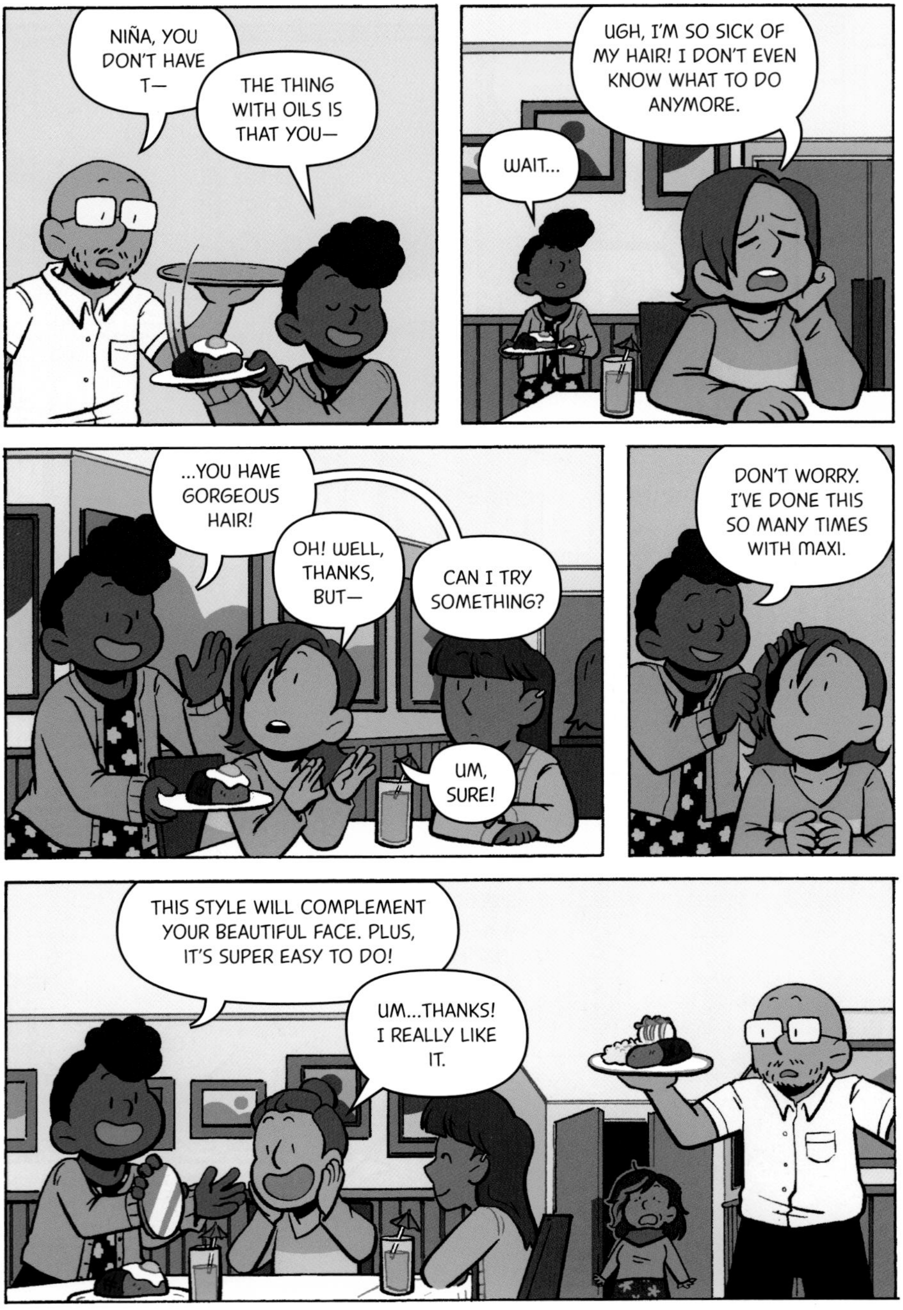
NIÑA, YOU DON'T HAVE T—
THE THING WITH OILS IS THAT YOU—
UGH, I'M SO SICK OF MY HAIR! I DON'T EVEN KNOW WHAT TO DO ANYMORE.
WAIT...
...YOU HAVE GORGEOUS HAIR!
OH! WELL, THANKS, BUT—
CAN I TRY SOMETHING?
UM, SURE!
DON'T WORRY. I'VE DONE THIS SO MANY TIMES WITH MAXI.
THIS STYLE WILL COMPLEMENT YOUR BEAUTIFUL FACE. PLUS, IT'S SUPER EASY TO DO!
UM...THANKS! I REALLY LIKE IT.

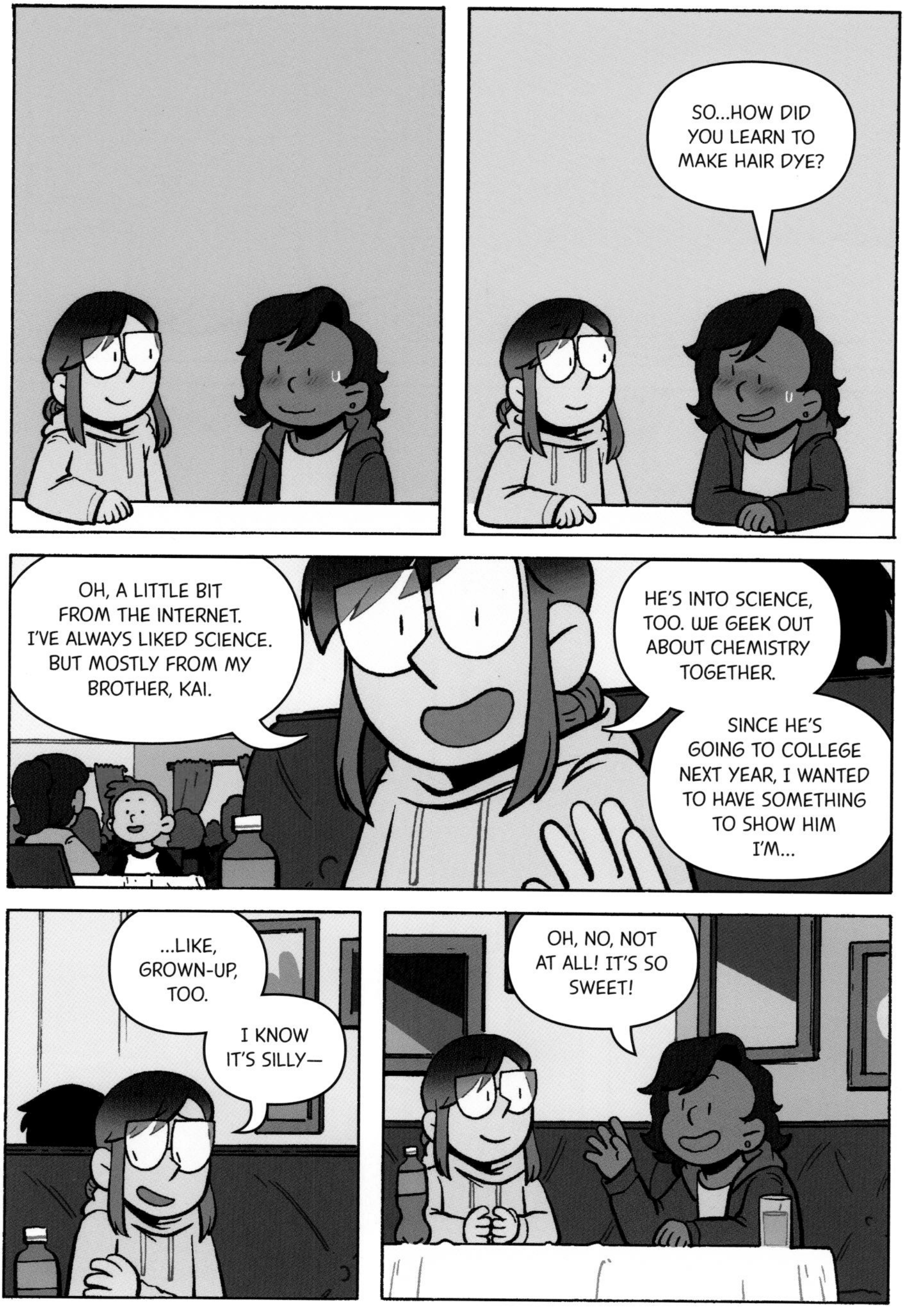
SO...HOW DID YOU LEARN TO MAKE HAIR DYE?
OH, A LITTLE BIT FROM THE INTERNET. I'VE ALWAYS LIKED SCIENCE. BUT MOSTLY FROM MY BROTHER, KAI.
HE'S INTO SCIENCE, TOO. WE GEEK OUT ABOUT CHEMISTRY TOGETHER.
SINCE HE'S GOING TO COLLEGE NEXT YEAR, I WANTED TO HAVE SOMETHING TO SHOW HIM I'M...
...LIKE, GROWN-UP, TOO.
I KNOW IT'S SILLY—
OH, NO, NOT AT ALL! IT'S SO SWEET!

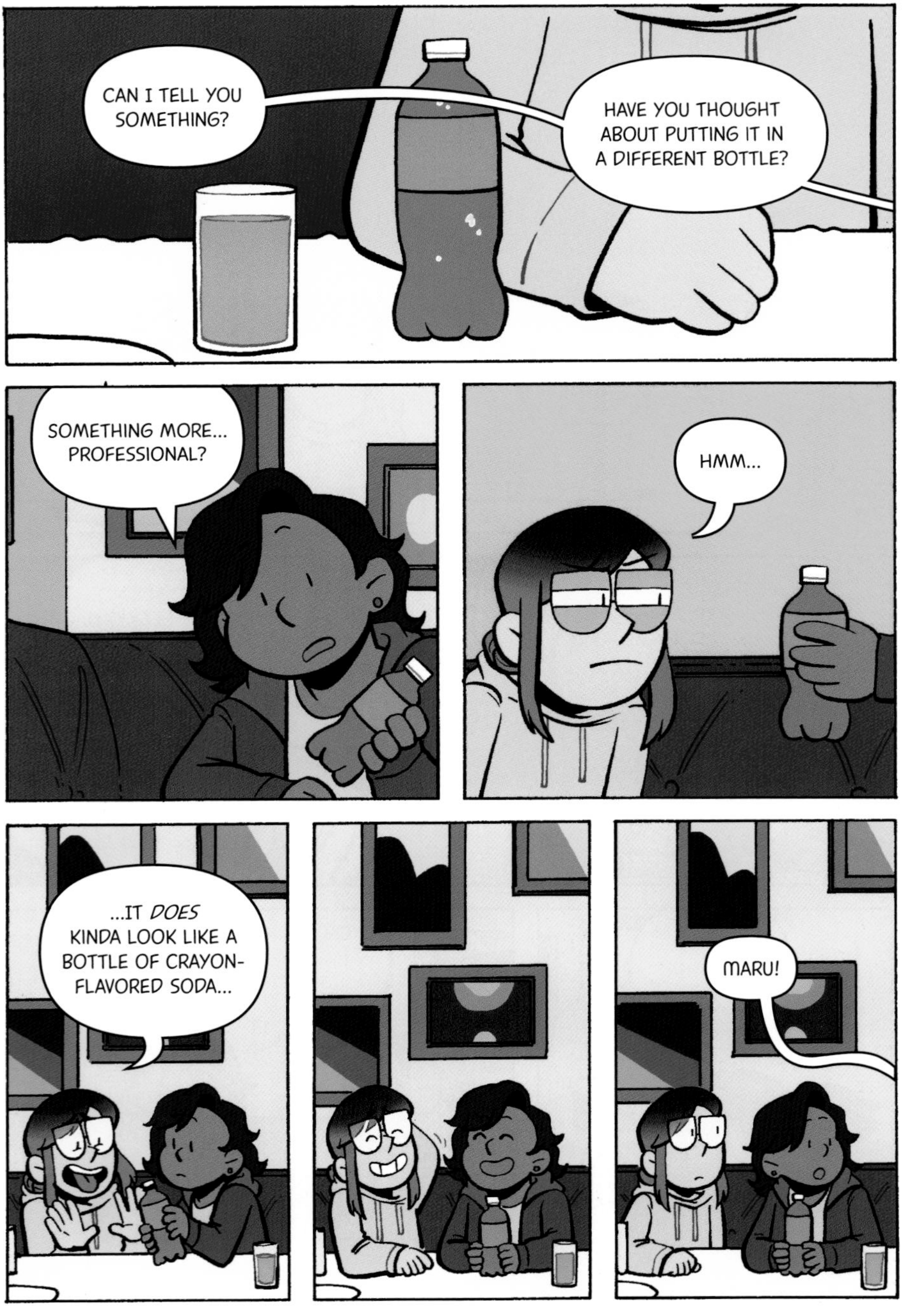
CAN I TELL YOU SOMETHING?
HAVE YOU THOUGHT ABOUT PUTTING IT IN A DIFFERENT BOTTLE?
SOMETHING MORE... PROFESSIONAL?
HMM...
...IT *DOES* KINDA LOOK LIKE A BOTTLE OF CRAYON-FLAVORED SODA...
MARU!

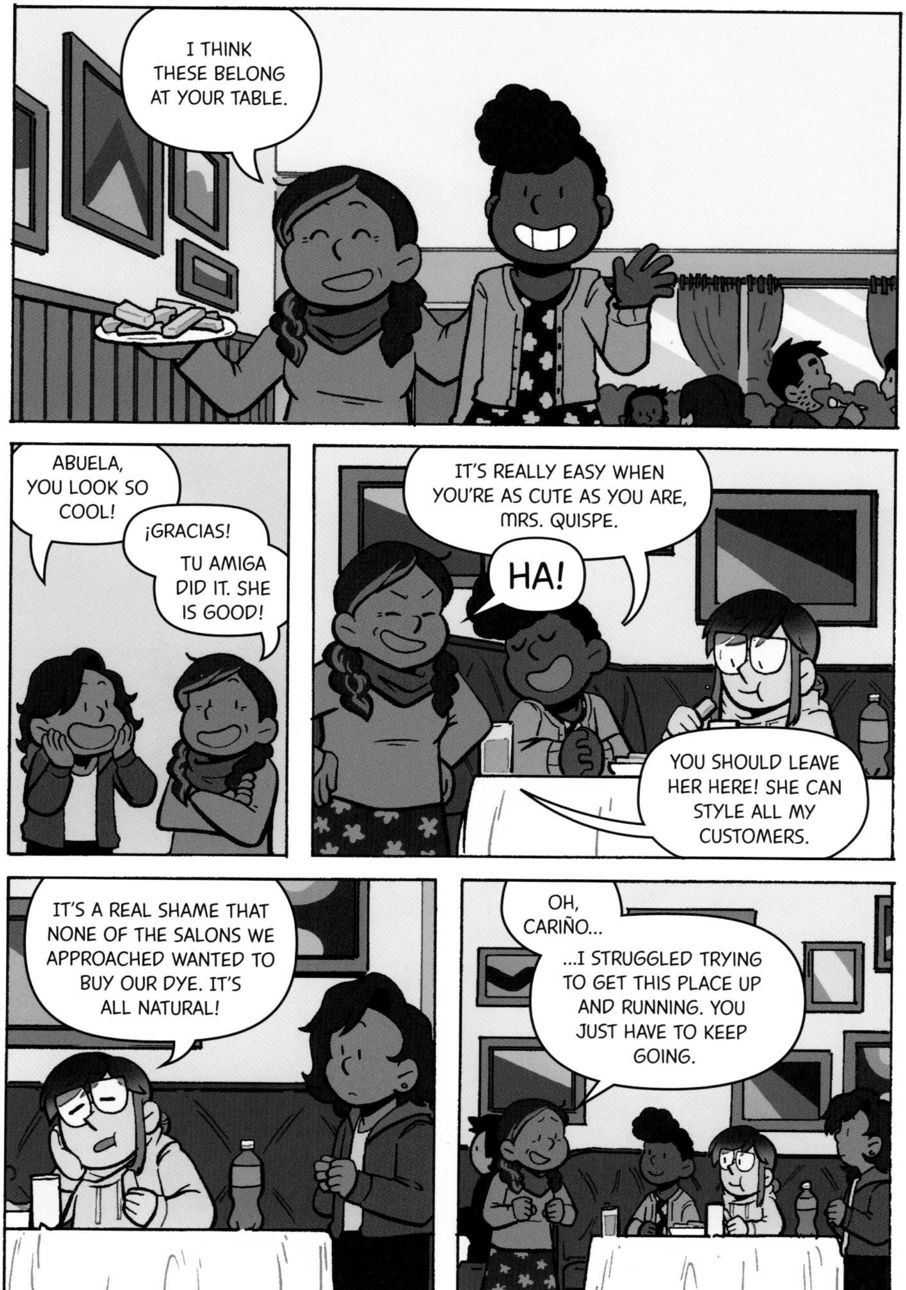
I THINK THESE BELONG AT YOUR TABLE.
ABUELA, YOU LOOK SO COOL!
¡GRACIAS!
TU AMIGA DID IT. SHE IS GOOD!
IT'S REALLY EASY WHEN YOU'RE AS CUTE AS YOU ARE, MRS. QUISPE.
HA!
YOU SHOULD LEAVE HER HERE! SHE CAN STYLE ALL MY CUSTOMERS.
IT'S A REAL SHAME THAT NONE OF THE SALONS WE APPROACHED WANTED TO BUY OUR DYE. IT'S ALL NATURAL!
OH, CARIÑO...
...I STRUGGLED TRYING TO GET THIS PLACE UP AND RUNNING. YOU JUST HAVE TO KEEP GOING.

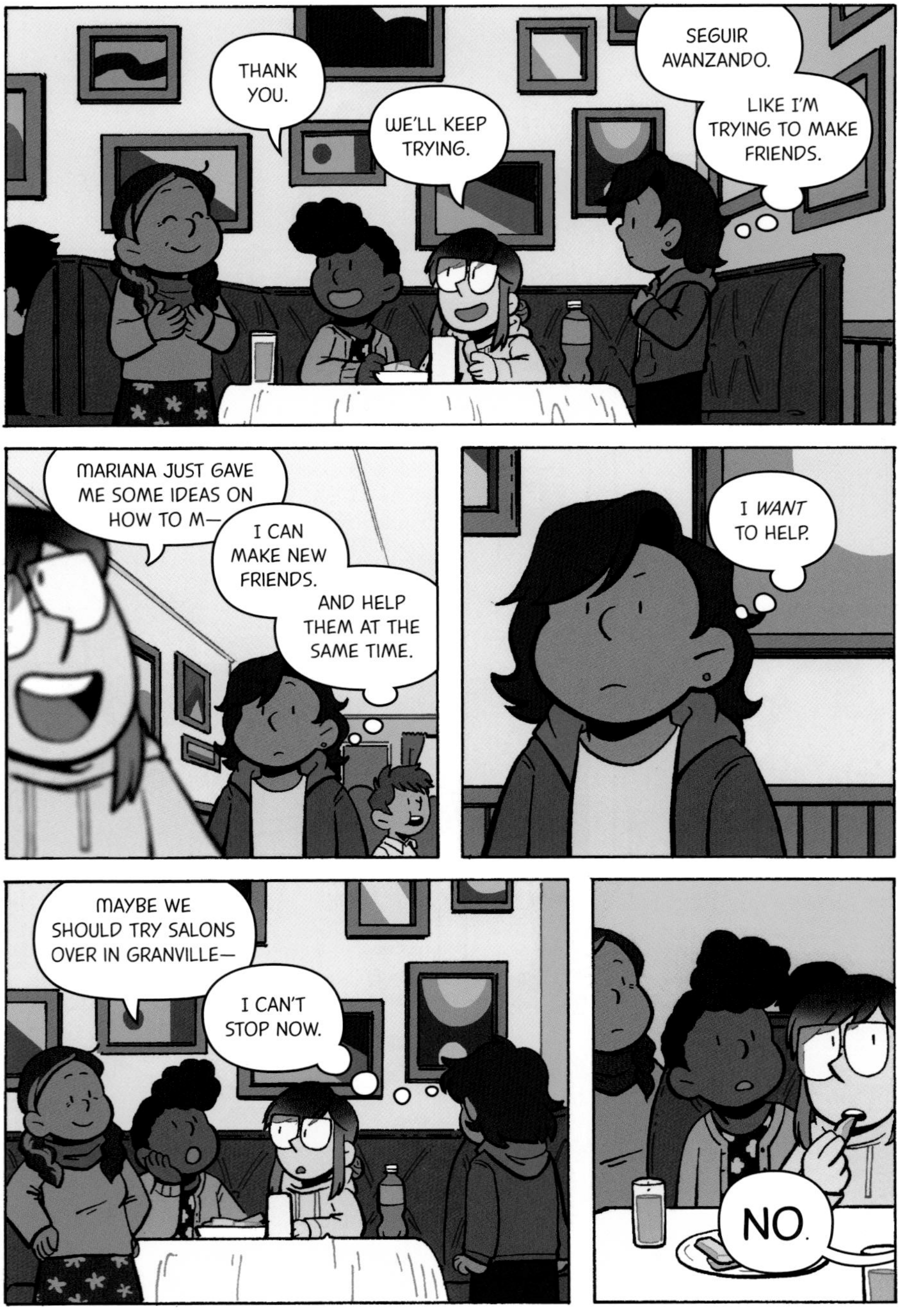
THANK YOU.
WE'LL KEEP TRYING.
SEGUIR AVANZANDO.
LIKE I'M TRYING TO MAKE FRIENDS.
MARIANA JUST GAVE ME SOME IDEAS ON HOW TO M—
I CAN MAKE NEW FRIENDS.
AND HELP THEM AT THE SAME TIME.
I *WANT* TO HELP.
MAYBE WE SHOULD TRY SALONS OVER IN GRANVILLE—
I CAN'T STOP NOW.
NO.

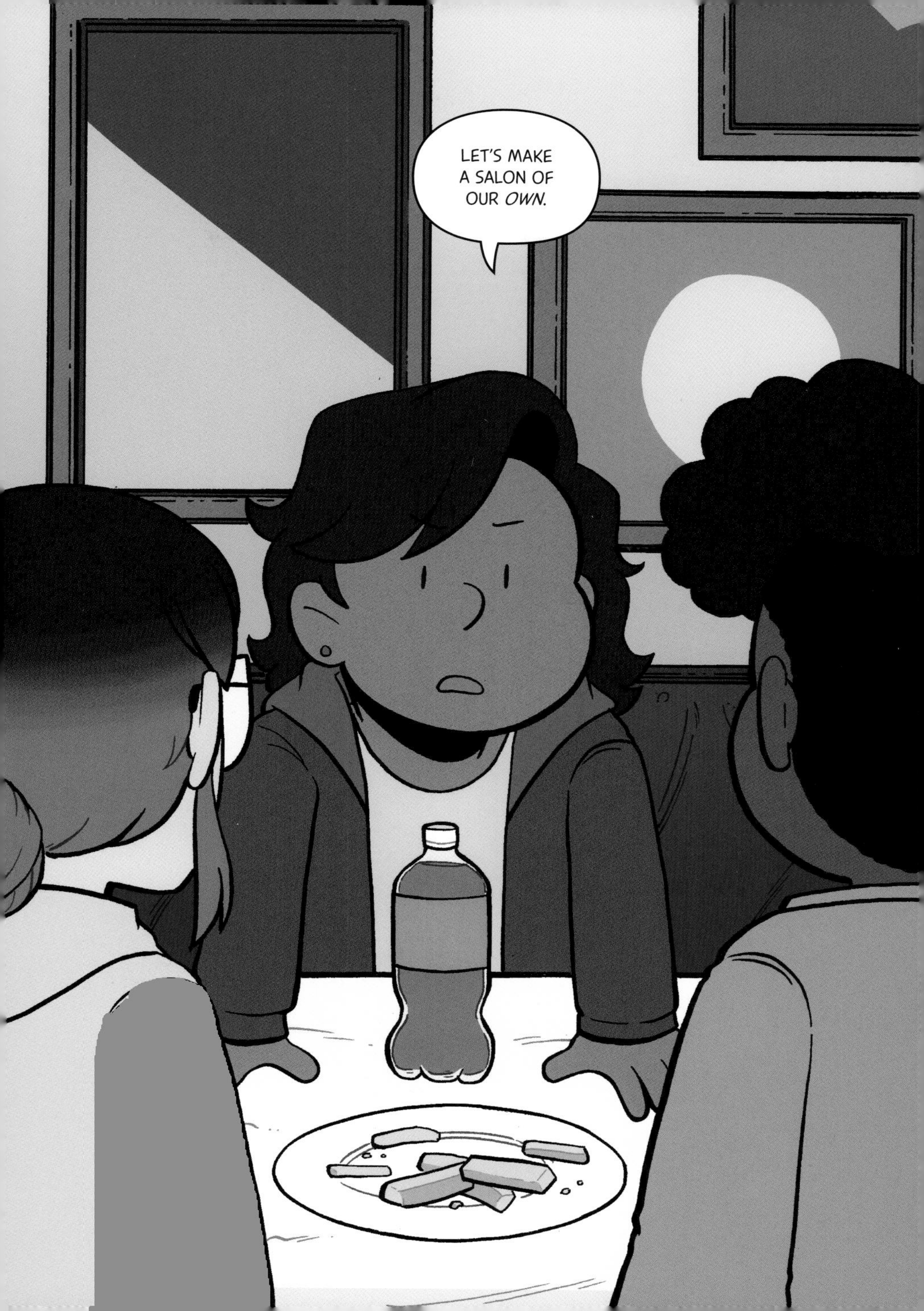
LET'S MAKE A SALON OF OUR *OWN*.

CHAPTER 3

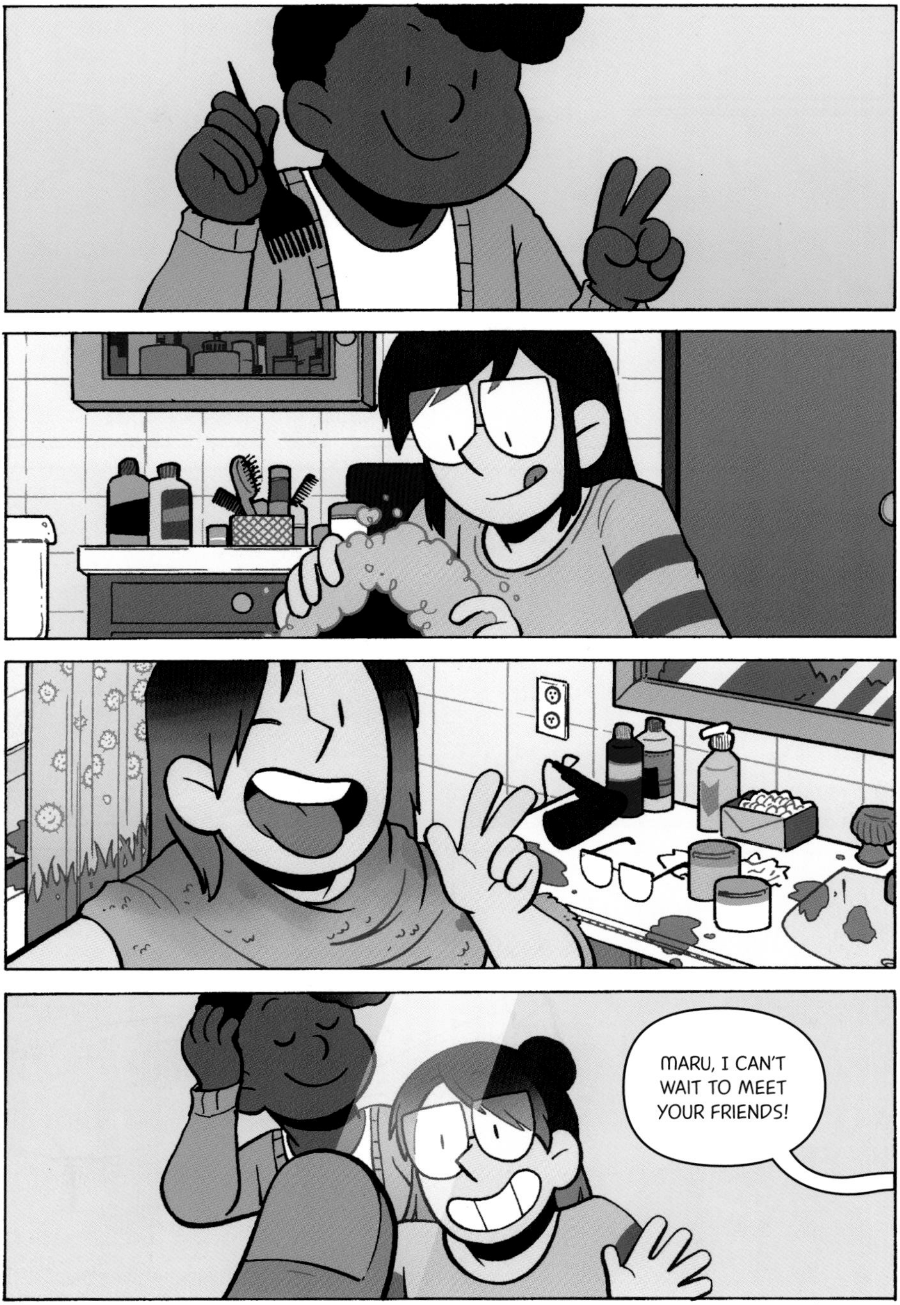
MARU, I CAN'T WAIT TO MEET YOUR FRIENDS!

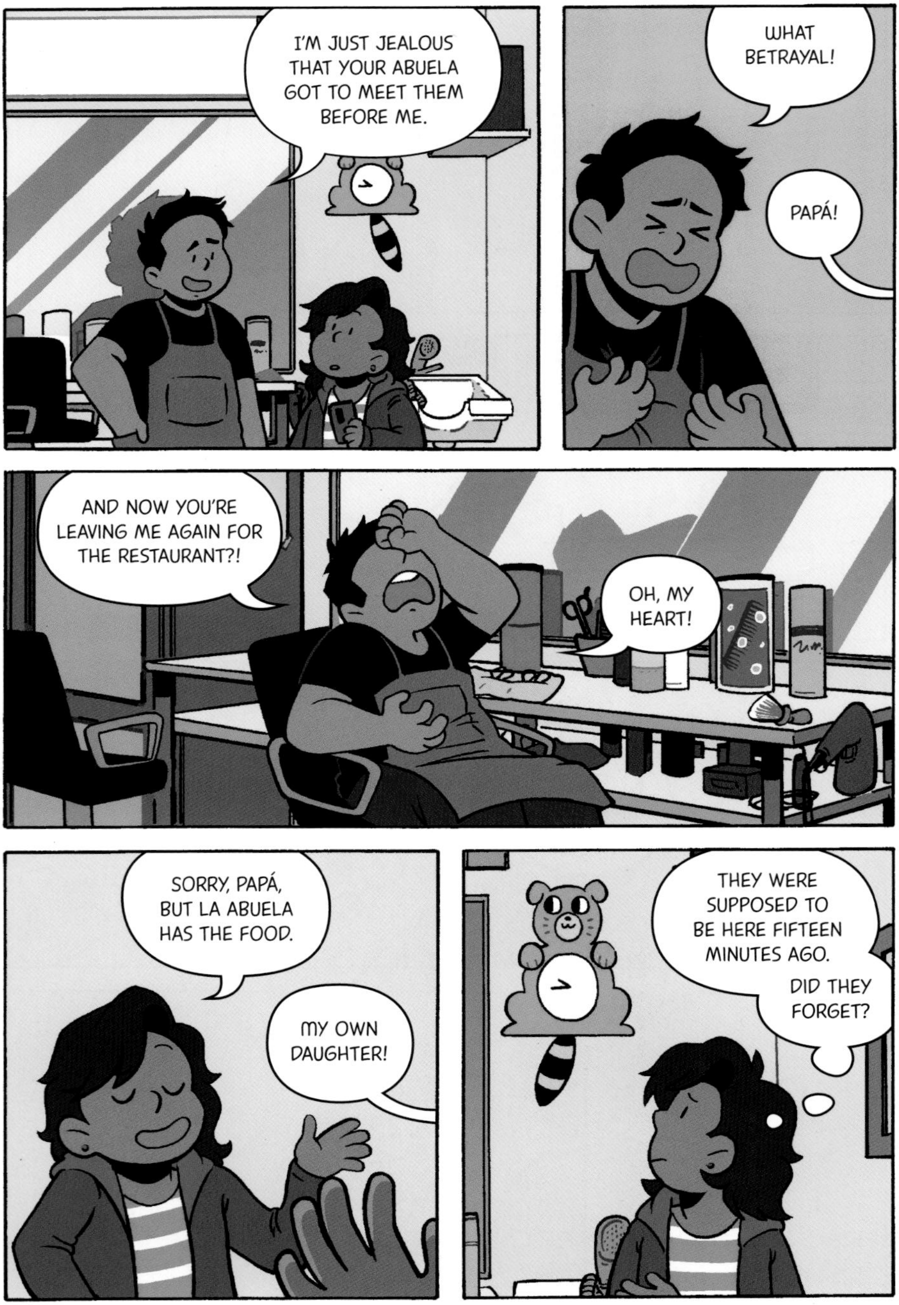
I'M JUST JEALOUS THAT YOUR ABUELA GOT TO MEET THEM BEFORE ME.
WHAT BETRAYAL!
PAPÁ!
AND NOW YOU'RE LEAVING ME AGAIN FOR THE RESTAURANT?!
OH, MY HEART!
SORRY, PAPÁ, BUT LA ABUELA HAS THE FOOD.
MY OWN DAUGHTER!
THEY WERE SUPPOSED TO BE HERE FIFTEEN MINUTES AGO.
DID THEY FORGET?

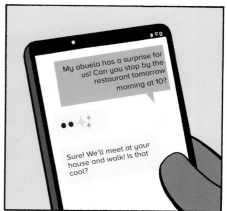

My abuela has a surprise for us! Can you stop by the restaurant tomorrow morning at 10?

Sure! We'll meet at your house and walk! Is that cool?

I'LL WAIT OUTSIDE. I'M SORT OF ANXIOUS ABOUT LA ABUELA'S SURPRISE.

OKAY...

PLEASE BE THERE, PLEASE BE THERE...

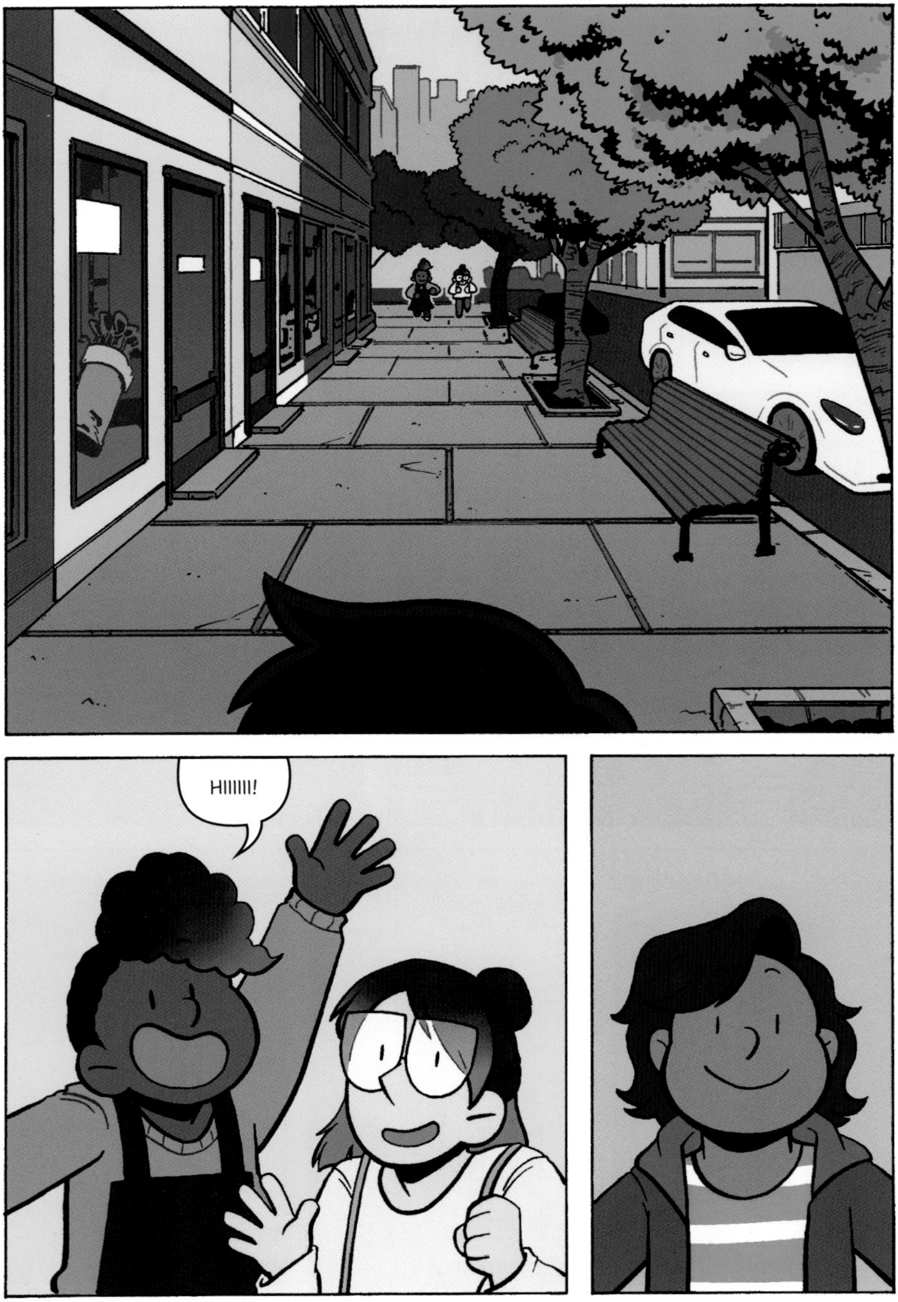
HIIIIII!

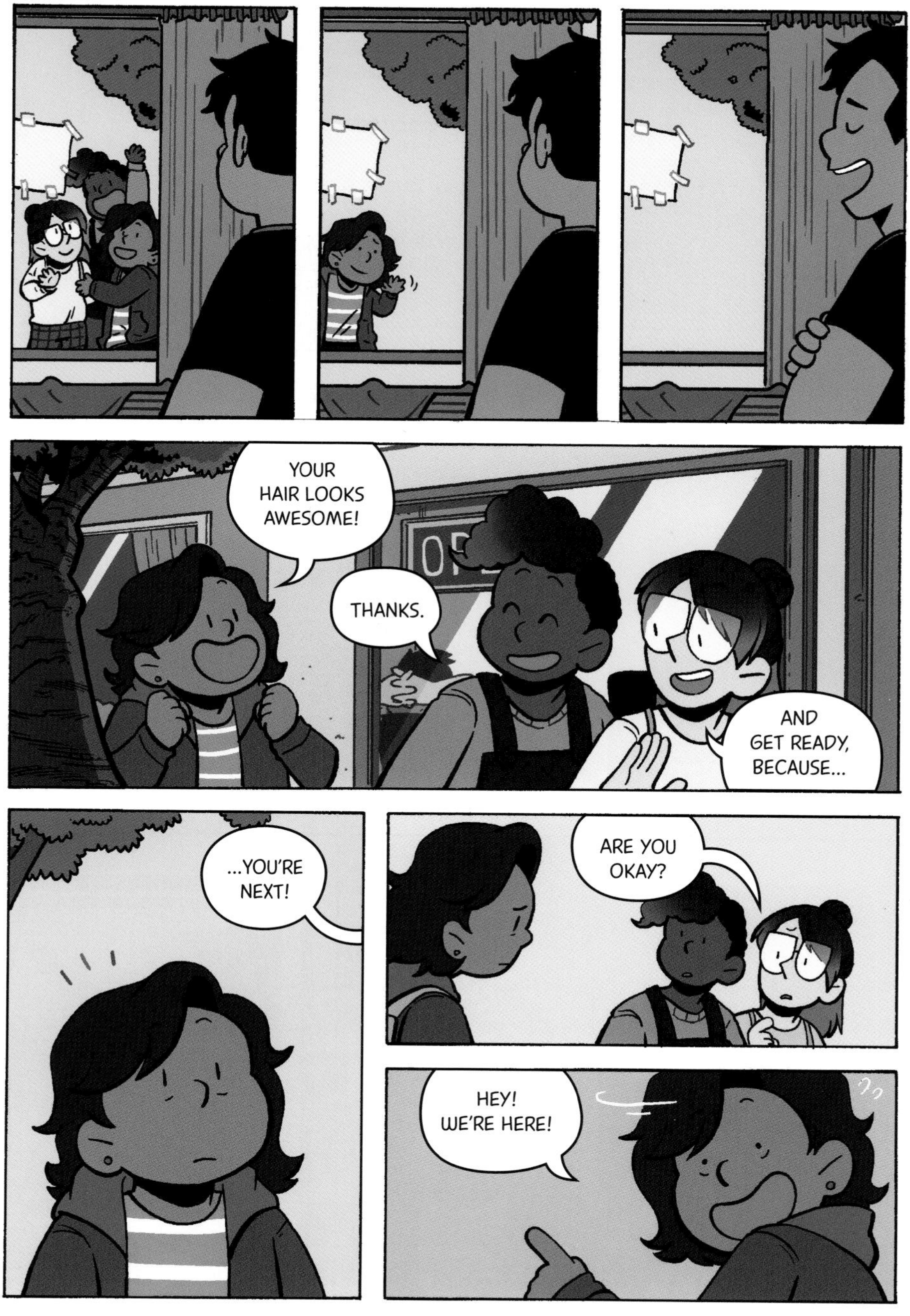
YOUR HAIR LOOKS AWESOME!
THANKS.
AND GET READY, BECAUSE...
...YOU'RE NEXT!
ARE YOU OKAY?
HEY! WE'RE HERE!

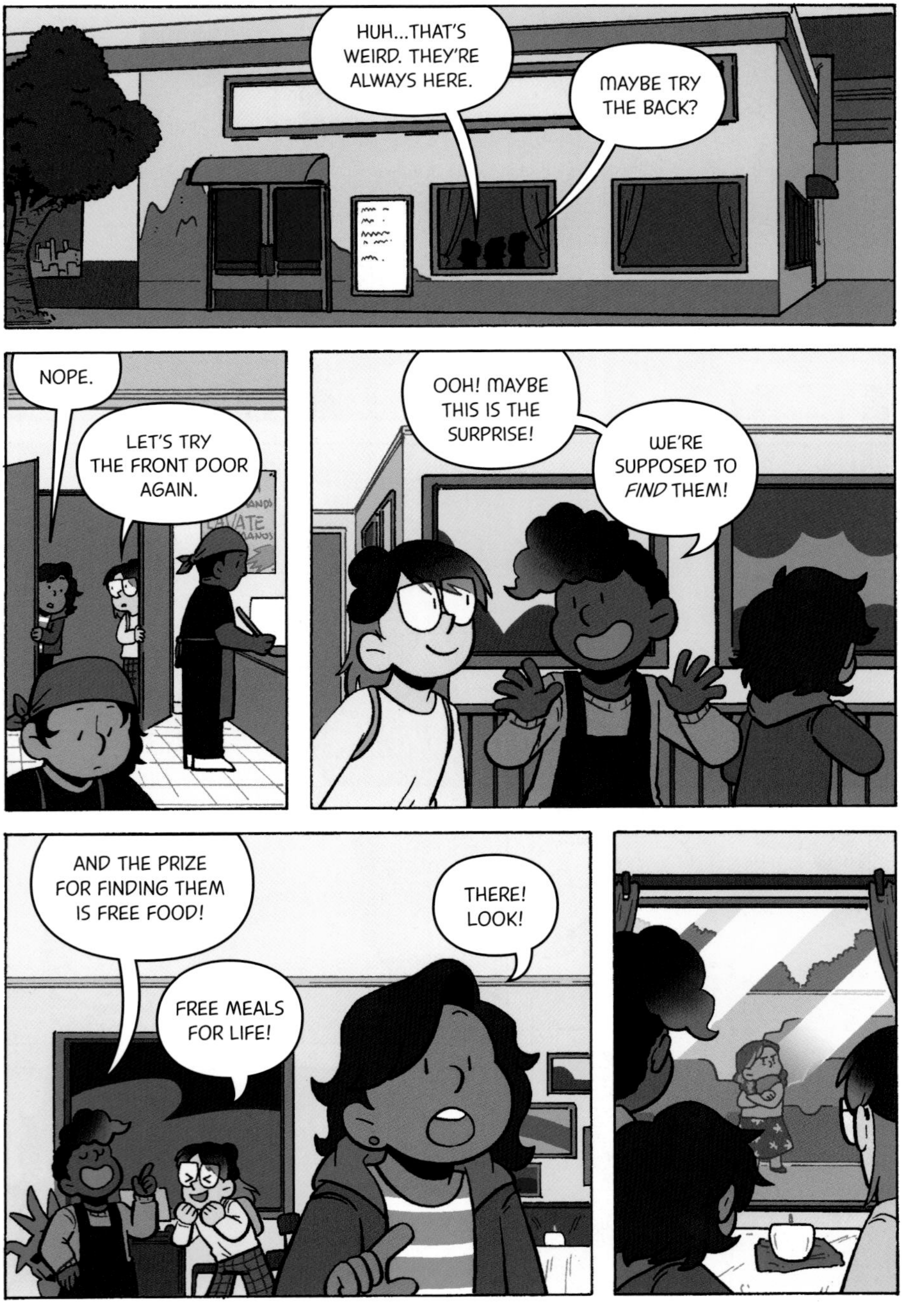
HUH...THAT'S WEIRD. THEY'RE ALWAYS HERE.
MAYBE TRY THE BACK?
NOPE.
LET'S TRY THE FRONT DOOR AGAIN.
OOH! MAYBE THIS IS THE SURPRISE!
WE'RE SUPPOSED TO *FIND* THEM!
AND THE PRIZE FOR FINDING THEM IS FREE FOOD!
FREE MEALS FOR LIFE!
THERE! LOOK!

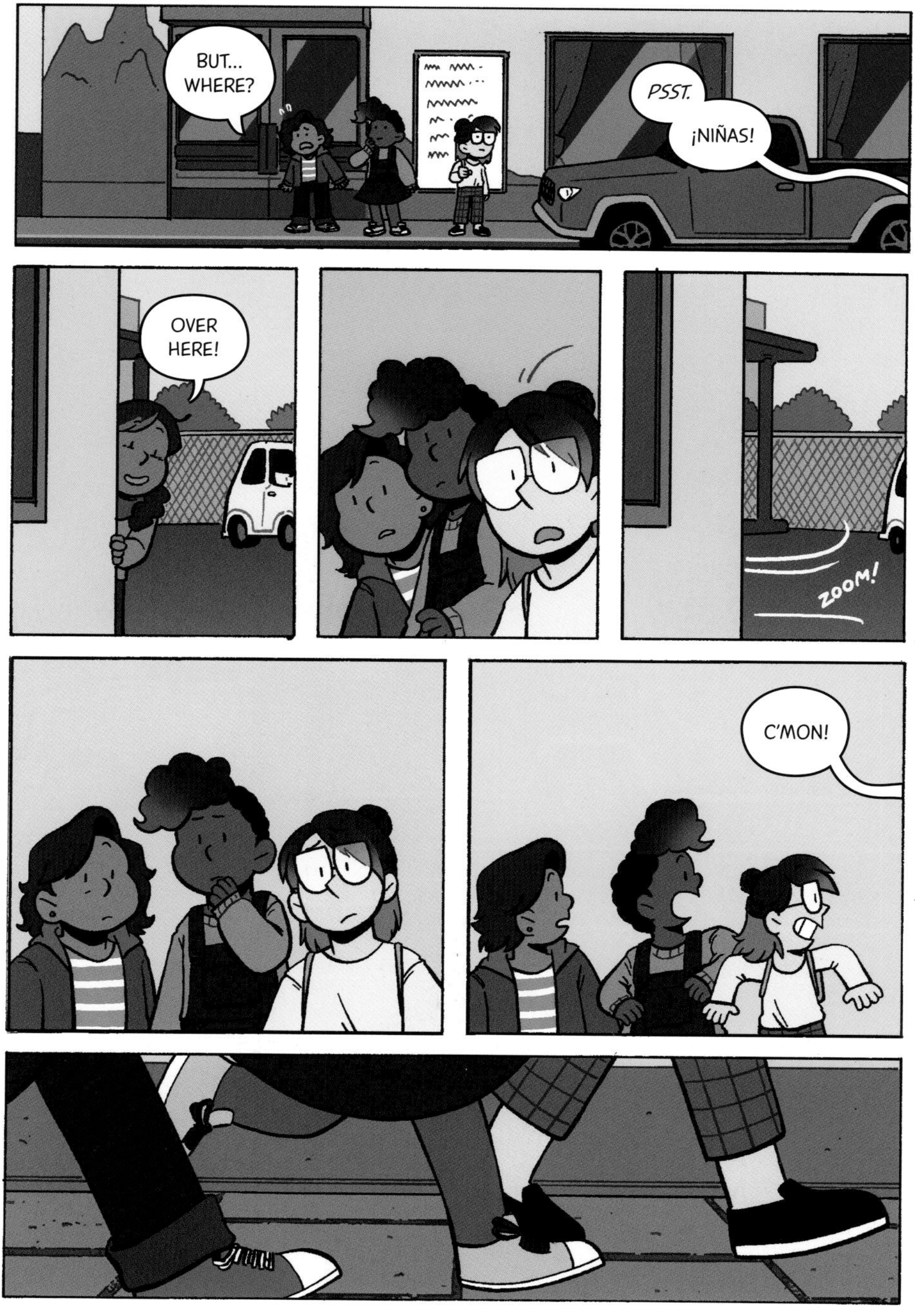

BUT... WHERE?
PSST.
¡NIÑAS!
OVER HERE!
ZOOM!
C'MON!

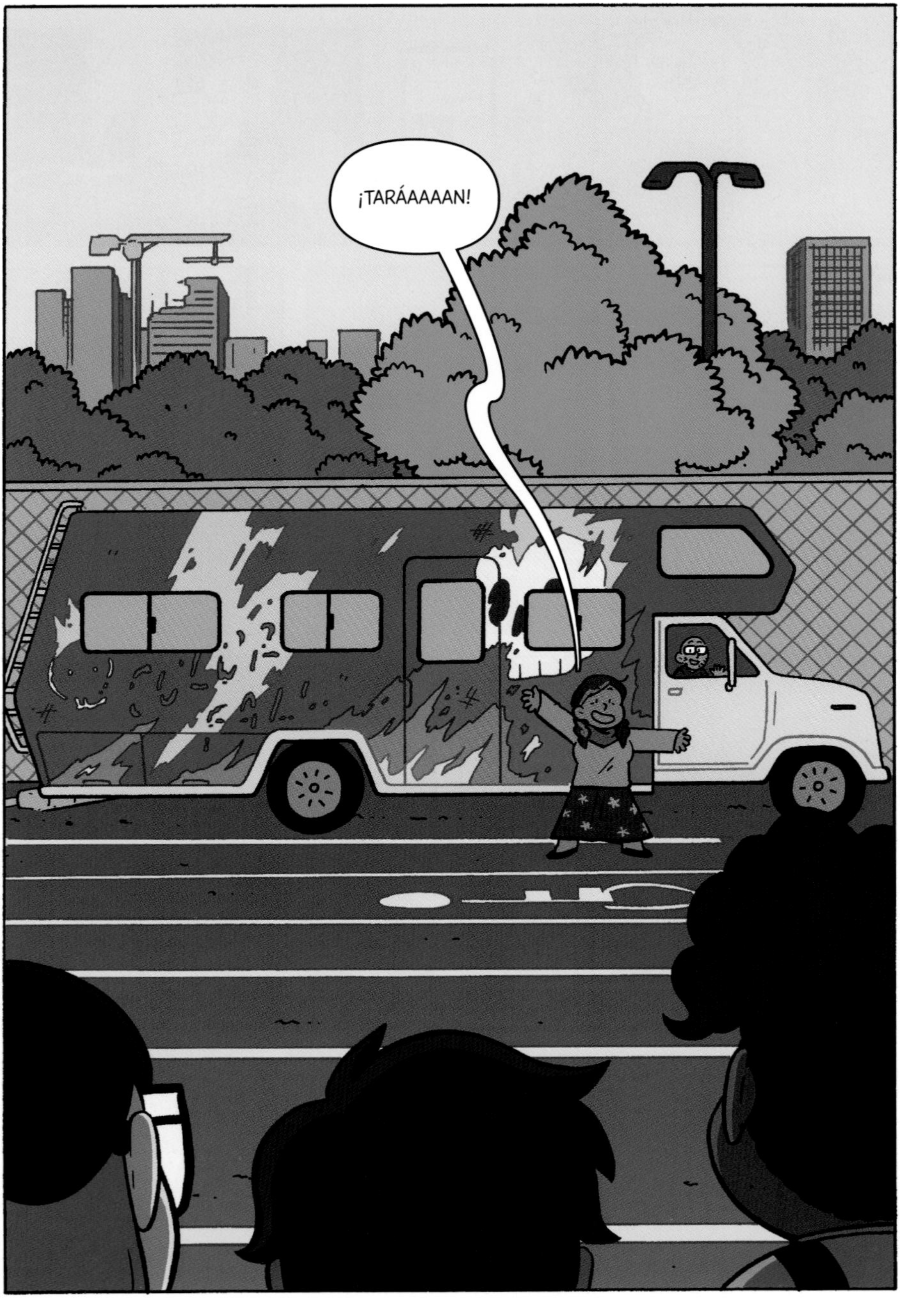
¡TARÁAAAAN!

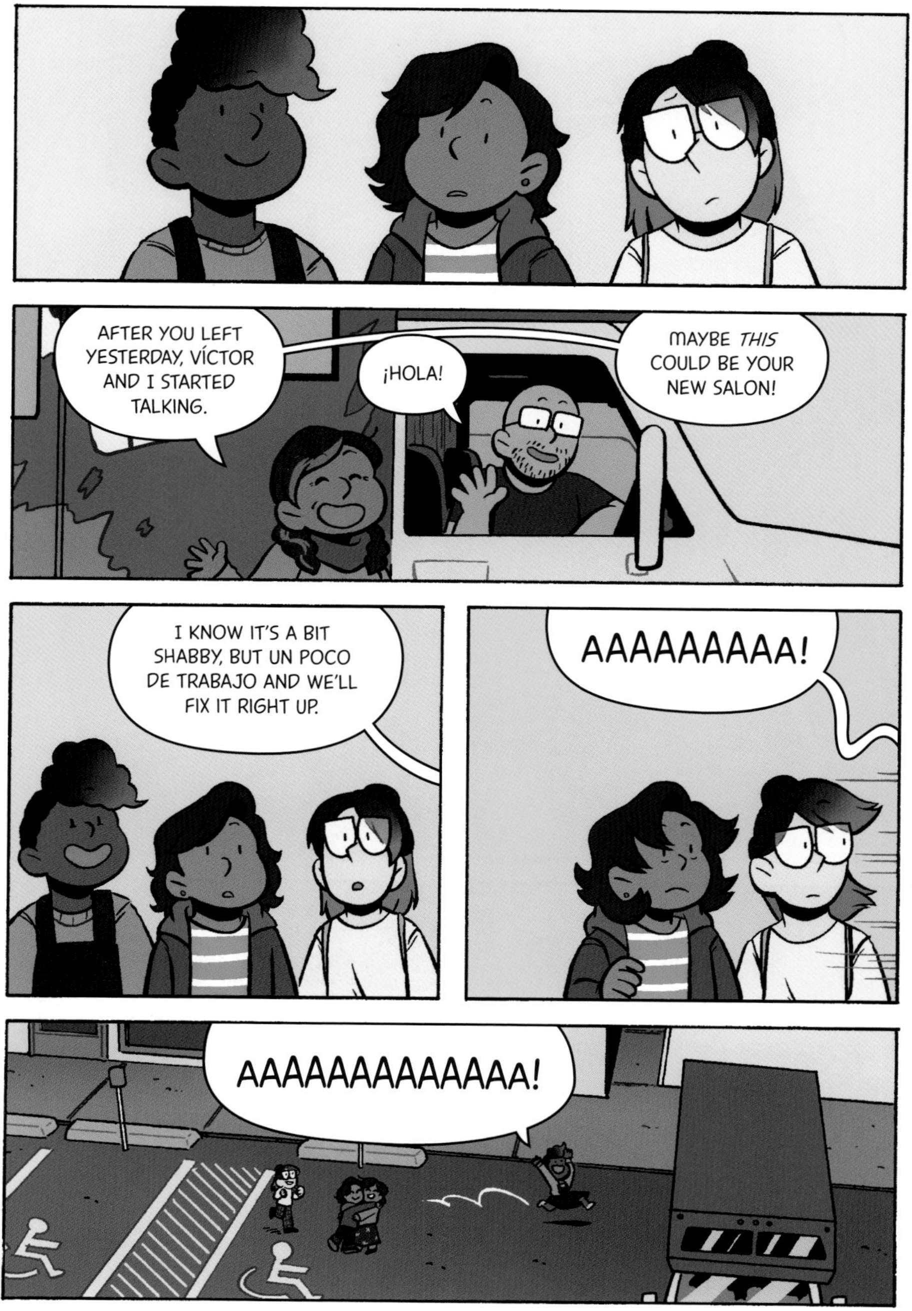
AFTER YOU LEFT YESTERDAY, VÍCTOR AND I STARTED TALKING.
¡HOLA!
MAYBE *THIS* COULD BE YOUR NEW SALON!
I KNOW IT'S A BIT SHABBY, BUT UN POCO DE TRABAJO AND WE'LL FIX IT RIGHT UP.
AAAAAAAAA!
AAAAAAAAAAAAAA!

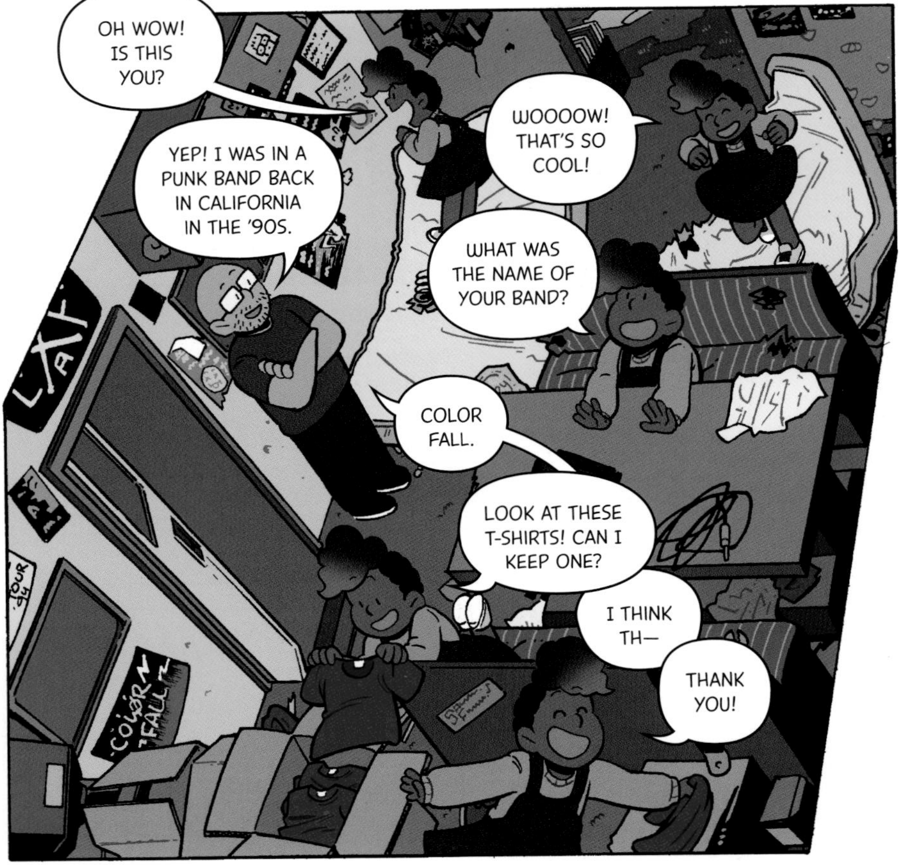
OH WOW! IS THIS YOU?
YEP! I WAS IN A PUNK BAND BACK IN CALIFORNIA IN THE '90S.
WOOOOW! THAT'S SO COOL!
WHAT WAS THE NAME OF YOUR BAND?
COLOR FALL.
LOOK AT THESE T-SHIRTS! CAN I KEEP ONE?
I THINK TH—
THANK YOU!
LAX
TOUR 94
COLOR FALL

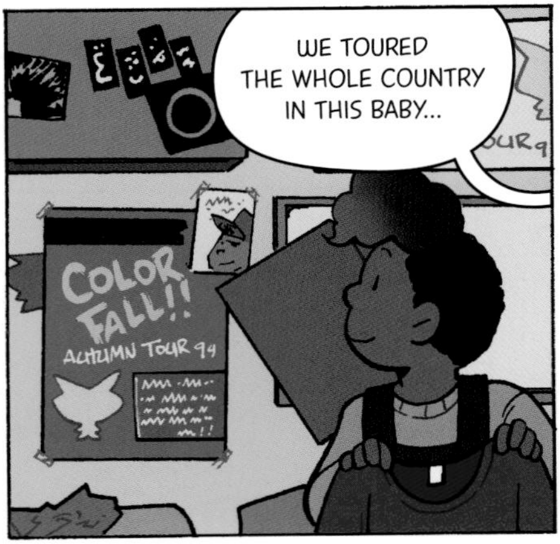
WE TOURED THE WHOLE COUNTRY IN THIS BABY...
COLOR FALL!!
AUTUMN TOUR 94

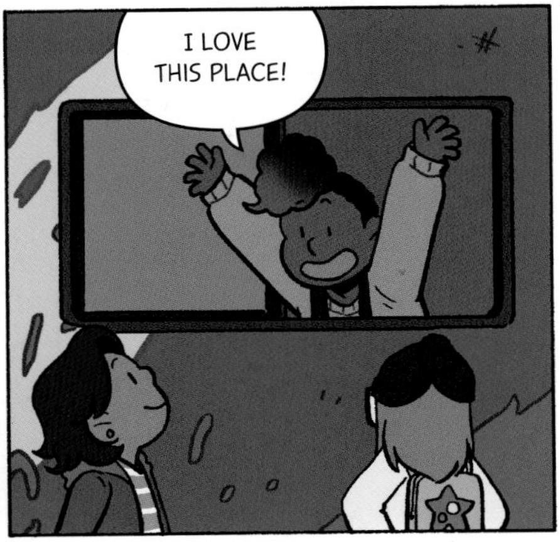
I LOVE THIS PLACE!

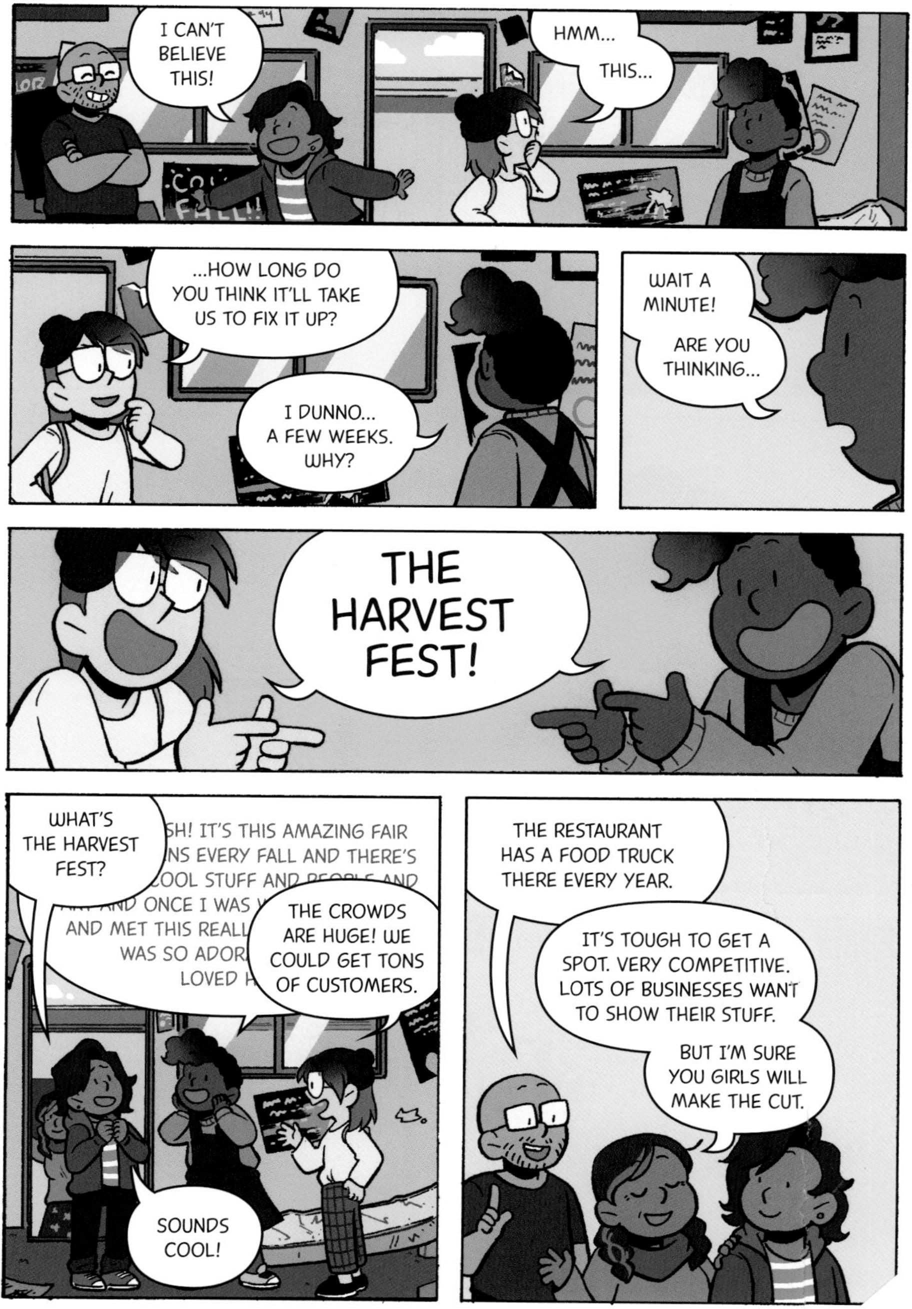

I CAN'T BELIEVE THIS!
HMM... THIS...
...HOW LONG DO YOU THINK IT'LL TAKE US TO FIX IT UP?
I DUNNO... A FEW WEEKS. WHY?
WAIT A MINUTE!
ARE YOU THINKING...
THE HARVEST FEST!
WHAT'S THE HARVEST FEST?
SH! IT'S THIS AMAZING FAIR
NS EVERY FALL AND THERE'S
COOL STUFF AND PEOPLE AND
AND ONCE I WAS
AND MET THIS REALL
WAS SO ADOR
LOVED H
THE CROWDS ARE HUGE! WE COULD GET TONS OF CUSTOMERS.
SOUNDS COOL!
THE RESTAURANT HAS A FOOD TRUCK THERE EVERY YEAR.
IT'S TOUGH TO GET A SPOT. VERY COMPETITIVE. LOTS OF BUSINESSES WANT TO SHOW THEIR STUFF.
BUT I'M SURE YOU GIRLS WILL MAKE THE CUT.

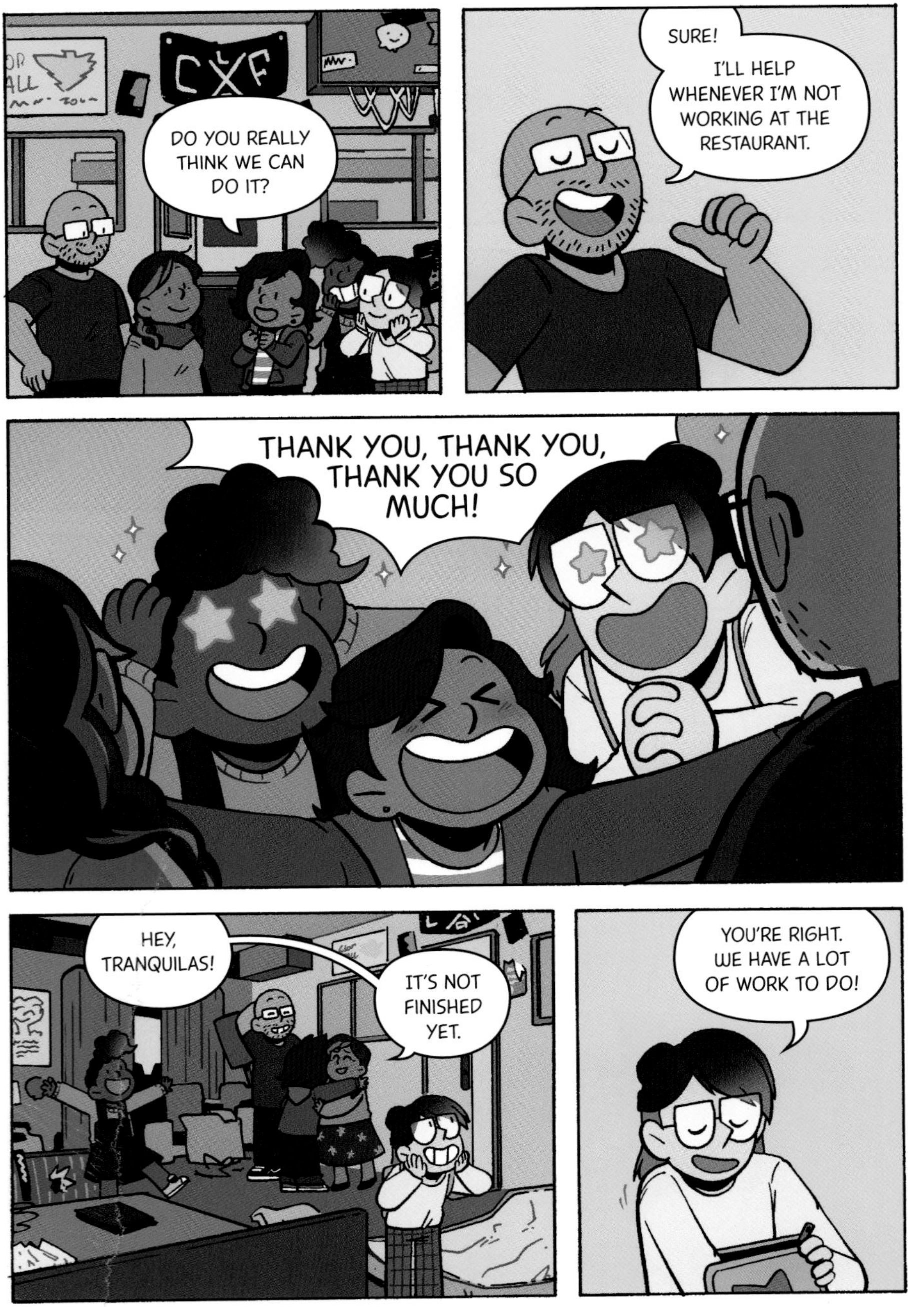
DO YOU REALLY THINK WE CAN DO IT?
SURE!
I'LL HELP WHENEVER I'M NOT WORKING AT THE RESTAURANT.
THANK YOU, THANK YOU, THANK YOU SO MUCH!
HEY, TRANQUILAS!
IT'S NOT FINISHED YET.
YOU'RE RIGHT. WE HAVE A LOT OF WORK TO DO!

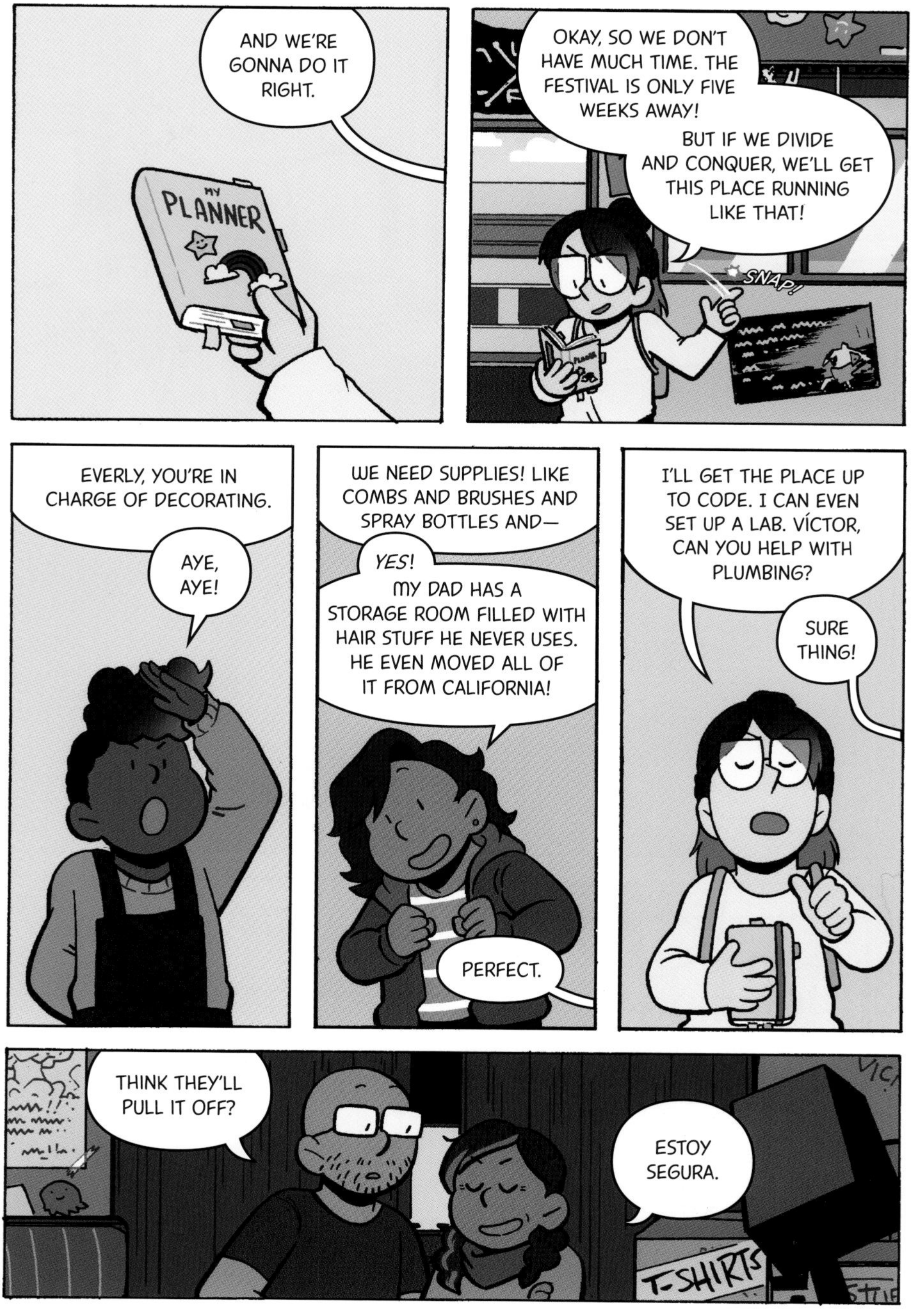
AND WE'RE GONNA DO IT RIGHT.
MY PLANNER
OKAY, SO WE DON'T HAVE MUCH TIME. THE FESTIVAL IS ONLY FIVE WEEKS AWAY!
BUT IF WE DIVIDE AND CONQUER, WE'LL GET THIS PLACE RUNNING LIKE THAT!
SNAP!
EVERLY, YOU'RE IN CHARGE OF DECORATING.
AYE, AYE!
WE NEED SUPPLIES! LIKE COMBS AND BRUSHES AND SPRAY BOTTLES AND—
YES!
MY DAD HAS A STORAGE ROOM FILLED WITH HAIR STUFF HE NEVER USES. HE EVEN MOVED ALL OF IT FROM CALIFORNIA!
PERFECT.
I'LL GET THE PLACE UP TO CODE. I CAN EVEN SET UP A LAB. VÍCTOR, CAN YOU HELP WITH PLUMBING?
SURE THING!
THINK THEY'LL PULL IT OFF?
ESTOY SEGURA.
T-SHIRTS

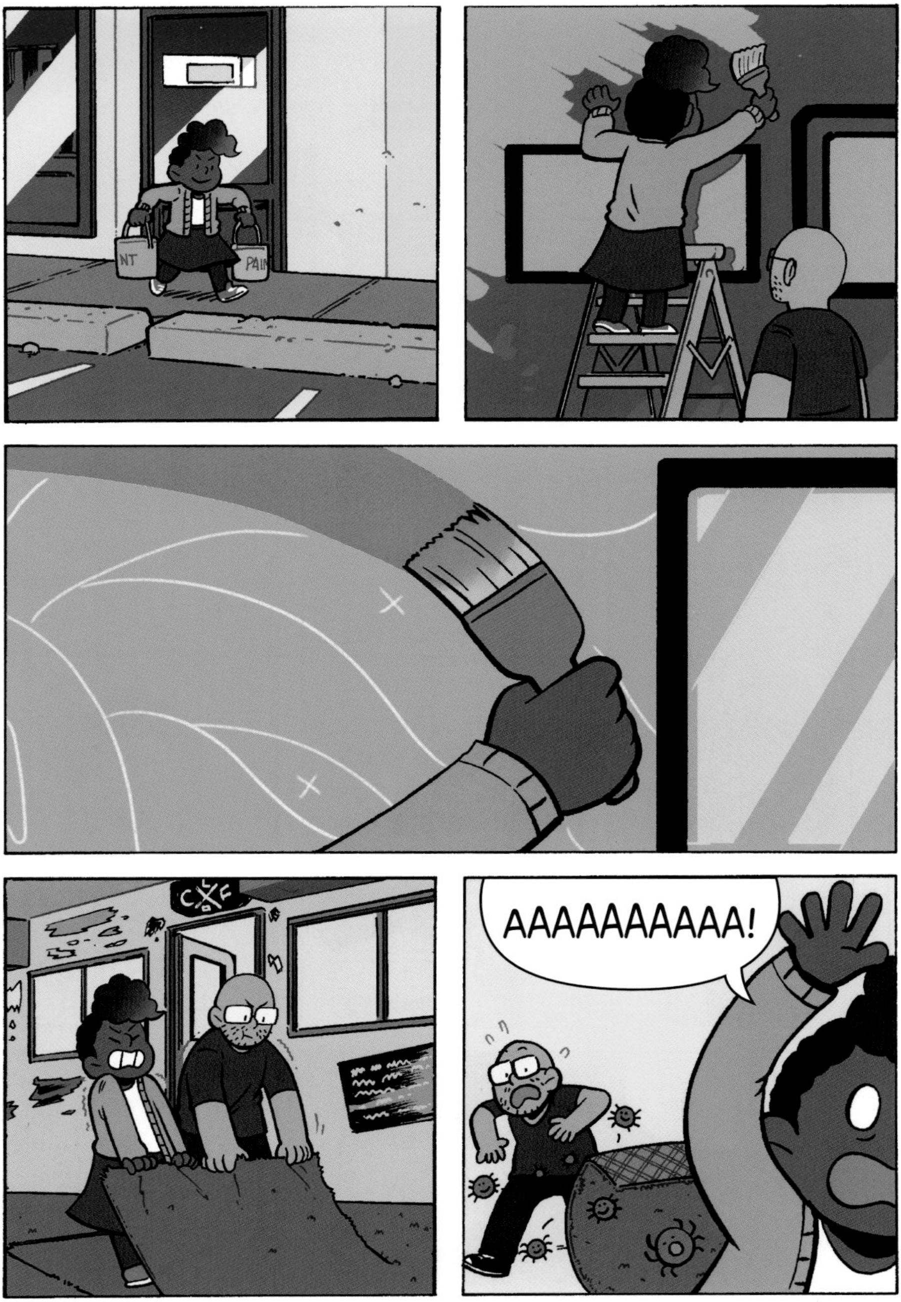
NT
PAIN
AAAAAAAAAA!

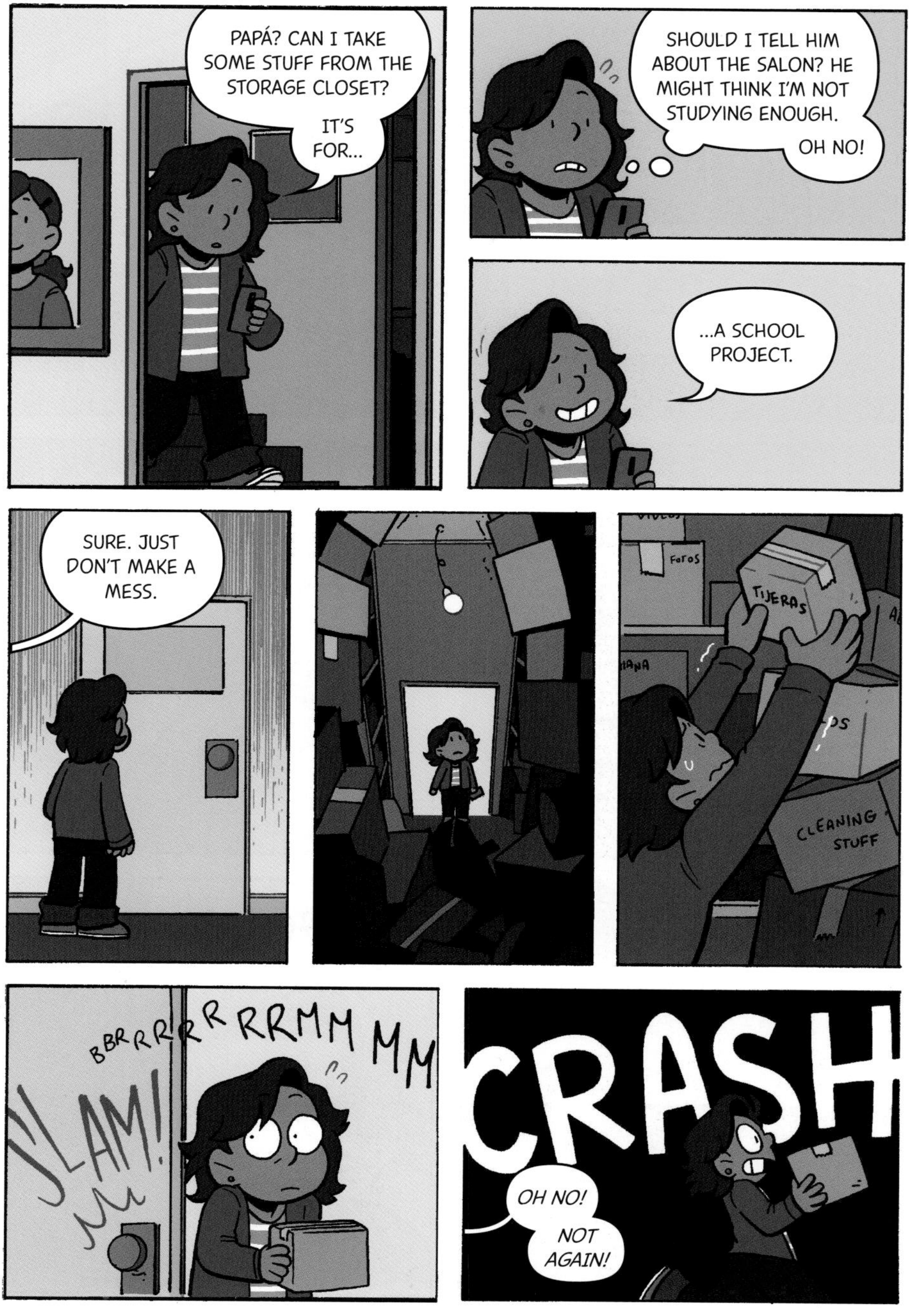
PAPÁ? CAN I TAKE SOME STUFF FROM THE STORAGE CLOSET?
IT'S FOR...
SHOULD I TELL HIM ABOUT THE SALON? HE MIGHT THINK I'M NOT STUDYING ENOUGH.
OH NO!
...A SCHOOL PROJECT.
SURE. JUST DON'T MAKE A MESS.
FOTOS
TIJERAS
CLEANING STUFF
BBRRRRRR RRMM MM
SLAM!
CRASH
OH NO!
NOT AGAIN!

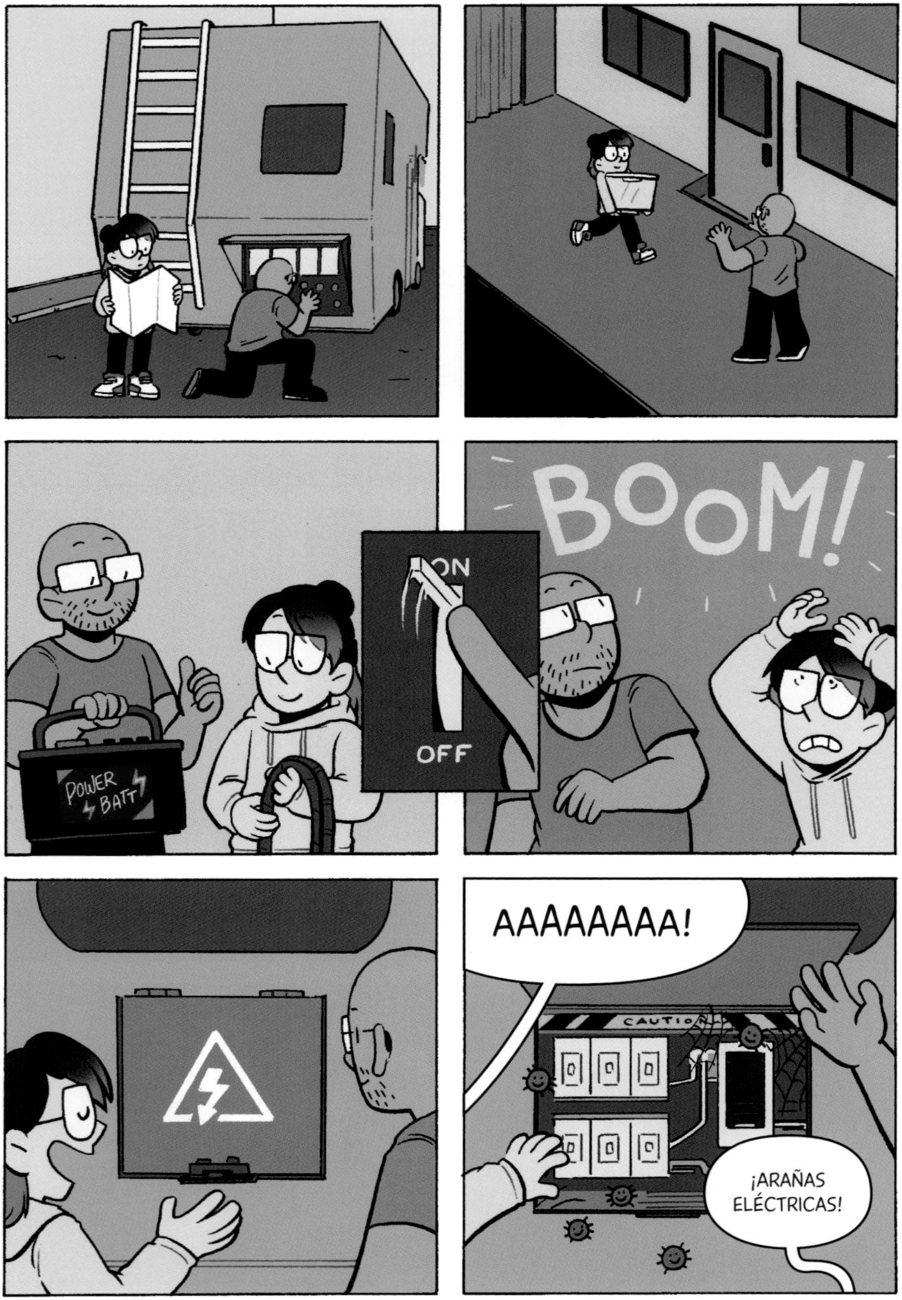
ON
OFF
BOOM!
POWER BATT
AAAAAAAA!
CAUTION
¡ARAÑAS ELÉCTRICAS!

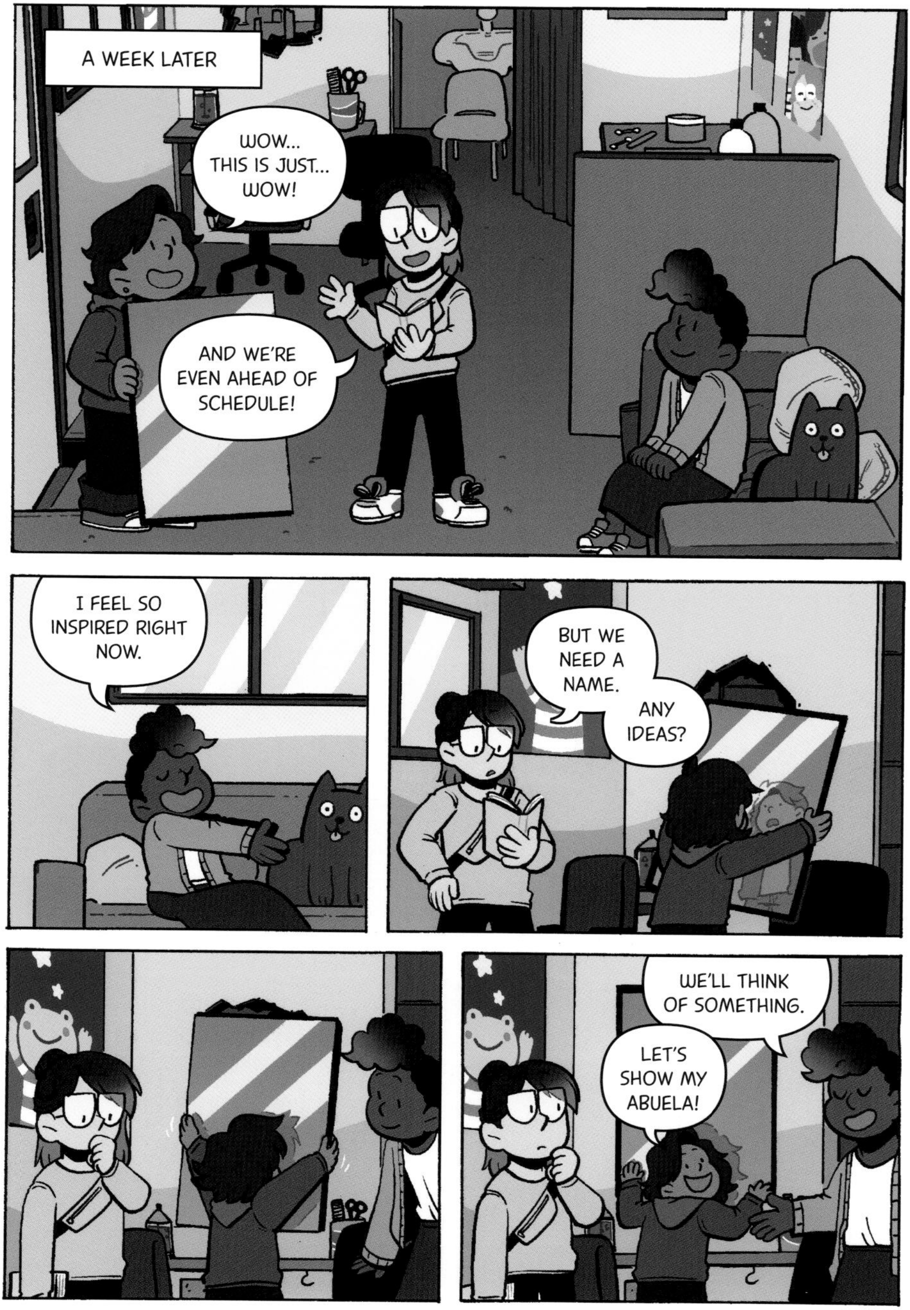
A WEEK LATER
WOW... THIS IS JUST... WOW!
AND WE'RE EVEN AHEAD OF SCHEDULE!
I FEEL SO INSPIRED RIGHT NOW.
BUT WE NEED A NAME.
ANY IDEAS?
WE'LL THINK OF SOMETHING.
LET'S SHOW MY ABUELA!

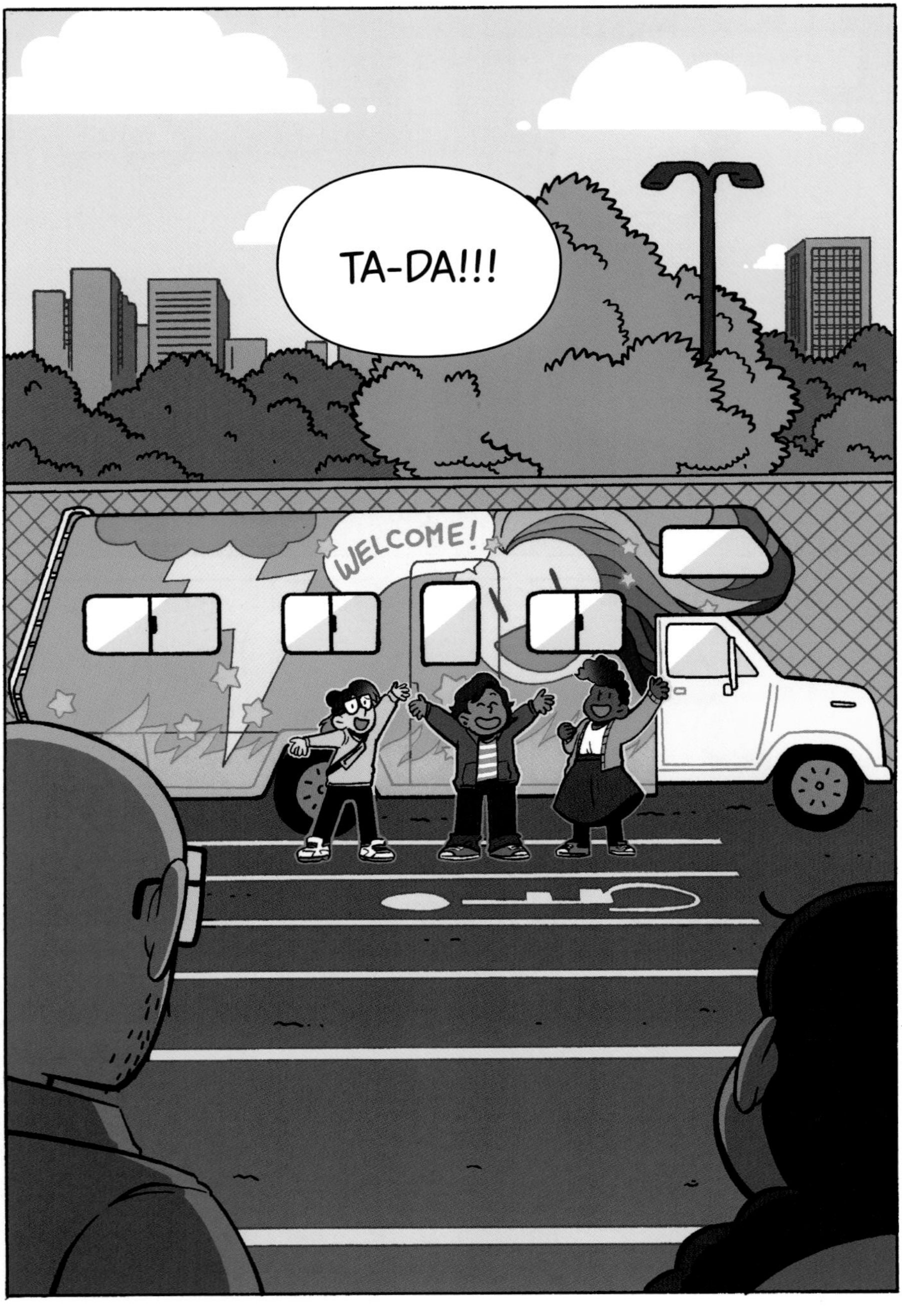
TA-DA!!!
WELCOME!

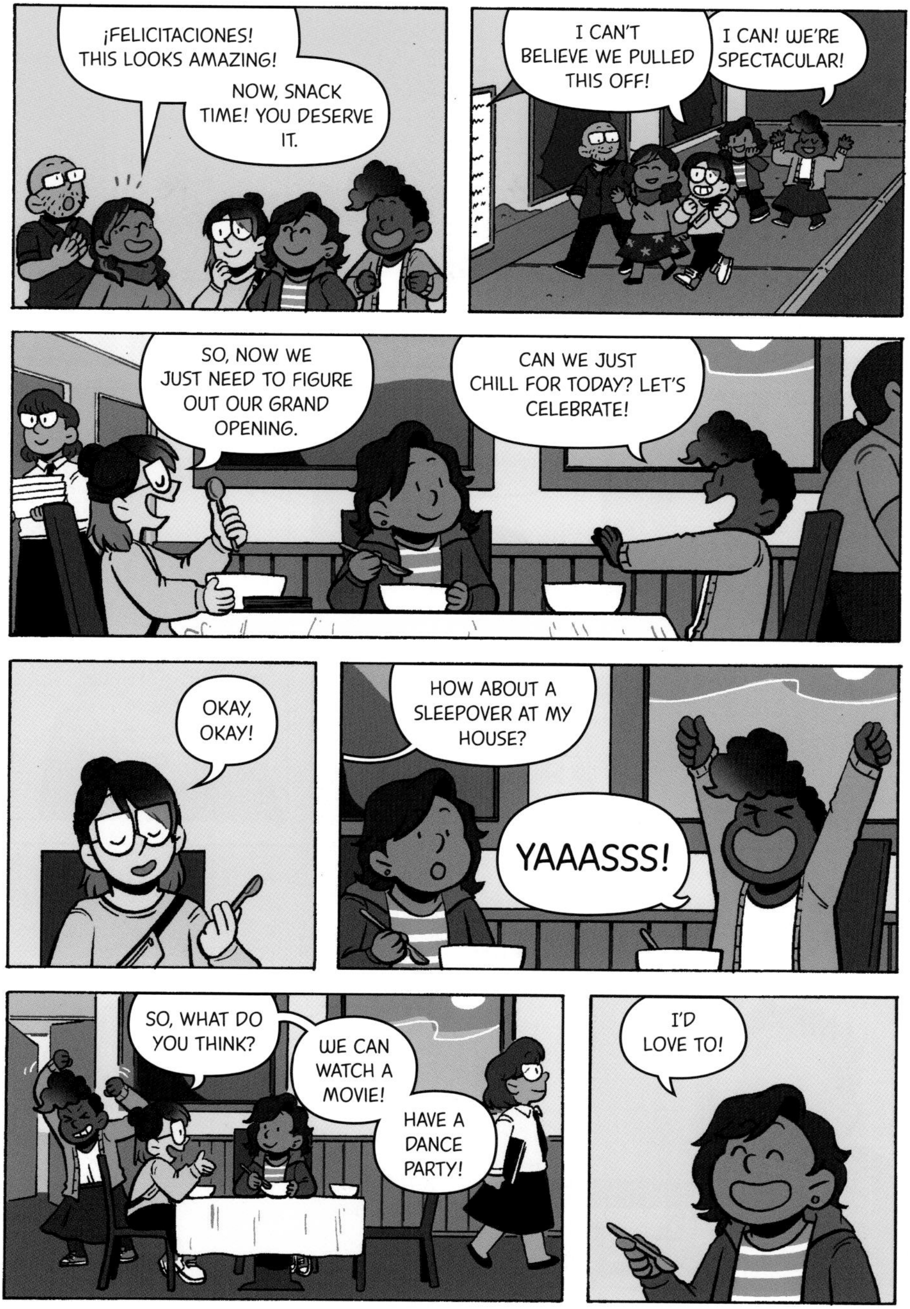
¡FELICITACIONES! THIS LOOKS AMAZING!
NOW, SNACK TIME! YOU DESERVE IT.
I CAN'T BELIEVE WE PULLED THIS OFF!
I CAN! WE'RE SPECTACULAR!
SO, NOW WE JUST NEED TO FIGURE OUT OUR GRAND OPENING.
CAN WE JUST CHILL FOR TODAY? LET'S CELEBRATE!
OKAY, OKAY!
HOW ABOUT A SLEEPOVER AT MY HOUSE?
YAAASSS!
SO, WHAT DO YOU THINK?
WE CAN WATCH A MOVIE!
HAVE A DANCE PARTY!
I'D LOVE TO!

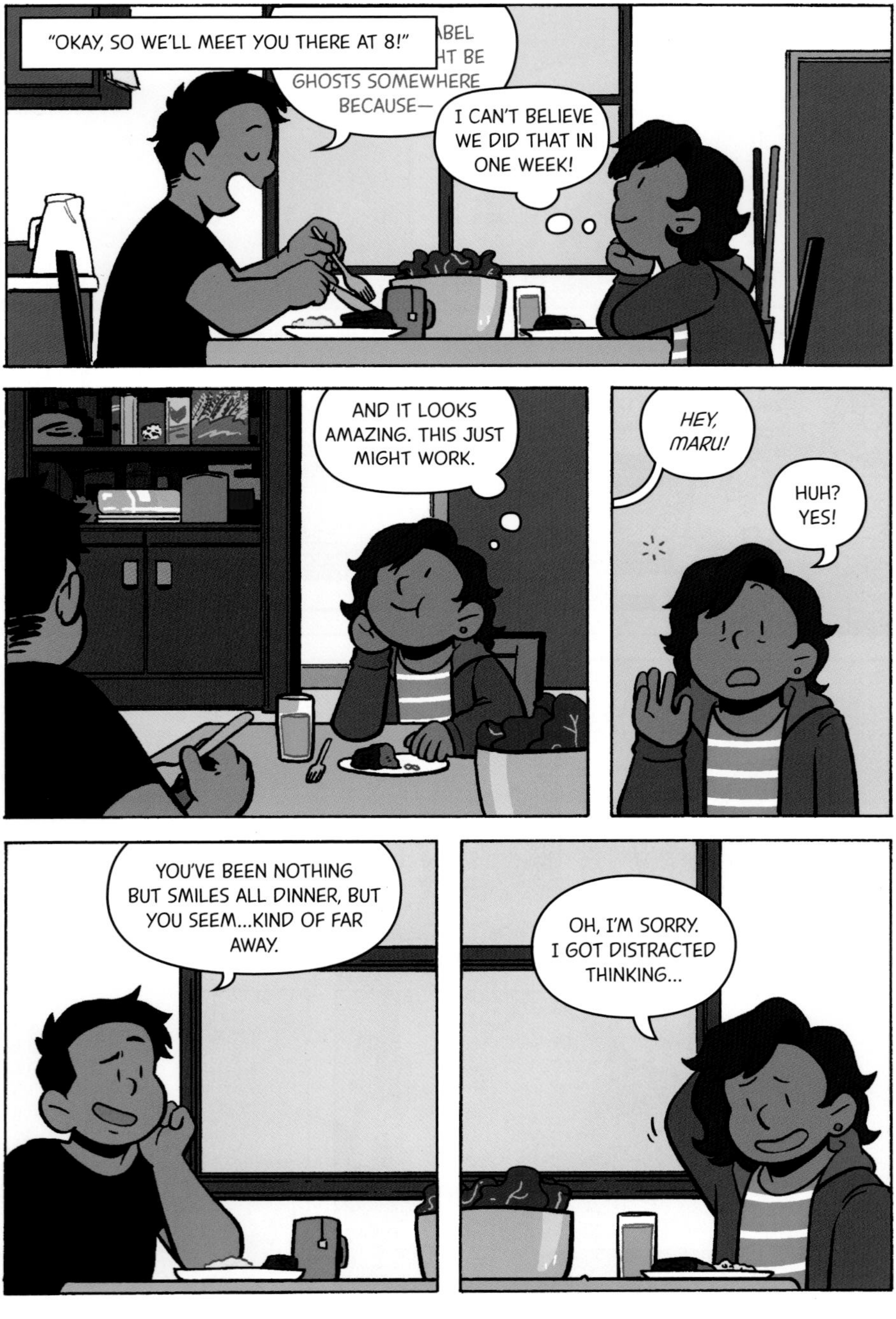
"OKAY, SO WE'LL MEET YOU THERE AT 8!"
GHOSTS SOMEWHERE
BECAUSE—
I CAN'T BELIEVE WE DID THAT IN ONE WEEK!
AND IT LOOKS AMAZING. THIS JUST MIGHT WORK.
HEY, MARU!
HUH? YES!
YOU'VE BEEN NOTHING BUT SMILES ALL DINNER, BUT YOU SEEM...KIND OF FAR AWAY.
OH, I'M SORRY. I GOT DISTRACTED THINKING...

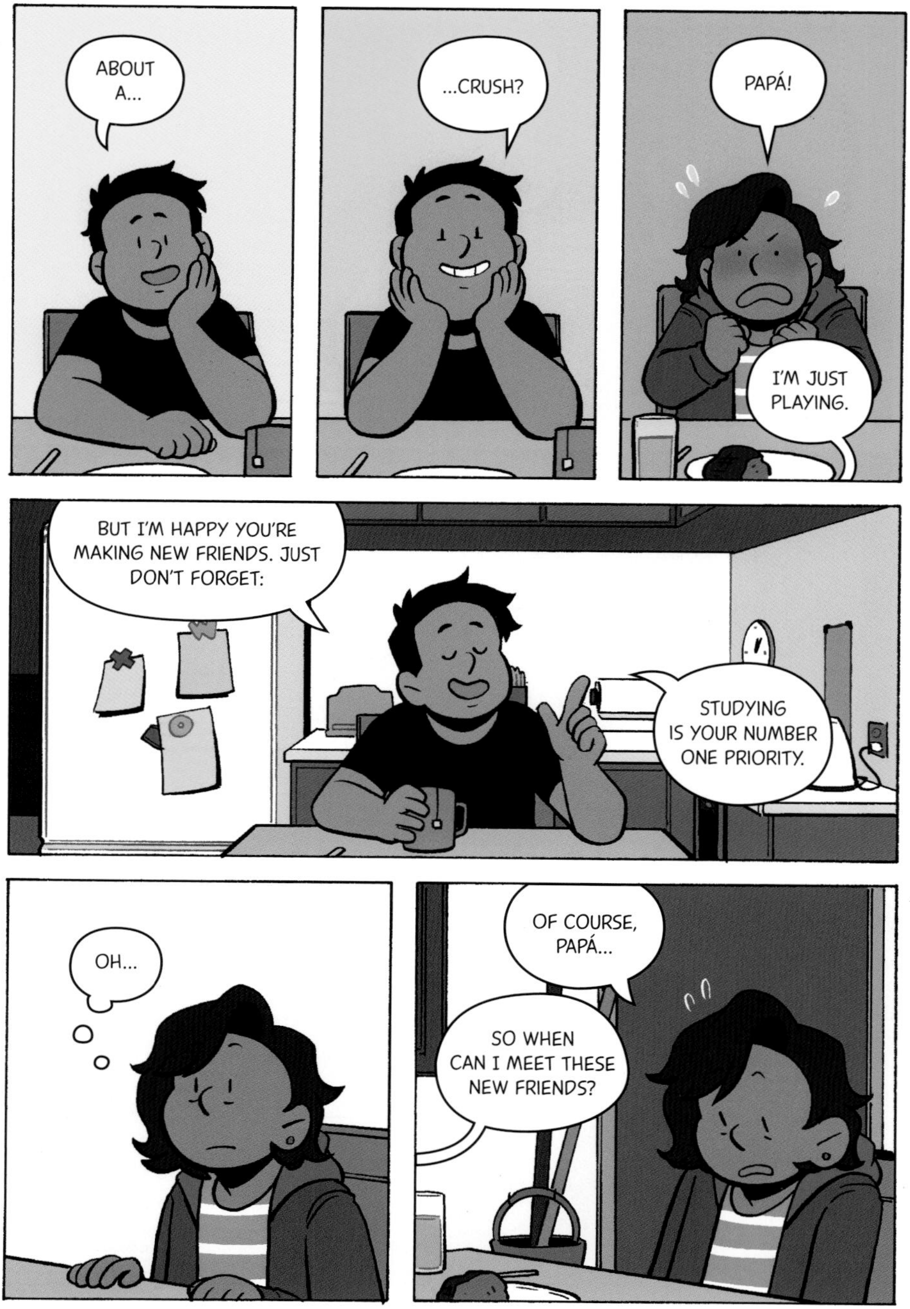

ABOUT A...
...CRUSH?
PAPÁ!
I'M JUST PLAYING.
BUT I'M HAPPY YOU'RE MAKING NEW FRIENDS. JUST DON'T FORGET:
STUDYING IS YOUR NUMBER ONE PRIORITY.
OH...
OF COURSE, PAPÁ...
SO WHEN CAN I MEET THESE NEW FRIENDS?

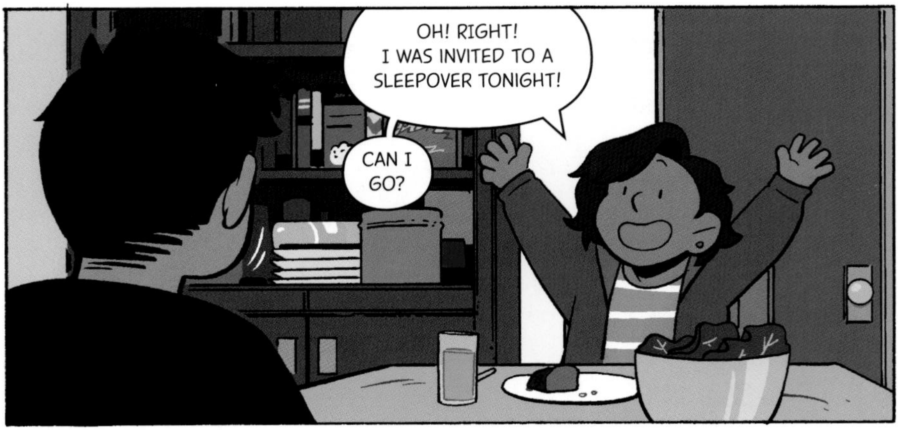
OH! RIGHT!
I WAS INVITED TO A
SLEEPOVER TONIGHT!
CAN I GO?

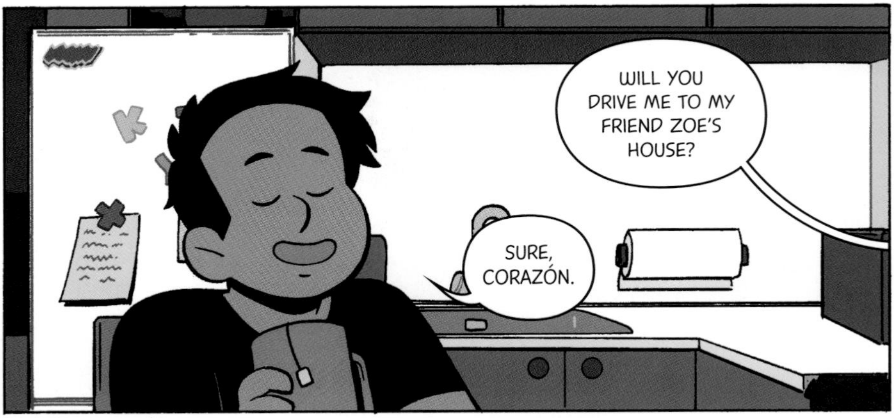
WILL YOU
DRIVE ME TO MY
FRIEND ZOE'S
HOUSE?
SURE,
CORAZÓN.

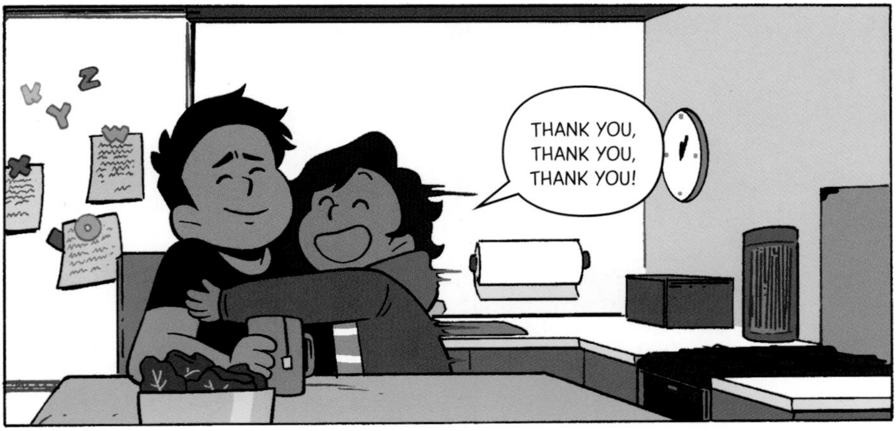
THANK YOU,
THANK YOU,
THANK YOU!

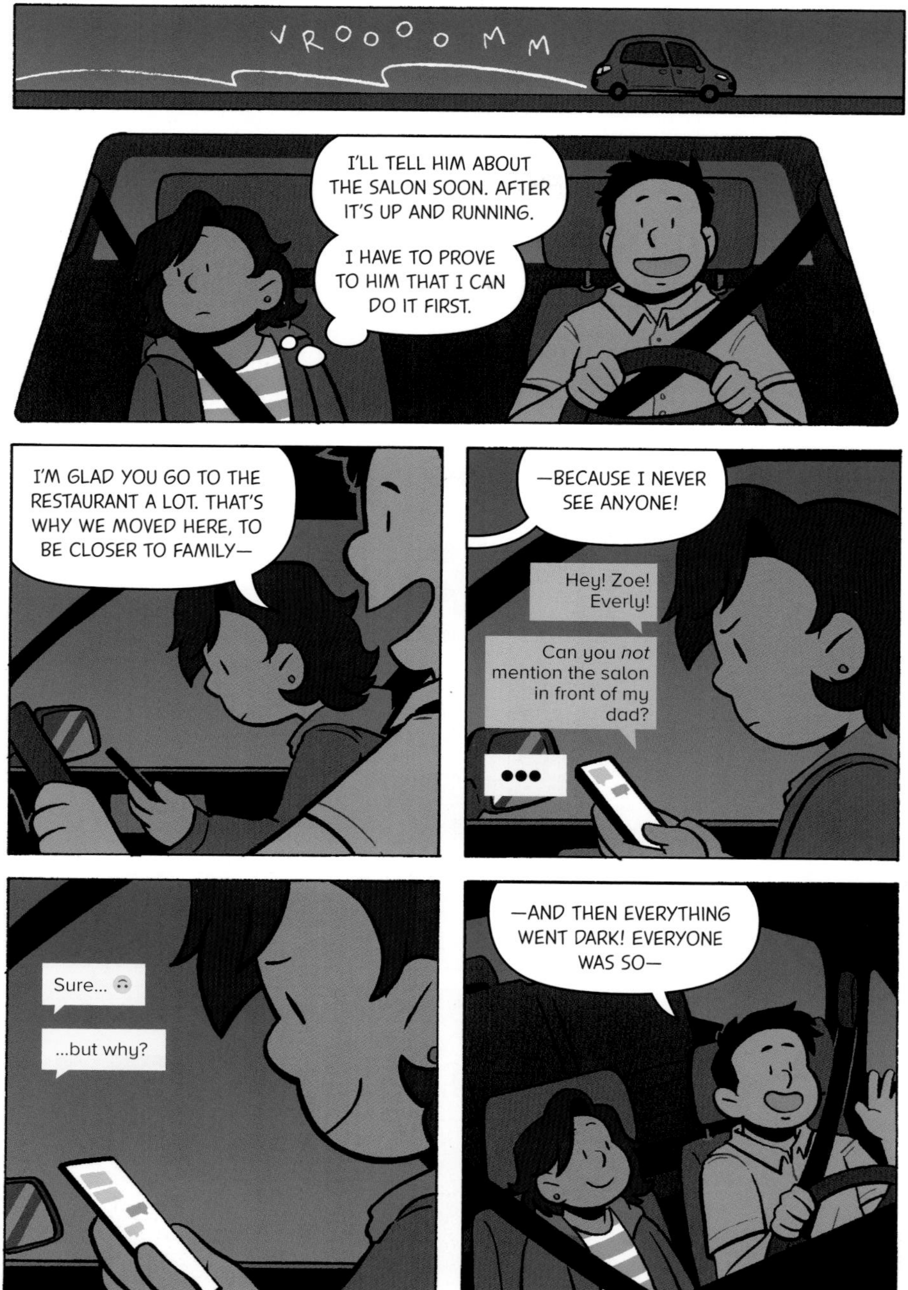
VROOOOMM
I'LL TELL HIM ABOUT THE SALON SOON. AFTER IT'S UP AND RUNNING.
I HAVE TO PROVE TO HIM THAT I CAN DO IT FIRST.
I'M GLAD YOU GO TO THE RESTAURANT A LOT. THAT'S WHY WE MOVED HERE, TO BE CLOSER TO FAMILY—
—BECAUSE I NEVER SEE ANYONE!
Hey! Zoe! Everly!
Can you *not* mention the salon in front of my dad?
Sure...
...but why?
—AND THEN EVERYTHING WENT DARK! EVERYONE WAS SO—

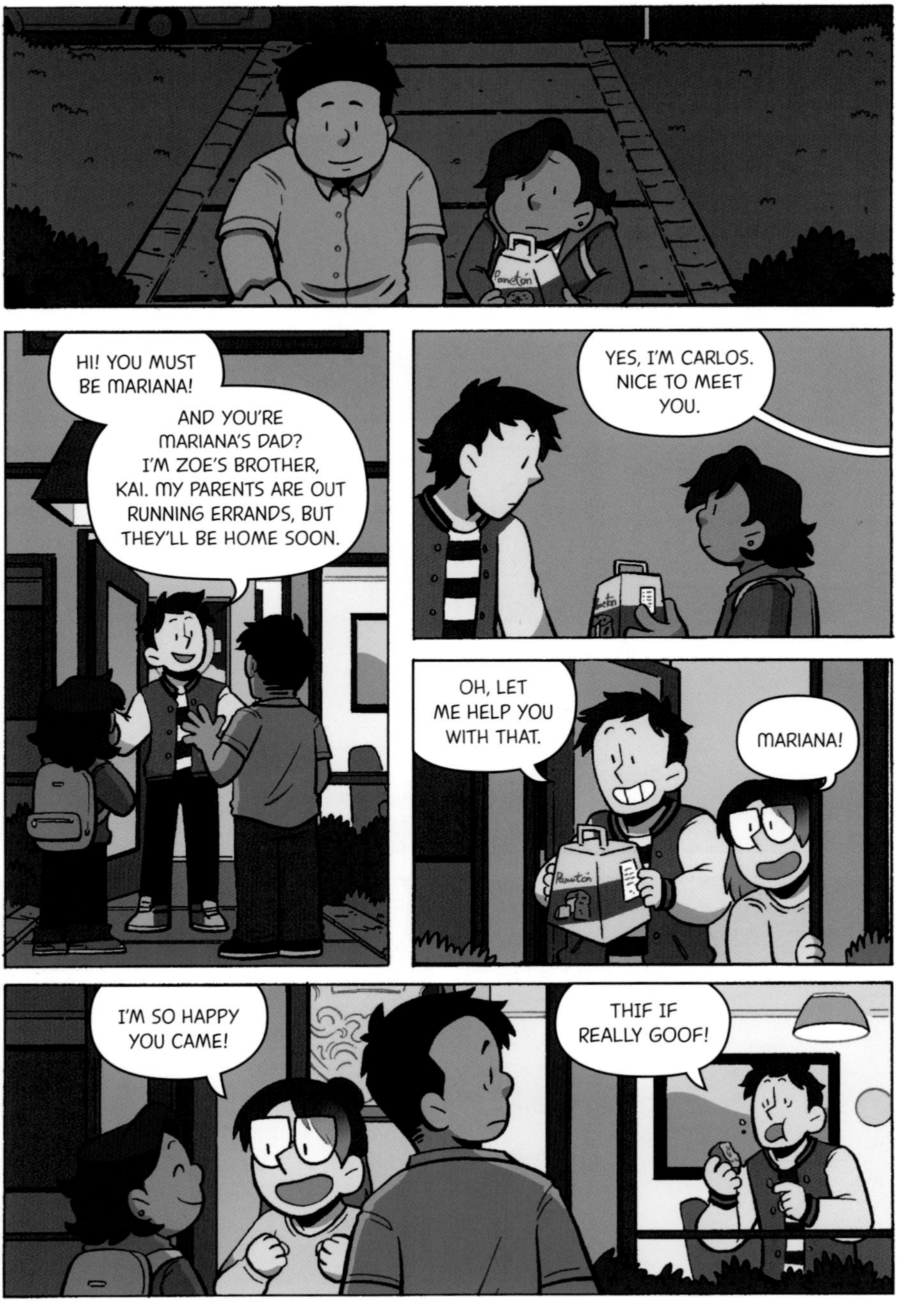
HI! YOU MUST BE MARIANA!
AND YOU'RE MARIANA'S DAD? I'M ZOE'S BROTHER, KAI. MY PARENTS ARE OUT RUNNING ERRANDS, BUT THEY'LL BE HOME SOON.
YES, I'M CARLOS. NICE TO MEET YOU.
OH, LET ME HELP YOU WITH THAT.
MARIANA!
I'M SO HAPPY YOU CAME!
THIF IF REALLY GOOF!

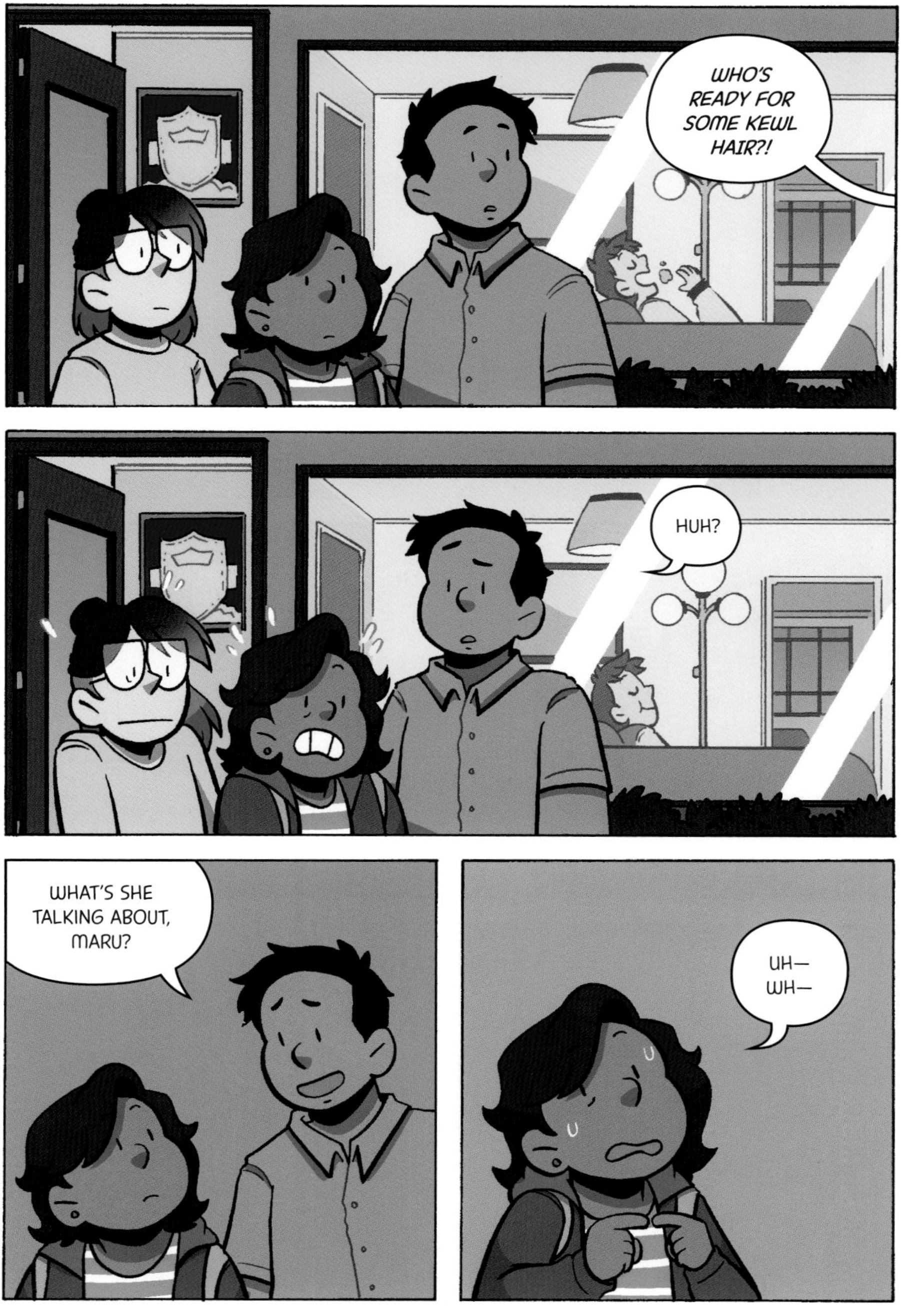
WHO'S READY FOR SOME KEWL HAIR?!
HUH?
WHAT'S SHE TALKING ABOUT, MARU?
UH— WH—

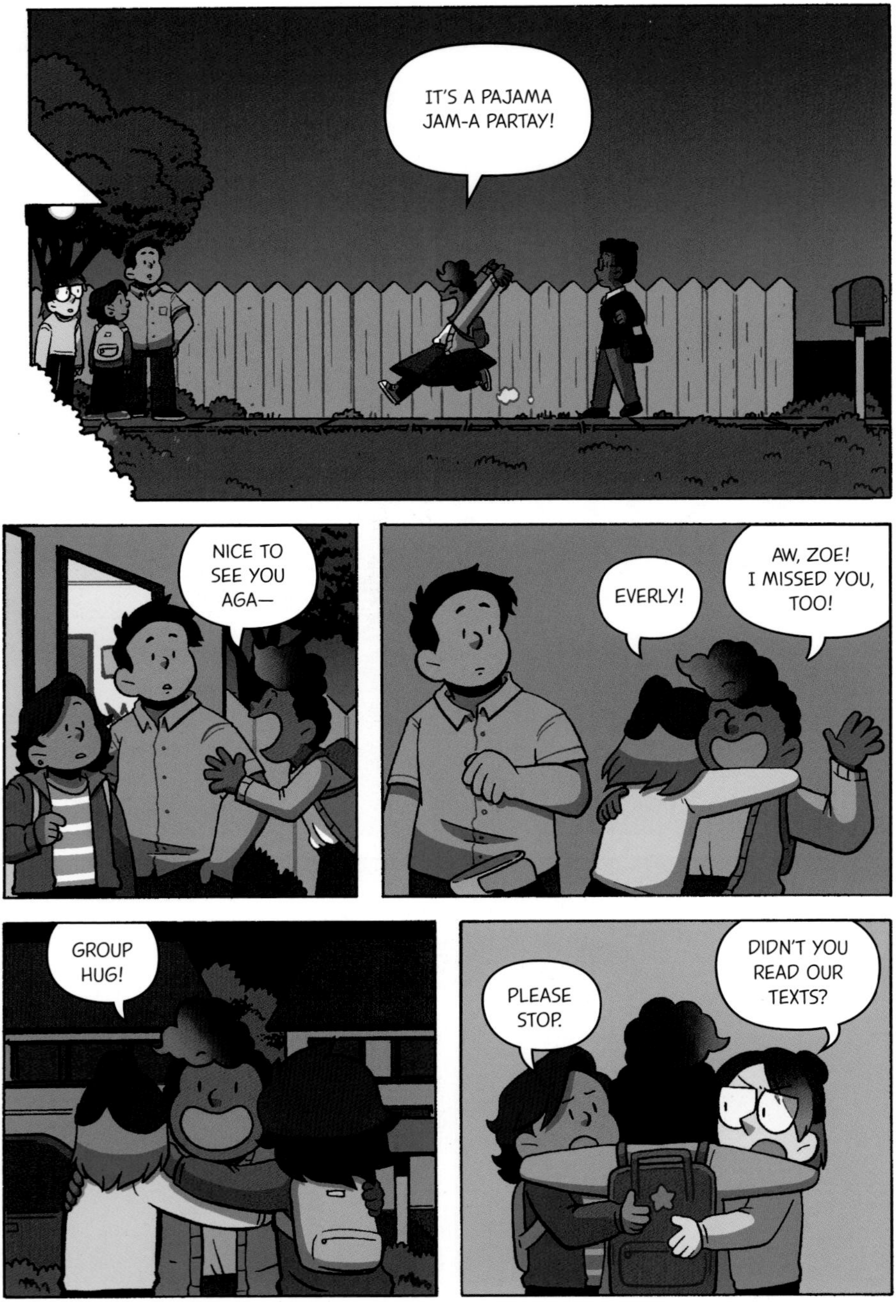
IT'S A PAJAMA JAM-A PARTAY!
NICE TO SEE YOU AGA—
EVERLY!
AW, ZOE! I MISSED YOU, TOO!
GROUP HUG!
PLEASE STOP.
DIDN'T YOU READ OUR TEXTS?

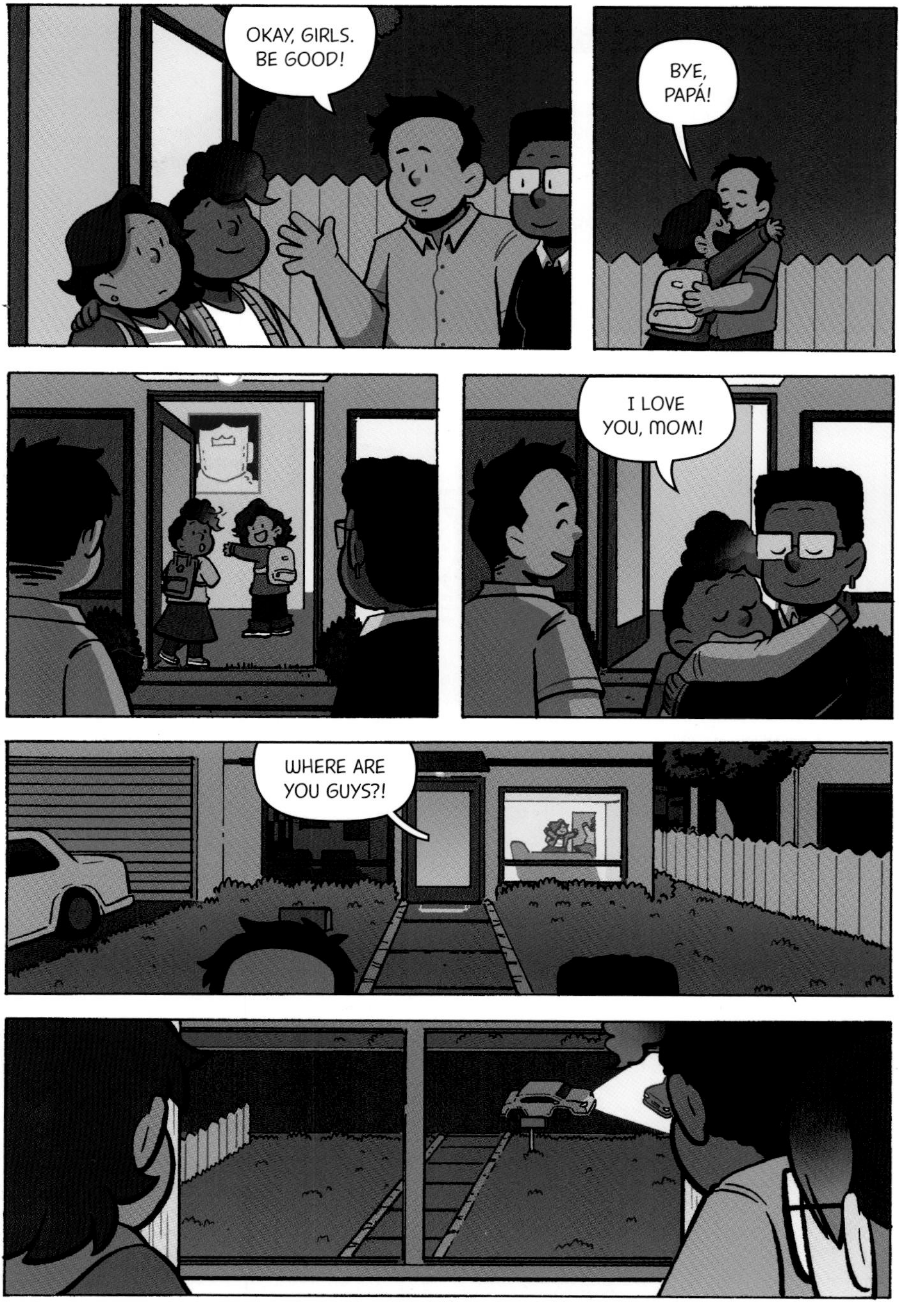
OKAY, GIRLS. BE GOOD!
BYE, PAPÁ!
I LOVE YOU, MOM!
WHERE ARE YOU GUYS?!

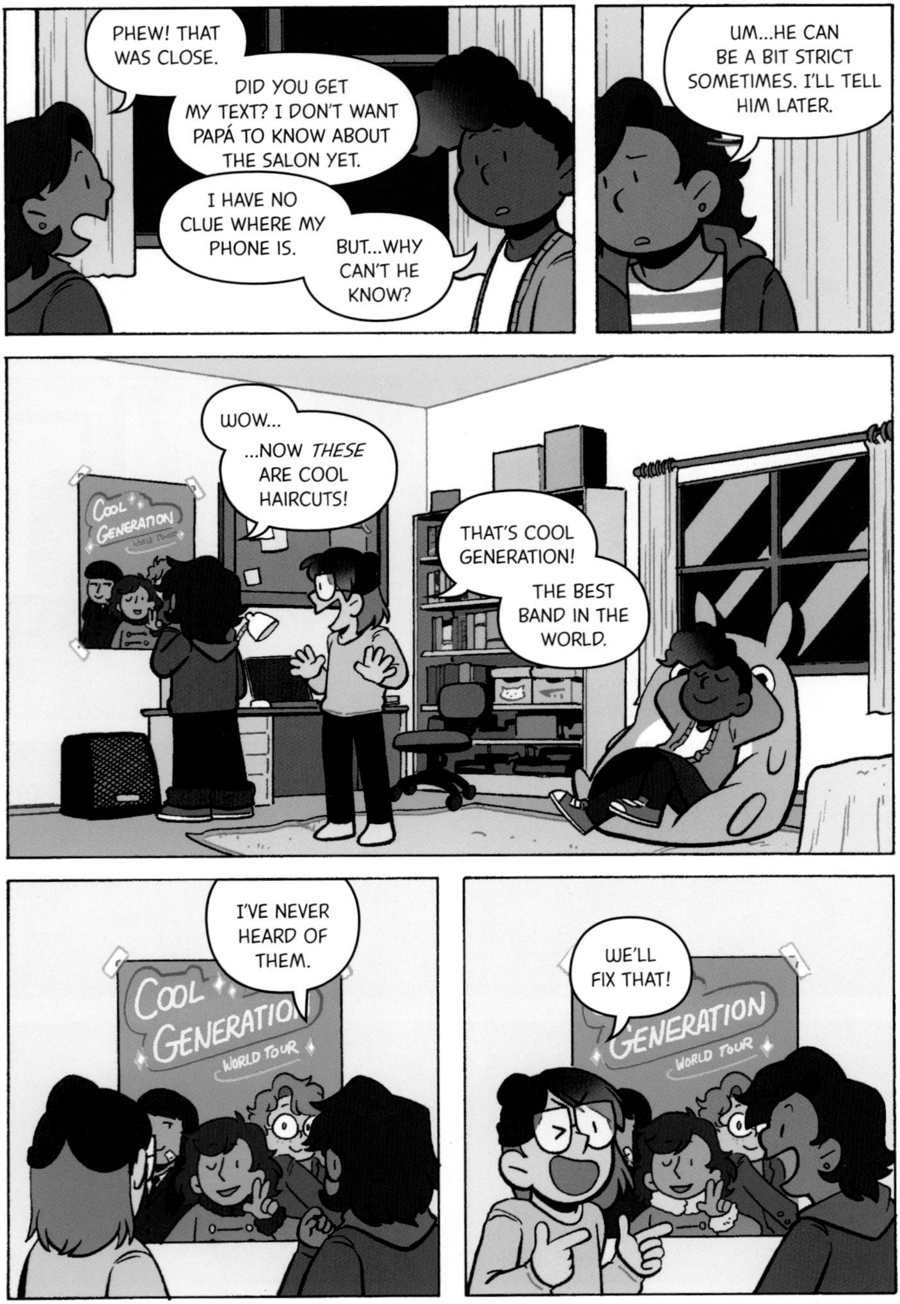
PHEW! THAT WAS CLOSE.
DID YOU GET MY TEXT? I DON'T WANT PAPÁ TO KNOW ABOUT THE SALON YET.
I HAVE NO CLUE WHERE MY PHONE IS.
BUT...WHY CAN'T HE KNOW?
UM...HE CAN BE A BIT STRICT SOMETIMES. I'LL TELL HIM LATER.
WOW...
...NOW *THESE* ARE COOL HAIRCUTS!
COOL GENERATION WORLD TOUR
THAT'S COOL GENERATION!
THE BEST BAND IN THE WORLD.
I'VE NEVER HEARD OF THEM.
COOL GENERATION WORLD TOUR
WE'LL FIX THAT!
GENERATION WORLD TOUR

ARE YOU READY?

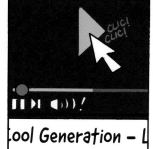

CLIC! CLIC!

ool Generation - L

C'MON, LET'S DANCE!

LET'S GO, MARU!

OKAY!

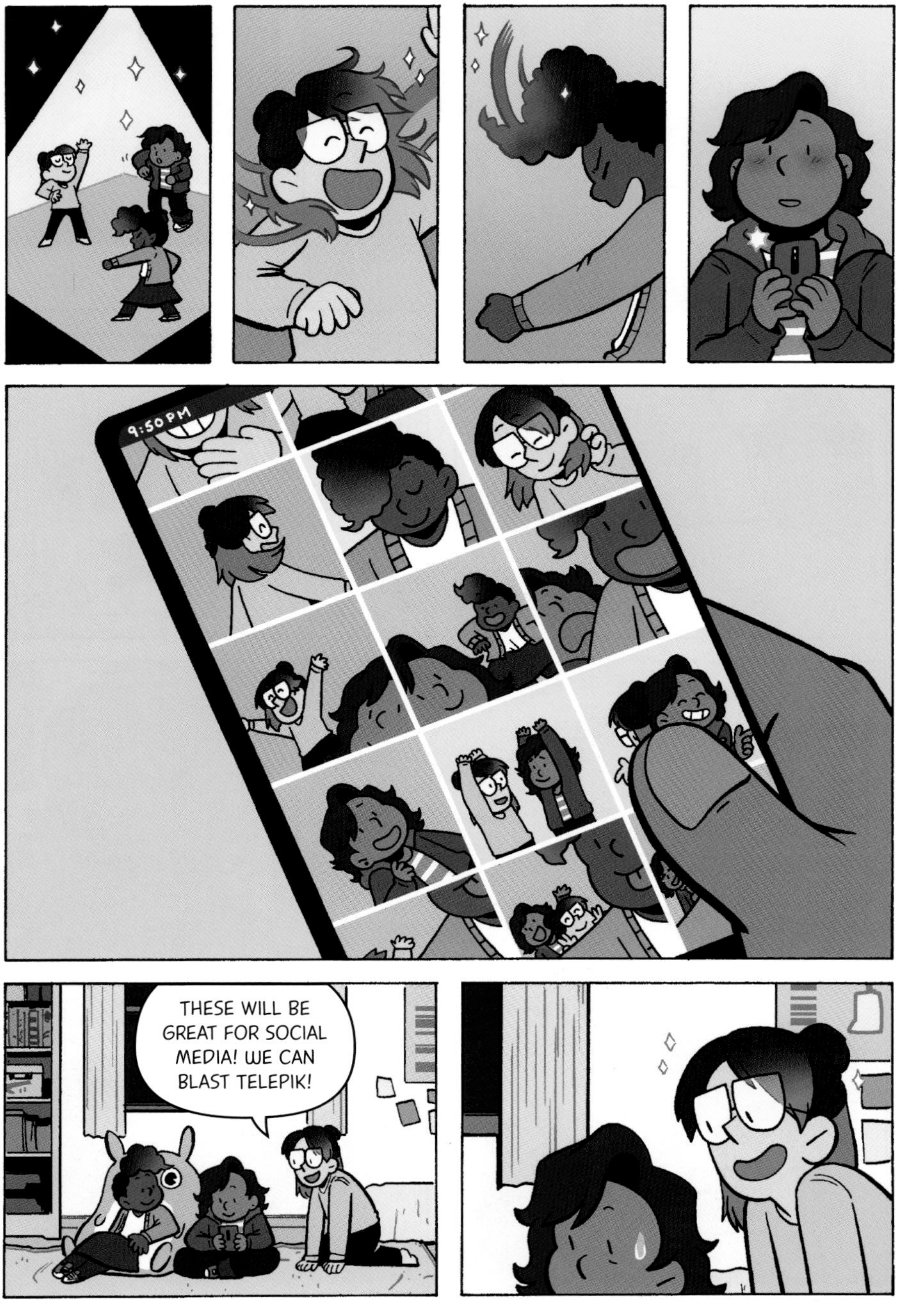
9:50 PM
THESE WILL BE GREAT FOR SOCIAL MEDIA! WE CAN BLAST TELEPIK!

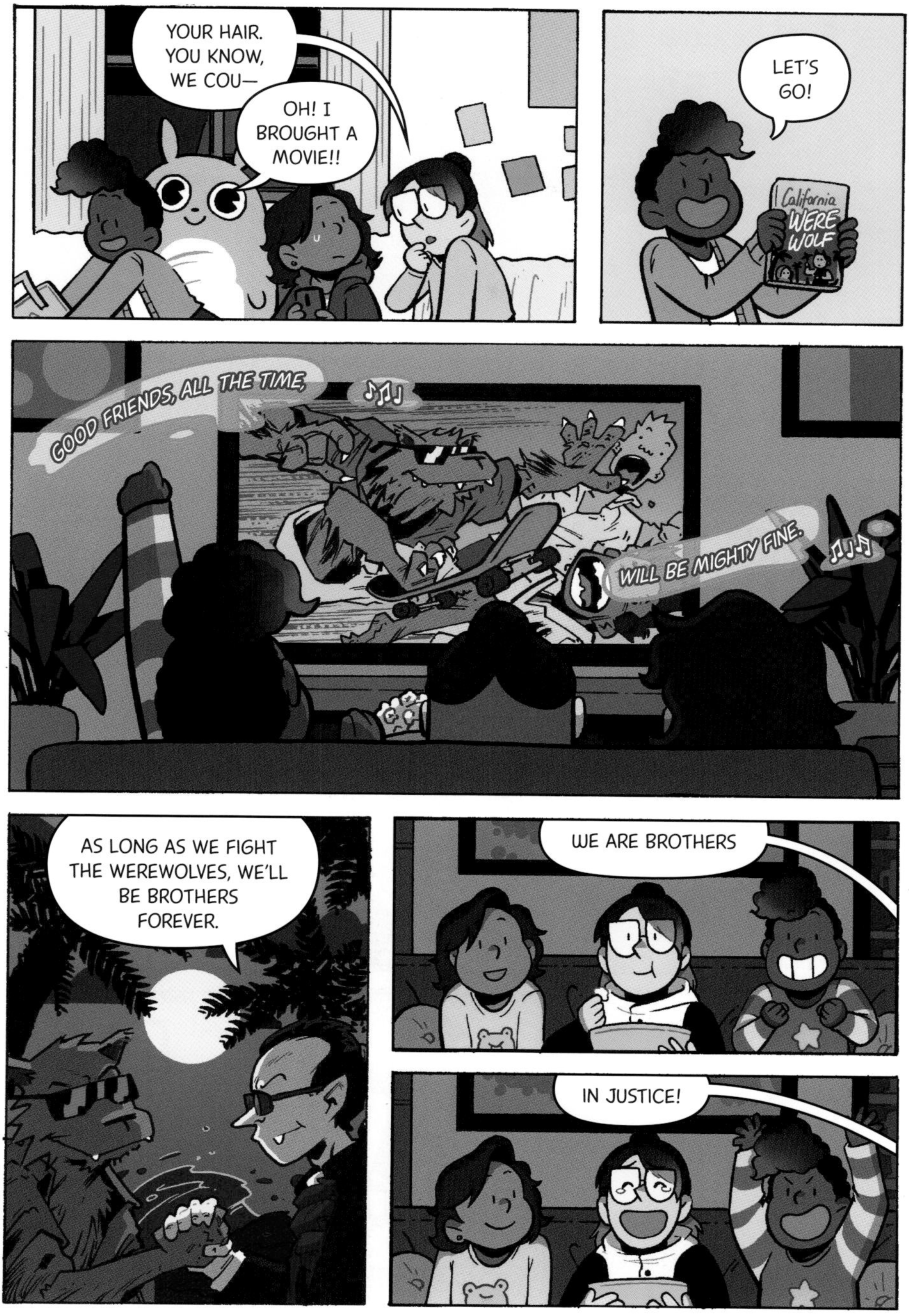

YOUR HAIR. YOU KNOW, WE COU—
OH! I BROUGHT A MOVIE!!
LET'S GO!
California WERE WOLF
GOOD FRIENDS, ALL THE TIME,
WILL BE MIGHTY FINE.
AS LONG AS WE FIGHT THE WEREWOLVES, WE'LL BE BROTHERS FOREVER.
WE ARE BROTHERS
IN JUSTICE!

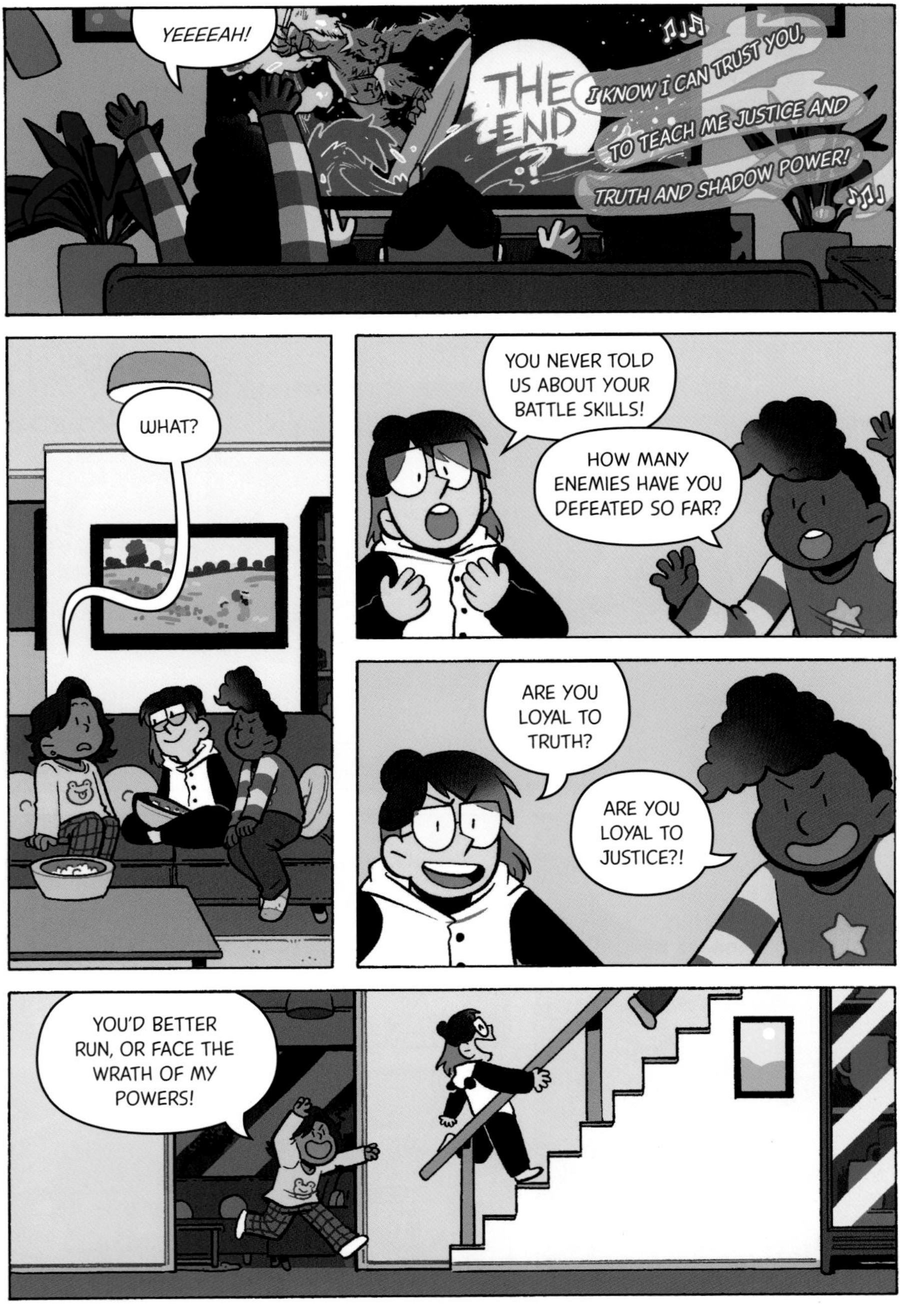
YEEEEAH!
THE END ?
I KNOW I CAN TRUST YOU,
TO TEACH ME JUSTICE AND
TRUTH AND SHADOW POWER!
WHAT?
YOU NEVER TOLD US ABOUT YOUR BATTLE SKILLS!
HOW MANY ENEMIES HAVE YOU DEFEATED SO FAR?
ARE YOU LOYAL TO TRUTH?
ARE YOU LOYAL TO JUSTICE?!
YOU'D BETTER RUN, OR FACE THE WRATH OF MY POWERS!

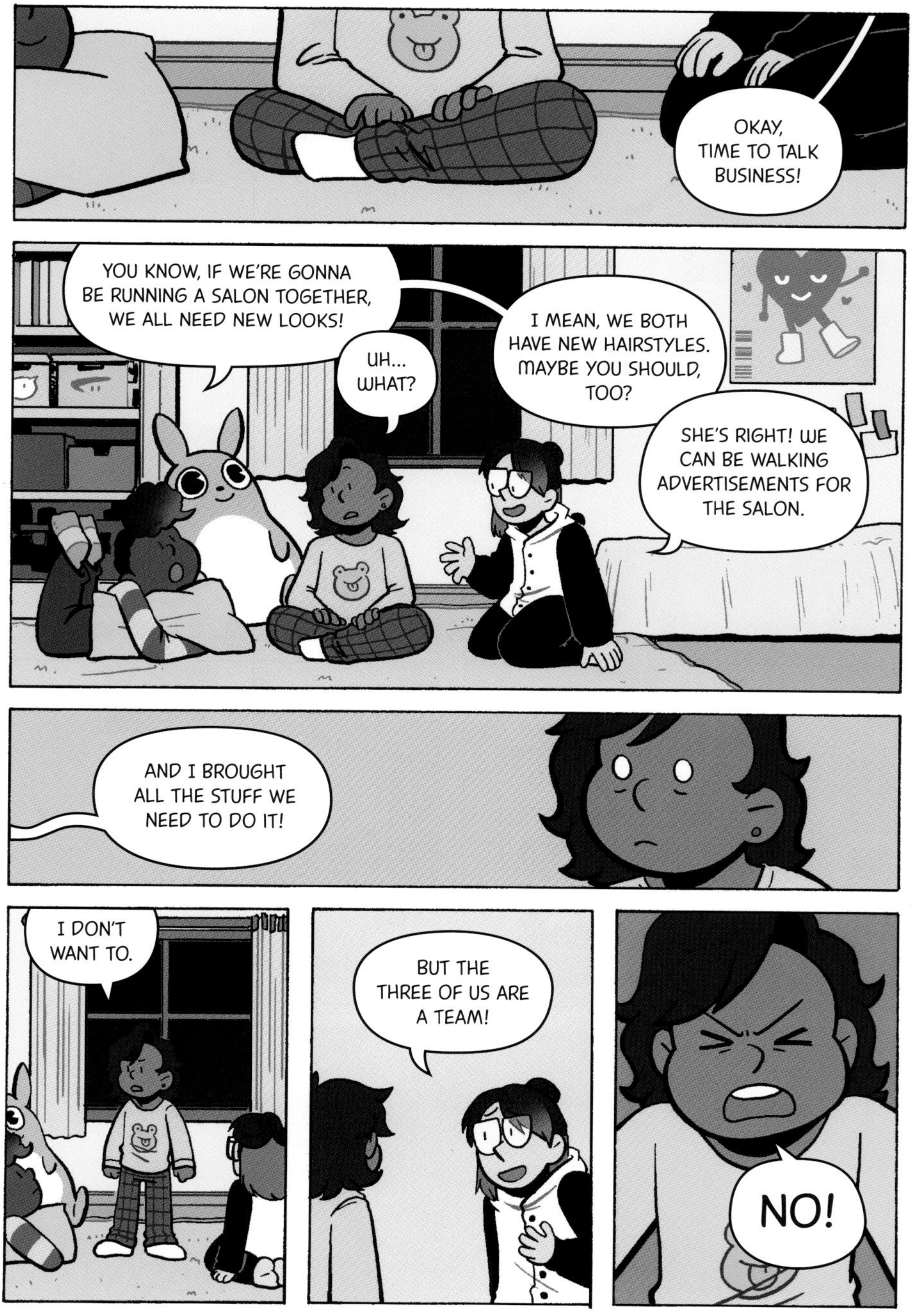
OKAY, TIME TO TALK BUSINESS!
YOU KNOW, IF WE'RE GONNA BE RUNNING A SALON TOGETHER, WE ALL NEED NEW LOOKS!
UH... WHAT?
I MEAN, WE BOTH HAVE NEW HAIRSTYLES. MAYBE YOU SHOULD, TOO?
SHE'S RIGHT! WE CAN BE WALKING ADVERTISEMENTS FOR THE SALON.
AND I BROUGHT ALL THE STUFF WE NEED TO DO IT!
I DON'T WANT TO.
BUT THE THREE OF US ARE A TEAM!
NO!

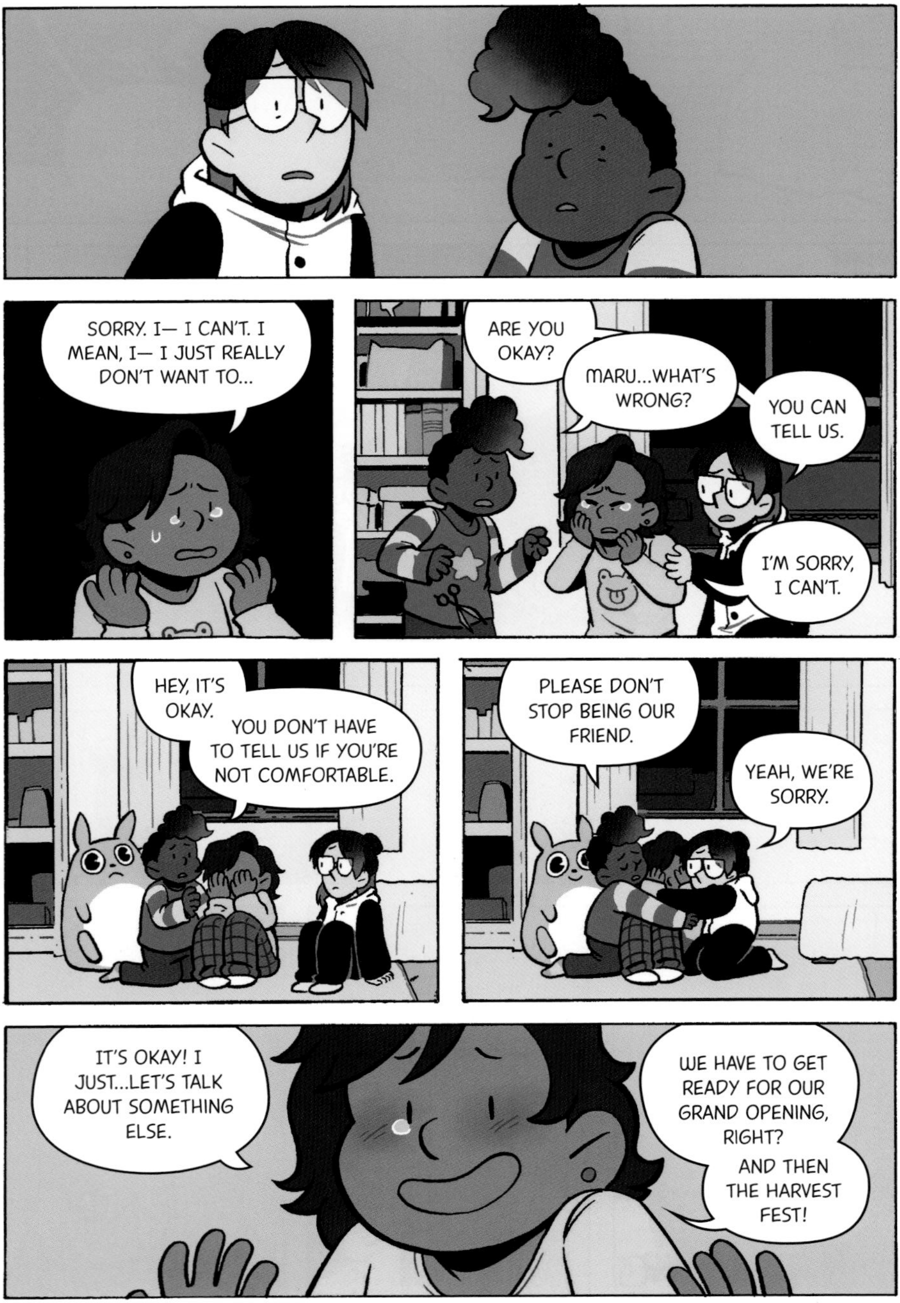
SORRY. I— I CAN'T. I MEAN, I— I JUST REALLY DON'T WANT TO...
ARE YOU OKAY?
MARU...WHAT'S WRONG?
YOU CAN TELL US.
I'M SORRY, I CAN'T.
HEY, IT'S OKAY.
YOU DON'T HAVE TO TELL US IF YOU'RE NOT COMFORTABLE.
PLEASE DON'T STOP BEING OUR FRIEND.
YEAH, WE'RE SORRY.
IT'S OKAY! I JUST...LET'S TALK ABOUT SOMETHING ELSE.
WE HAVE TO GET READY FOR OUR GRAND OPENING, RIGHT?
AND THEN THE HARVEST FEST!

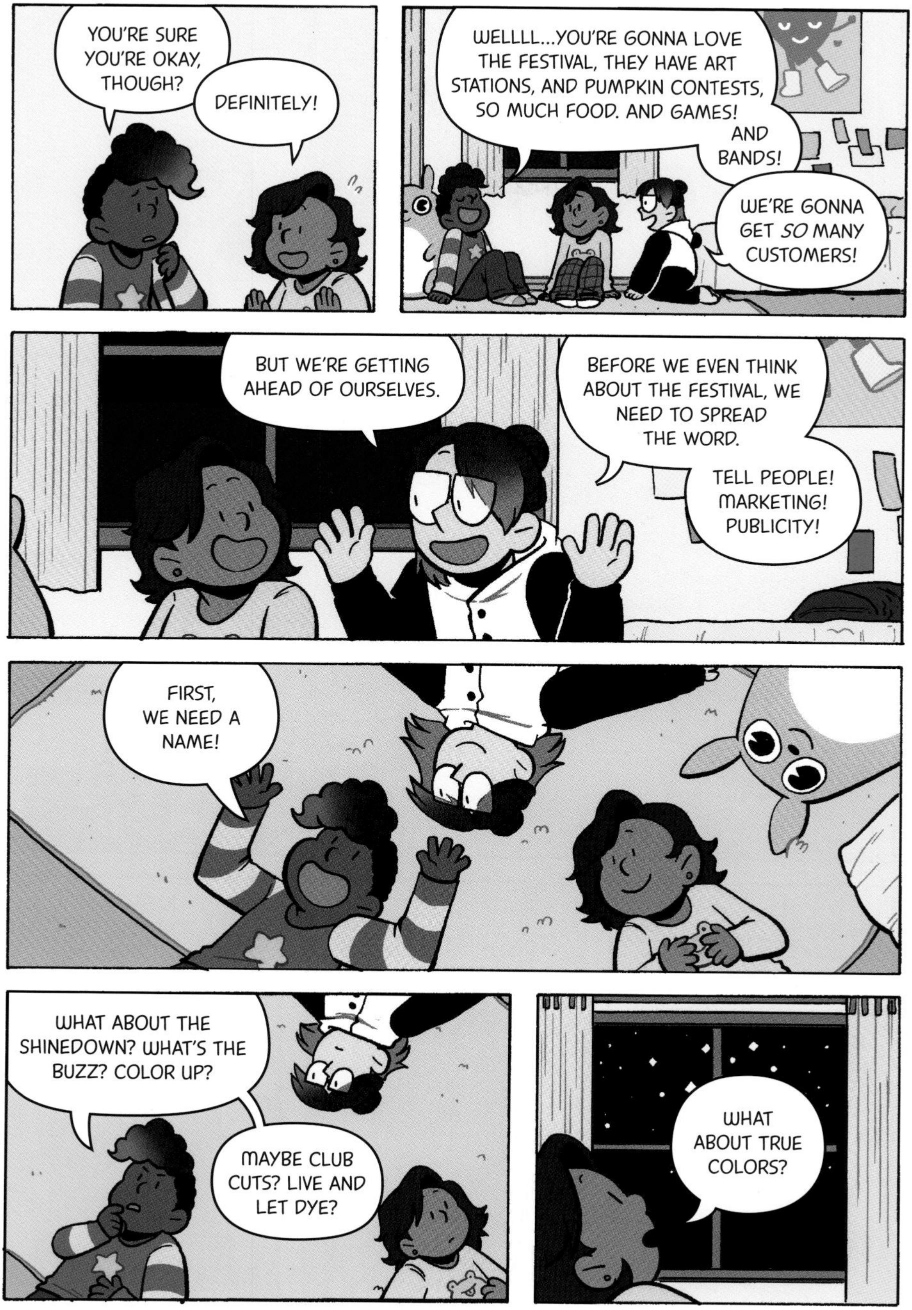
YOU'RE SURE YOU'RE OKAY, THOUGH?
DEFINITELY!
WELLLL...YOU'RE GONNA LOVE THE FESTIVAL, THEY HAVE ART STATIONS, AND PUMPKIN CONTESTS, SO MUCH FOOD. AND GAMES!
AND BANDS!
WE'RE GONNA GET *SO* MANY CUSTOMERS!
BUT WE'RE GETTING AHEAD OF OURSELVES.
BEFORE WE EVEN THINK ABOUT THE FESTIVAL, WE NEED TO SPREAD THE WORD.
TELL PEOPLE! MARKETING! PUBLICITY!
FIRST, WE NEED A NAME!
WHAT ABOUT THE SHINEDOWN? WHAT'S THE BUZZ? COLOR UP?
MAYBE CLUB CUTS? LIVE AND LET DYE?
WHAT ABOUT TRUE COLORS?

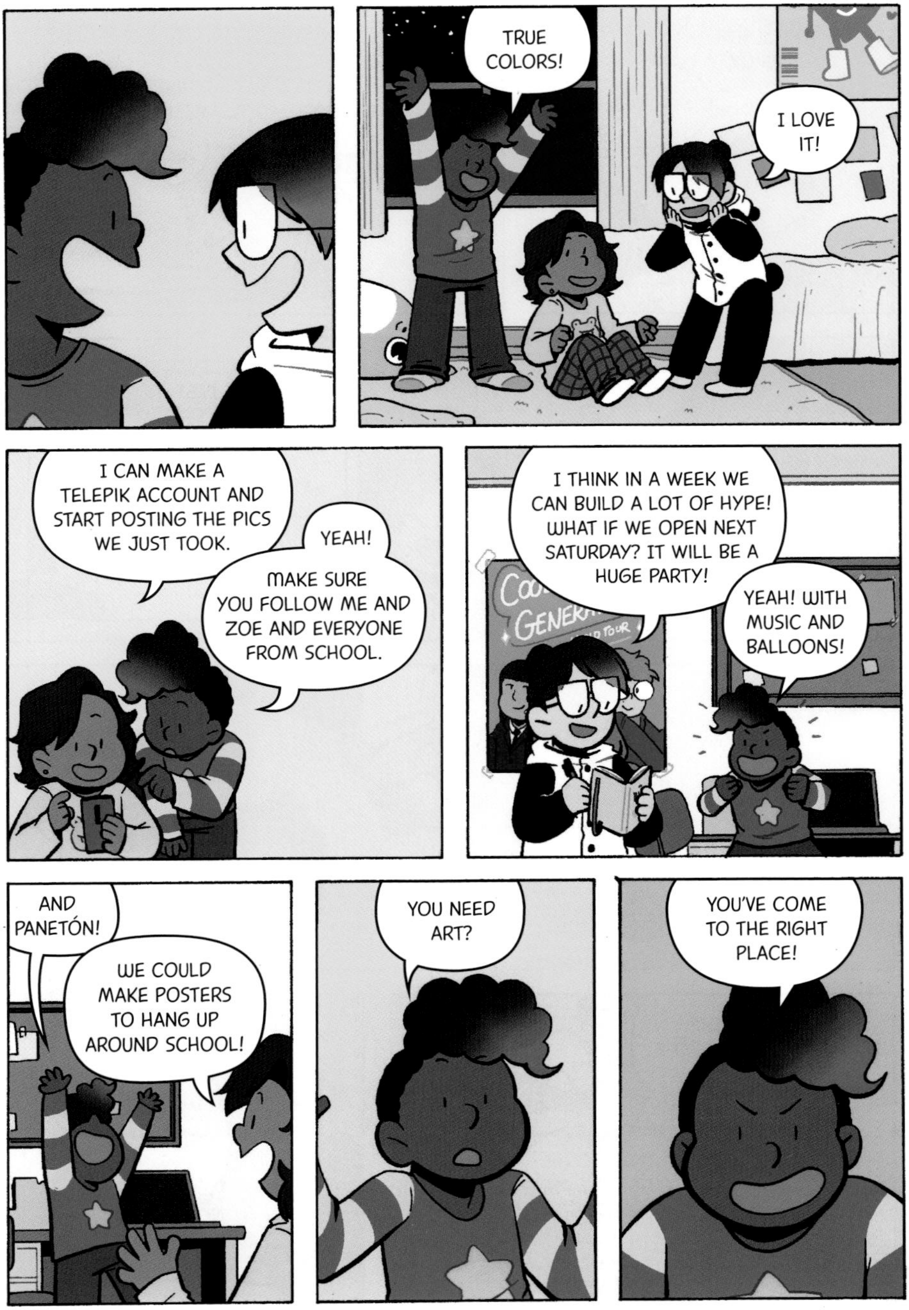
TRUE COLORS!
I LOVE IT!
I CAN MAKE A TELEPIK ACCOUNT AND START POSTING THE PICS WE JUST TOOK.
YEAH!
MAKE SURE YOU FOLLOW ME AND ZOE AND EVERYONE FROM SCHOOL.
I THINK IN A WEEK WE CAN BUILD A LOT OF HYPE! WHAT IF WE OPEN NEXT SATURDAY? IT WILL BE A HUGE PARTY!
YEAH! WITH MUSIC AND BALLOONS!
AND PANETÓN!
WE COULD MAKE POSTERS TO HANG UP AROUND SCHOOL!
YOU NEED ART?
YOU'VE COME TO THE RIGHT PLACE!

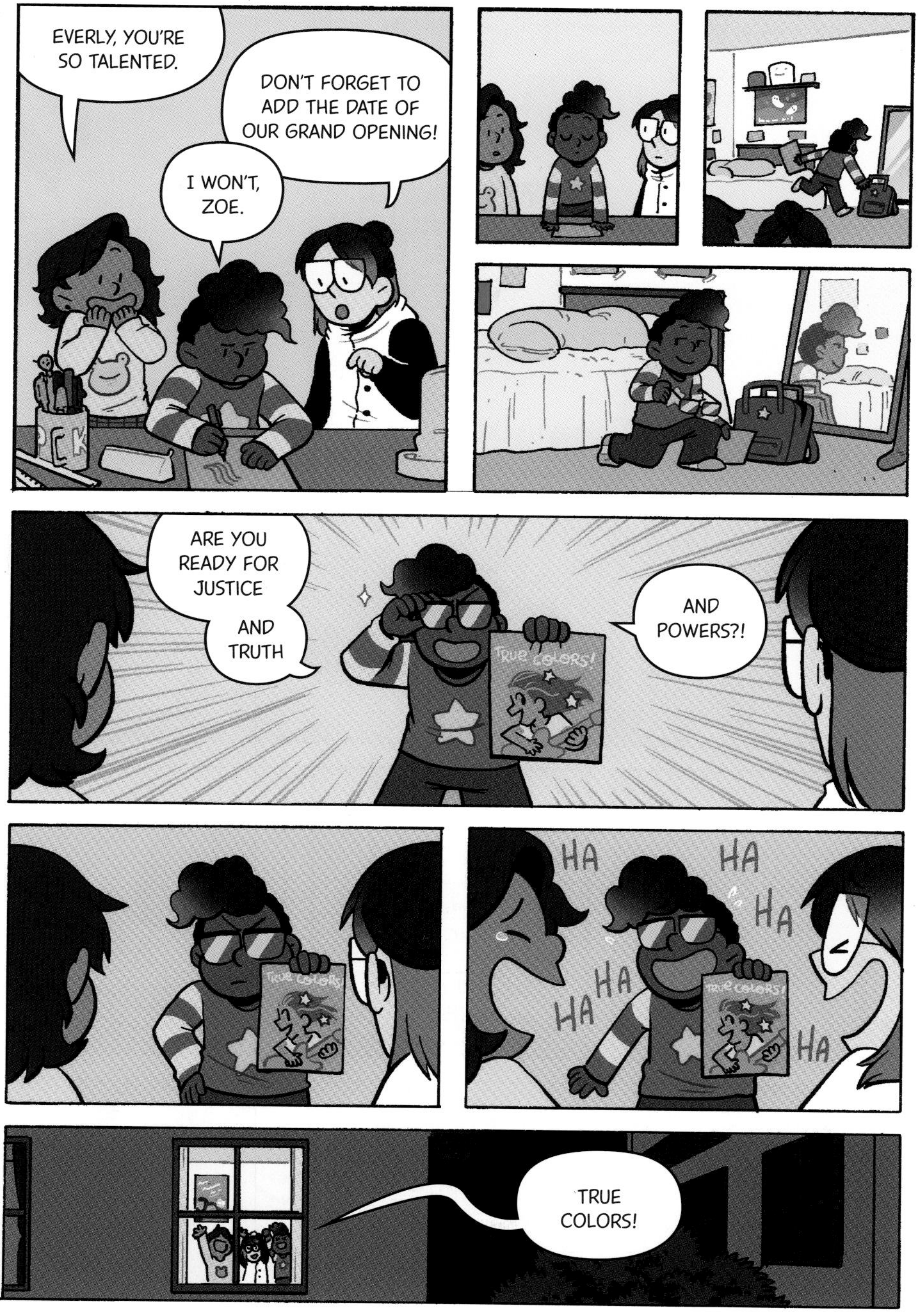
EVERLY, YOU'RE SO TALENTED.
DON'T FORGET TO ADD THE DATE OF OUR GRAND OPENING!
I WON'T, ZOE.
ARE YOU READY FOR JUSTICE AND TRUTH
AND POWERS?!
TRUE COLORS!
TRUE COLORS!
TRUE COLORS!
HA HA HA HA HA HA HA
TRUE COLORS!

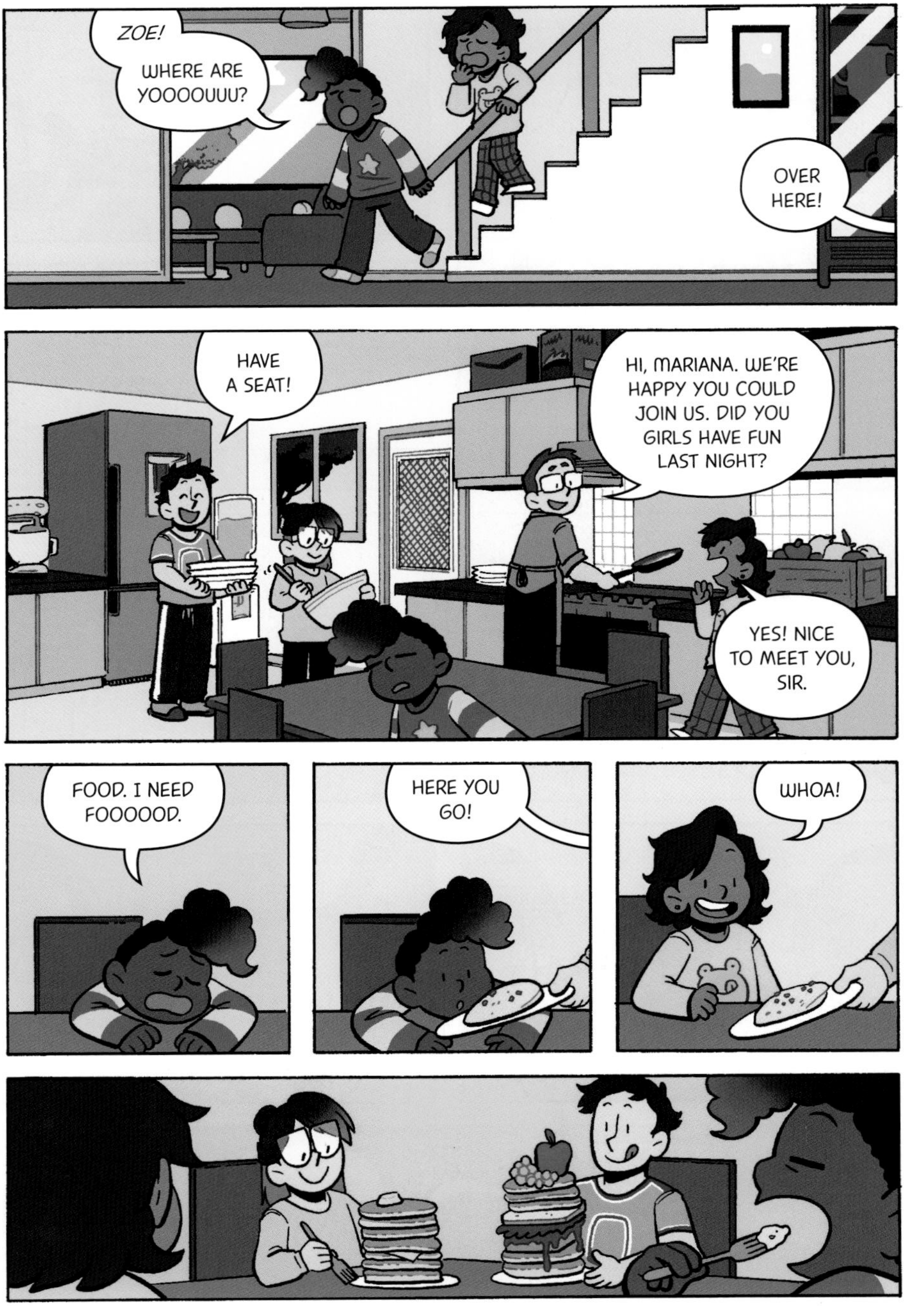
ZOE!
WHERE ARE YOOOOUUU?
OVER HERE!
HAVE A SEAT!
HI, MARIANA. WE'RE HAPPY YOU COULD JOIN US. DID YOU GIRLS HAVE FUN LAST NIGHT?
YES! NICE TO MEET YOU, SIR.
FOOD. I NEED FOOOOOD.
HERE YOU GO!
WHOA!

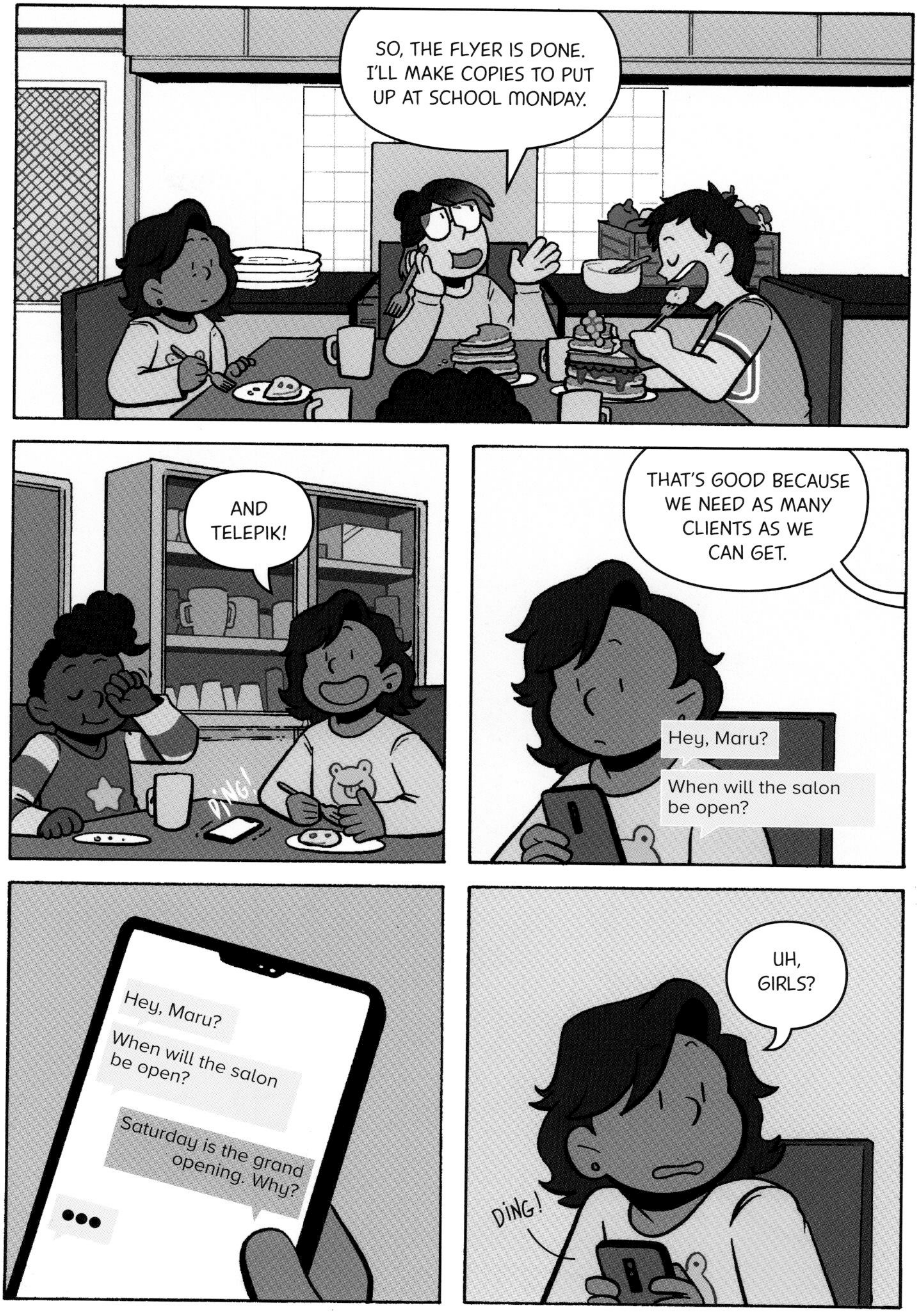
SO, THE FLYER IS DONE. I'LL MAKE COPIES TO PUT UP AT SCHOOL MONDAY.
AND TELEPIK!
DING!
THAT'S GOOD BECAUSE WE NEED AS MANY CLIENTS AS WE CAN GET.
Hey, Maru?
When will the salon be open?
Hey, Maru?
When will the salon be open?
Saturday is the grand opening. Why?
UH, GIRLS?
DING!

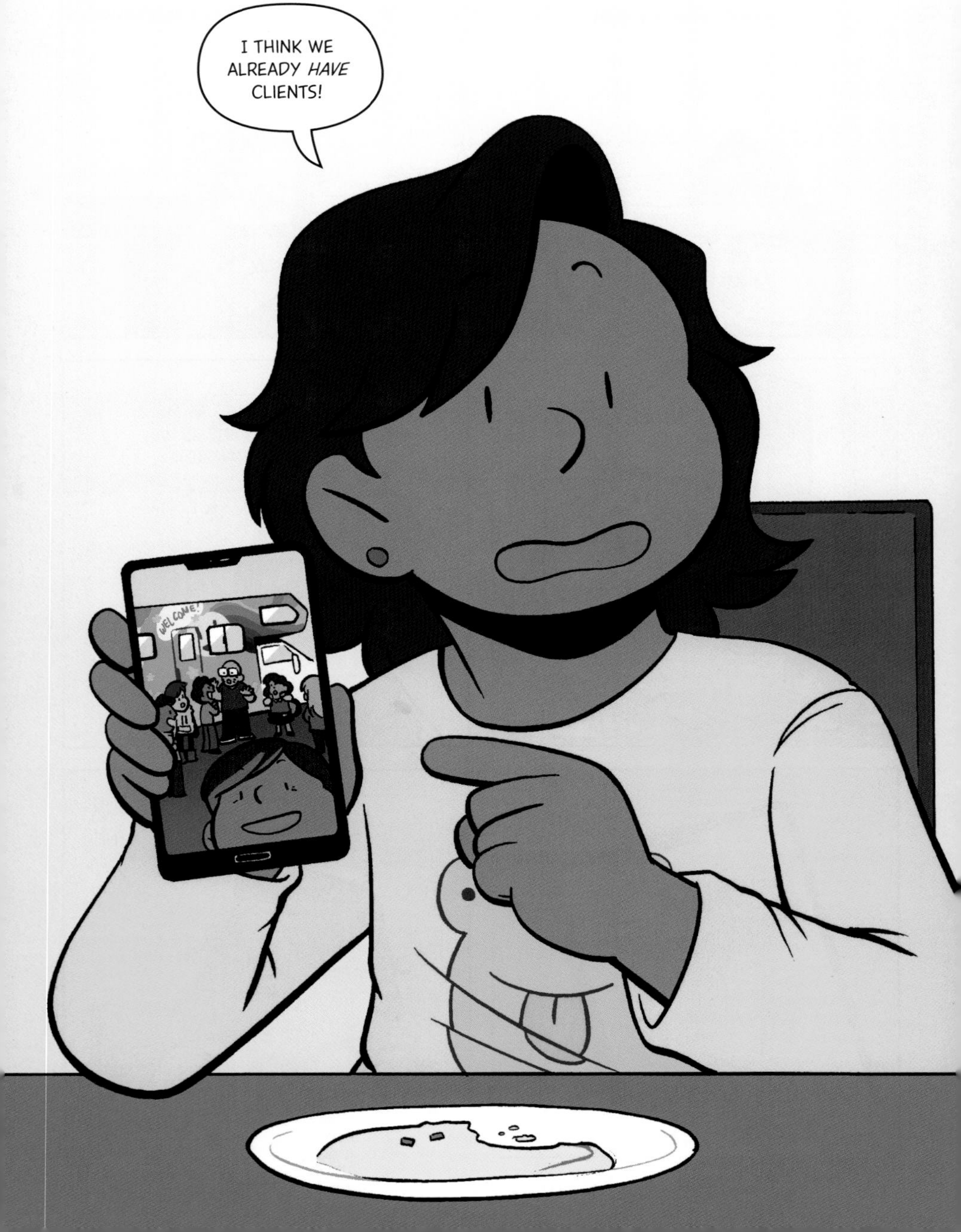
I THINK WE ALREADY *HAVE* CLIENTS!
WELCOME!

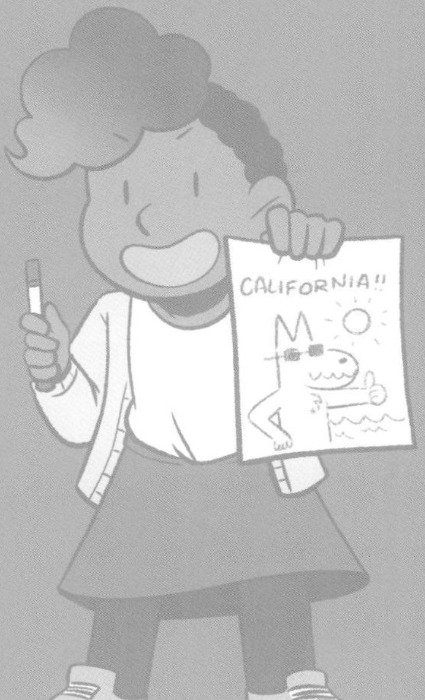
CALIFORNIA!!

CHAPTER 4

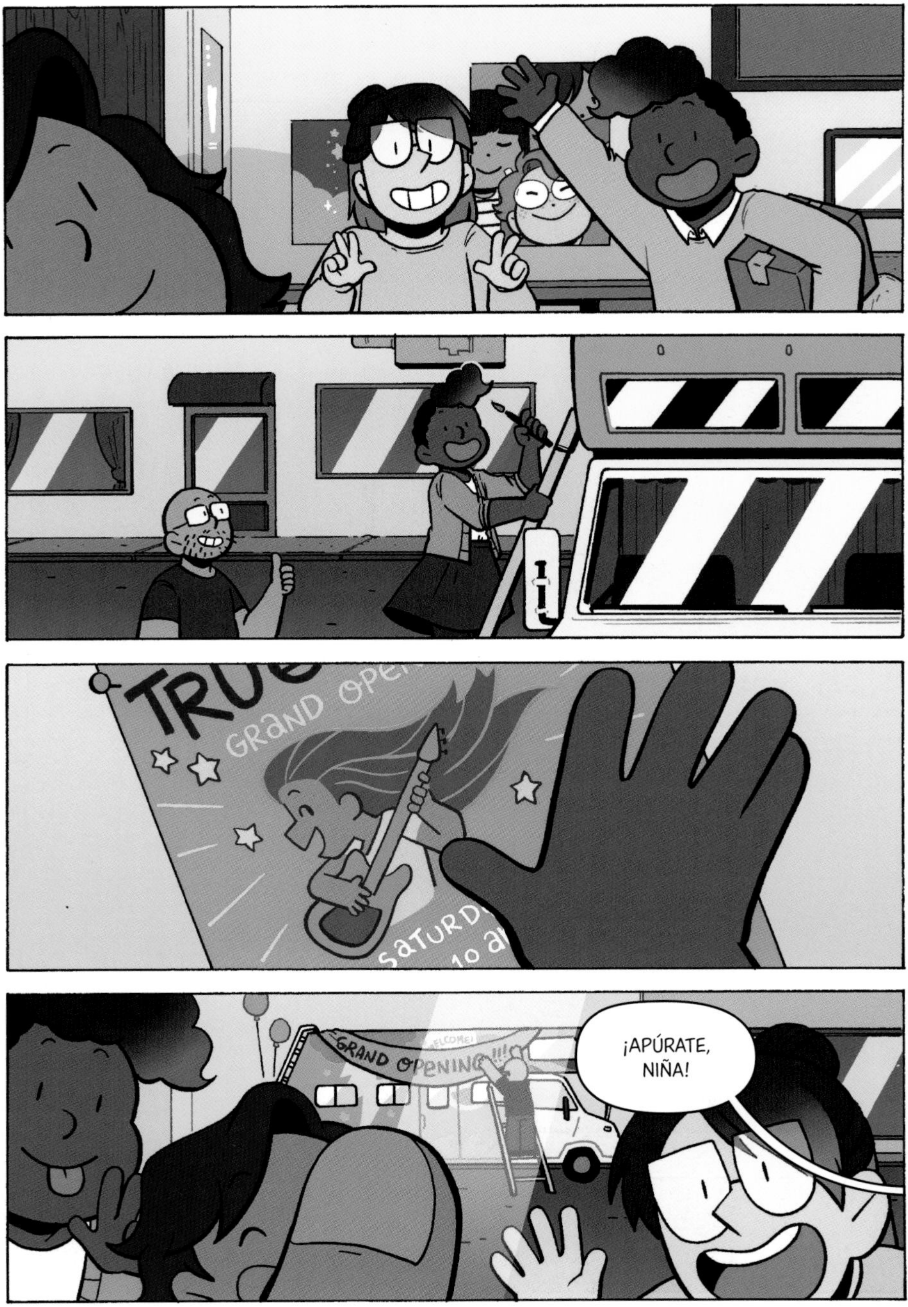
GRAND OPENING!!!
¡APÚRATE, NIÑA!

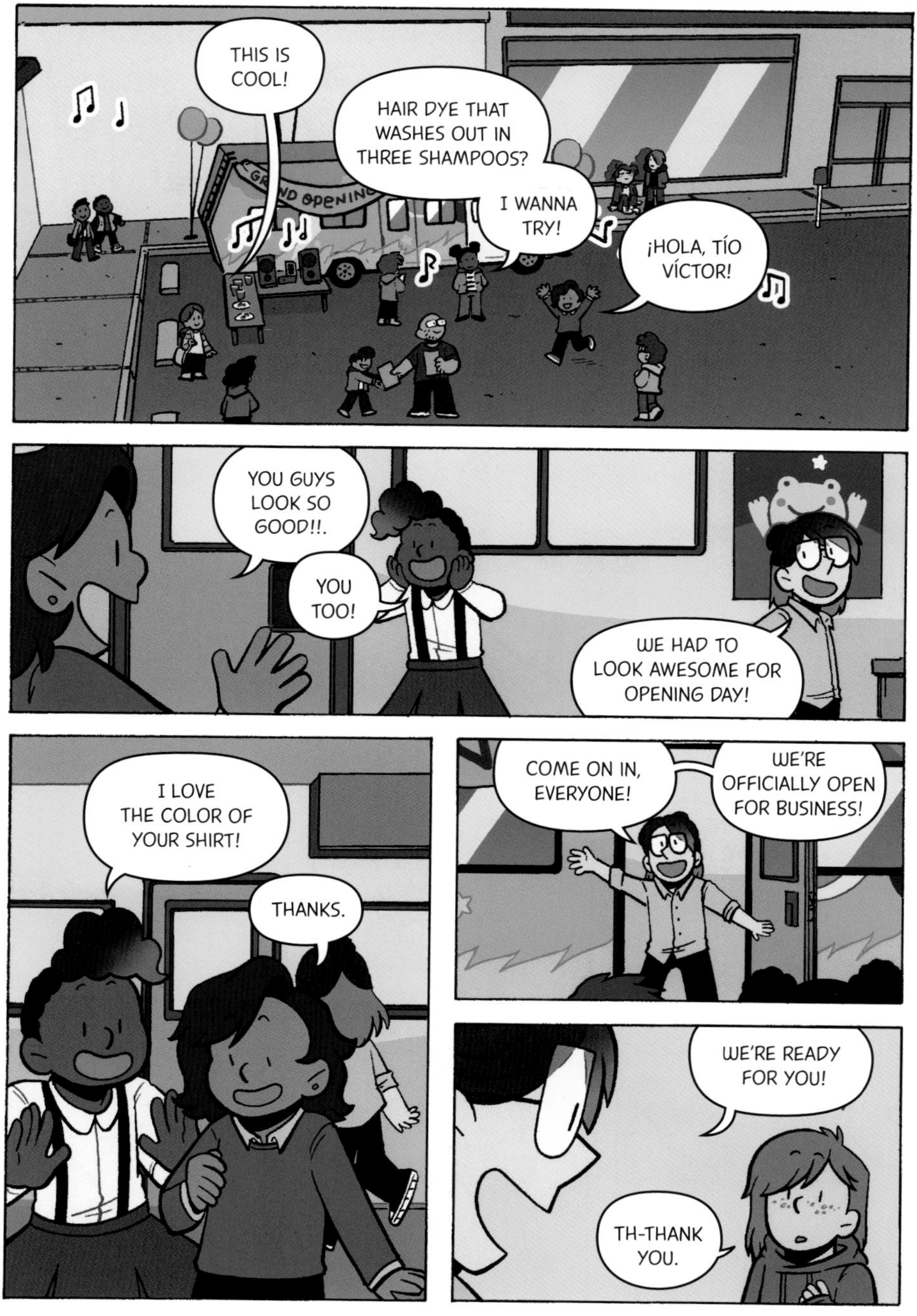
THIS IS COOL!
HAIR DYE THAT WASHES OUT IN THREE SHAMPOOS?
I WANNA TRY!
¡HOLA, TÍO VÍCTOR!
GRAND OPENING
YOU GUYS LOOK SO GOOD!!.
YOU TOO!
WE HAD TO LOOK AWESOME FOR OPENING DAY!
I LOVE THE COLOR OF YOUR SHIRT!
THANKS.
COME ON IN, EVERYONE!
WE'RE OFFICIALLY OPEN FOR BUSINESS!
WE'RE READY FOR YOU!
TH-THANK YOU.

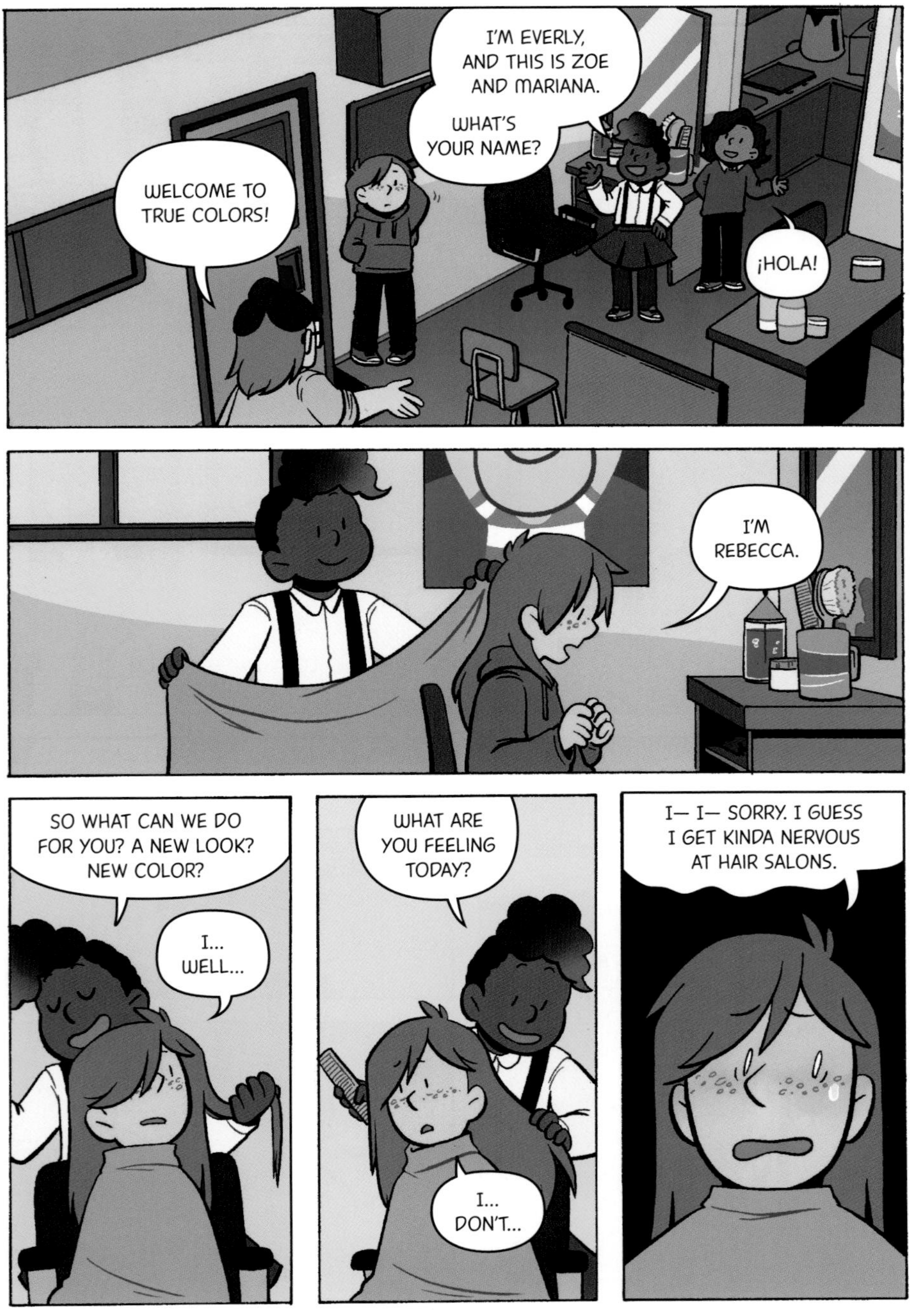
WELCOME TO TRUE COLORS!
I'M EVERLY, AND THIS IS ZOE AND MARIANA.
WHAT'S YOUR NAME?
¡HOLA!
I'M REBECCA.
SO WHAT CAN WE DO FOR YOU? A NEW LOOK? NEW COLOR?
I... WELL...
WHAT ARE YOU FEELING TODAY?
I... DON'T...
I— I— SORRY. I GUESS I GET KINDA NERVOUS AT HAIR SALONS.

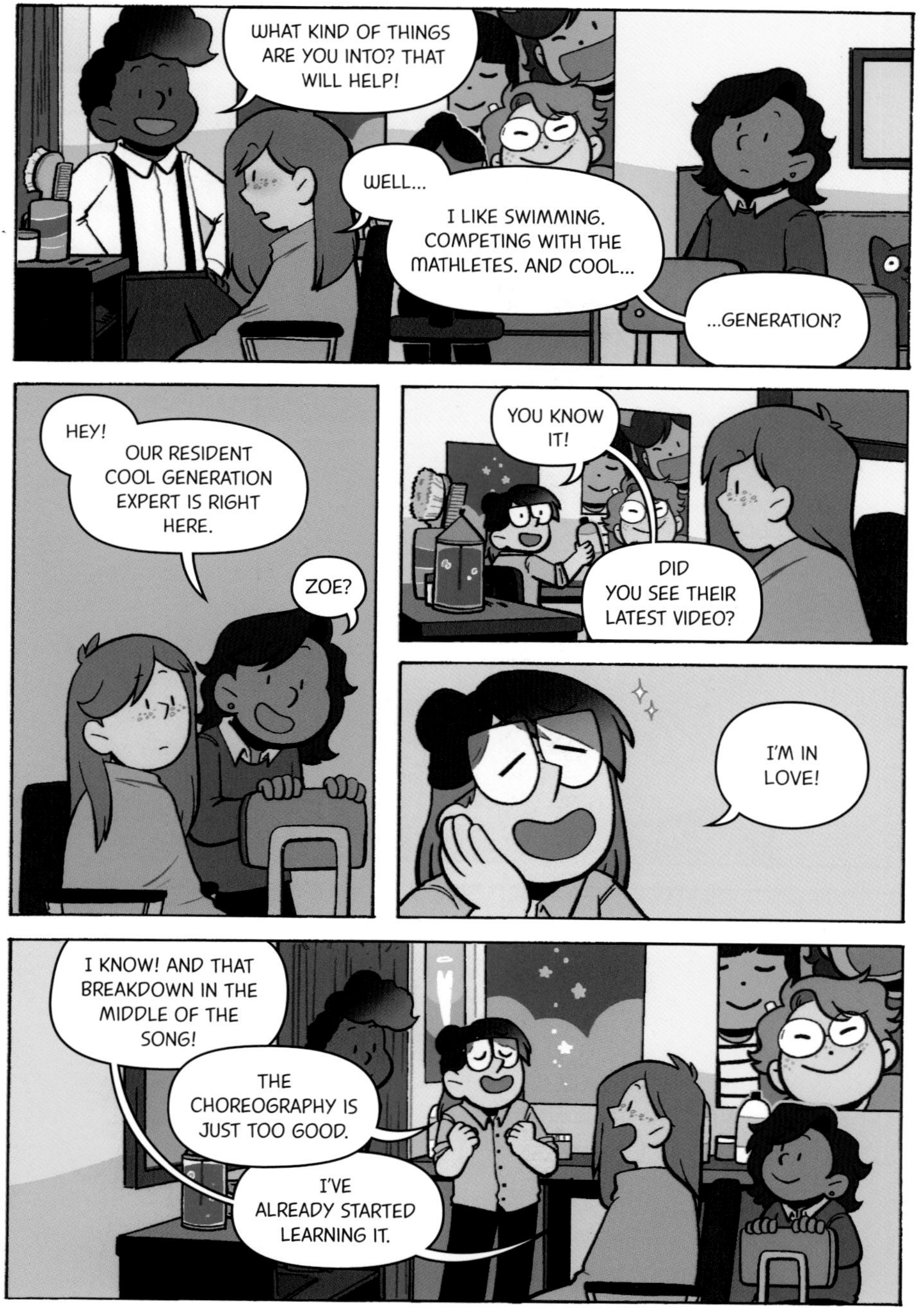
WHAT KIND OF THINGS ARE YOU INTO? THAT WILL HELP!
WELL...
I LIKE SWIMMING. COMPETING WITH THE MATHLETES. AND COOL...
...GENERATION?
HEY!
OUR RESIDENT COOL GENERATION EXPERT IS RIGHT HERE.
ZOE?
YOU KNOW IT!
DID YOU SEE THEIR LATEST VIDEO?
I'M IN LOVE!
I KNOW! AND THAT BREAKDOWN IN THE MIDDLE OF THE SONG!
THE CHOREOGRAPHY IS JUST TOO GOOD.
I'VE ALREADY STARTED LEARNING IT.

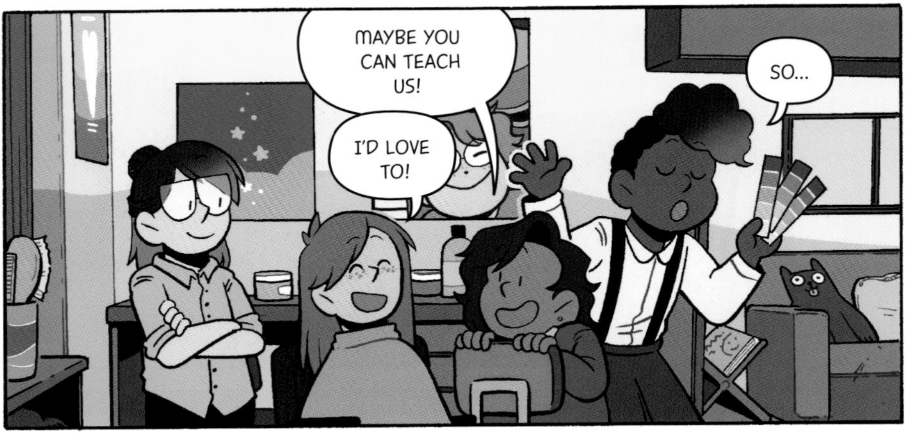
MAYBE YOU CAN TEACH US!
I'D LOVE TO!
SO...

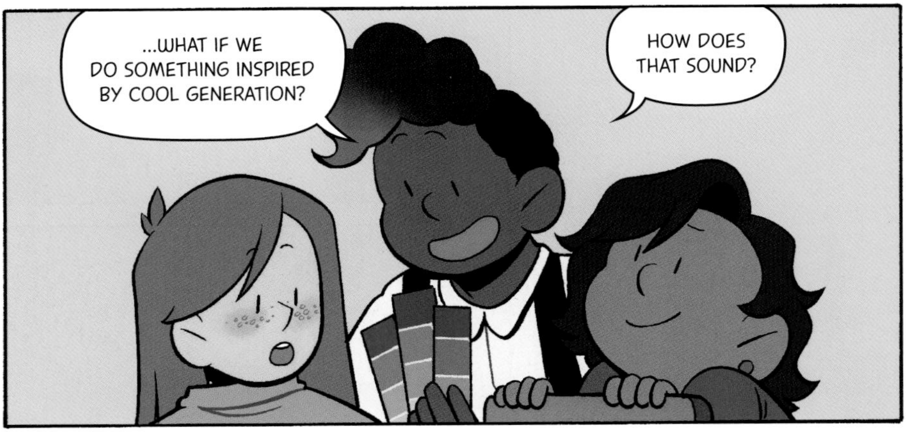
...WHAT IF WE DO SOMETHING INSPIRED BY COOL GENERATION?
HOW DOES THAT SOUND?

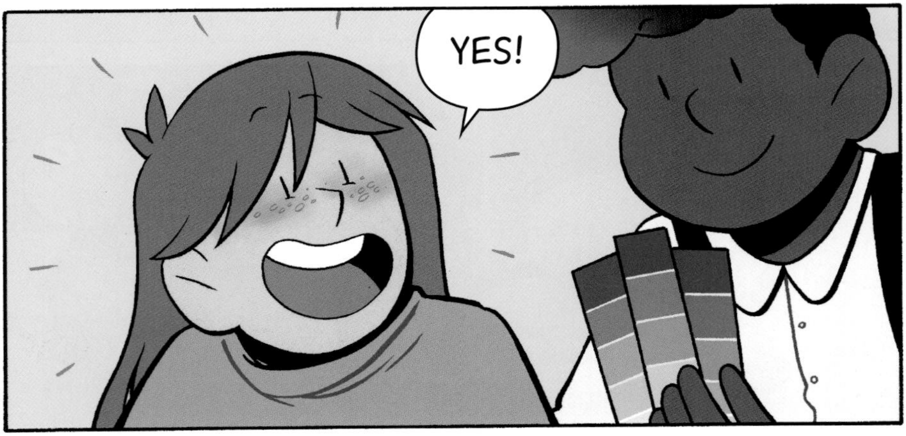
YES!

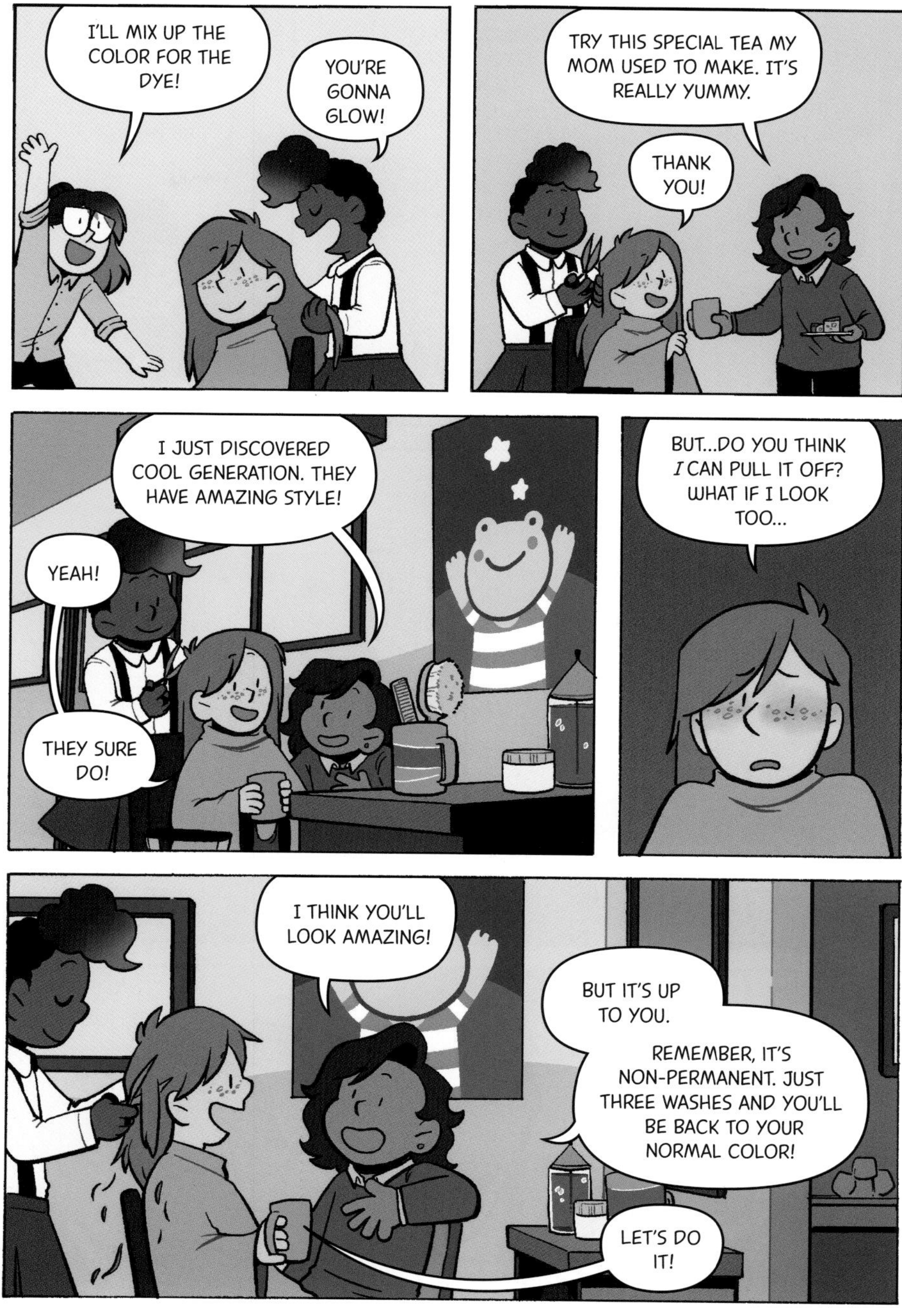
I'LL MIX UP THE COLOR FOR THE DYE!
YOU'RE GONNA GLOW!
TRY THIS SPECIAL TEA MY MOM USED TO MAKE. IT'S REALLY YUMMY.
THANK YOU!
I JUST DISCOVERED COOL GENERATION. THEY HAVE AMAZING STYLE!
YEAH!
THEY SURE DO!
BUT...DO YOU THINK *I* CAN PULL IT OFF? WHAT IF I LOOK TOO...
I THINK YOU'LL LOOK AMAZING!
BUT IT'S UP TO YOU.
REMEMBER, IT'S NON-PERMANENT. JUST THREE WASHES AND YOU'LL BE BACK TO YOUR NORMAL COLOR!
LET'S DO IT!

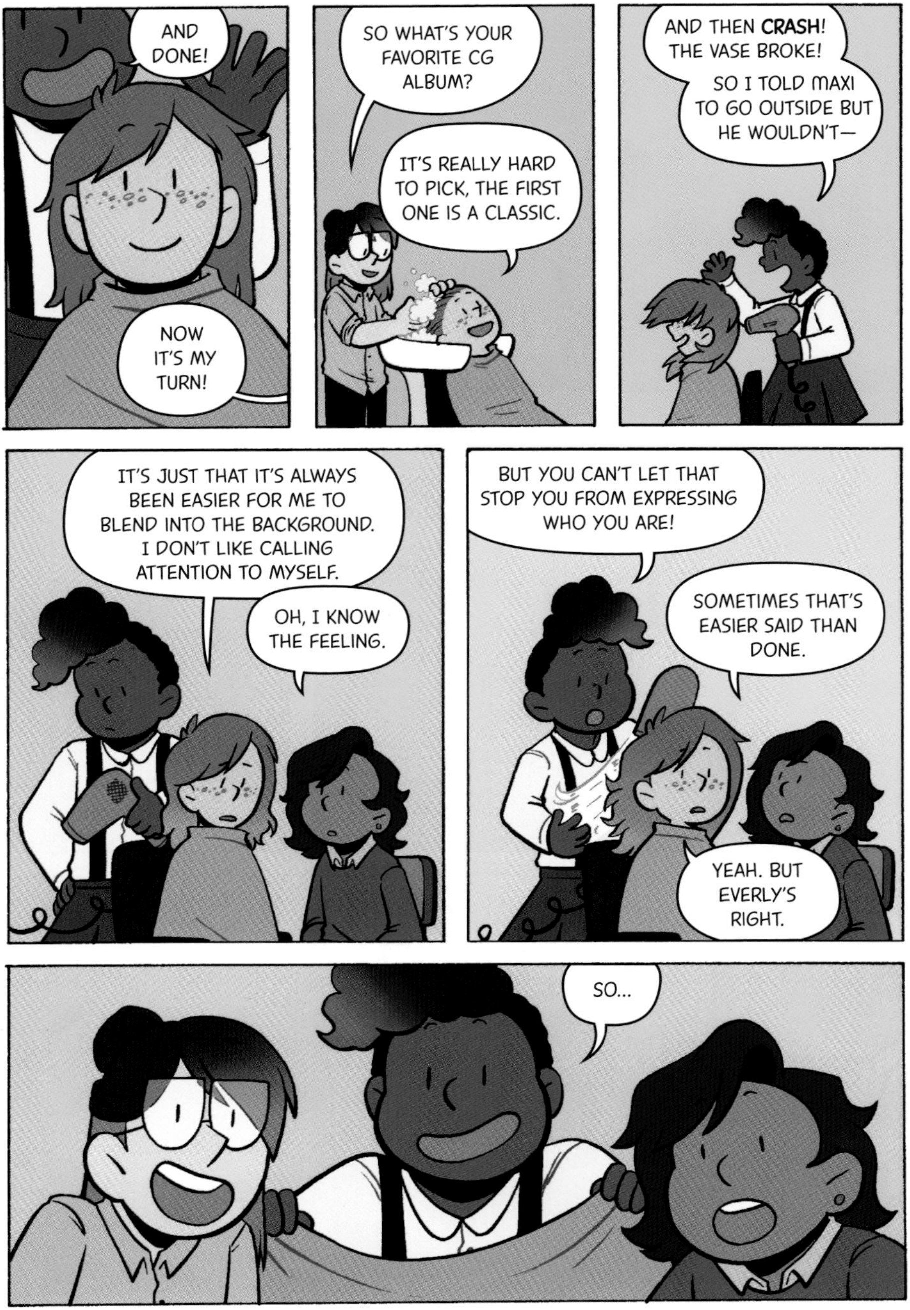
AND DONE!
NOW IT'S MY TURN!
SO WHAT'S YOUR FAVORITE CG ALBUM?
IT'S REALLY HARD TO PICK, THE FIRST ONE IS A CLASSIC.
AND THEN CRASH! THE VASE BROKE!
SO I TOLD MAXI TO GO OUTSIDE BUT HE WOULDN'T—
IT'S JUST THAT IT'S ALWAYS BEEN EASIER FOR ME TO BLEND INTO THE BACKGROUND. I DON'T LIKE CALLING ATTENTION TO MYSELF.
OH, I KNOW THE FEELING.
BUT YOU CAN'T LET THAT STOP YOU FROM EXPRESSING WHO YOU ARE!
SOMETIMES THAT'S EASIER SAID THAN DONE.
YEAH. BUT EVERLY'S RIGHT.
SO...

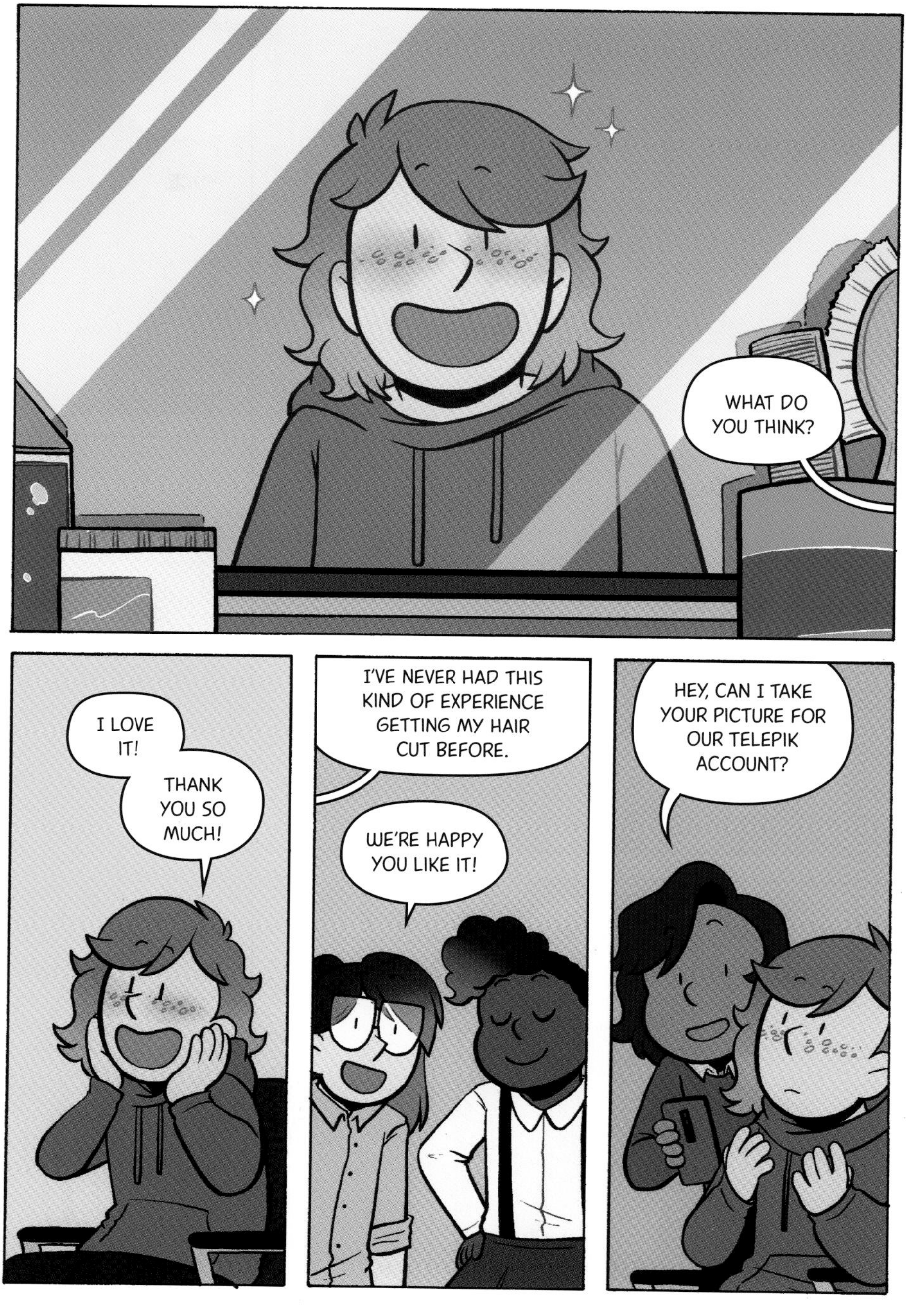
WHAT DO YOU THINK?
I LOVE IT!
THANK YOU SO MUCH!
I'VE NEVER HAD THIS KIND OF EXPERIENCE GETTING MY HAIR CUT BEFORE.
WE'RE HAPPY YOU LIKE IT!
HEY, CAN I TAKE YOUR PICTURE FOR OUR TELEPIK ACCOUNT?

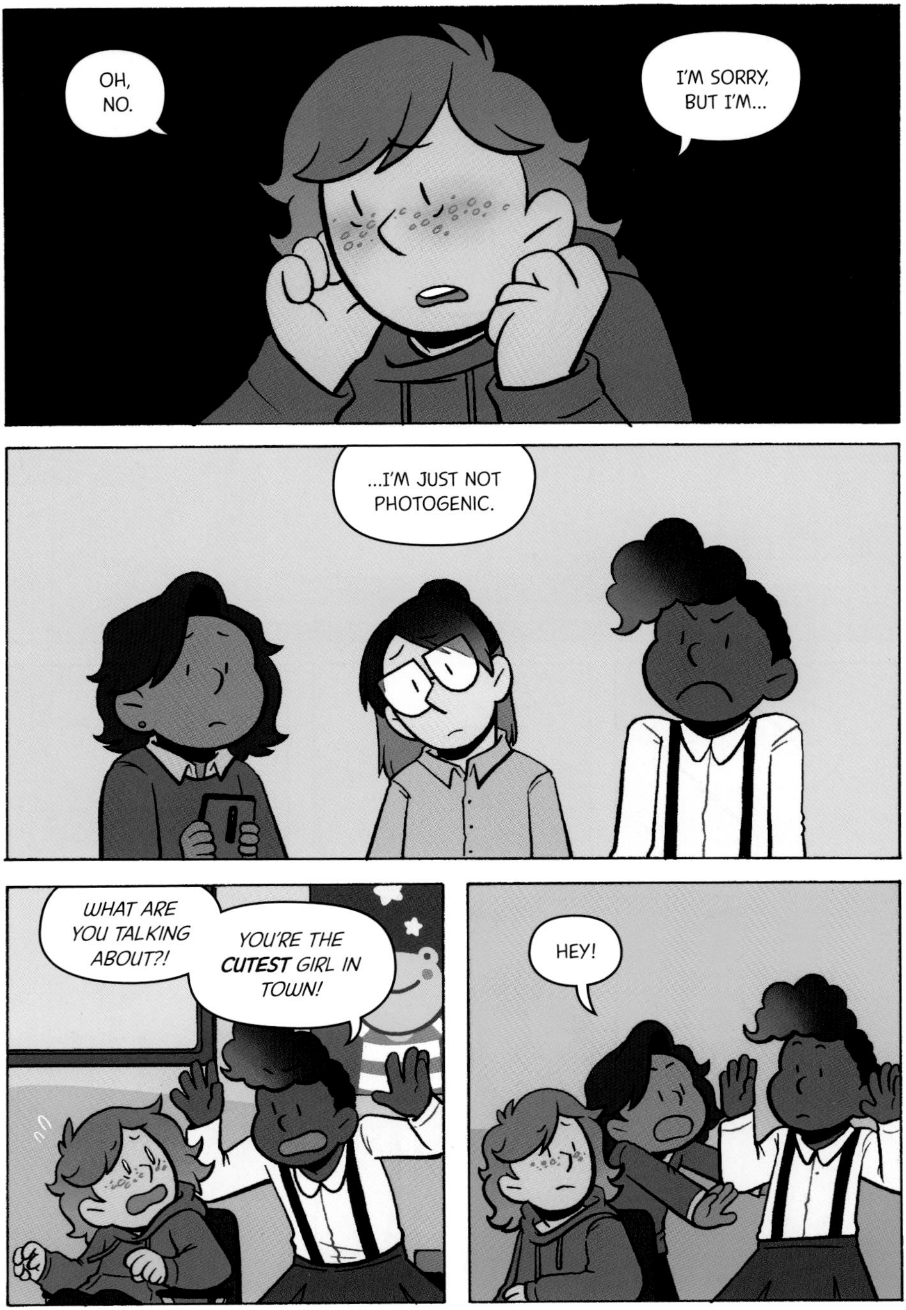
OH, NO.
I'M SORRY, BUT I'M...
...I'M JUST NOT PHOTOGENIC.
WHAT ARE YOU TALKING ABOUT?!
YOU'RE THE **CUTEST** GIRL IN TOWN!
HEY!

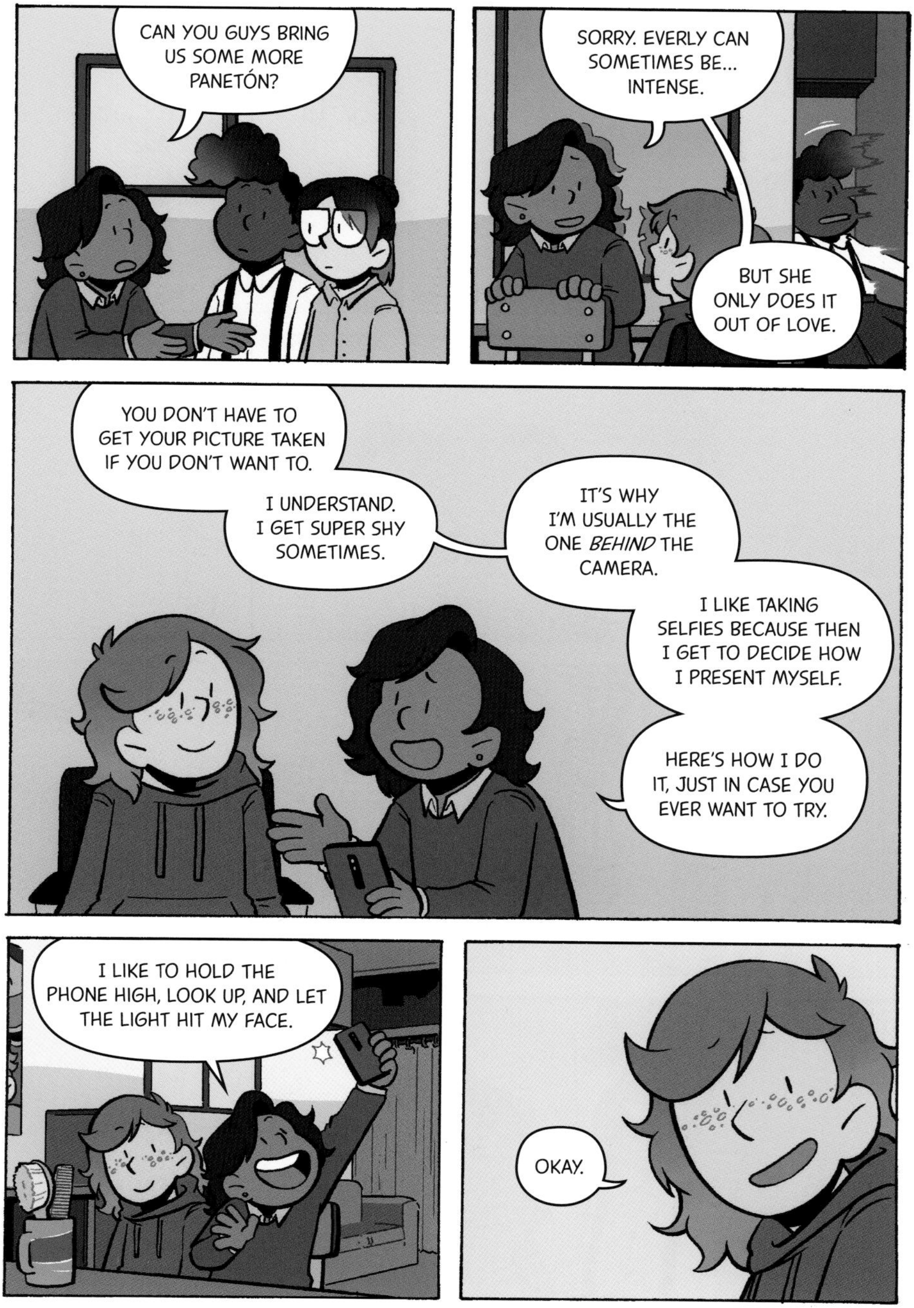
CAN YOU GUYS BRING US SOME MORE PANETÓN?
SORRY. EVERLY CAN SOMETIMES BE... INTENSE.
BUT SHE ONLY DOES IT OUT OF LOVE.
YOU DON'T HAVE TO GET YOUR PICTURE TAKEN IF YOU DON'T WANT TO.
I UNDERSTAND. I GET SUPER SHY SOMETIMES.
IT'S WHY I'M USUALLY THE ONE *BEHIND* THE CAMERA.
I LIKE TAKING SELFIES BECAUSE THEN I GET TO DECIDE HOW I PRESENT MYSELF.
HERE'S HOW I DO IT, JUST IN CASE YOU EVER WANT TO TRY.
I LIKE TO HOLD THE PHONE HIGH, LOOK UP, AND LET THE LIGHT HIT MY FACE.
OKAY.

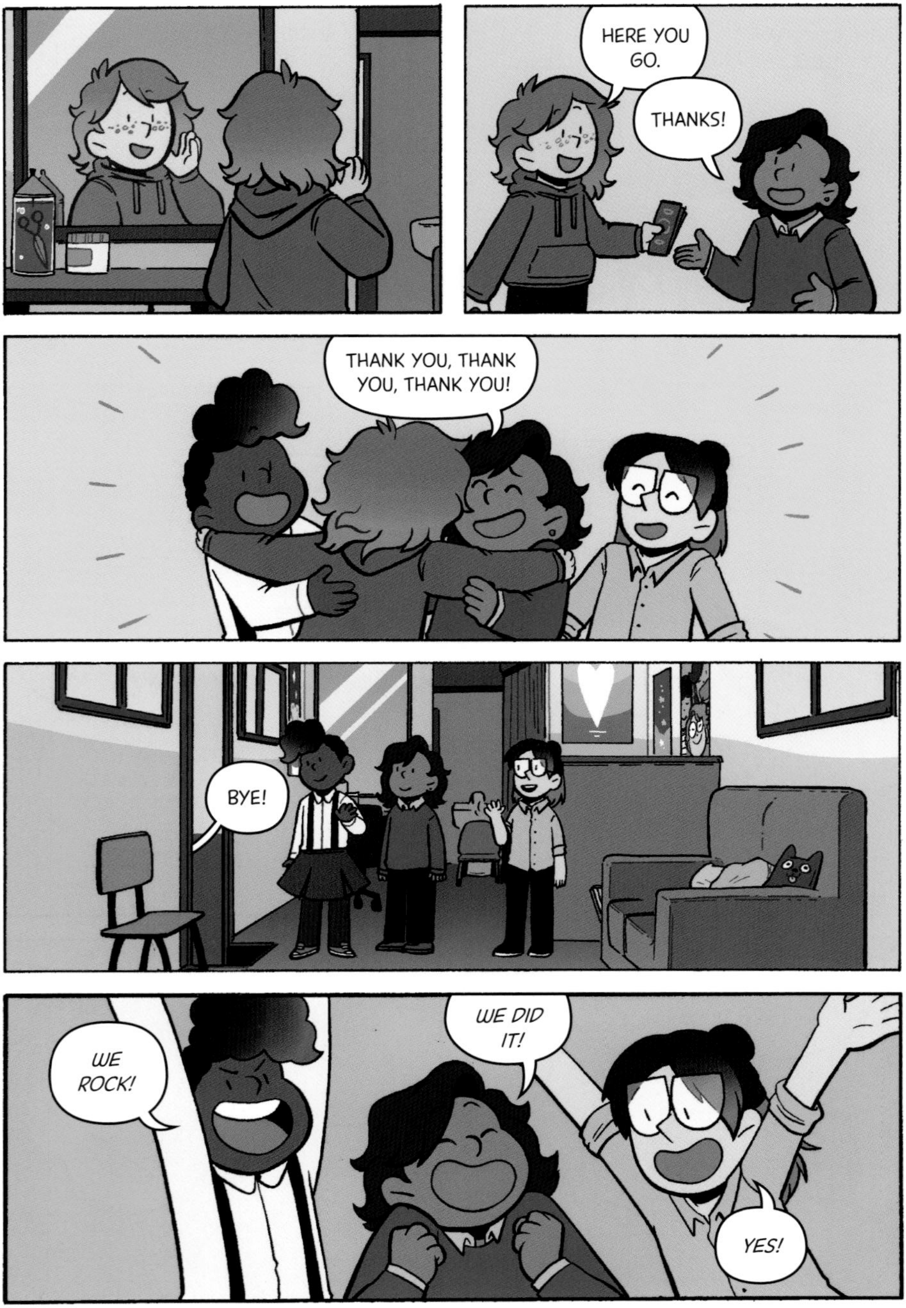
HERE YOU GO.
THANKS!
THANK YOU, THANK YOU, THANK YOU!
BYE!
WE ROCK!
WE DID IT!
YES!

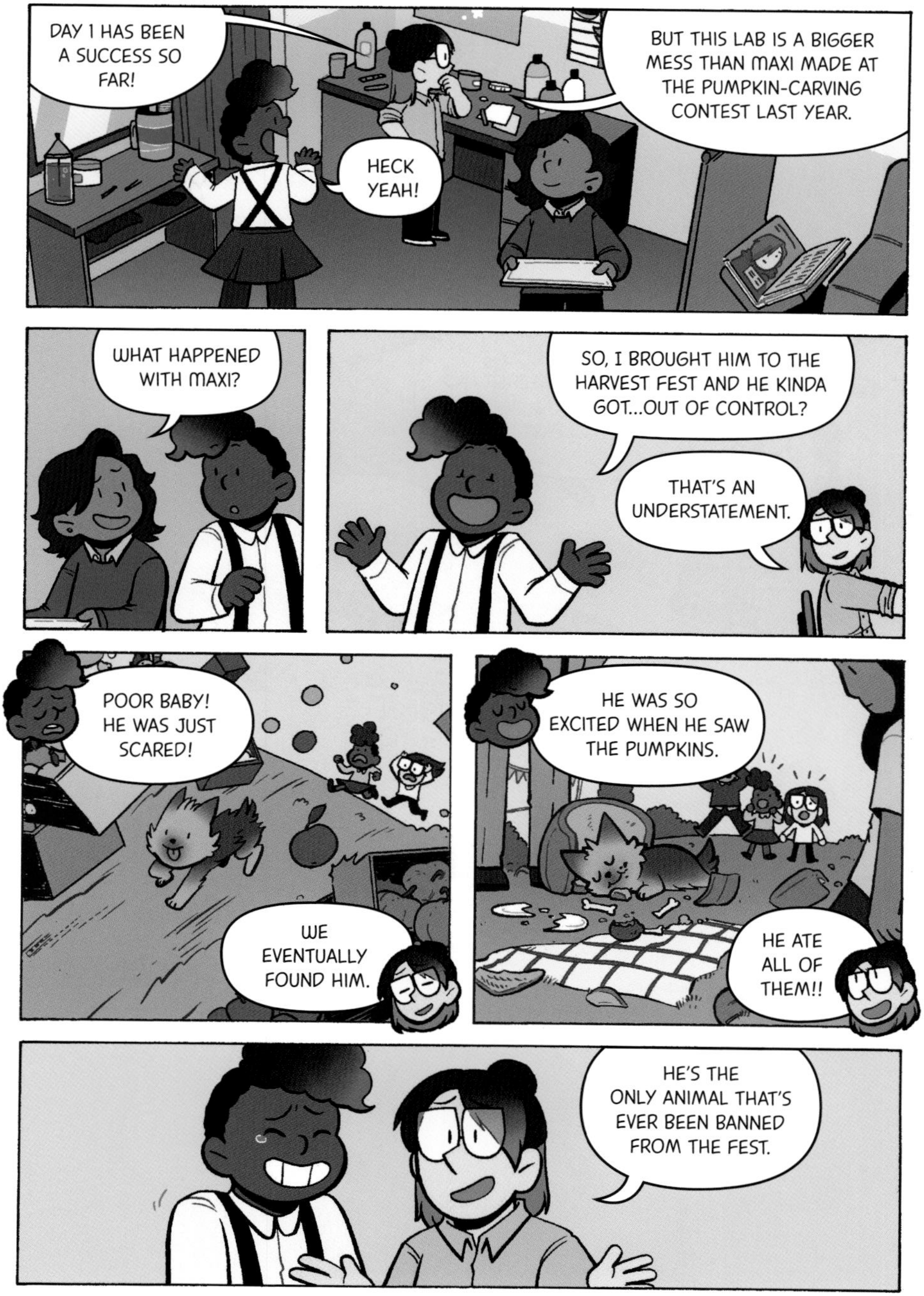
DAY 1 HAS BEEN A SUCCESS SO FAR!
BUT THIS LAB IS A BIGGER MESS THAN MAXI MADE AT THE PUMPKIN-CARVING CONTEST LAST YEAR.
HECK YEAH!
WHAT HAPPENED WITH MAXI?
SO, I BROUGHT HIM TO THE HARVEST FEST AND HE KINDA GOT...OUT OF CONTROL?
THAT'S AN UNDERSTATEMENT.
POOR BABY! HE WAS JUST SCARED!
WE EVENTUALLY FOUND HIM.
HE WAS SO EXCITED WHEN HE SAW THE PUMPKINS.
HE ATE ALL OF THEM!!
HE'S THE ONLY ANIMAL THAT'S EVER BEEN BANNED FROM THE FEST.

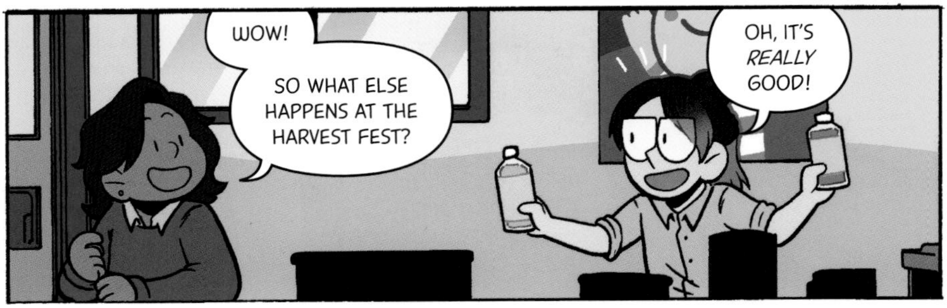
WOW!
SO WHAT ELSE HAPPENS AT THE HARVEST FEST?
OH, IT'S *REALLY* GOOD!

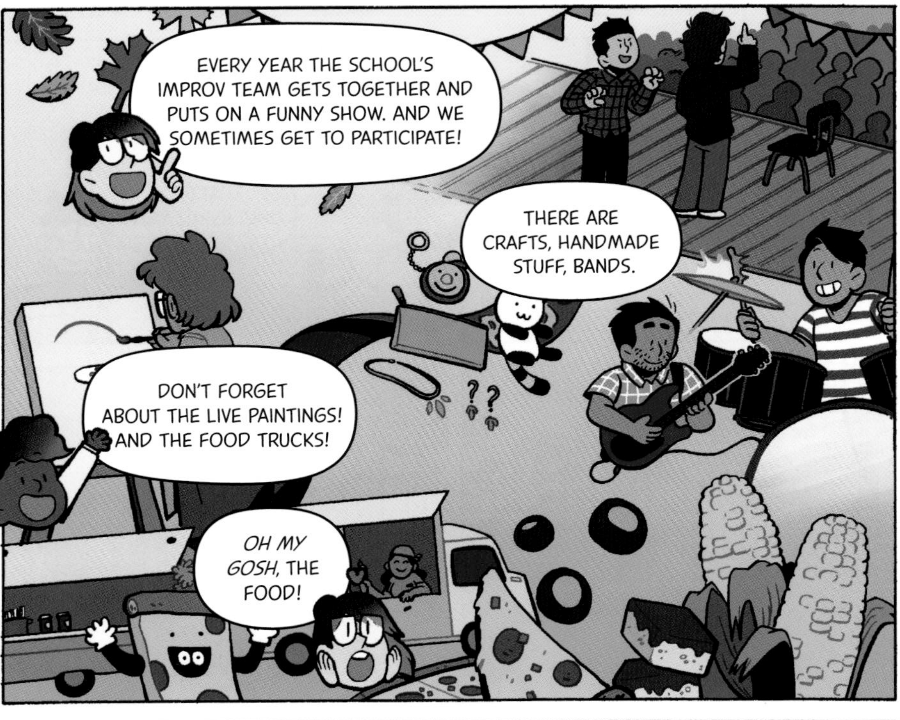
EVERY YEAR THE SCHOOL'S IMPROV TEAM GETS TOGETHER AND PUTS ON A FUNNY SHOW. AND WE SOMETIMES GET TO PARTICIPATE!
THERE ARE CRAFTS, HANDMADE STUFF, BANDS.
DON'T FORGET ABOUT THE LIVE PAINTINGS! AND THE FOOD TRUCKS!
OH MY GOSH, THE FOOD!

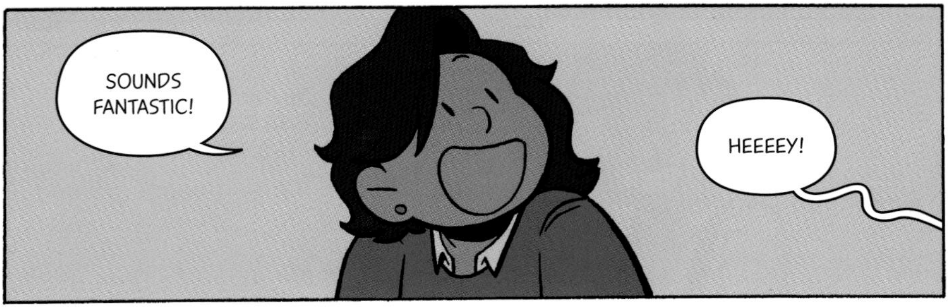
SOUNDS FANTASTIC!
HEEEEY!

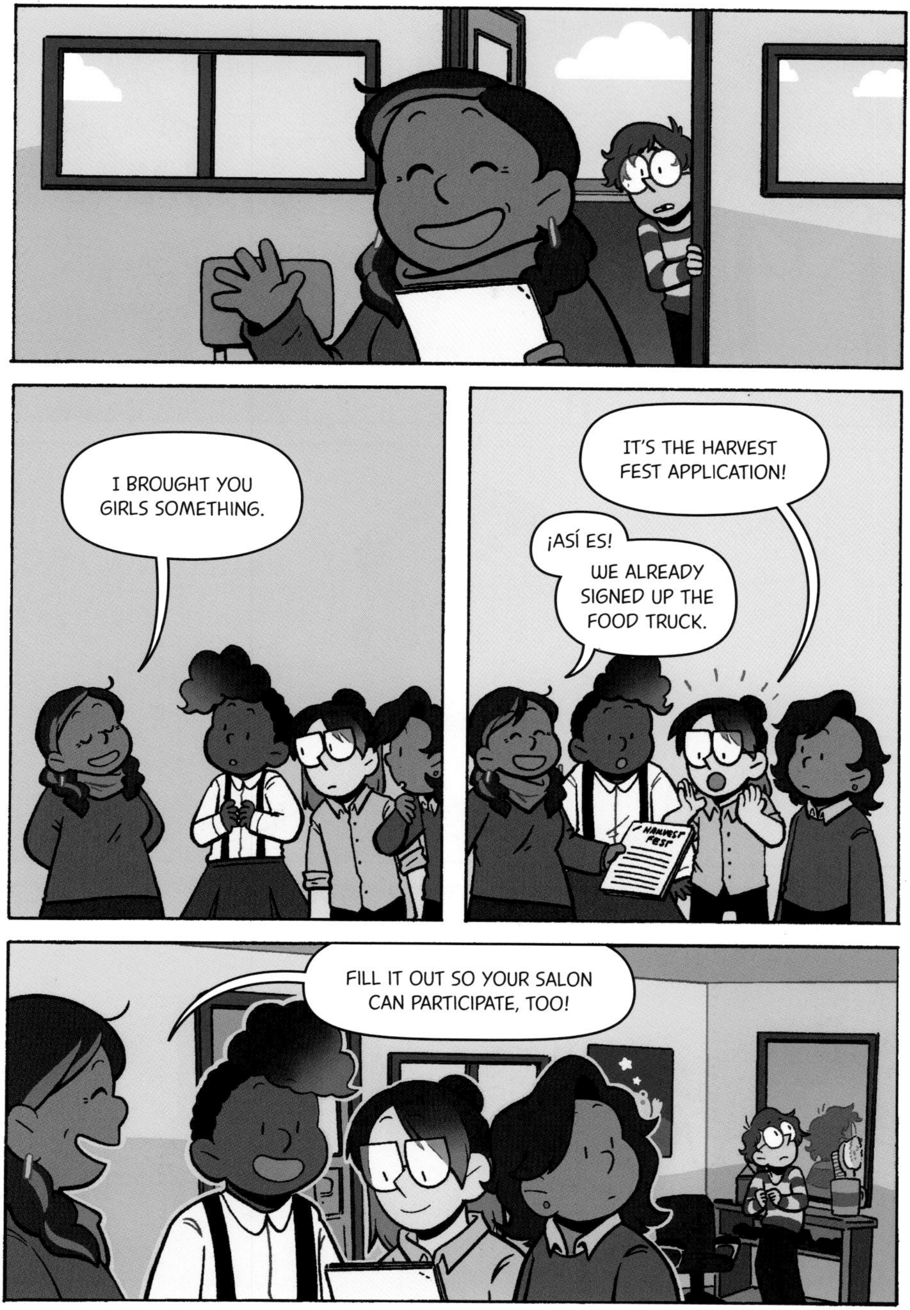
I BROUGHT YOU GIRLS SOMETHING.
IT'S THE HARVEST FEST APPLICATION!
¡ASÍ ES!
WE ALREADY SIGNED UP THE FOOD TRUCK.
HARVEST FEST
FILL IT OUT SO YOUR SALON CAN PARTICIPATE, TOO!

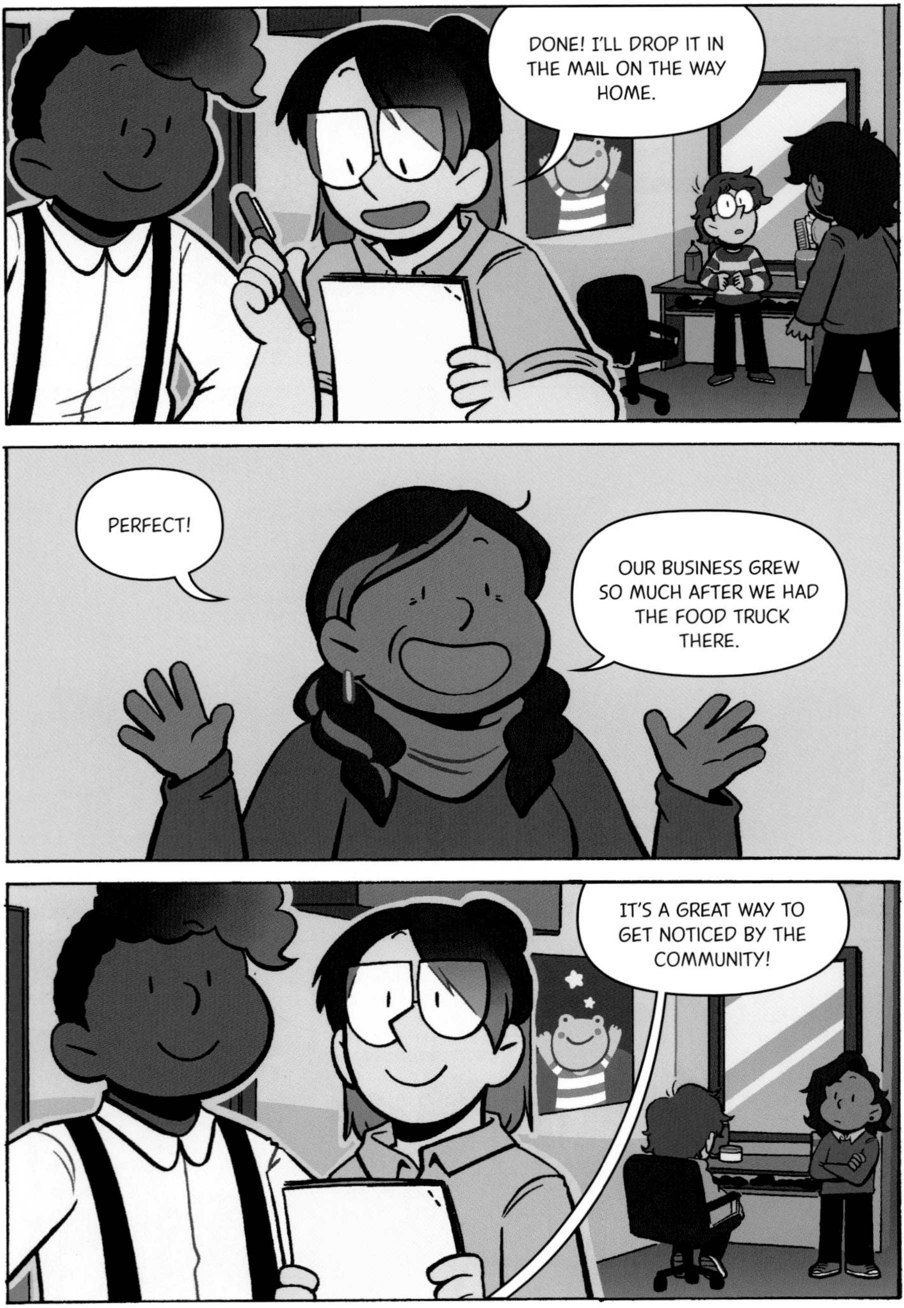
DONE! I'LL DROP IT IN THE MAIL ON THE WAY HOME.
PERFECT!
OUR BUSINESS GREW SO MUCH AFTER WE HAD THE FOOD TRUCK THERE.
IT'S A GREAT WAY TO GET NOTICED BY THE COMMUNITY!

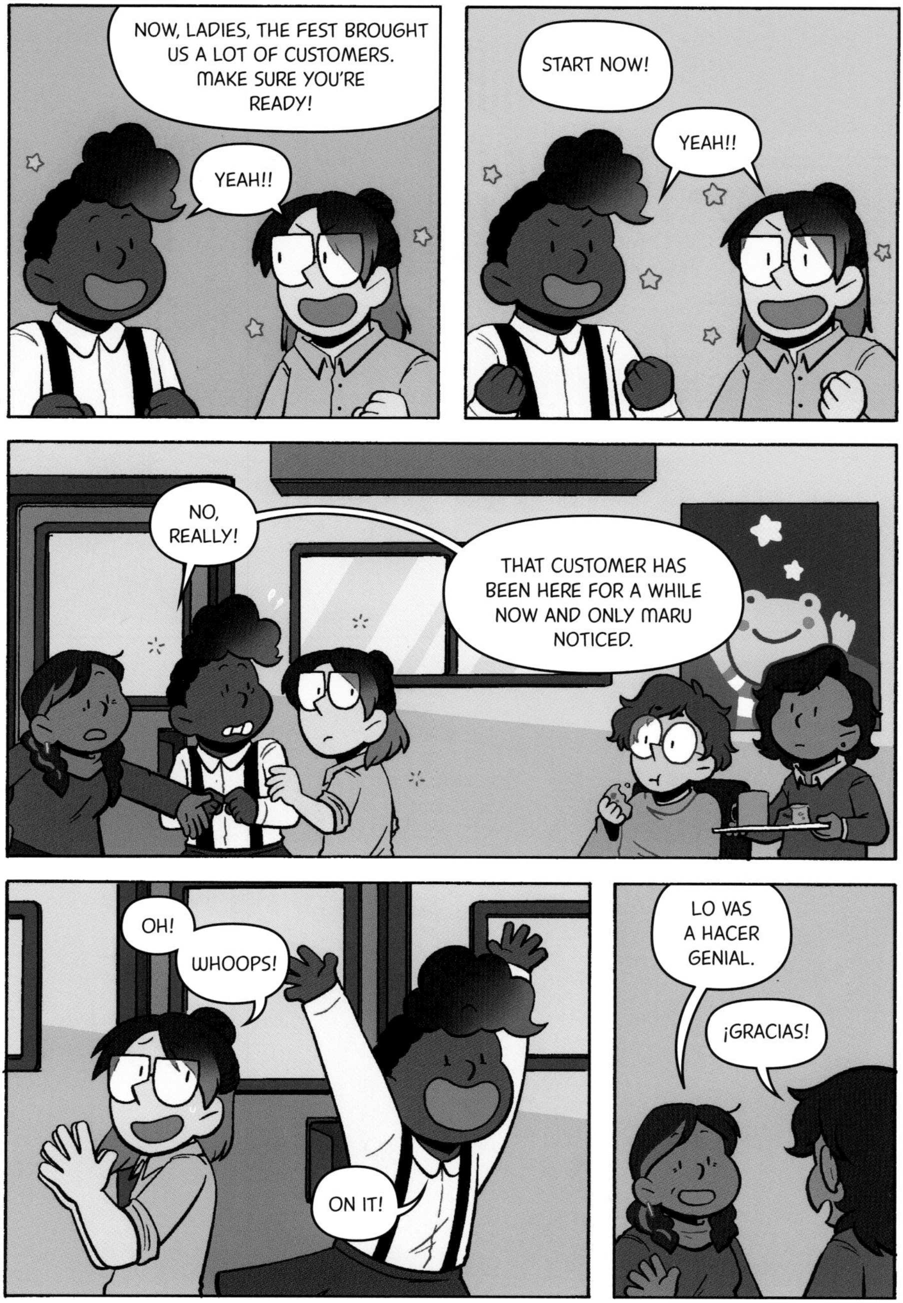
NOW, LADIES, THE FEST BROUGHT US A LOT OF CUSTOMERS. MAKE SURE YOU'RE READY!
YEAH!!
START NOW!
YEAH!!
NO, REALLY!
THAT CUSTOMER HAS BEEN HERE FOR A WHILE NOW AND ONLY MARU NOTICED.
OH!
WHOOPS!
ON IT!
LO VAS A HACER GENIAL.
¡GRACIAS!

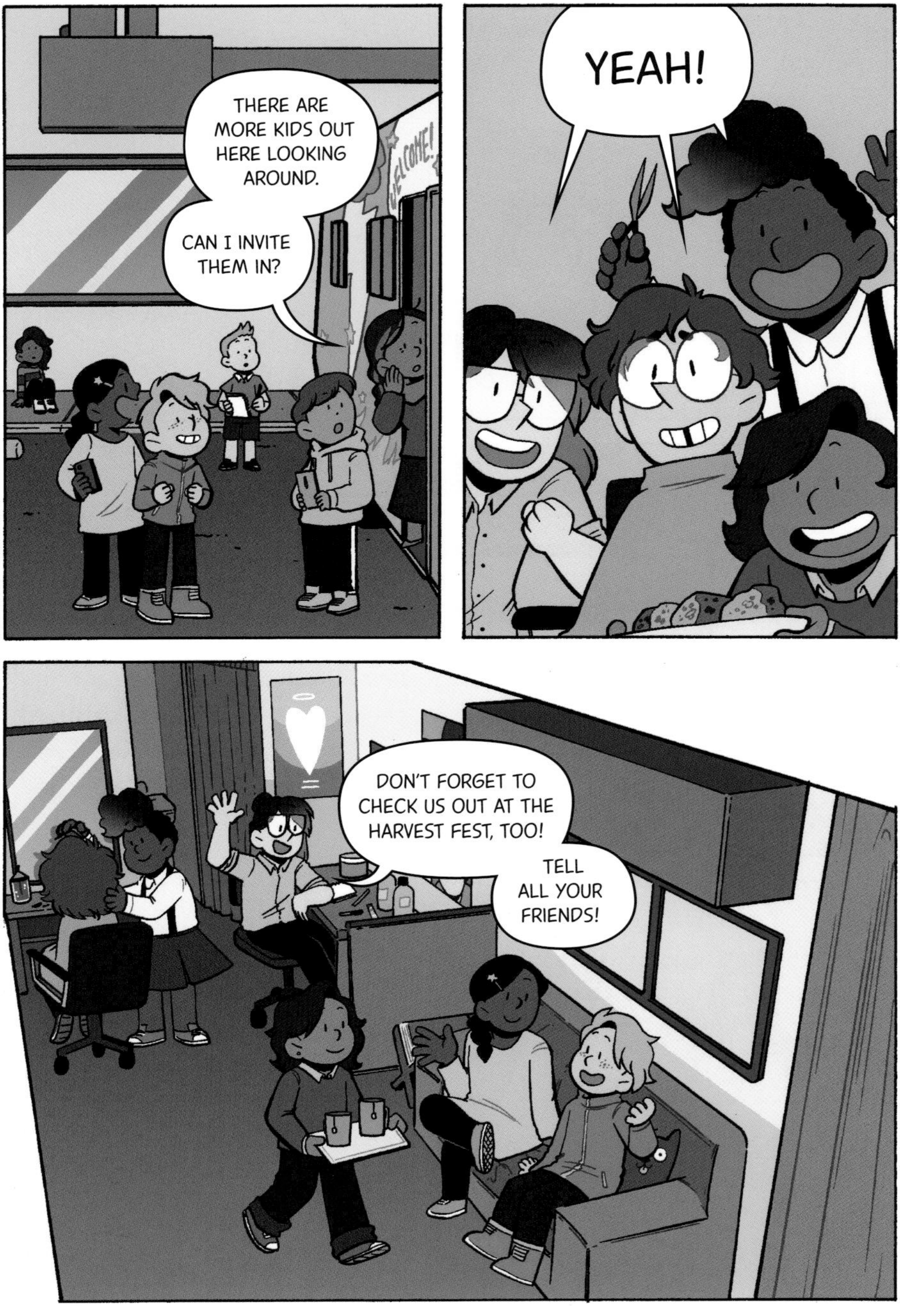

THERE ARE MORE KIDS OUT HERE LOOKING AROUND.
CAN I INVITE THEM IN?
WELCOME!
YEAH!
DON'T FORGET TO CHECK US OUT AT THE HARVEST FEST, TOO!
TELL ALL YOUR FRIENDS!

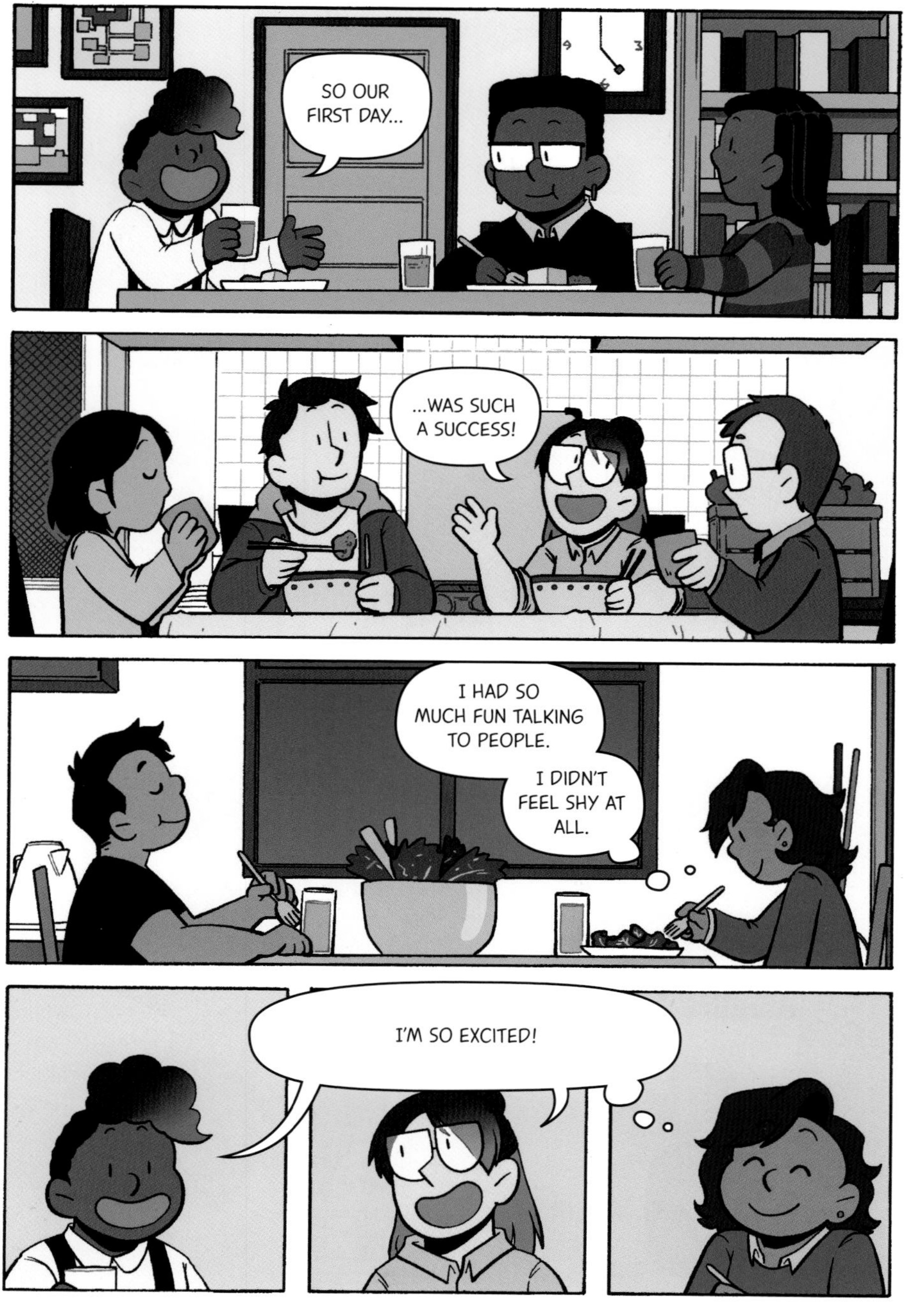
SO OUR FIRST DAY...
...WAS SUCH A SUCCESS!
I HAD SO MUCH FUN TALKING TO PEOPLE.
I DIDN'T FEEL SHY AT ALL.
I'M SO EXCITED!

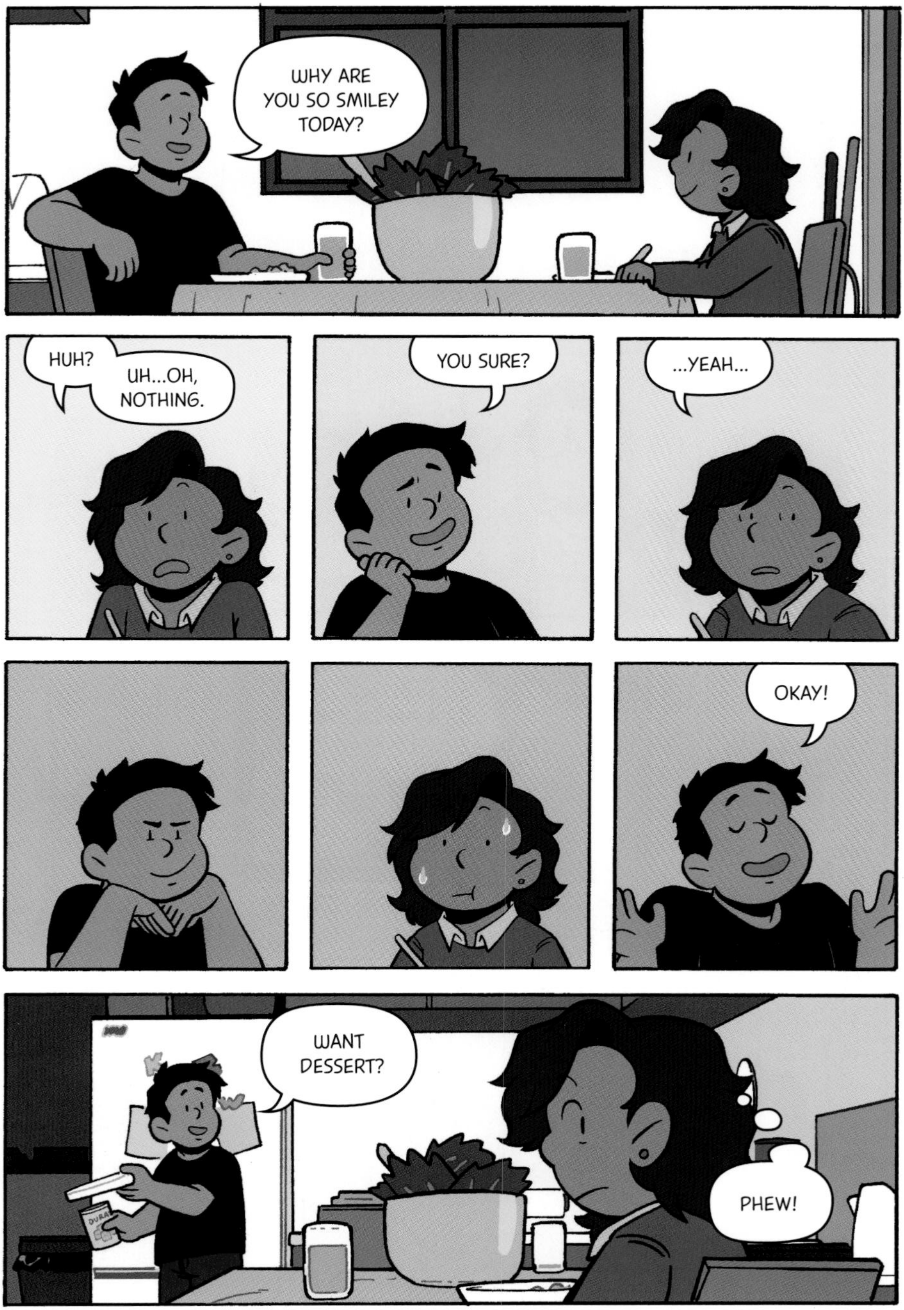
WHY ARE YOU SO SMILEY TODAY?
HUH?
UH...OH, NOTHING.
YOU SURE?
...YEAH...
OKAY!
WANT DESSERT?
PHEW!

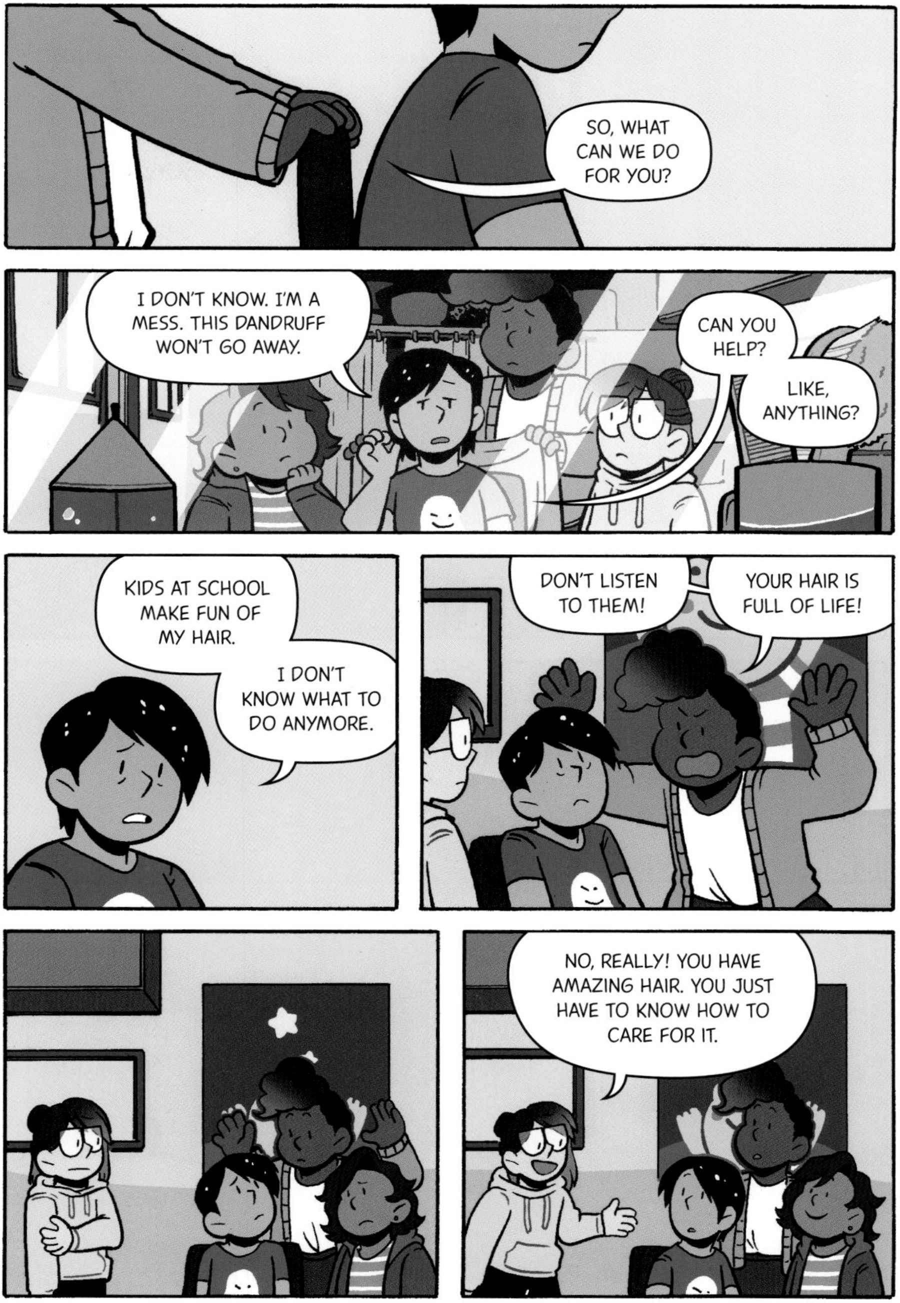
SO, WHAT CAN WE DO FOR YOU?
I DON'T KNOW. I'M A MESS. THIS DANDRUFF WON'T GO AWAY.
CAN YOU HELP?
LIKE, ANYTHING?
KIDS AT SCHOOL MAKE FUN OF MY HAIR.
I DON'T KNOW WHAT TO DO ANYMORE.
DON'T LISTEN TO THEM!
YOUR HAIR IS FULL OF LIFE!
NO, REALLY! YOU HAVE AMAZING HAIR. YOU JUST HAVE TO KNOW HOW TO CARE FOR IT.

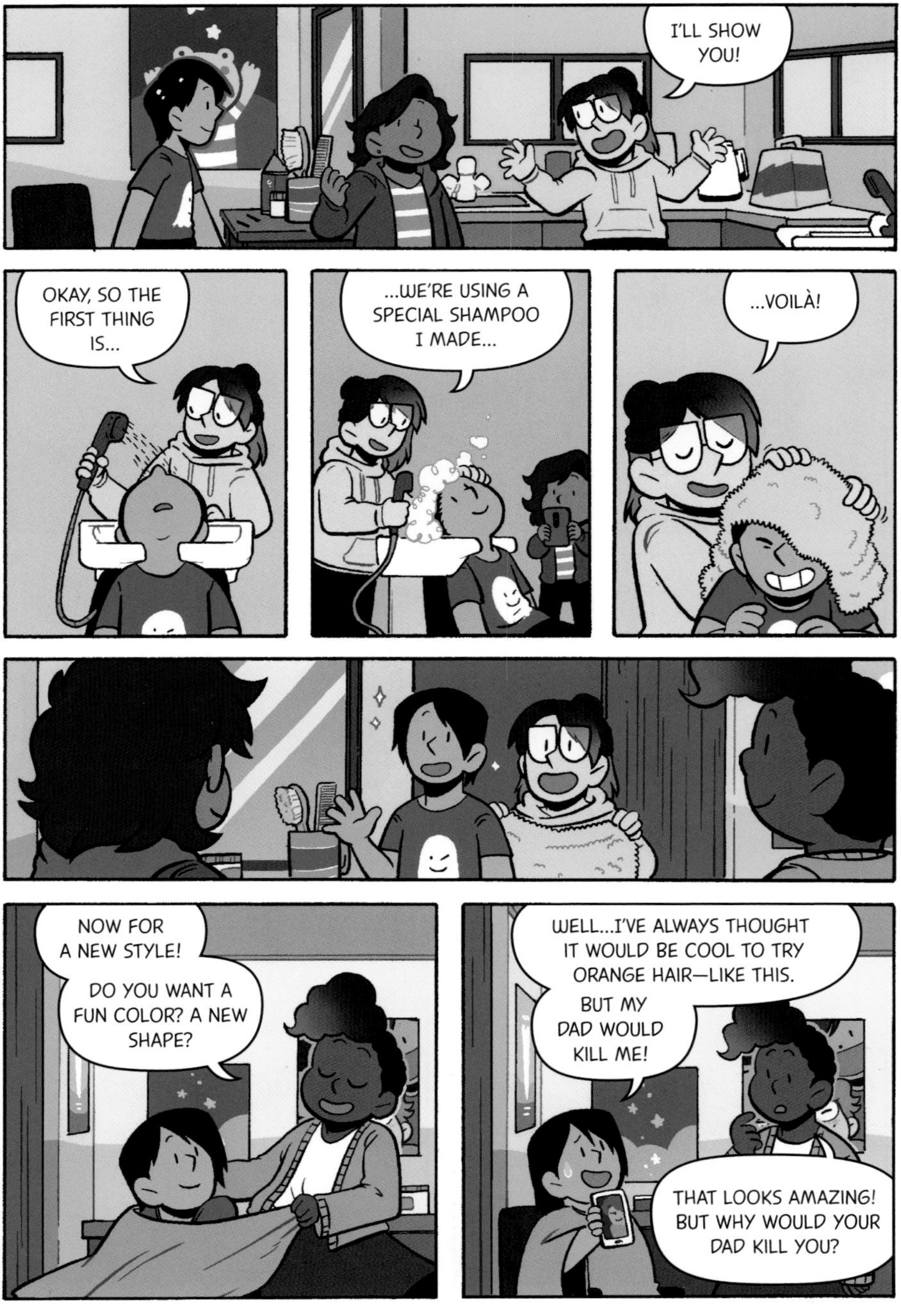
I'LL SHOW YOU!
OKAY, SO THE FIRST THING IS...
...WE'RE USING A SPECIAL SHAMPOO I MADE...
...VOILÀ!
NOW FOR A NEW STYLE!
DO YOU WANT A FUN COLOR? A NEW SHAPE?
WELL...I'VE ALWAYS THOUGHT IT WOULD BE COOL TO TRY ORANGE HAIR—LIKE THIS.
BUT MY DAD WOULD KILL ME!
THAT LOOKS AMAZING! BUT WHY WOULD YOUR DAD KILL YOU?

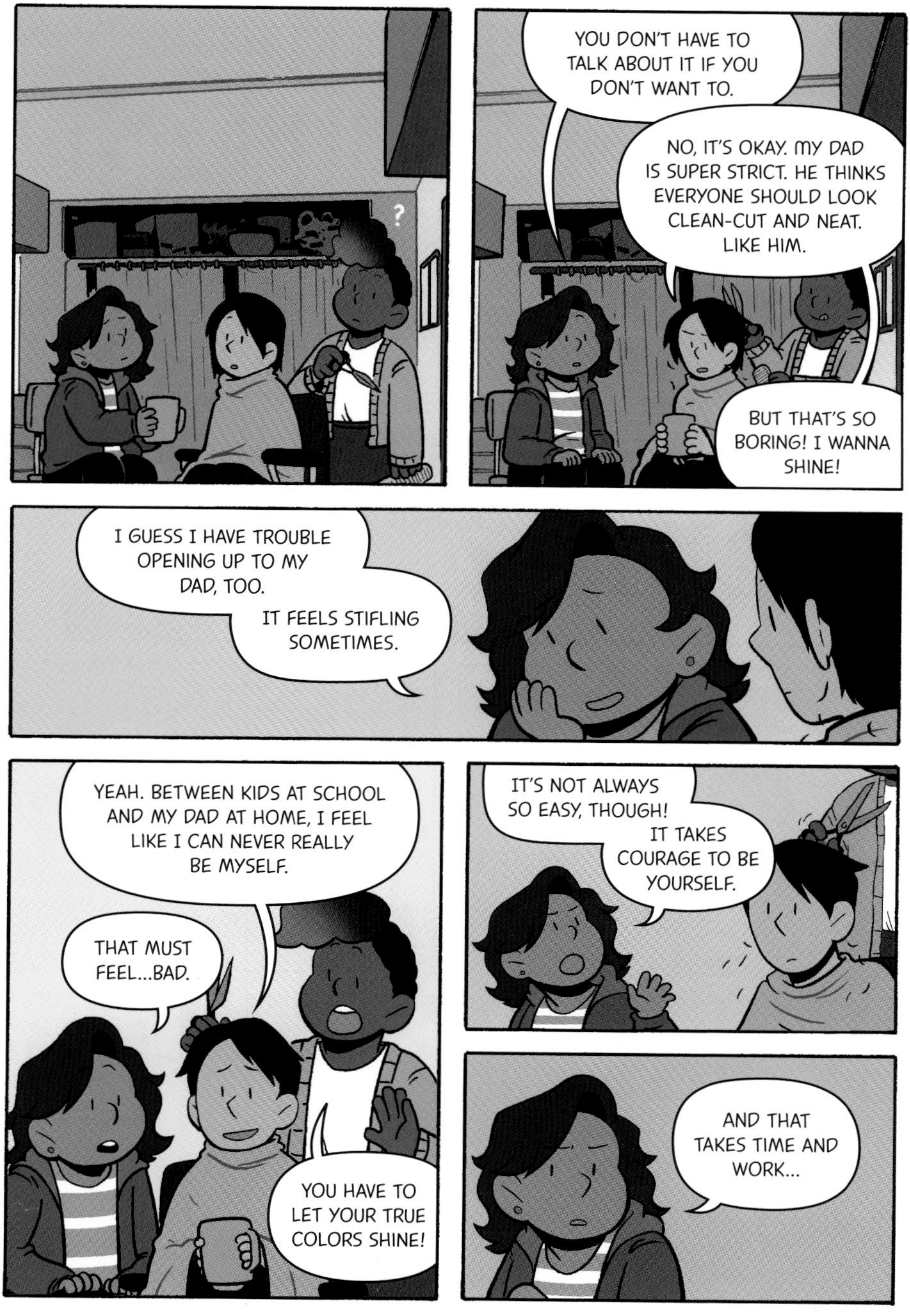
?
YOU DON'T HAVE TO TALK ABOUT IT IF YOU DON'T WANT TO.
NO, IT'S OKAY. MY DAD IS SUPER STRICT. HE THINKS EVERYONE SHOULD LOOK CLEAN-CUT AND NEAT. LIKE HIM.
BUT THAT'S SO BORING! I WANNA SHINE!
I GUESS I HAVE TROUBLE OPENING UP TO MY DAD, TOO.
IT FEELS STIFLING SOMETIMES.
YEAH. BETWEEN KIDS AT SCHOOL AND MY DAD AT HOME, I FEEL LIKE I CAN NEVER REALLY BE MYSELF.
THAT MUST FEEL...BAD.
YOU HAVE TO LET YOUR TRUE COLORS SHINE!
IT'S NOT ALWAYS SO EASY, THOUGH!
IT TAKES COURAGE TO BE YOURSELF.
AND THAT TAKES TIME AND WORK...

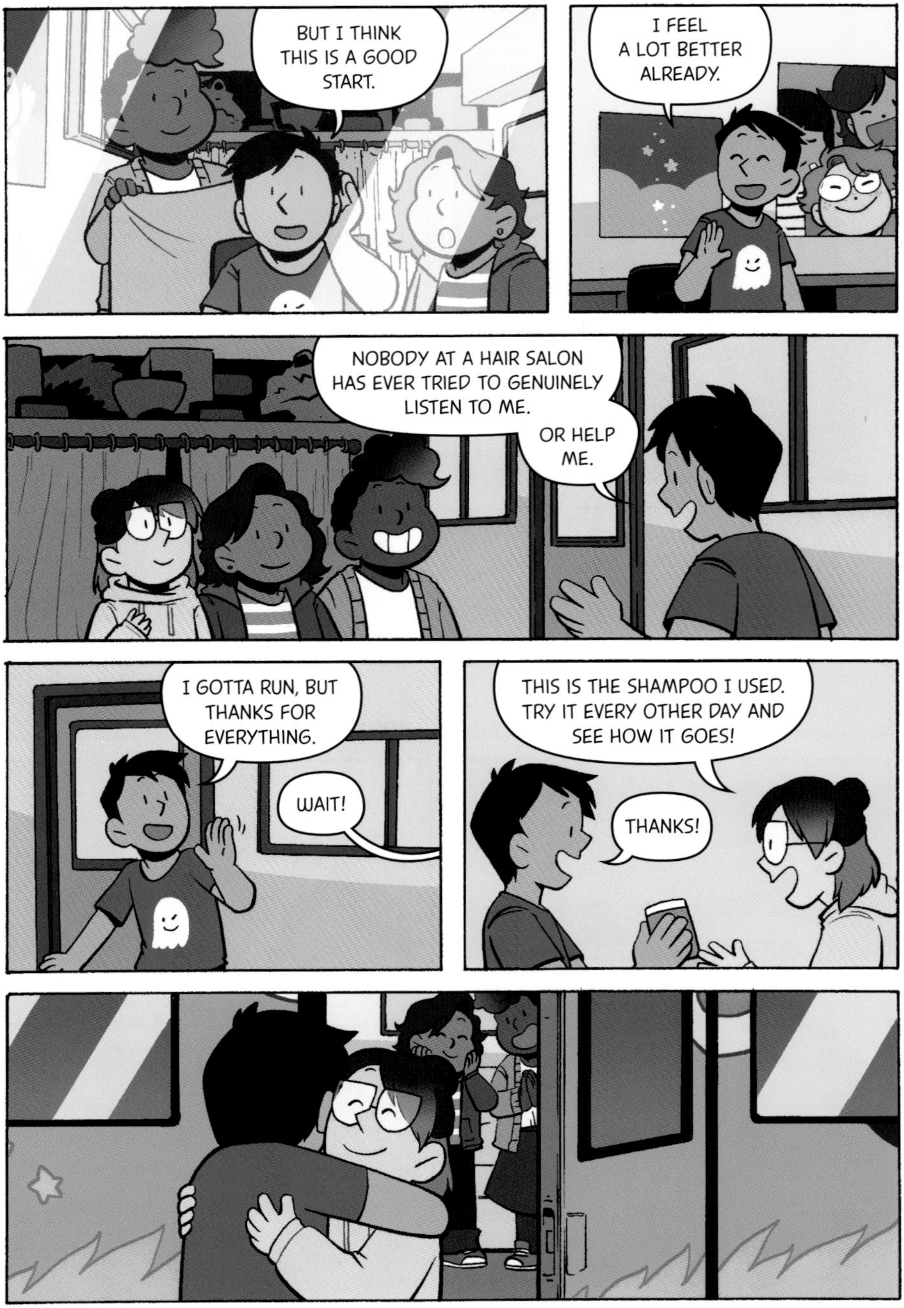
BUT I THINK THIS IS A GOOD START.
I FEEL A LOT BETTER ALREADY.
NOBODY AT A HAIR SALON HAS EVER TRIED TO GENUINELY LISTEN TO ME.
OR HELP ME.
I GOTTA RUN, BUT THANKS FOR EVERYTHING.
WAIT!
THIS IS THE SHAMPOO I USED. TRY IT EVERY OTHER DAY AND SEE HOW IT GOES!
THANKS!

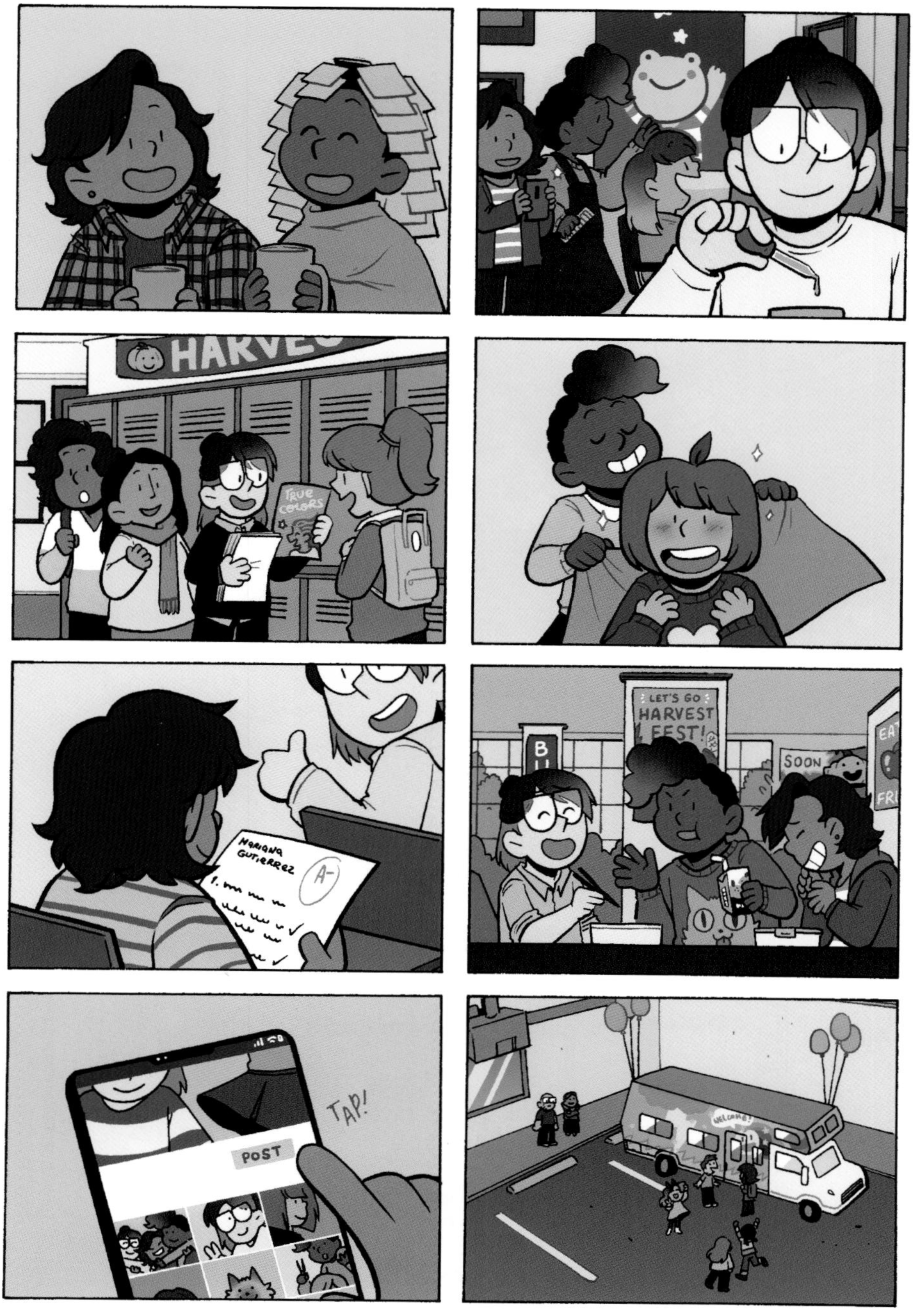
HARVES
TRUE COLORS
Mariana Gutierrez
A-
LET'S GO HARVEST FEST!
SOON
POST
TAP!
WELCOME!

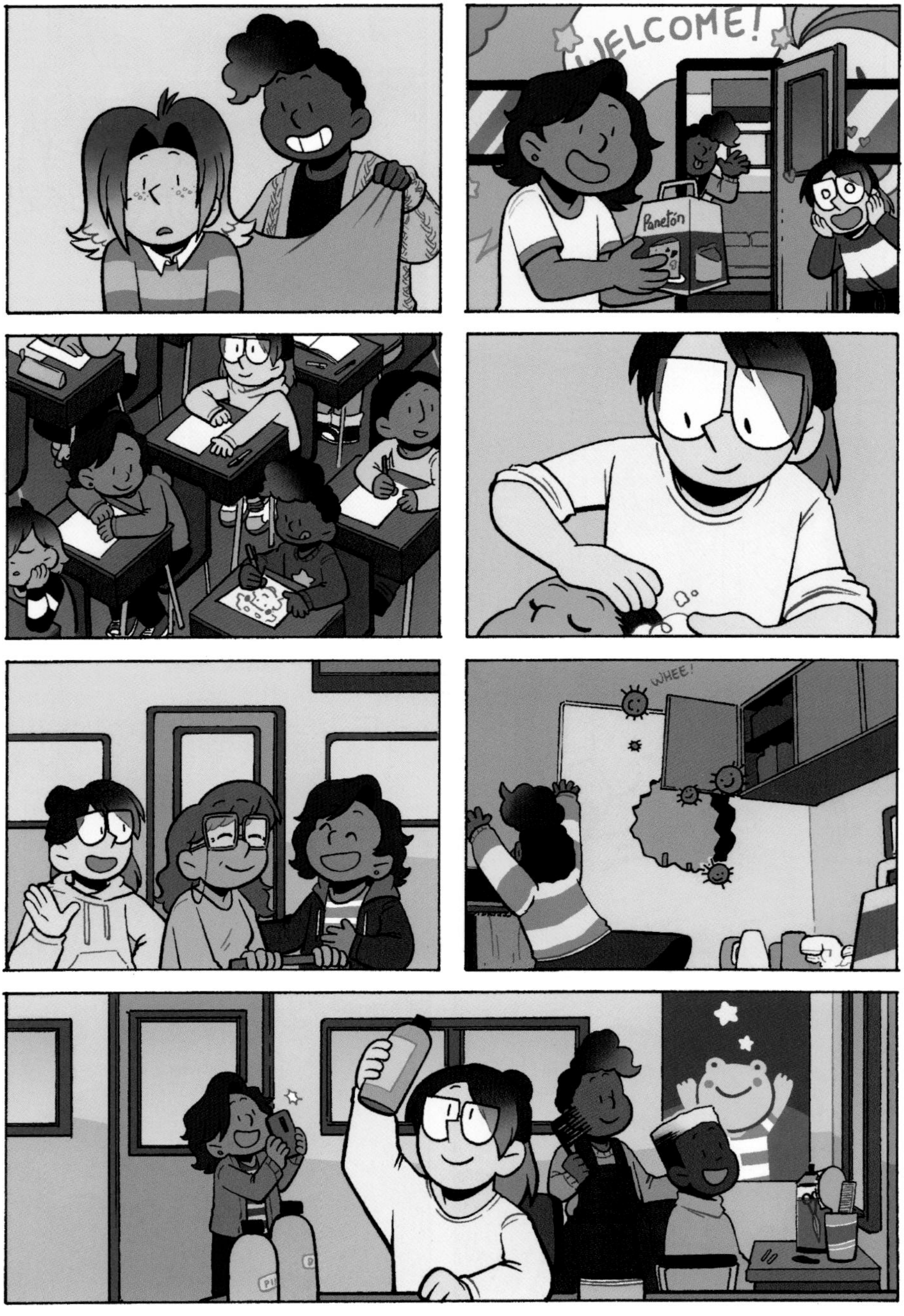
WELCOME!
Panetón
WHEE!

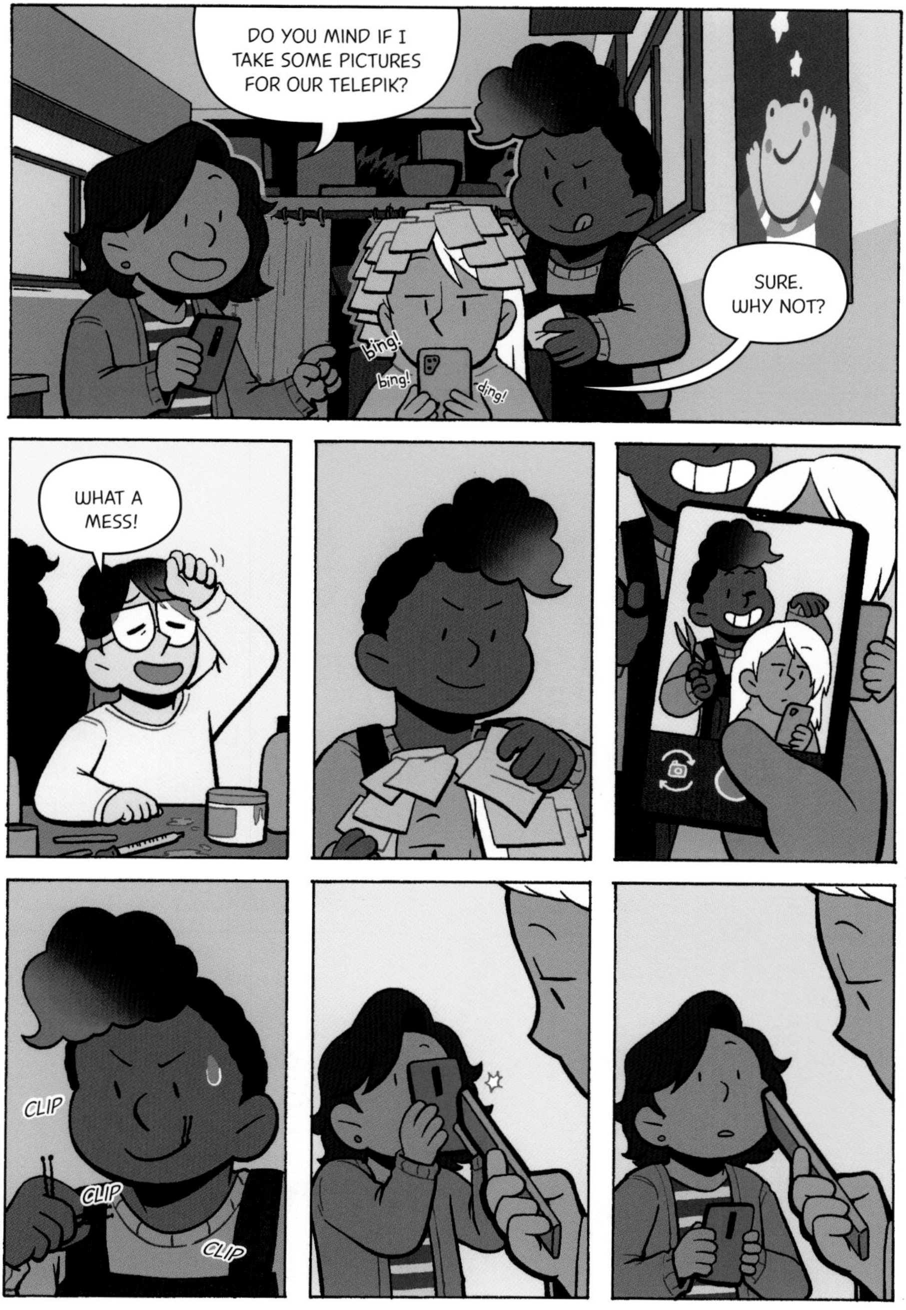
DO YOU MIND IF I TAKE SOME PICTURES FOR OUR TELEPIK?
bing!
bing!
ding!
SURE. WHY NOT?
WHAT A MESS!
CLIP
CLIP
CLIP

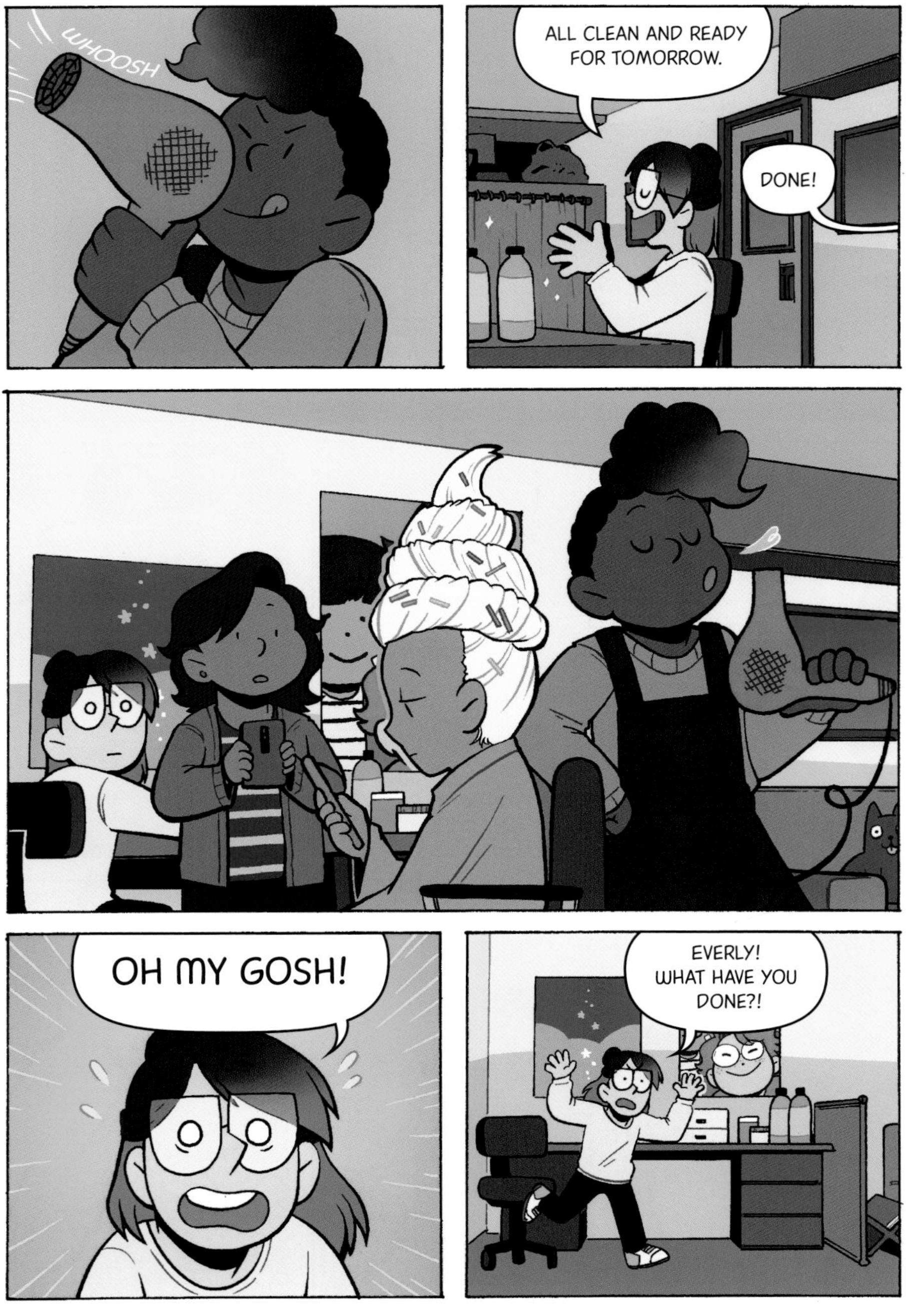
WHOOSH
ALL CLEAN AND READY FOR TOMORROW.
DONE!
OH MY GOSH!
EVERLY! WHAT HAVE YOU DONE?!

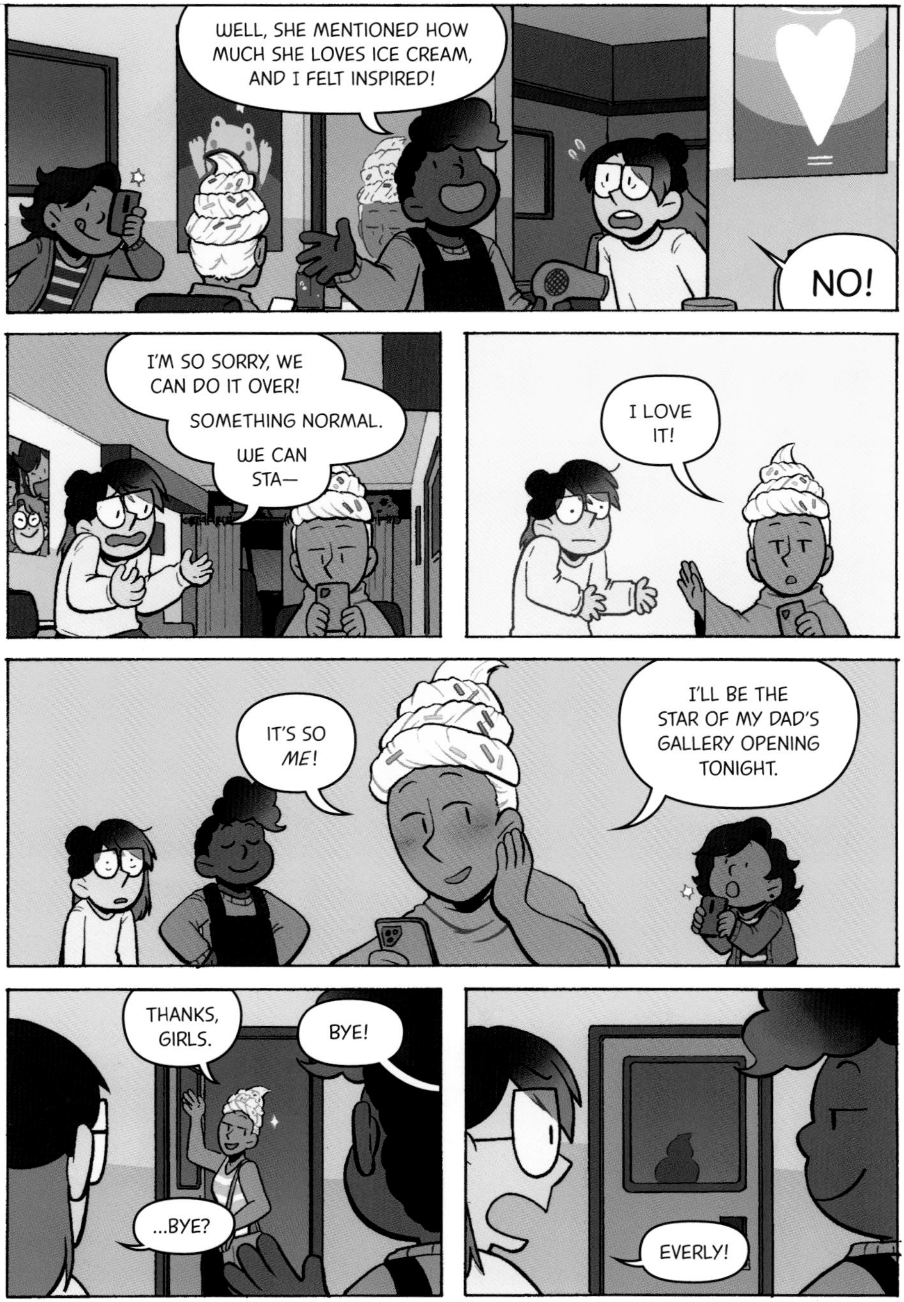
WELL, SHE MENTIONED HOW MUCH SHE LOVES ICE CREAM, AND I FELT INSPIRED!
NO!
I'M SO SORRY, WE CAN DO IT OVER!
SOMETHING NORMAL.
WE CAN STA—
I LOVE IT!
IT'S SO *ME*!
I'LL BE THE STAR OF MY DAD'S GALLERY OPENING TONIGHT.
THANKS, GIRLS.
BYE!
...BYE?
EVERLY!

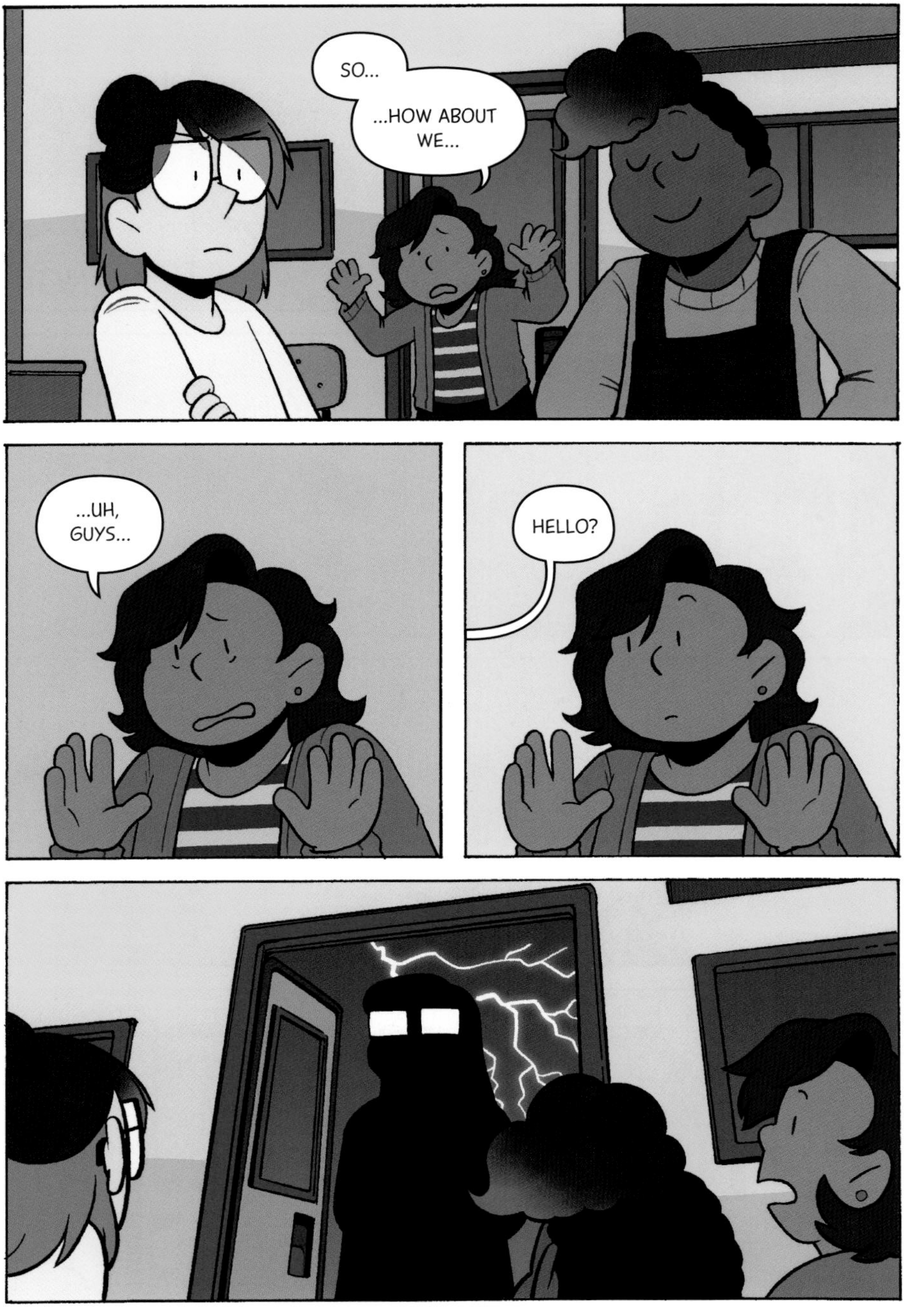
SO...
...HOW ABOUT WE...
...UH, GUYS...
HELLO?

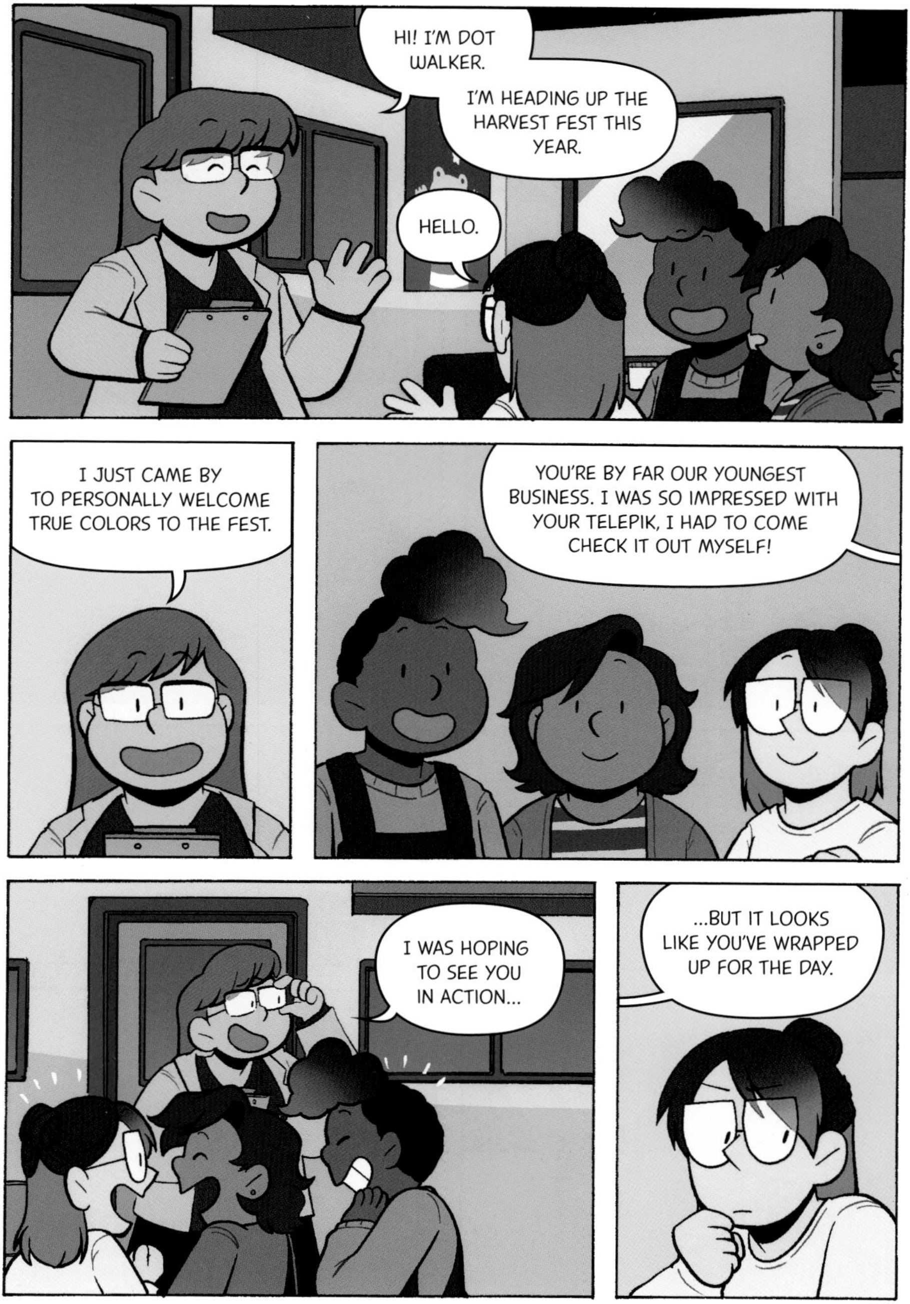
HI! I'M DOT WALKER.
I'M HEADING UP THE HARVEST FEST THIS YEAR.
HELLO.
I JUST CAME BY TO PERSONALLY WELCOME TRUE COLORS TO THE FEST.
YOU'RE BY FAR OUR YOUNGEST BUSINESS. I WAS SO IMPRESSED WITH YOUR TELEPIK, I HAD TO COME CHECK IT OUT MYSELF!
I WAS HOPING TO SEE YOU IN ACTION...
...BUT IT LOOKS LIKE YOU'VE WRAPPED UP FOR THE DAY.

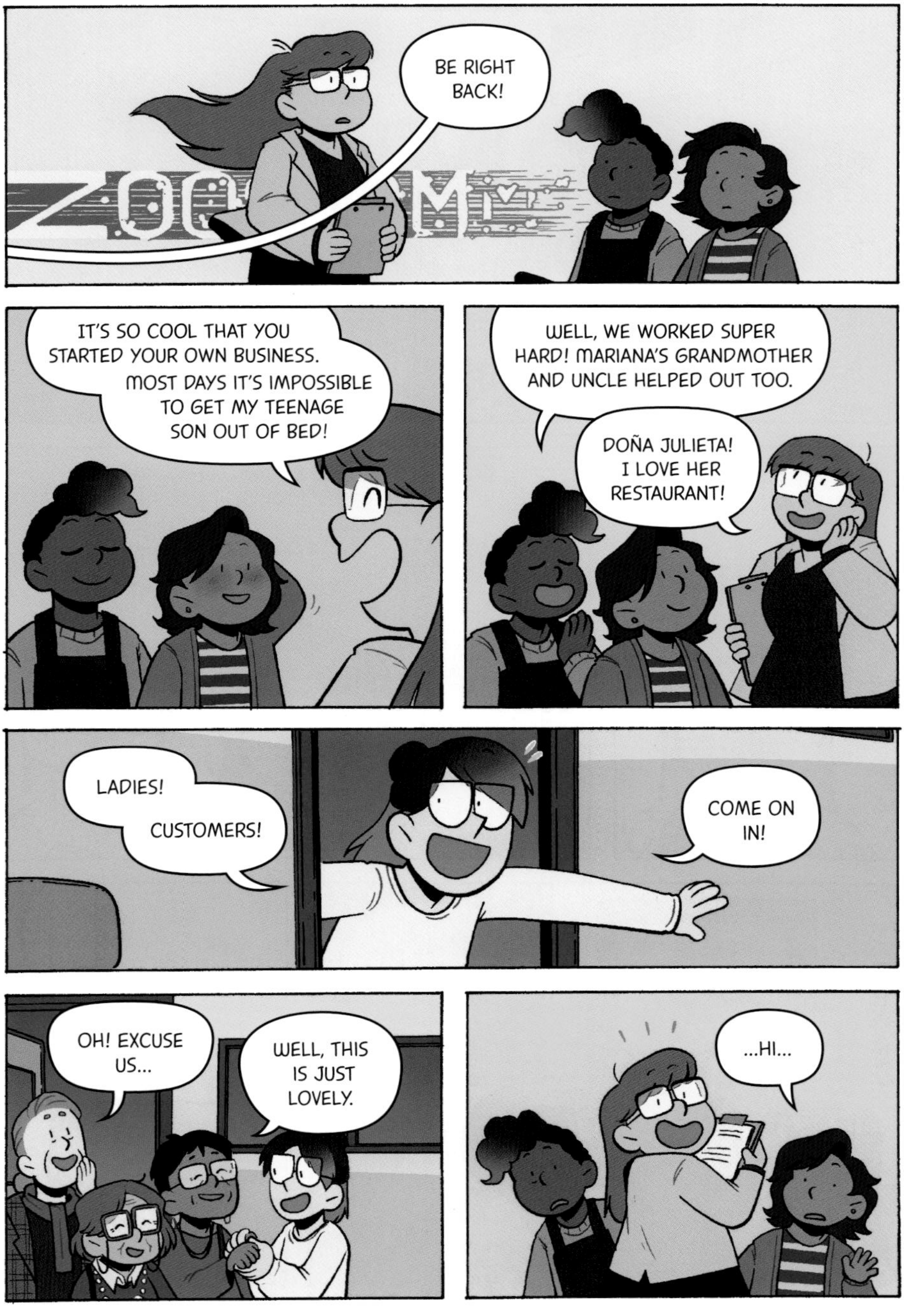
BE RIGHT BACK!
ZOOOM
IT'S SO COOL THAT YOU STARTED YOUR OWN BUSINESS.
MOST DAYS IT'S IMPOSSIBLE TO GET MY TEENAGE SON OUT OF BED!
WELL, WE WORKED SUPER HARD! MARIANA'S GRANDMOTHER AND UNCLE HELPED OUT TOO.
DOÑA JULIETA! I LOVE HER RESTAURANT!
LADIES!
CUSTOMERS!
COME ON IN!
OH! EXCUSE US...
WELL, THIS IS JUST LOVELY.
...HI...

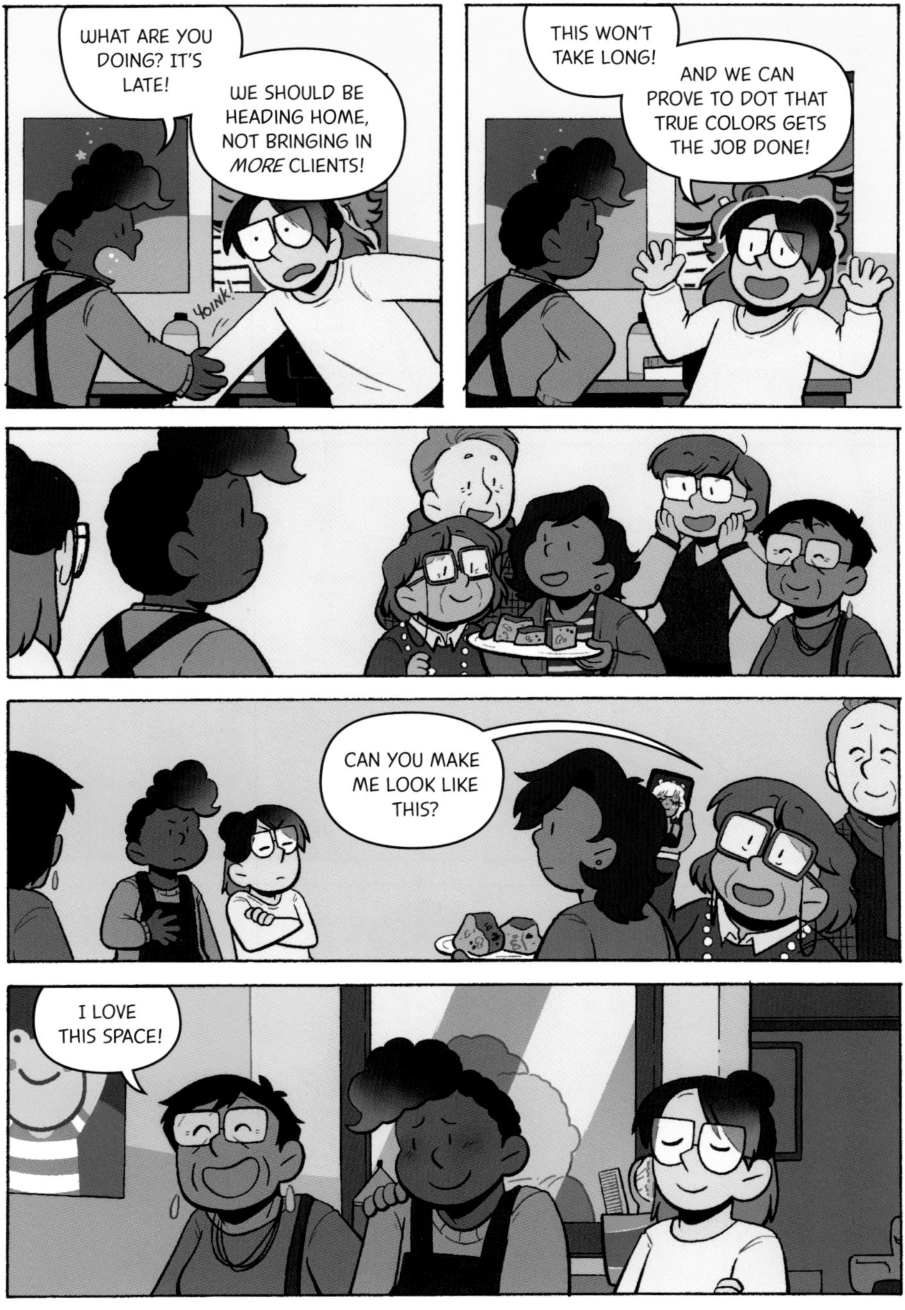
WHAT ARE YOU DOING? IT'S LATE!
WE SHOULD BE HEADING HOME, NOT BRINGING IN *MORE* CLIENTS!
YOINK!
THIS WON'T TAKE LONG!
AND WE CAN PROVE TO DOT THAT TRUE COLORS GETS THE JOB DONE!
CAN YOU MAKE ME LOOK LIKE THIS?
I LOVE THIS SPACE!

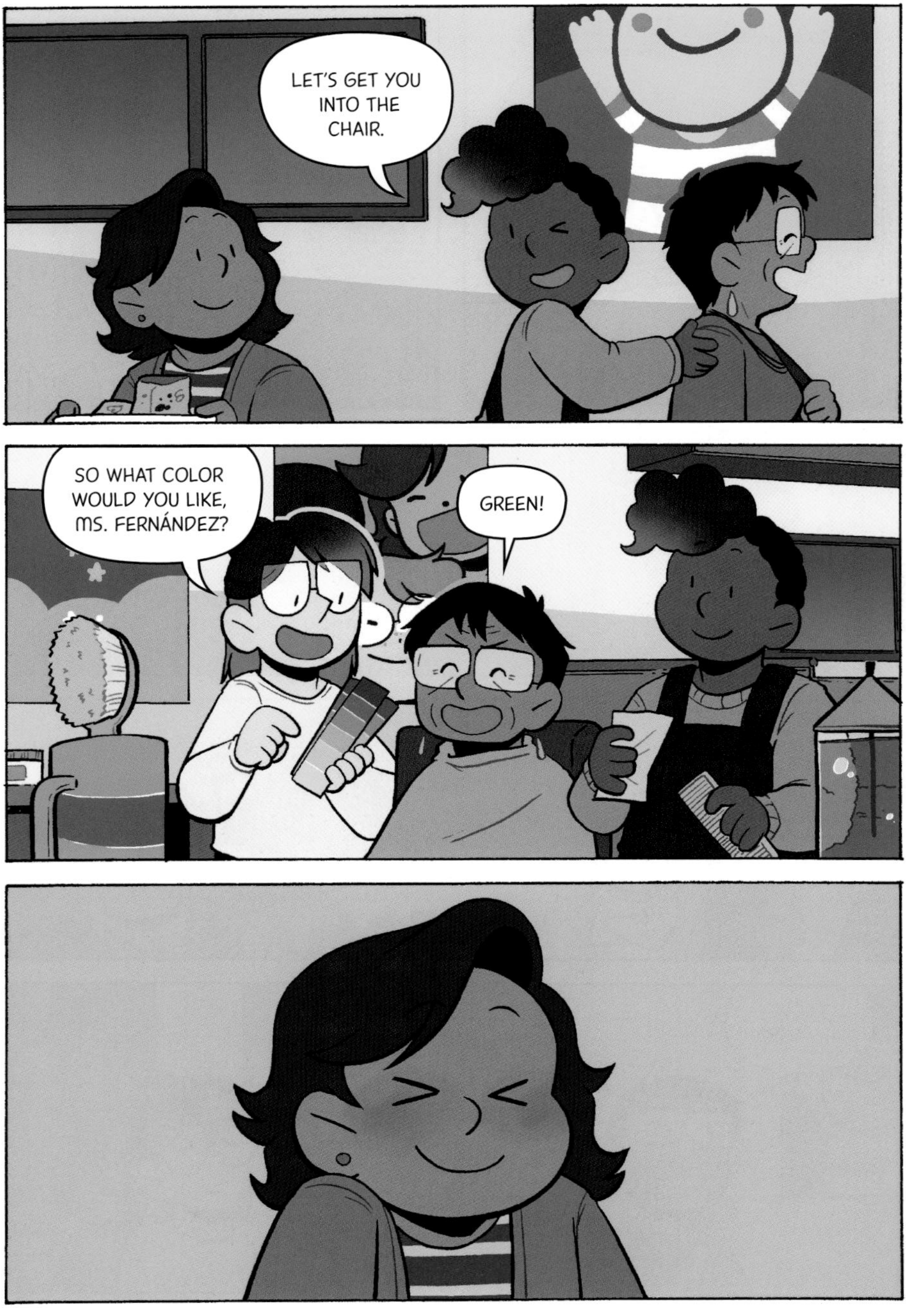
LET'S GET YOU INTO THE CHAIR.
SO WHAT COLOR WOULD YOU LIKE, MS. FERNÁNDEZ?
GREEN!

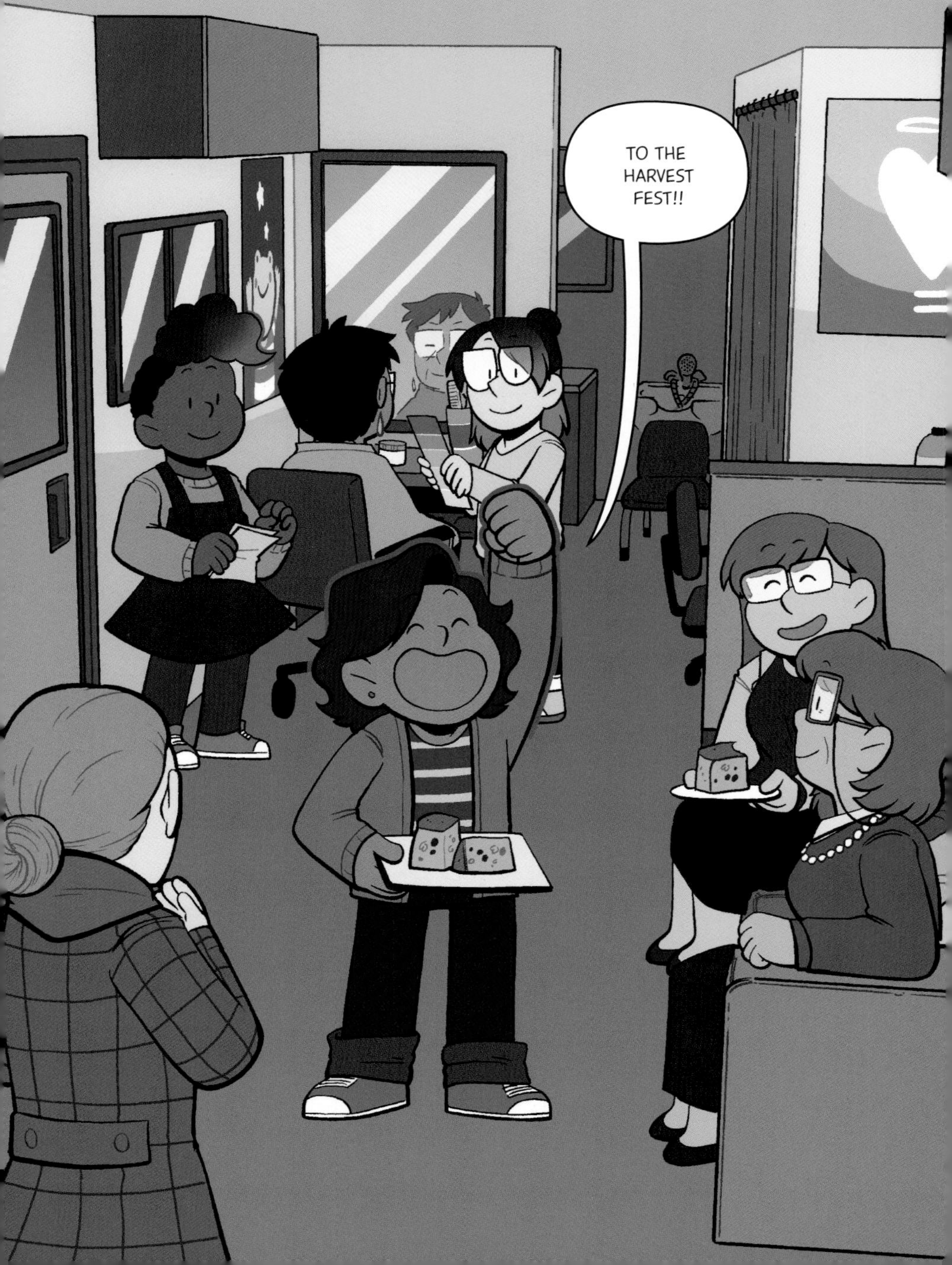
TO THE HARVEST FEST!!

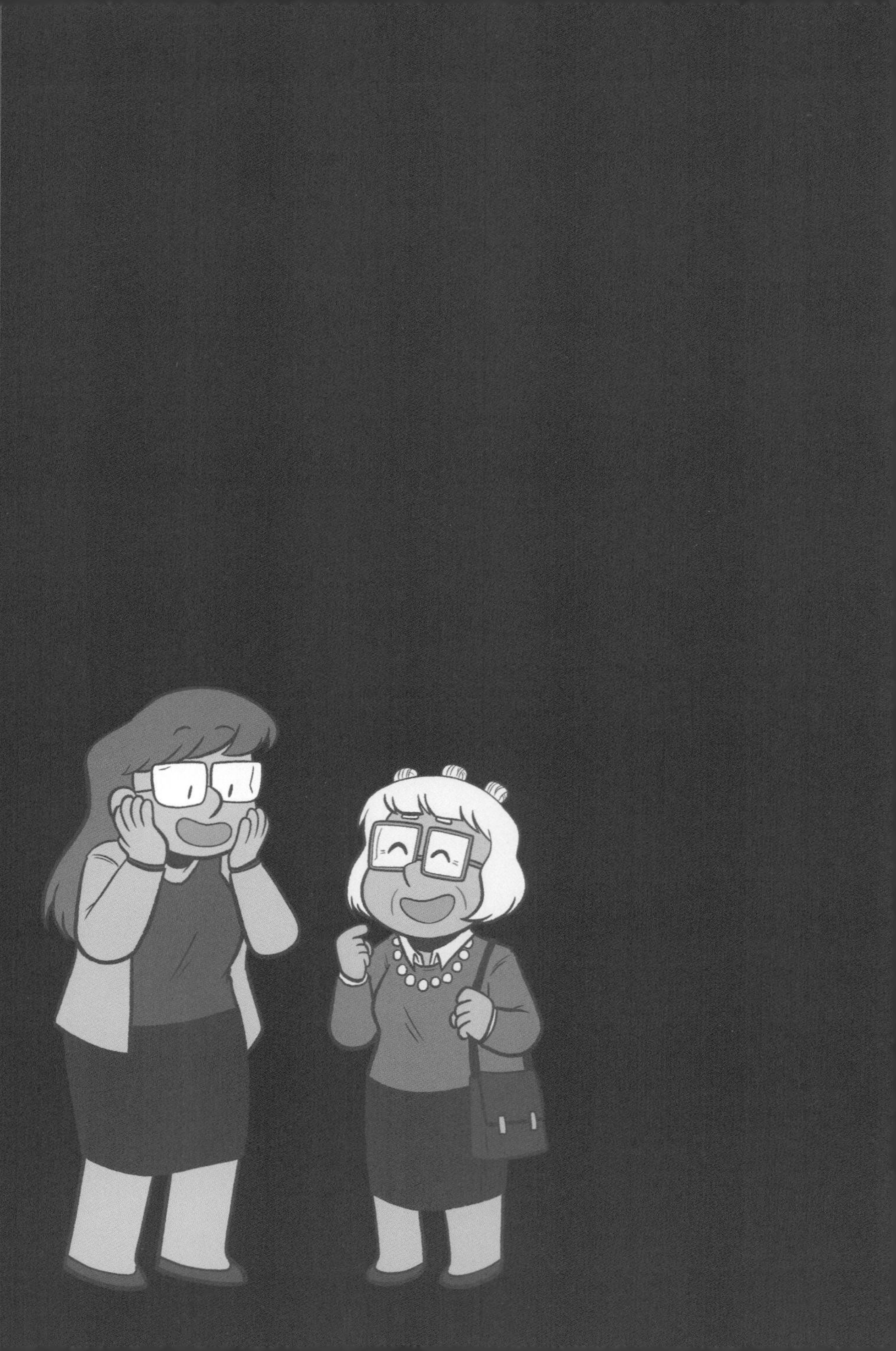

CHAPTER 5

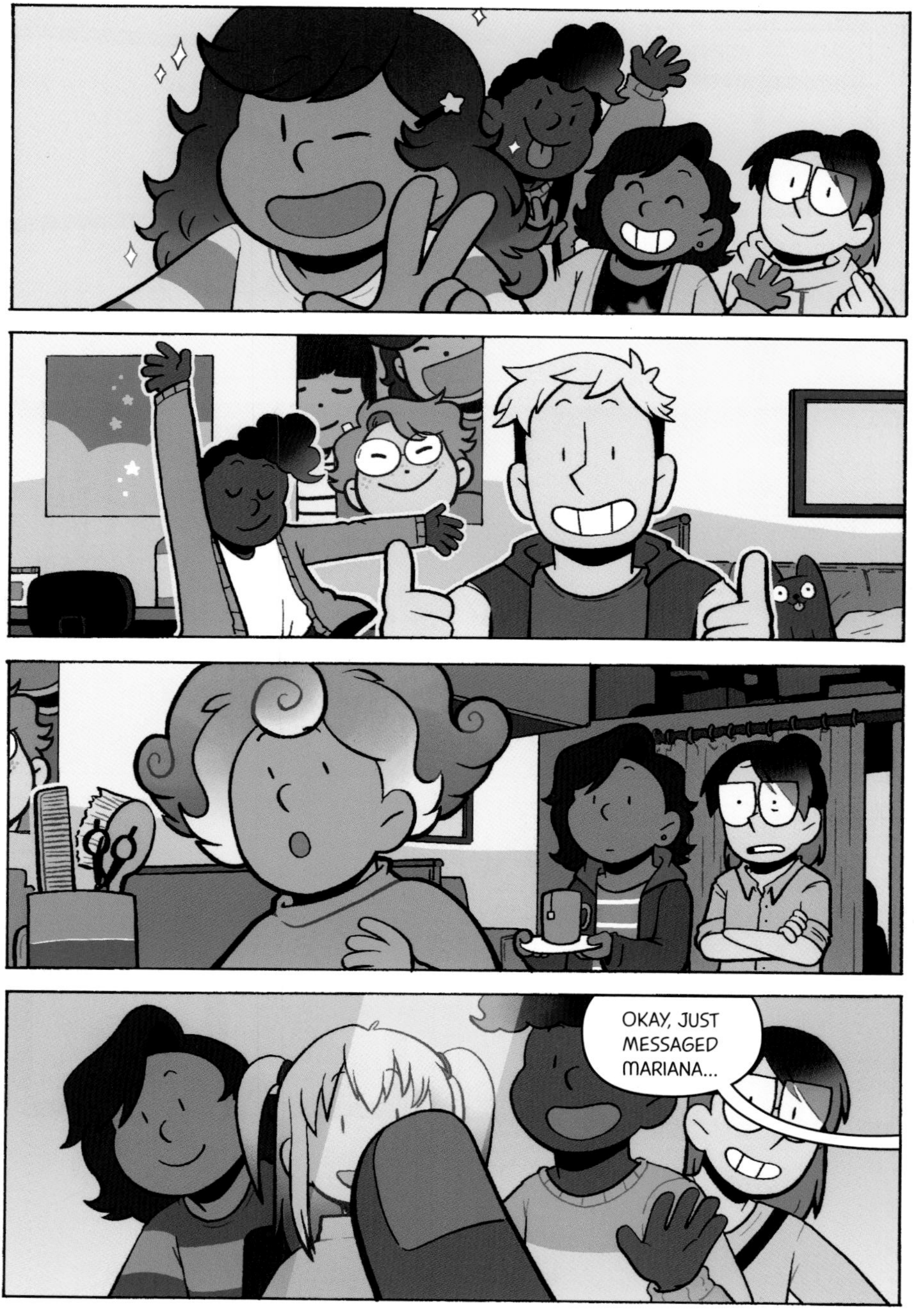
OKAY, JUST
MESSAGED
MARIANA...

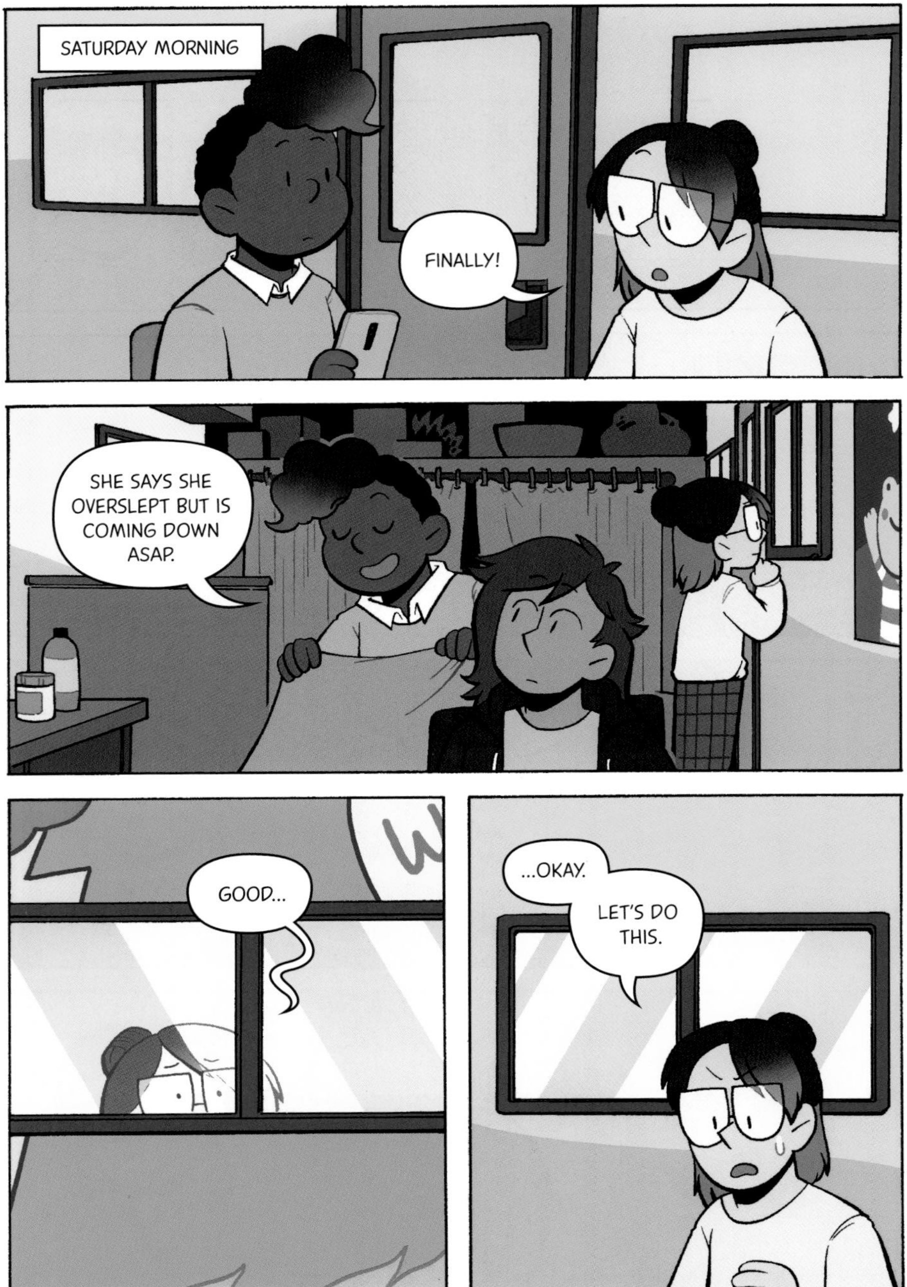
SATURDAY MORNING
FINALLY!
SHE SAYS SHE OVERSLEPT BUT IS COMING DOWN ASAP.
GOOD...
...OKAY.
LET'S DO THIS.

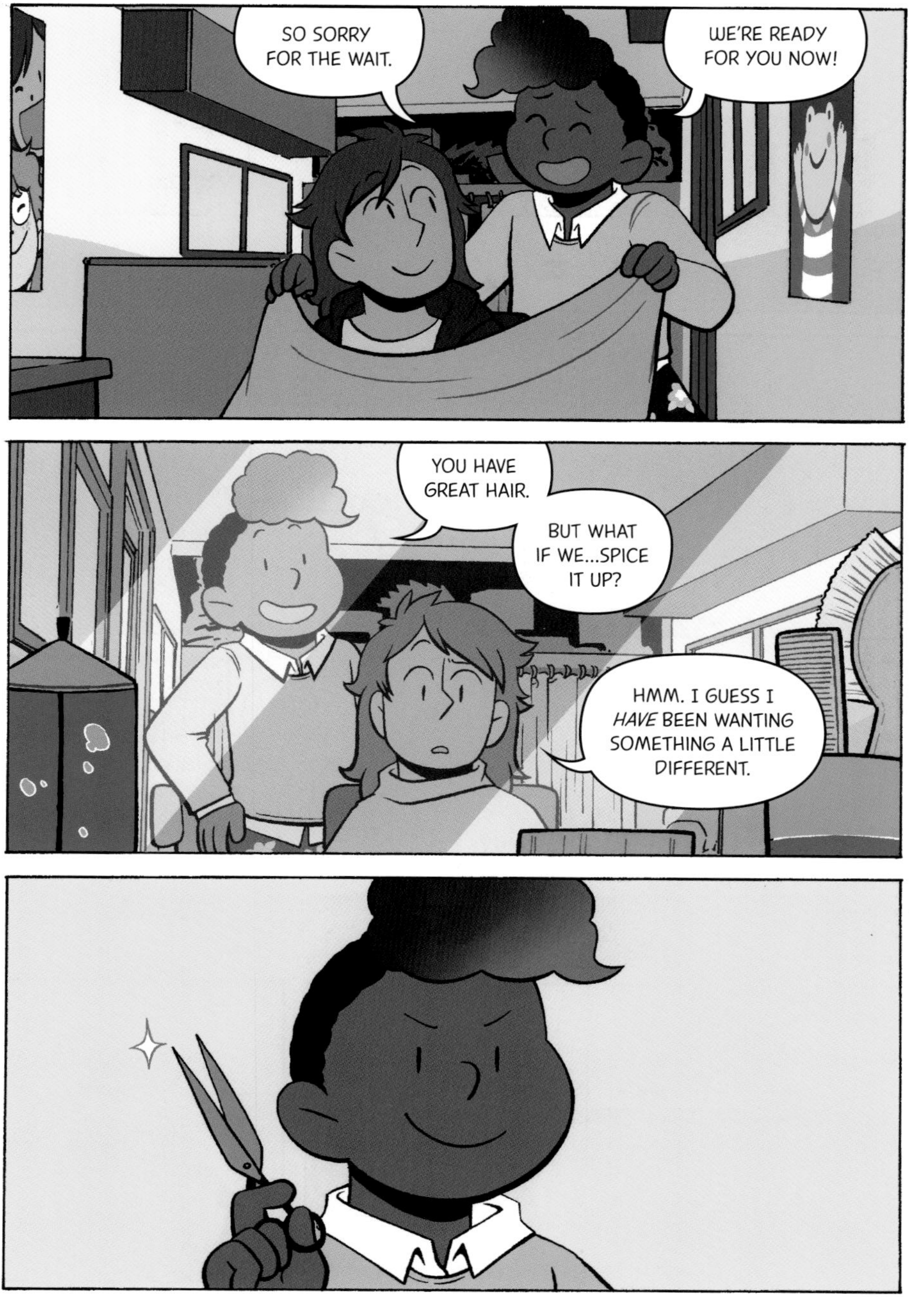
SO SORRY FOR THE WAIT.
WE'RE READY FOR YOU NOW!
YOU HAVE GREAT HAIR.
BUT WHAT IF WE...SPICE IT UP?
HMM. I GUESS I *HAVE* BEEN WANTING SOMETHING A LITTLE DIFFERENT.

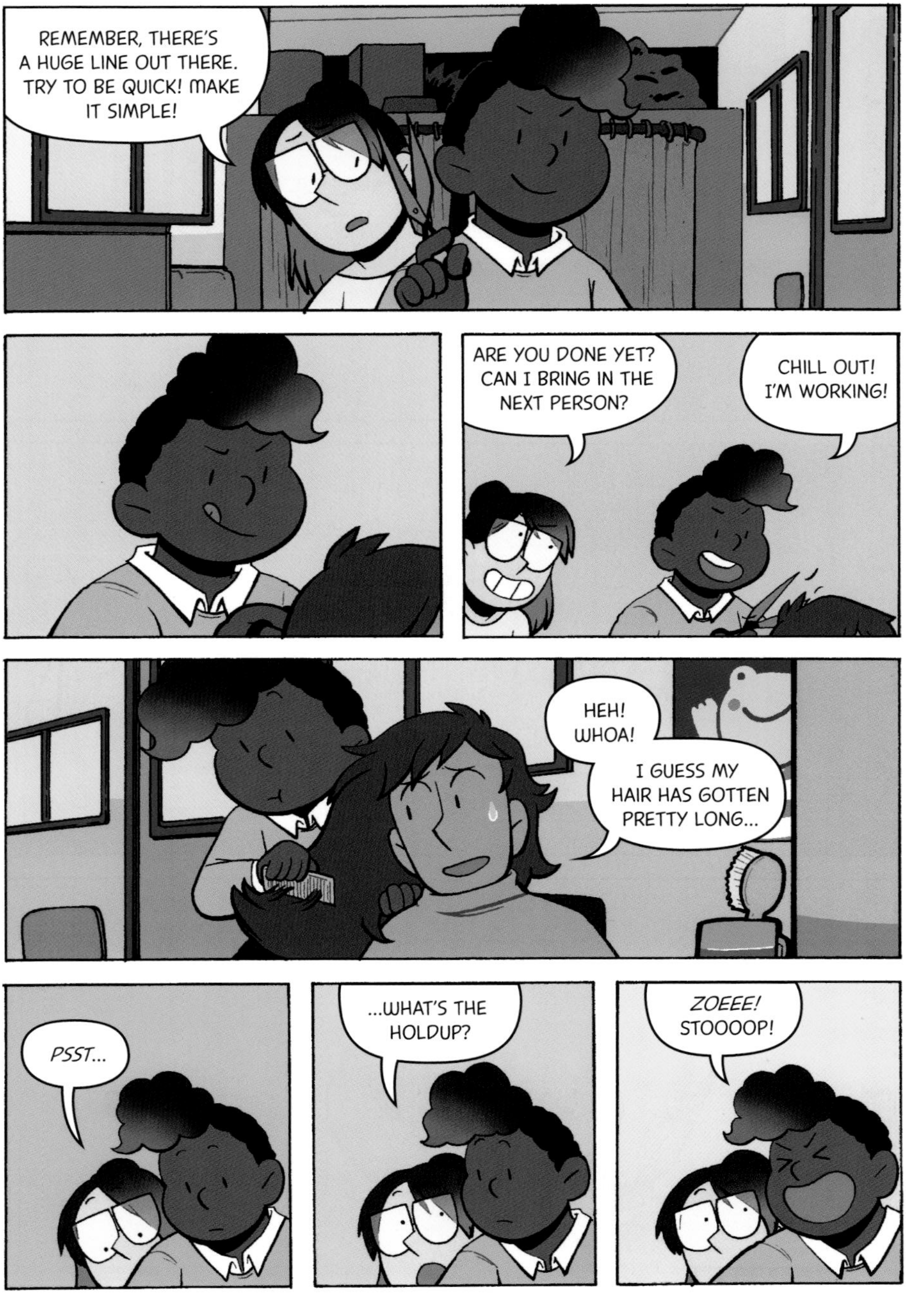
REMEMBER, THERE'S A HUGE LINE OUT THERE. TRY TO BE QUICK! MAKE IT SIMPLE!
ARE YOU DONE YET? CAN I BRING IN THE NEXT PERSON?
CHILL OUT! I'M WORKING!
HEH! WHOA!
I GUESS MY HAIR HAS GOTTEN PRETTY LONG...
PSST...
...WHAT'S THE HOLDUP?
ZOEEE! STOOOOP!

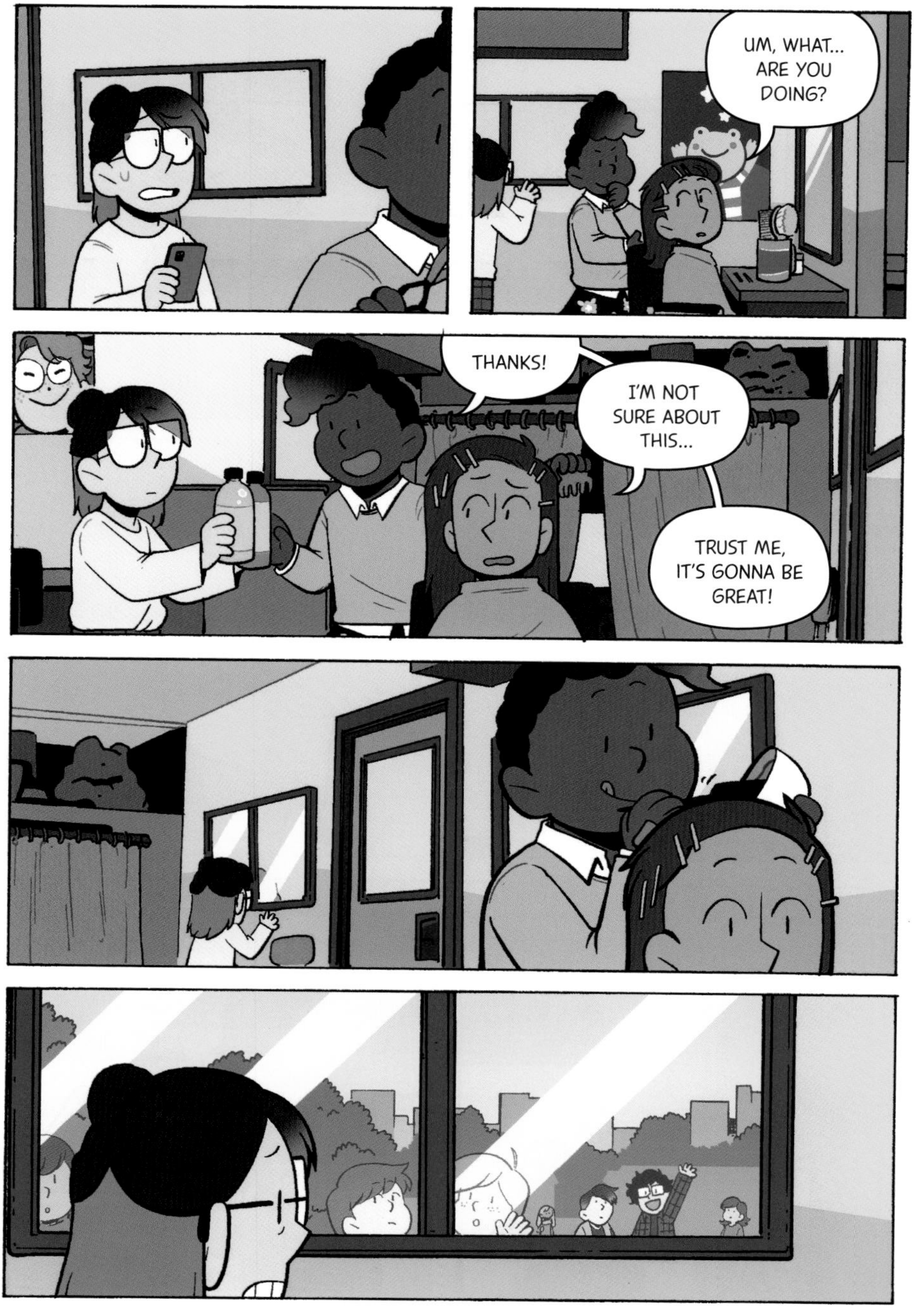
UM, WHAT... ARE YOU DOING?
THANKS!
I'M NOT SURE ABOUT THIS...
TRUST ME, IT'S GONNA BE GREAT!

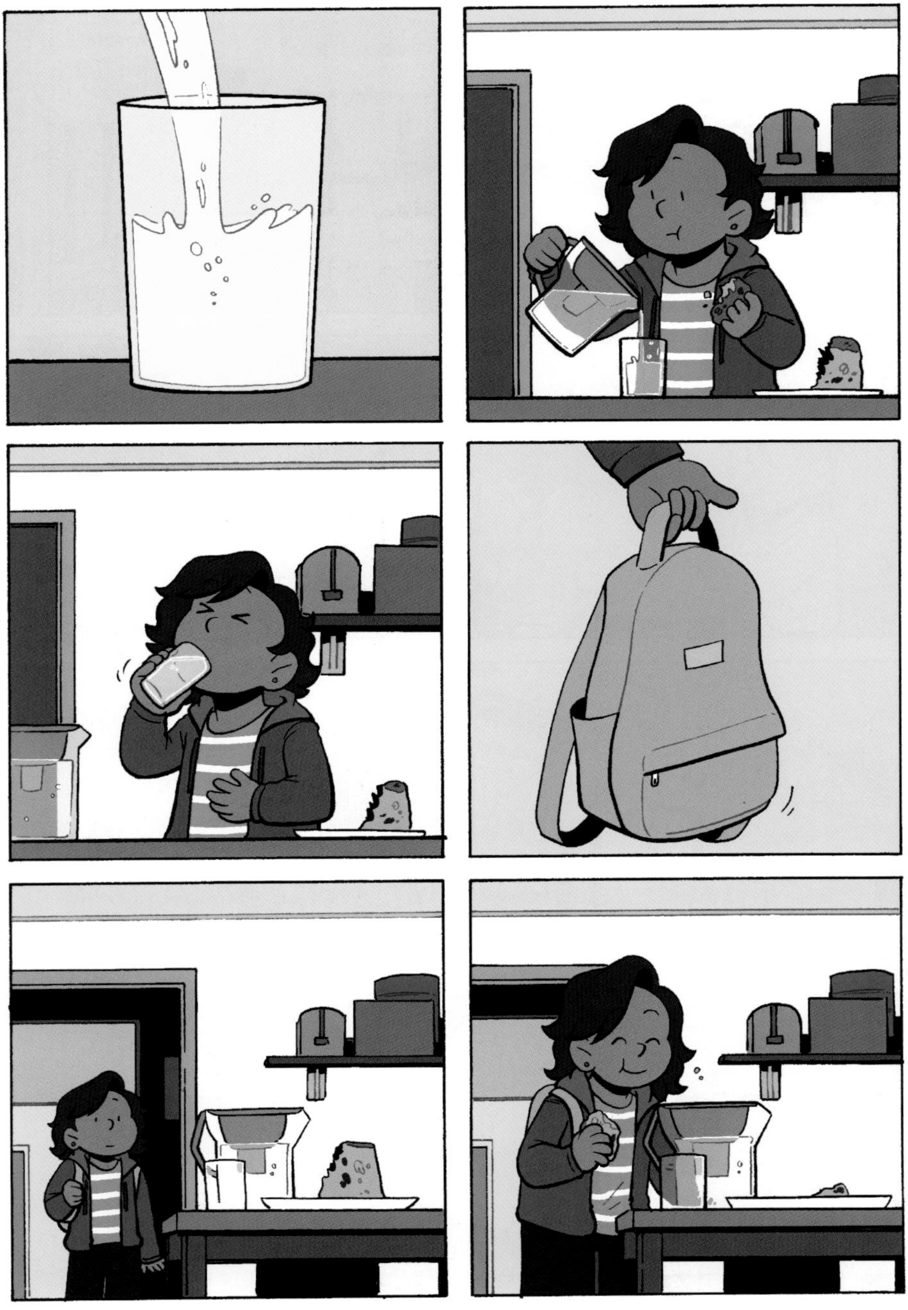

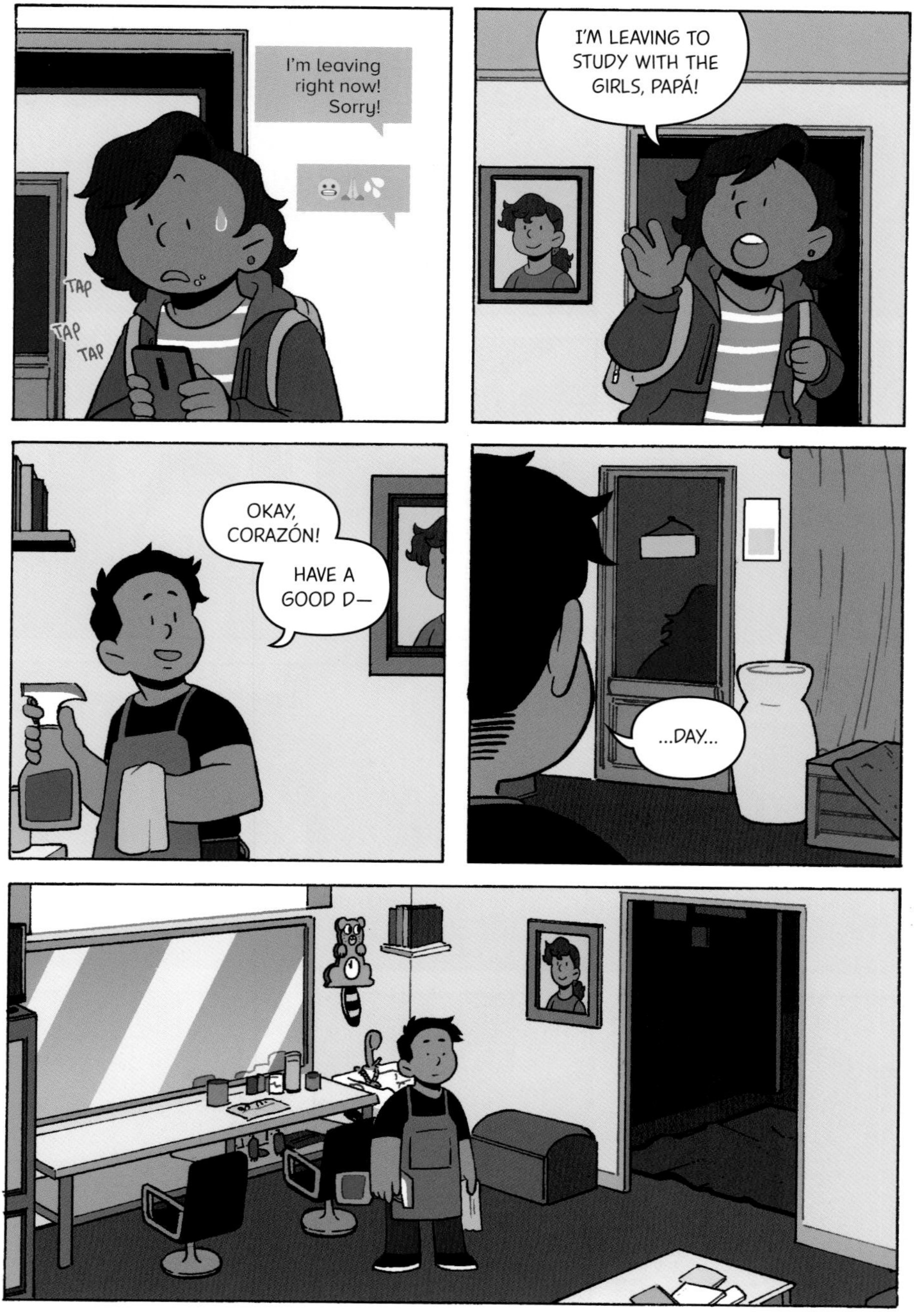
I'm leaving right now! Sorry!
TAP
TAP
TAP
I'M LEAVING TO STUDY WITH THE GIRLS, PAPÁ!
OKAY, CORAZÓN!
HAVE A GOOD D—
...DAY...

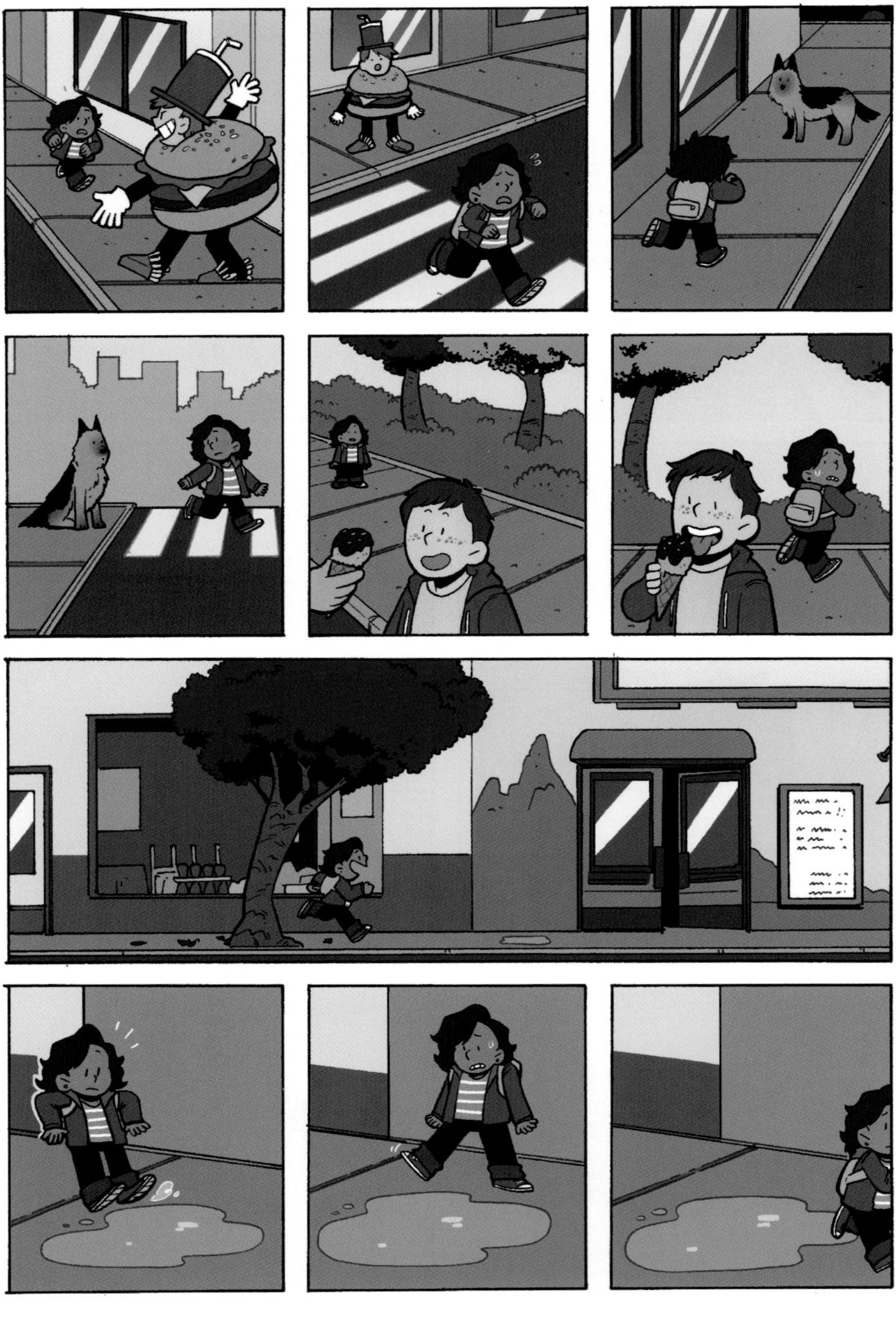

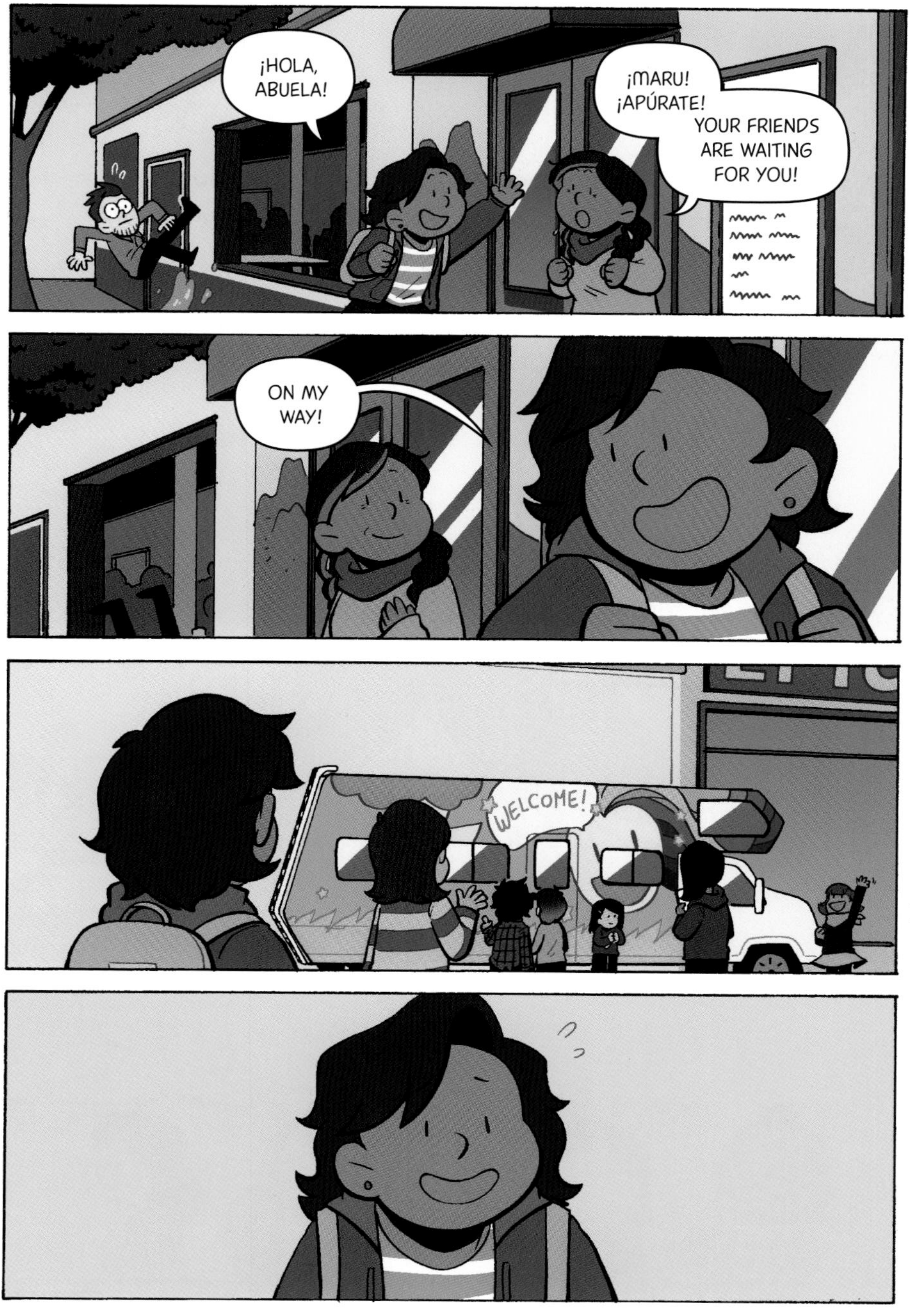
¡HOLA, ABUELA!
¡MARU! ¡APÚRATE!
YOUR FRIENDS ARE WAITING FOR YOU!
ON MY WAY!
WELCOME!

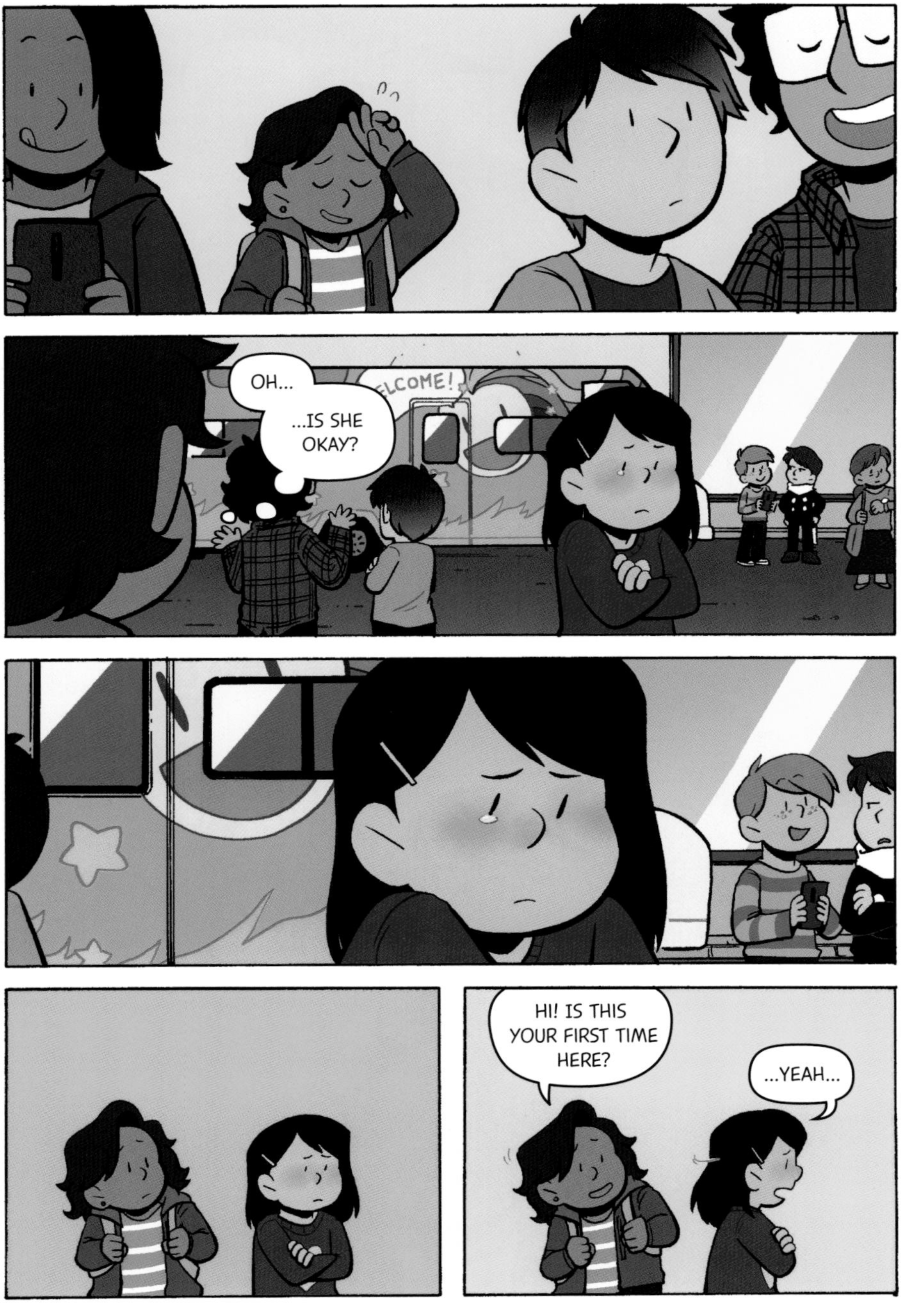
OH...
...IS SHE OKAY?
ELCOME!
HI! IS THIS YOUR FIRST TIME HERE?
...YEAH...

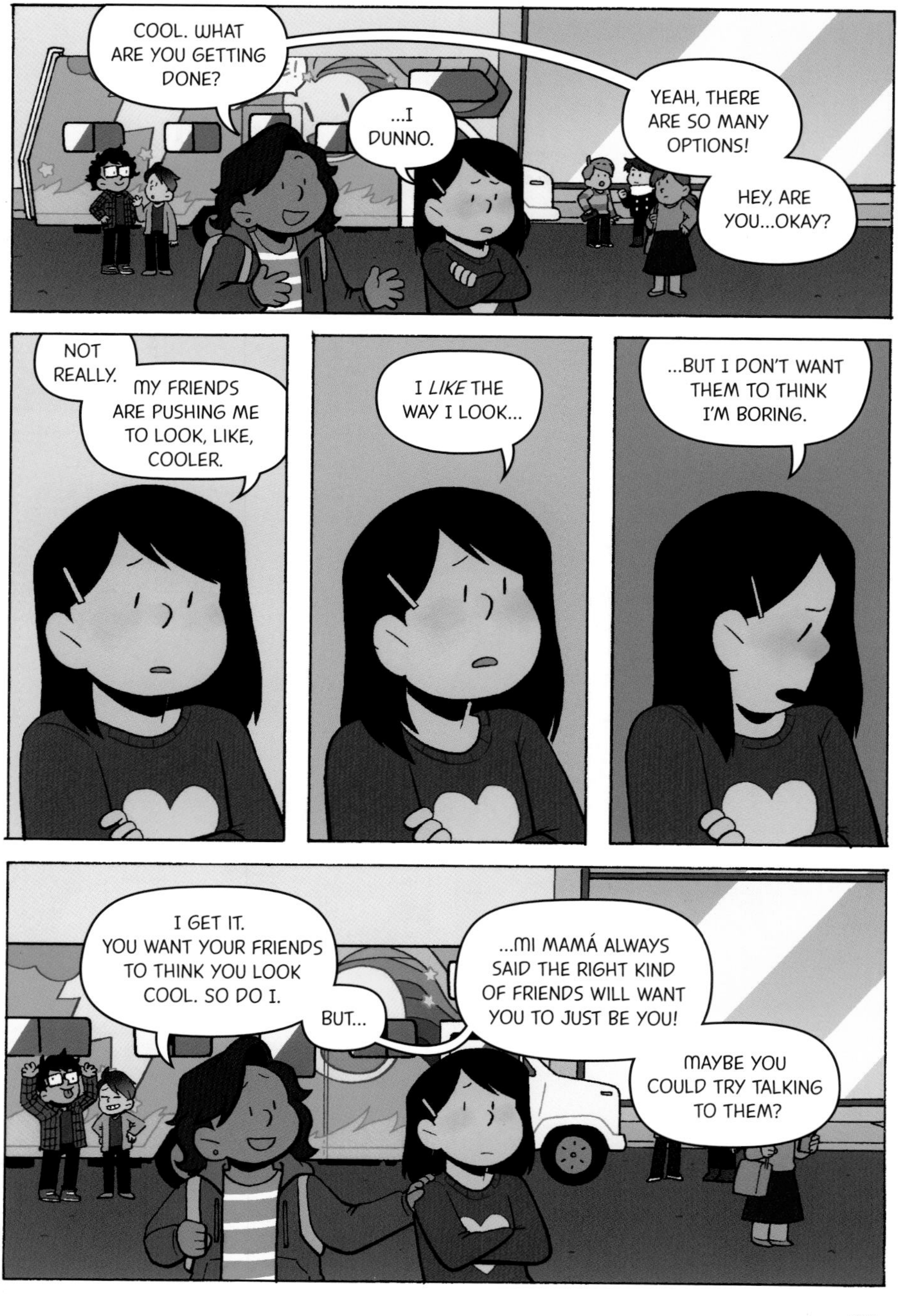
COOL. WHAT ARE YOU GETTING DONE?
...I DUNNO.
YEAH, THERE ARE SO MANY OPTIONS!
HEY, ARE YOU...OKAY?
NOT REALLY.
MY FRIENDS ARE PUSHING ME TO LOOK, LIKE, COOLER.
I *LIKE* THE WAY I LOOK...
...BUT I DON'T WANT THEM TO THINK I'M BORING.
I GET IT. YOU WANT YOUR FRIENDS TO THINK YOU LOOK COOL. SO DO I.
BUT...
...MI MAMÁ ALWAYS SAID THE RIGHT KIND OF FRIENDS WILL WANT YOU TO JUST BE YOU!
MAYBE YOU COULD TRY TALKING TO THEM?

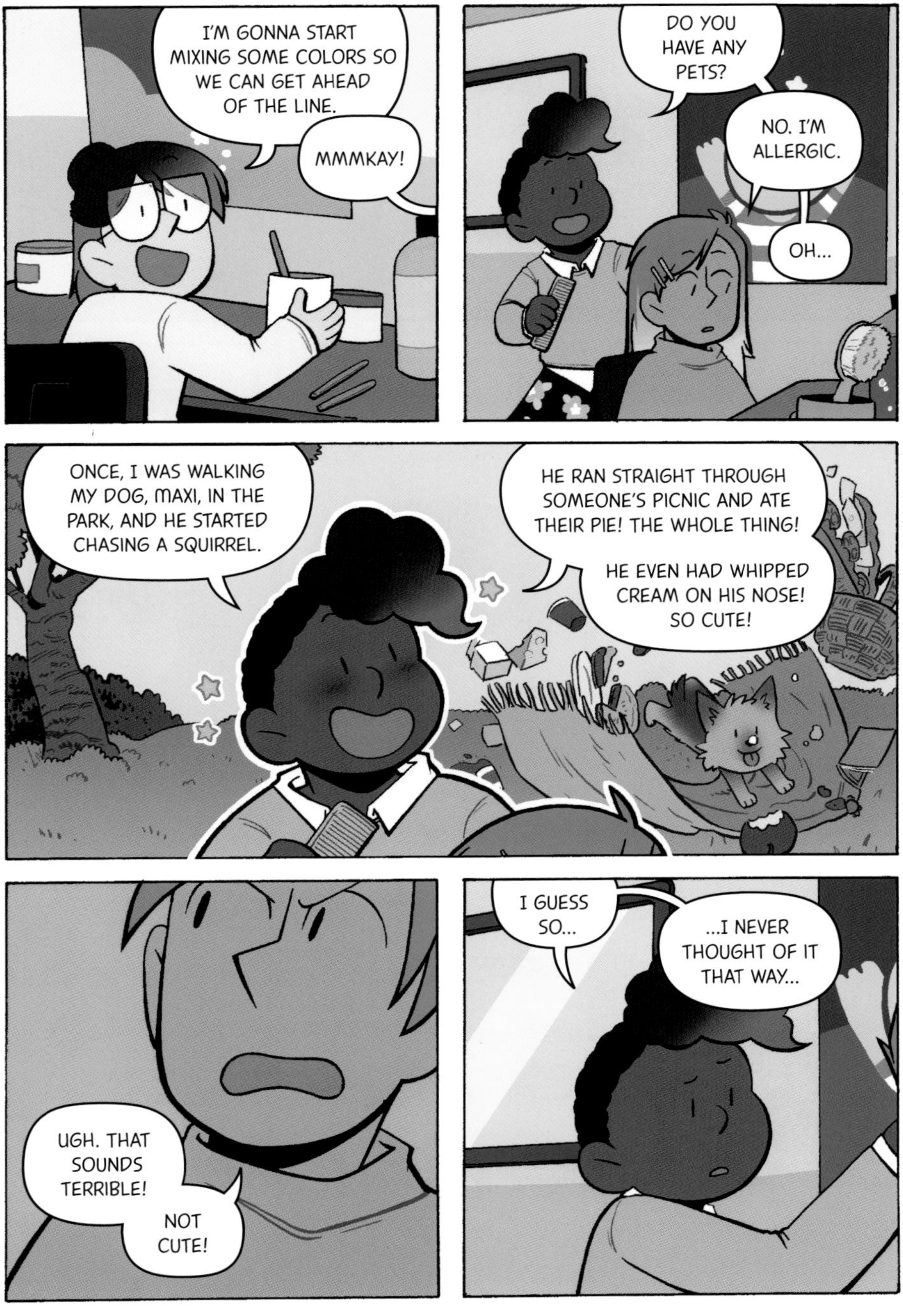
I'M GONNA START MIXING SOME COLORS SO WE CAN GET AHEAD OF THE LINE.
MMMKAY!
DO YOU HAVE ANY PETS?
NO. I'M ALLERGIC.
OH...
ONCE, I WAS WALKING MY DOG, MAXI, IN THE PARK, AND HE STARTED CHASING A SQUIRREL.
HE RAN STRAIGHT THROUGH SOMEONE'S PICNIC AND ATE THEIR PIE! THE WHOLE THING!
HE EVEN HAD WHIPPED CREAM ON HIS NOSE! SO CUTE!
UGH. THAT SOUNDS TERRIBLE!
NOT CUTE!
I GUESS SO...
...I NEVER THOUGHT OF IT THAT WAY...

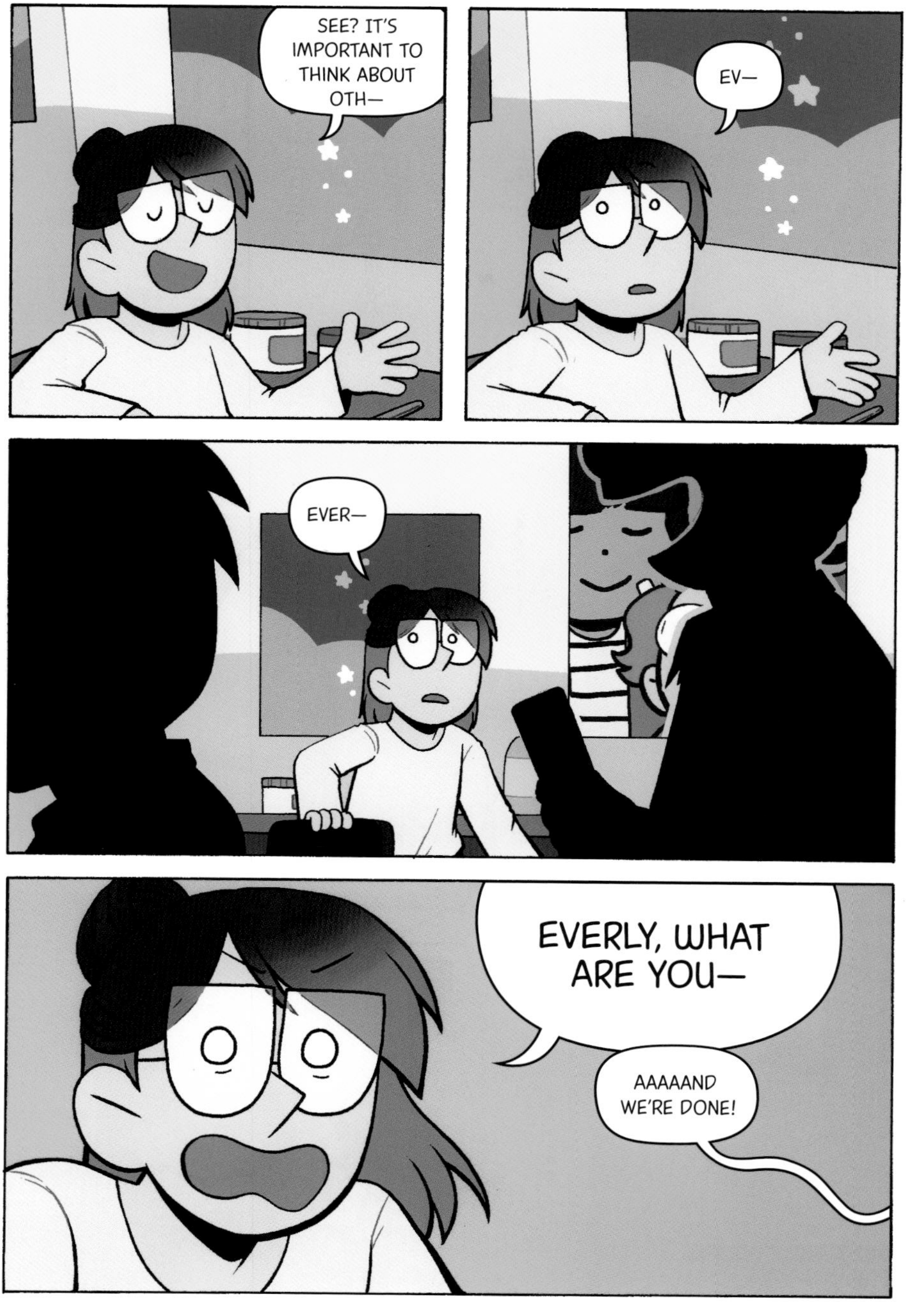
SEE? IT'S IMPORTANT TO THINK ABOUT OTH—
EV—
EVER—
EVERLY, WHAT ARE YOU—
AAAAAND WE'RE DONE!

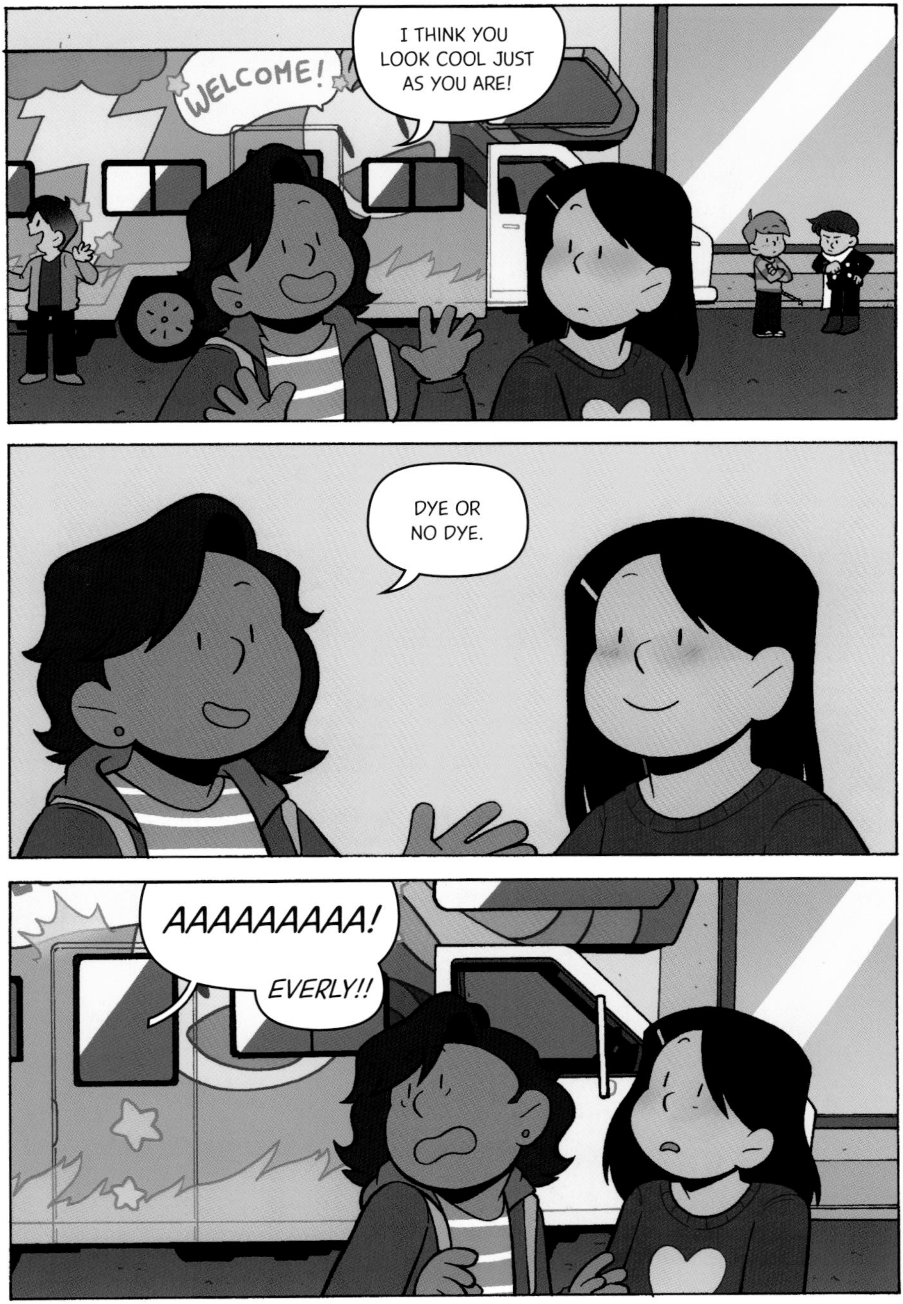
WELCOME!
I THINK YOU LOOK COOL JUST AS YOU ARE!
DYE OR NO DYE.
AAAAAAAAA!
EVERLY!!

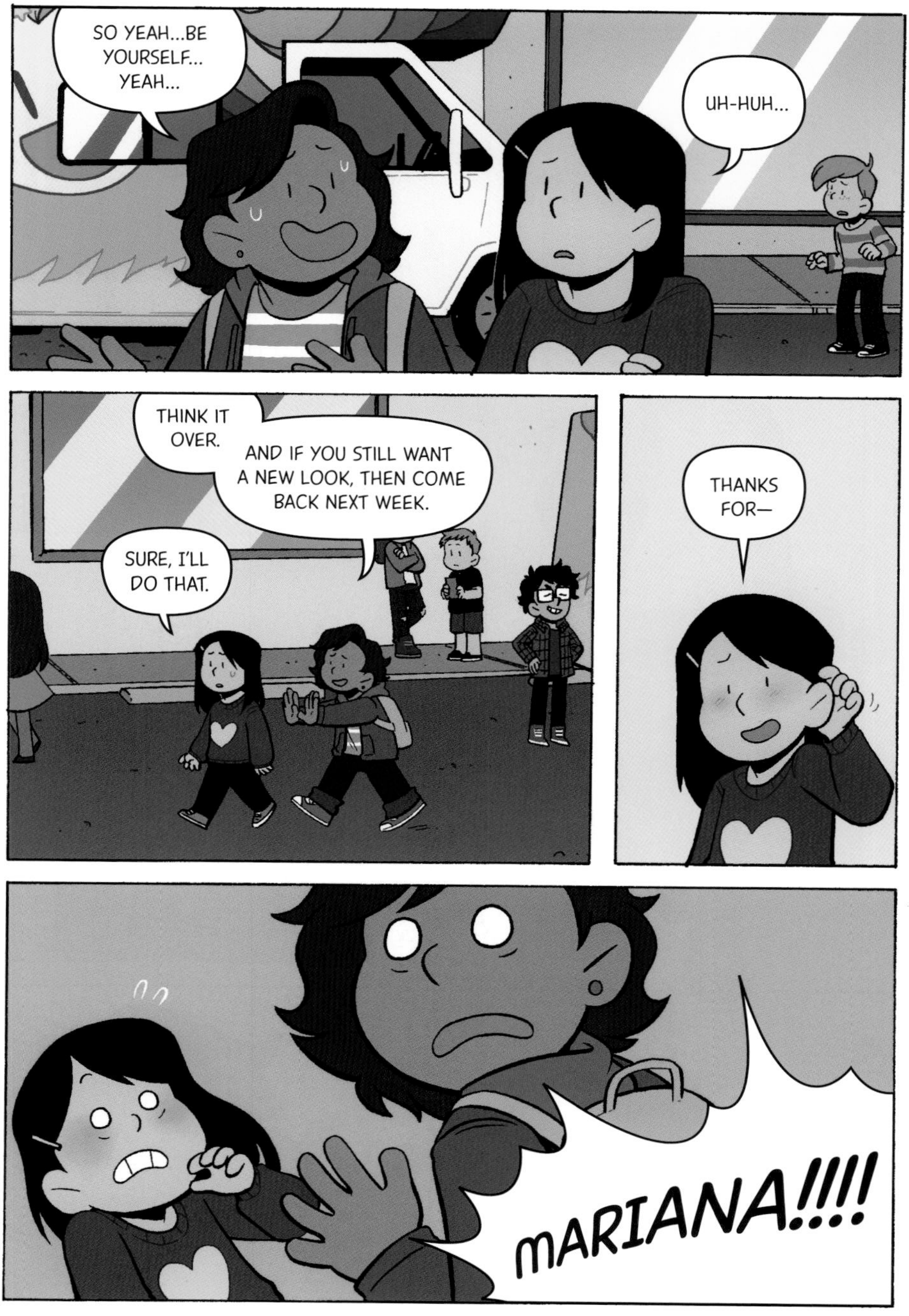
SO YEAH...BE YOURSELF... YEAH...
UH-HUH...
THINK IT OVER.
AND IF YOU STILL WANT A NEW LOOK, THEN COME BACK NEXT WEEK.
SURE, I'LL DO THAT.
THANKS FOR—
MARIANA!!!!

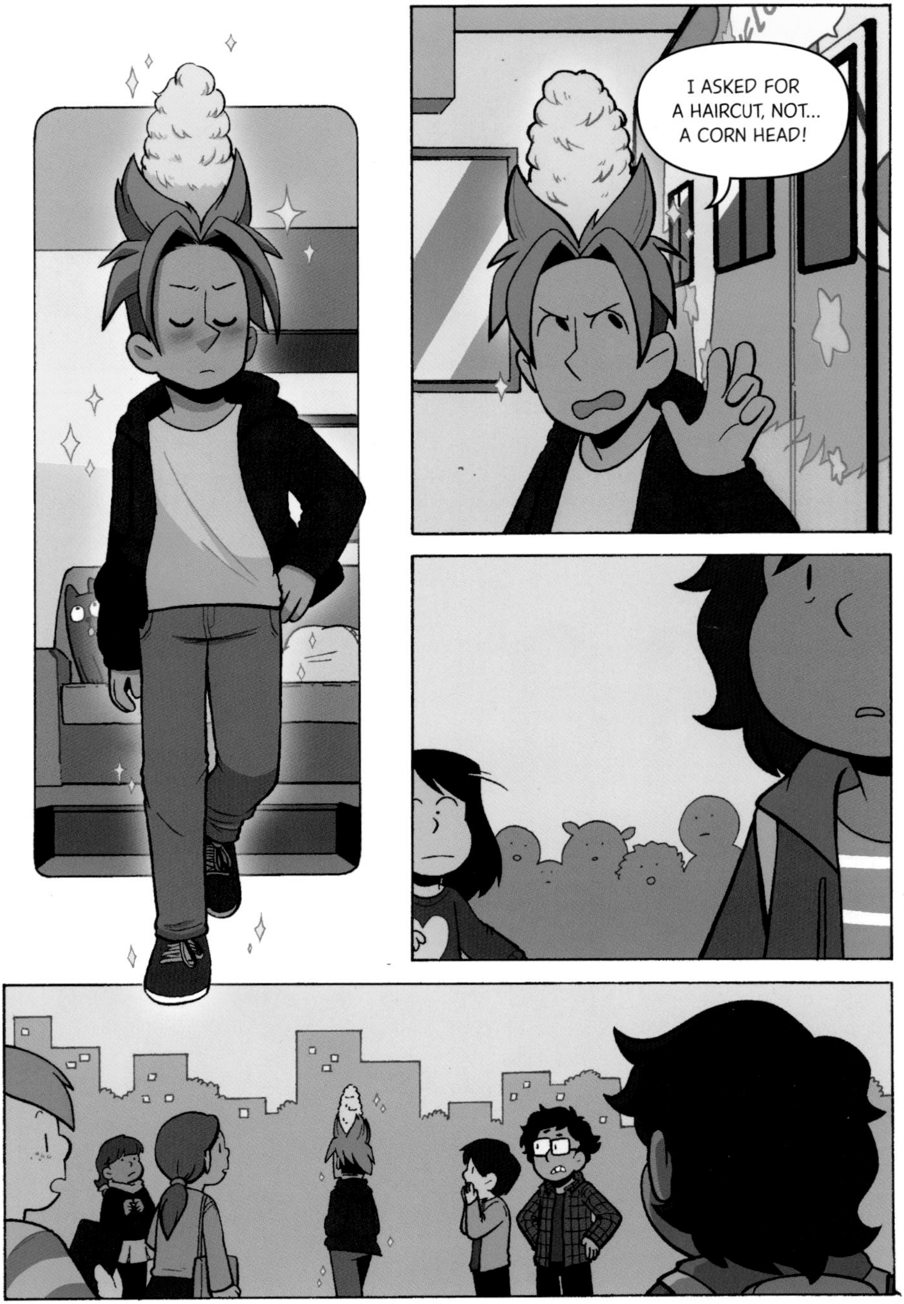
I ASKED FOR A HAIRCUT, NOT... A CORN HEAD!

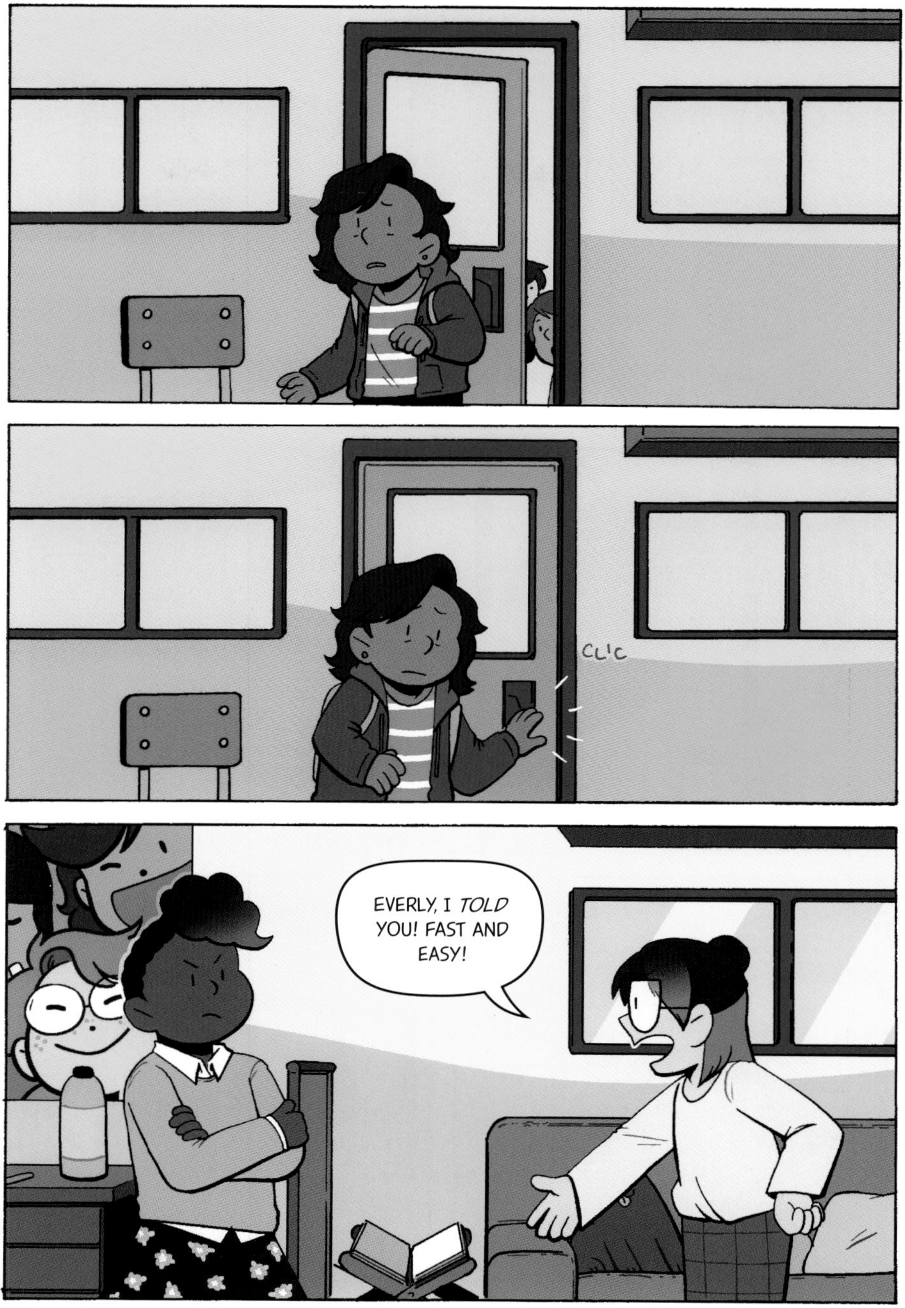
CLIC
EVERLY, I TOLD YOU! FAST AND EASY!

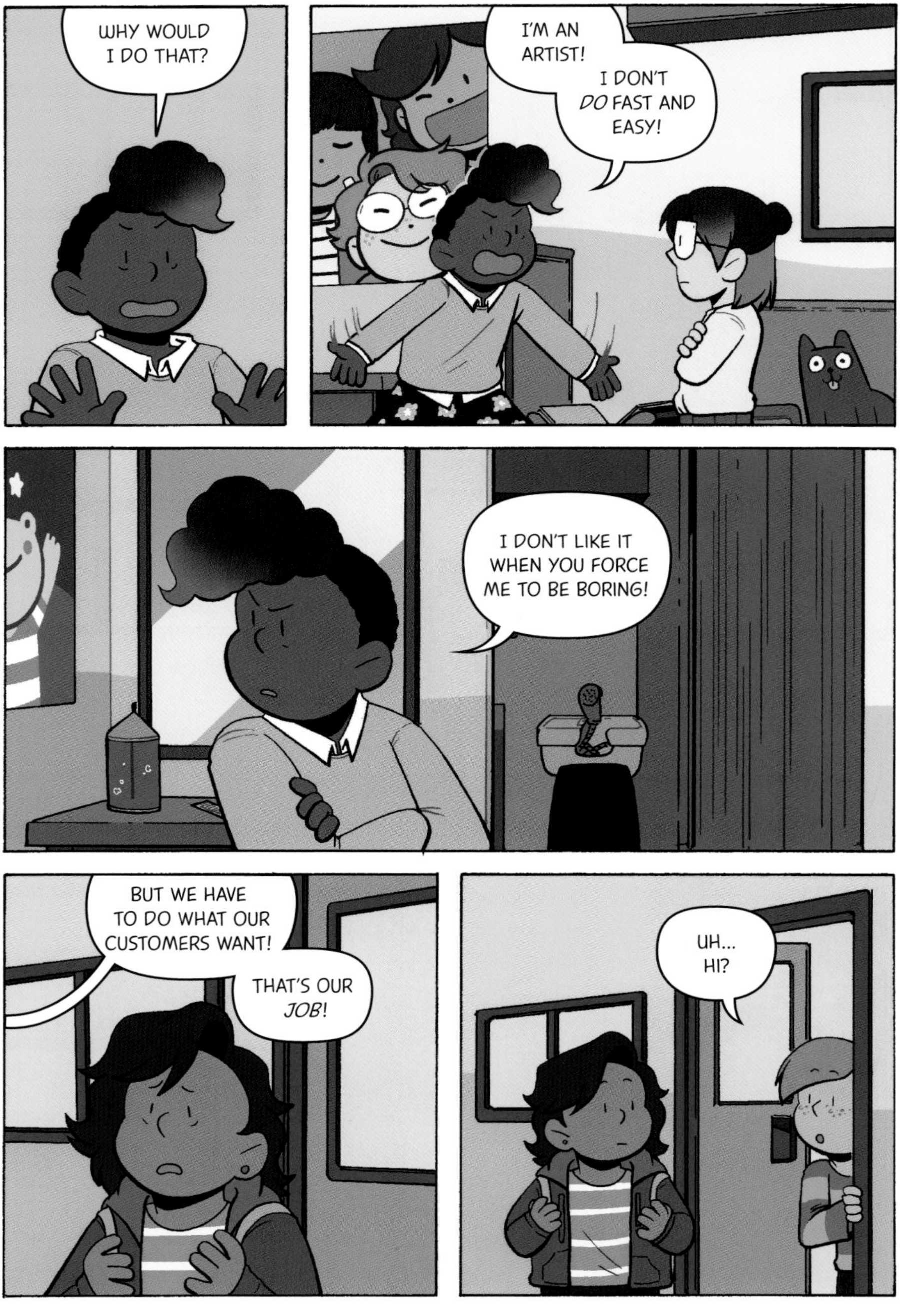
WHY WOULD I DO THAT?
I'M AN ARTIST!
I DON'T *DO* FAST AND EASY!
I DON'T LIKE IT WHEN YOU FORCE ME TO BE BORING!
BUT WE HAVE TO DO WHAT OUR CUSTOMERS WANT!
THAT'S OUR *JOB*!
UH... HI?

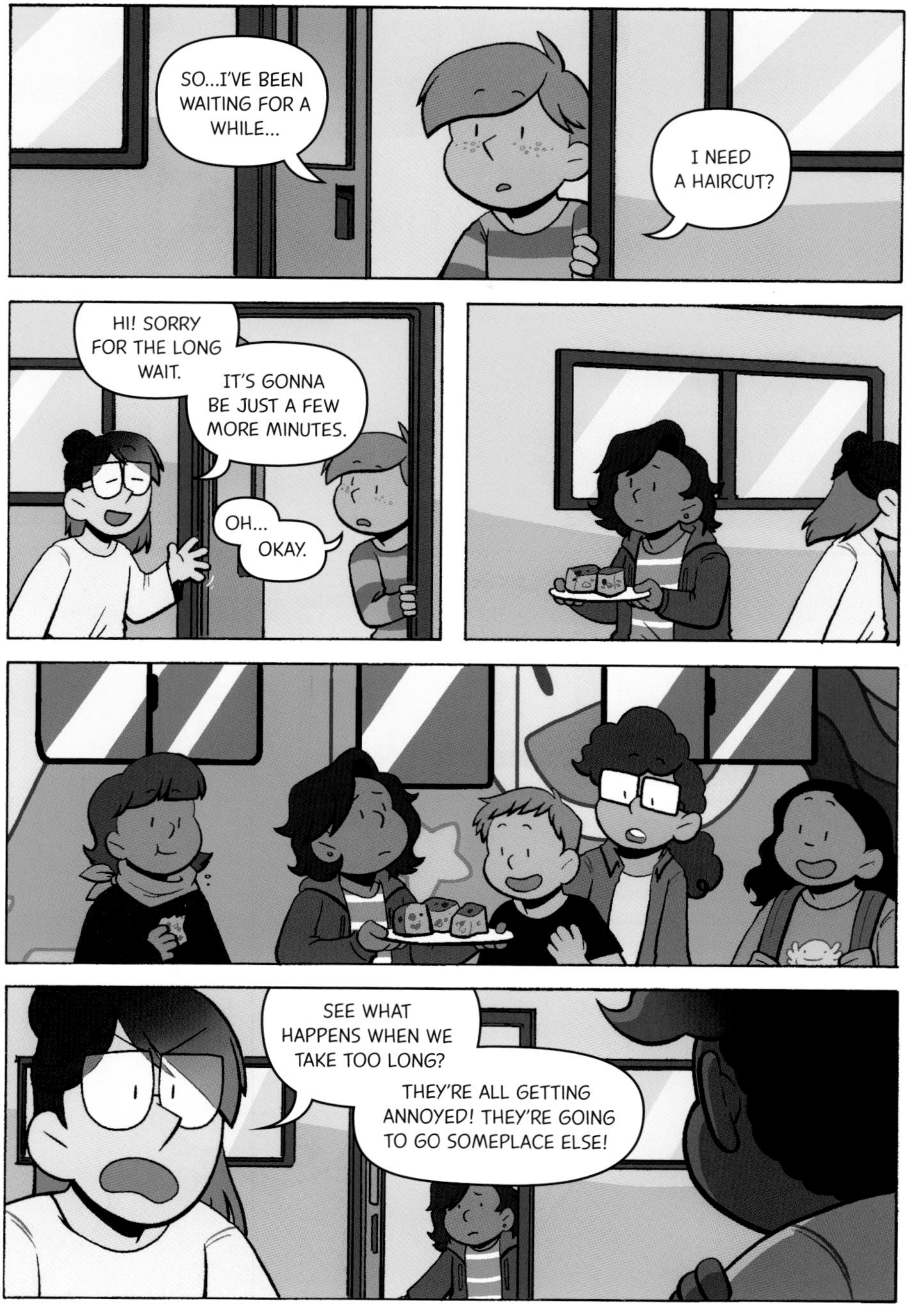
SO...I'VE BEEN WAITING FOR A WHILE...
I NEED A HAIRCUT?
HI! SORRY FOR THE LONG WAIT.
IT'S GONNA BE JUST A FEW MORE MINUTES.
OH... OKAY.
SEE WHAT HAPPENS WHEN WE TAKE TOO LONG?
THEY'RE ALL GETTING ANNOYED! THEY'RE GOING TO GO SOMEPLACE ELSE!

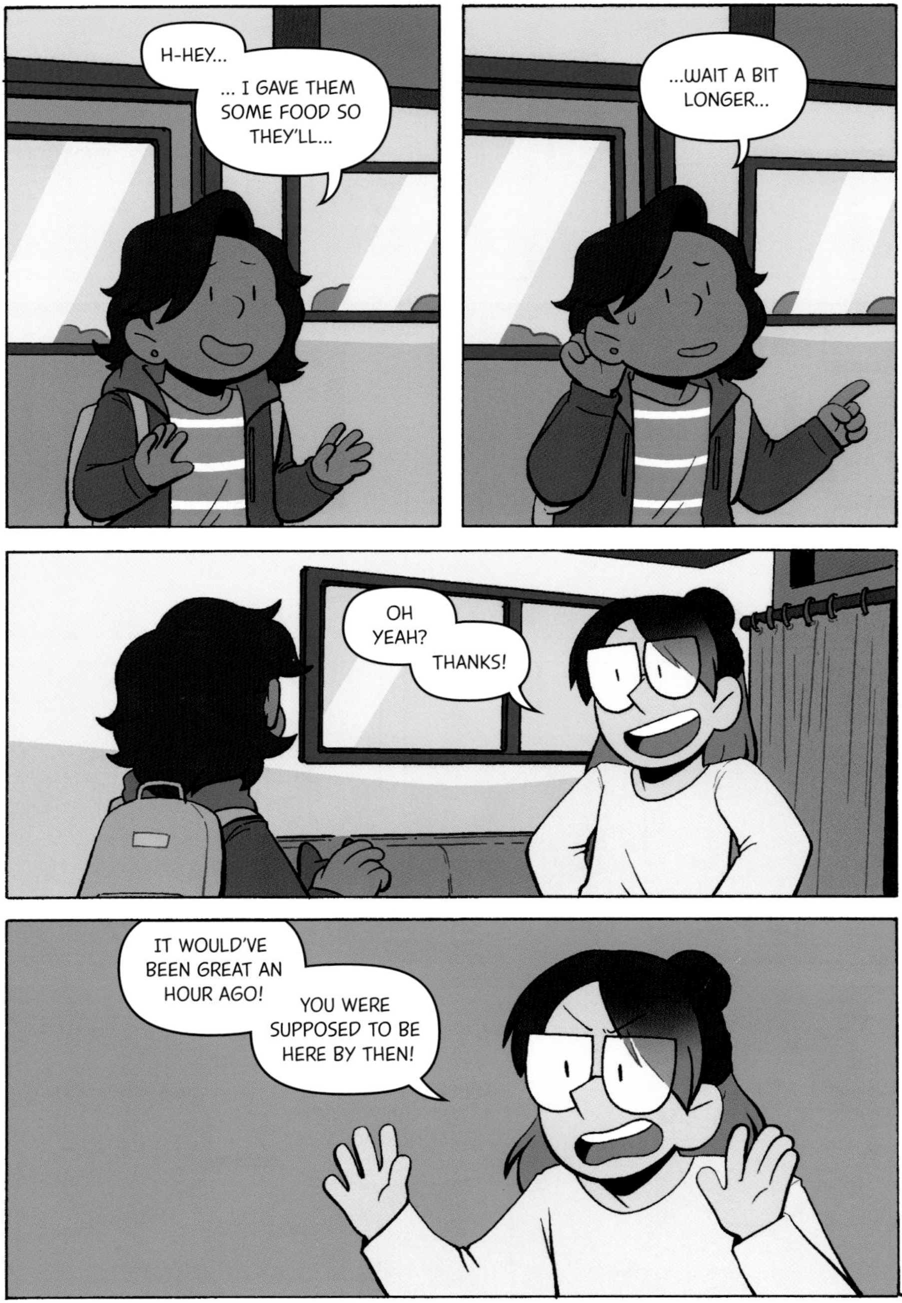
H-HEY...
... I GAVE THEM SOME FOOD SO THEY'LL...
...WAIT A BIT LONGER...
OH YEAH?
THANKS!
IT WOULD'VE BEEN GREAT AN HOUR AGO!
YOU WERE SUPPOSED TO BE HERE BY THEN!

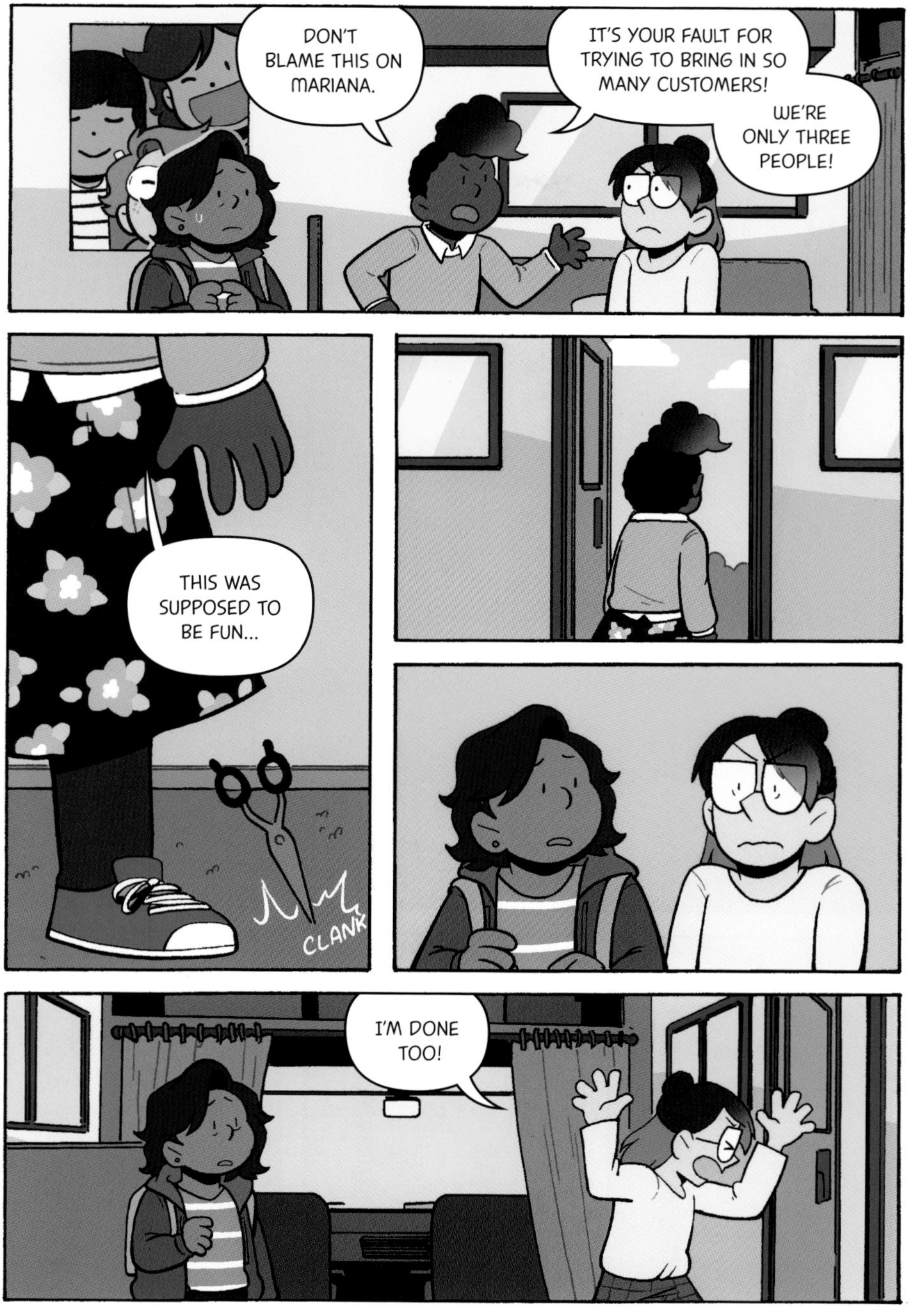
DON'T BLAME THIS ON MARIANA.
IT'S YOUR FAULT FOR TRYING TO BRING IN SO MANY CUSTOMERS!
WE'RE ONLY THREE PEOPLE!
THIS WAS SUPPOSED TO BE FUN...
CLANK
I'M DONE TOO!

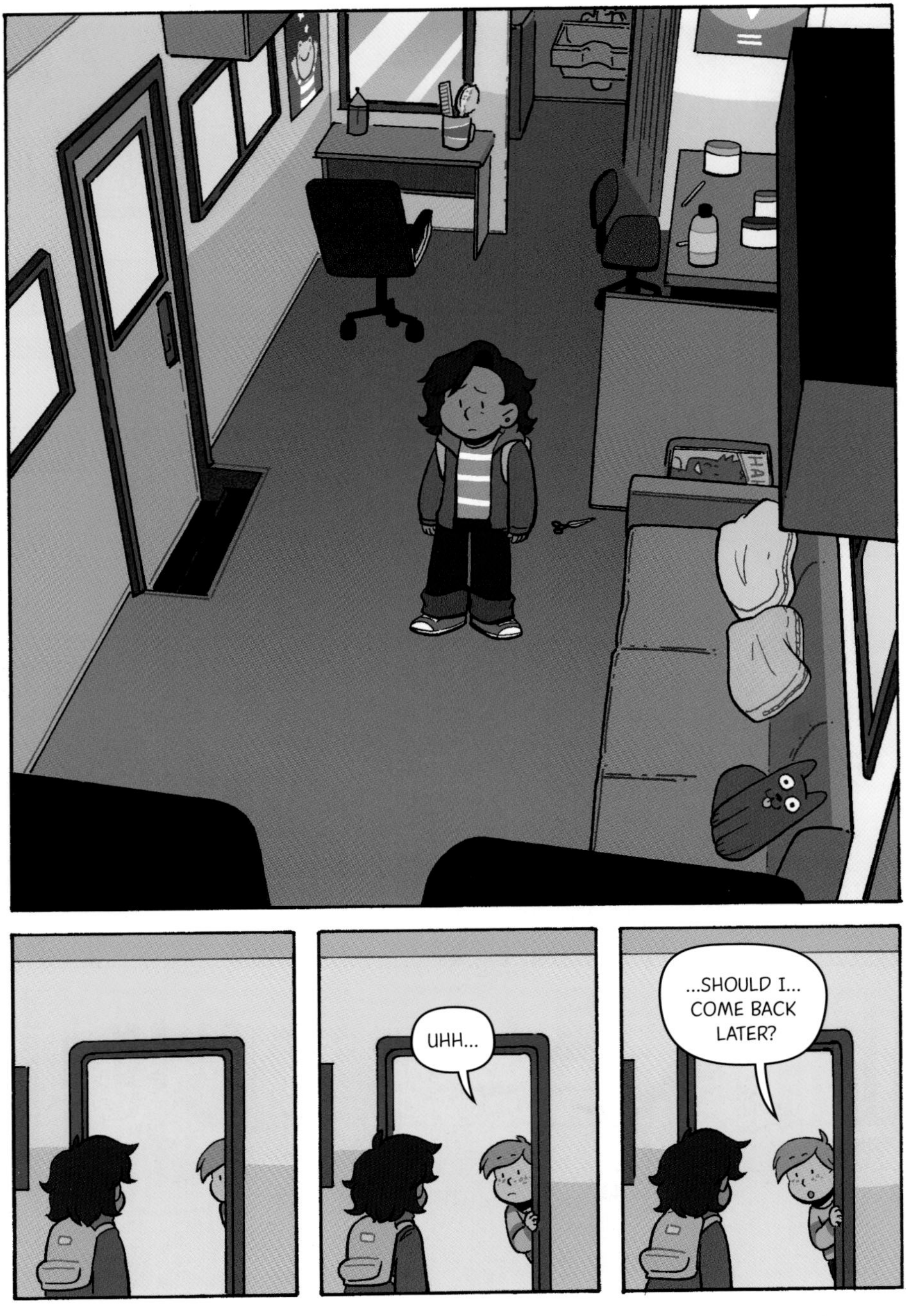
UHH...
...SHOULD I... COME BACK LATER?

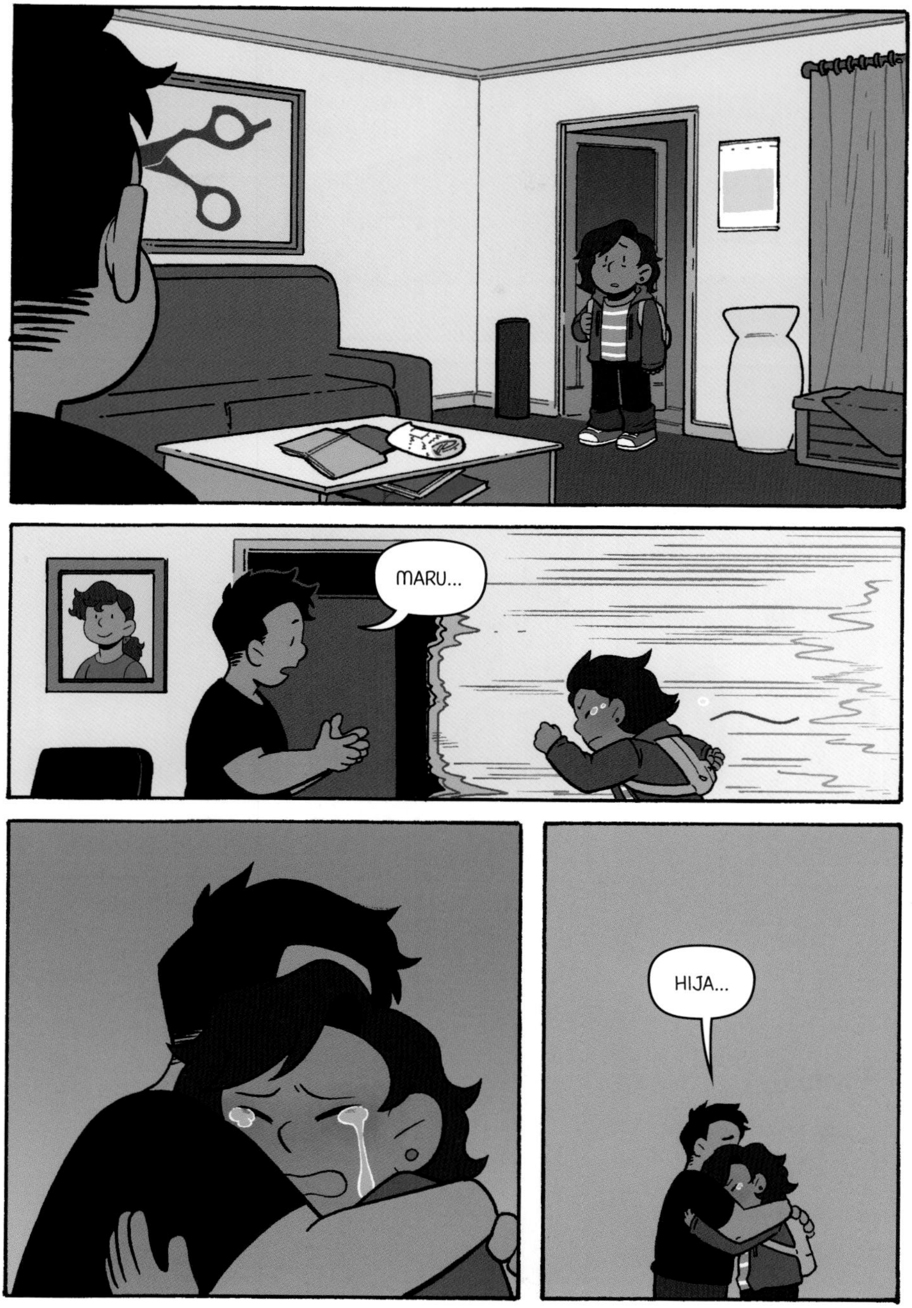
MARU...
HIJA...

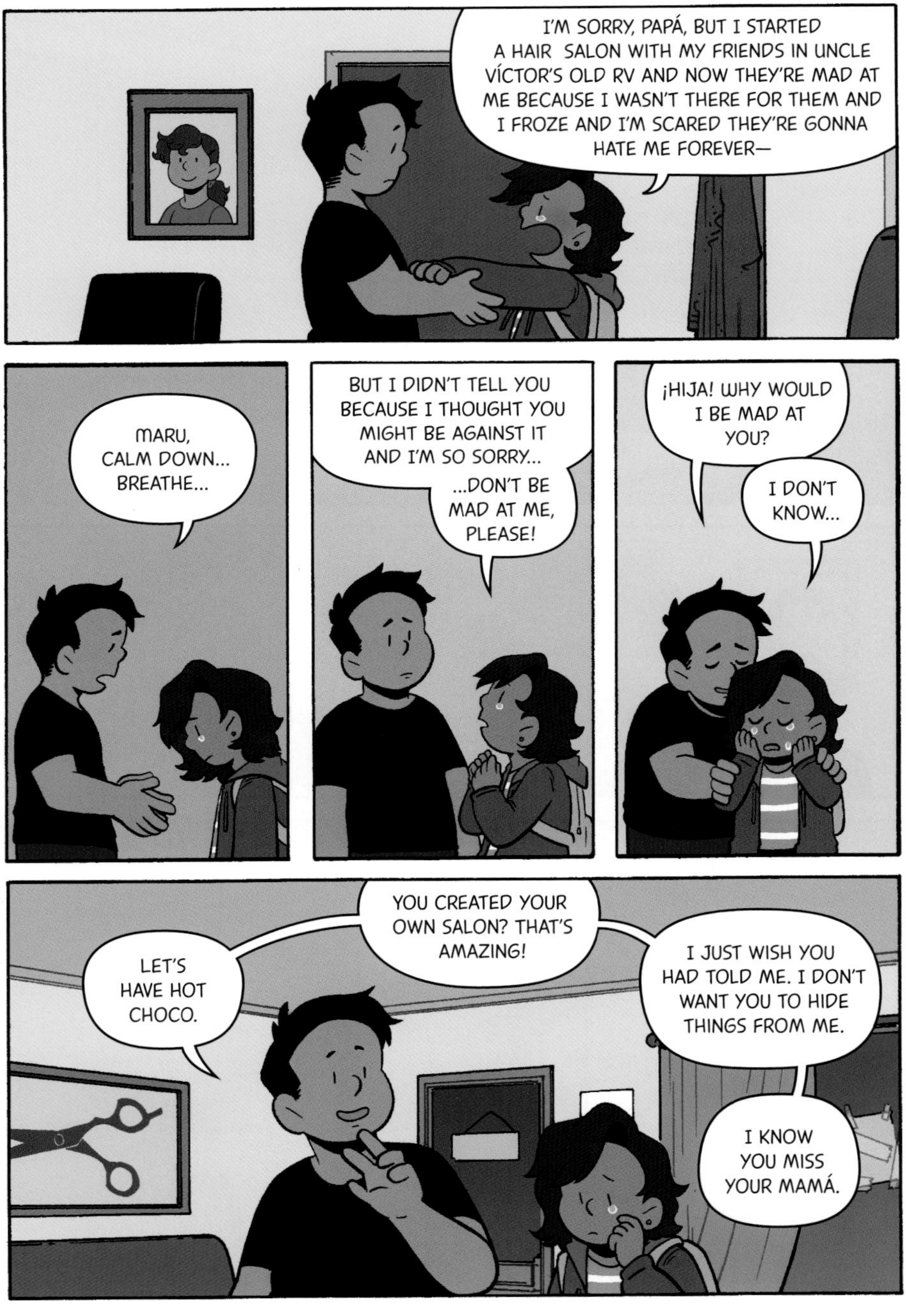

I'M SORRY, PAPÁ, BUT I STARTED A HAIR SALON WITH MY FRIENDS IN UNCLE VÍCTOR'S OLD RV AND NOW THEY'RE MAD AT ME BECAUSE I WASN'T THERE FOR THEM AND I FROZE AND I'M SCARED THEY'RE GONNA HATE ME FOREVER—
MARU, CALM DOWN... BREATHE...
BUT I DIDN'T TELL YOU BECAUSE I THOUGHT YOU MIGHT BE AGAINST IT AND I'M SO SORRY...
...DON'T BE MAD AT ME, PLEASE!
¡HIJA! WHY WOULD I BE MAD AT YOU?
I DON'T KNOW...
LET'S HAVE HOT CHOCO.
YOU CREATED YOUR OWN SALON? THAT'S AMAZING!
I JUST WISH YOU HAD TOLD ME. I DON'T WANT YOU TO HIDE THINGS FROM ME.
I KNOW YOU MISS YOUR MAMÁ.

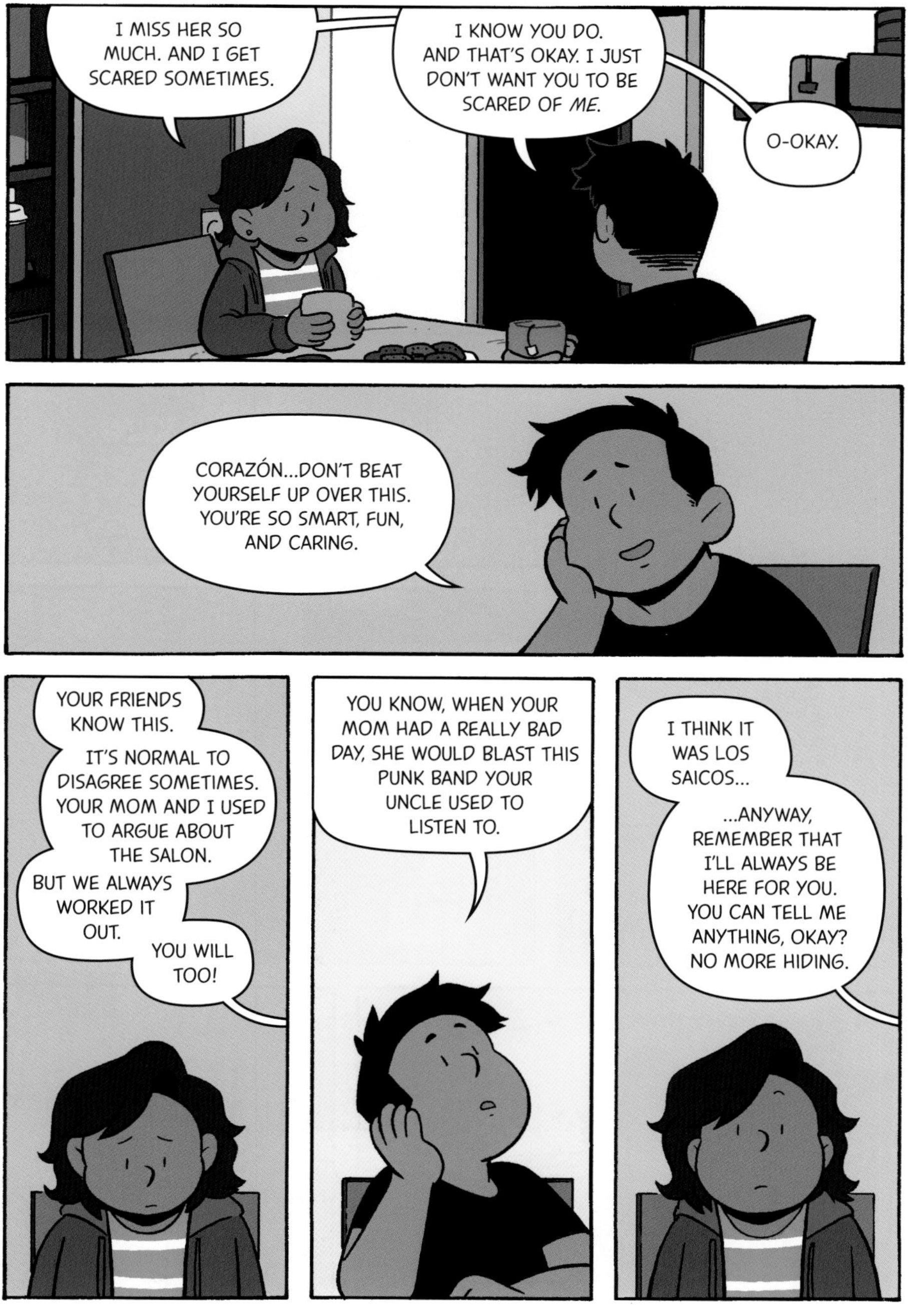
I MISS HER SO MUCH. AND I GET SCARED SOMETIMES.
I KNOW YOU DO. AND THAT'S OKAY. I JUST DON'T WANT YOU TO BE SCARED OF *ME*.
O-OKAY.
CORAZÓN...DON'T BEAT YOURSELF UP OVER THIS. YOU'RE SO SMART, FUN, AND CARING.
YOUR FRIENDS KNOW THIS.
IT'S NORMAL TO DISAGREE SOMETIMES. YOUR MOM AND I USED TO ARGUE ABOUT THE SALON.
BUT WE ALWAYS WORKED IT OUT.
YOU WILL TOO!
YOU KNOW, WHEN YOUR MOM HAD A REALLY BAD DAY, SHE WOULD BLAST THIS PUNK BAND YOUR UNCLE USED TO LISTEN TO.
I THINK IT WAS LOS SAICOS...
...ANYWAY, REMEMBER THAT I'LL ALWAYS BE HERE FOR YOU. YOU CAN TELL ME ANYTHING, OKAY? NO MORE HIDING.

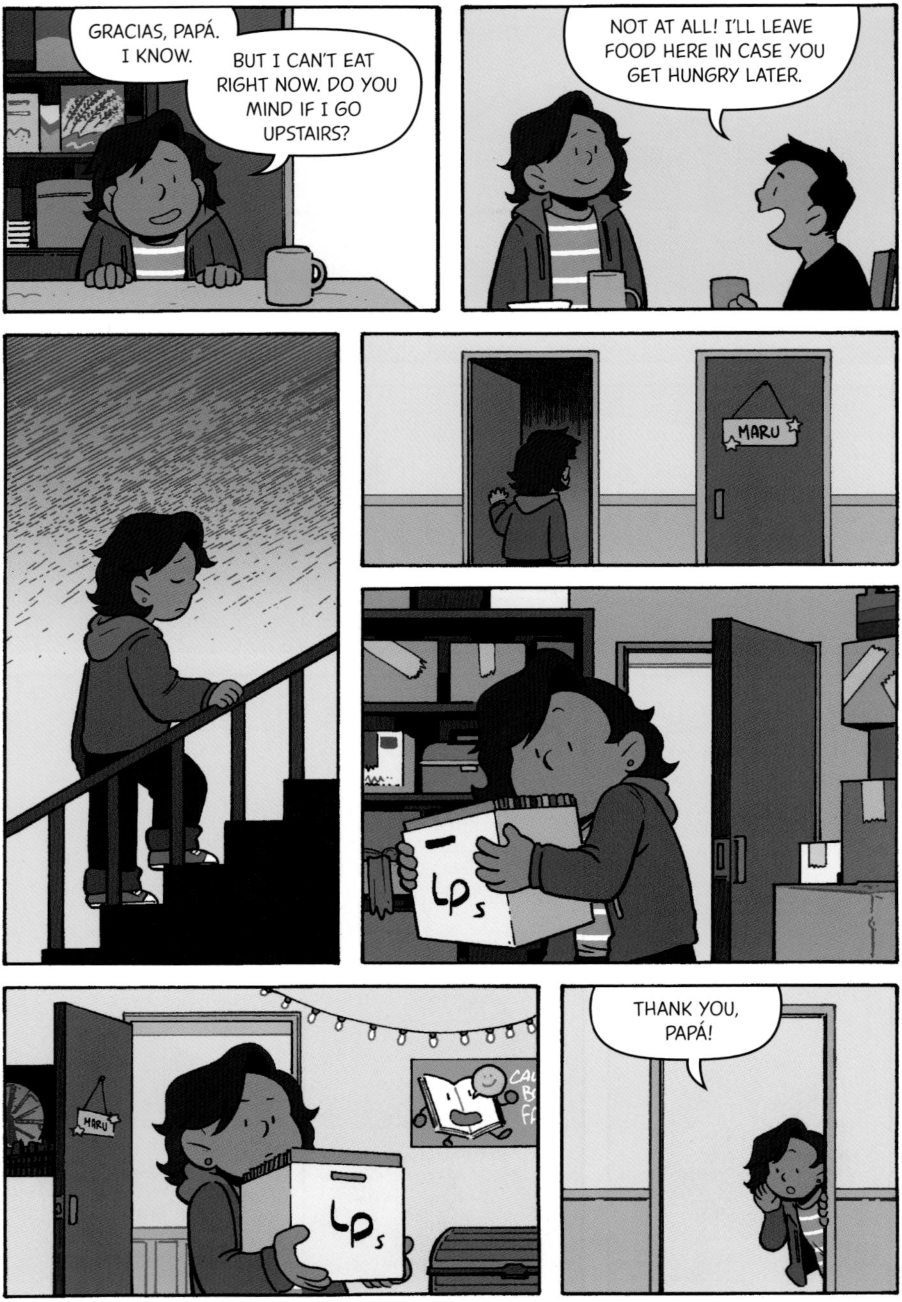
GRACIAS, PAPÁ. I KNOW.
BUT I CAN'T EAT RIGHT NOW. DO YOU MIND IF I GO UPSTAIRS?
NOT AT ALL! I'LL LEAVE FOOD HERE IN CASE YOU GET HUNGRY LATER.
MARU
LPs
MARU
LPs
THANK YOU, PAPÁ!

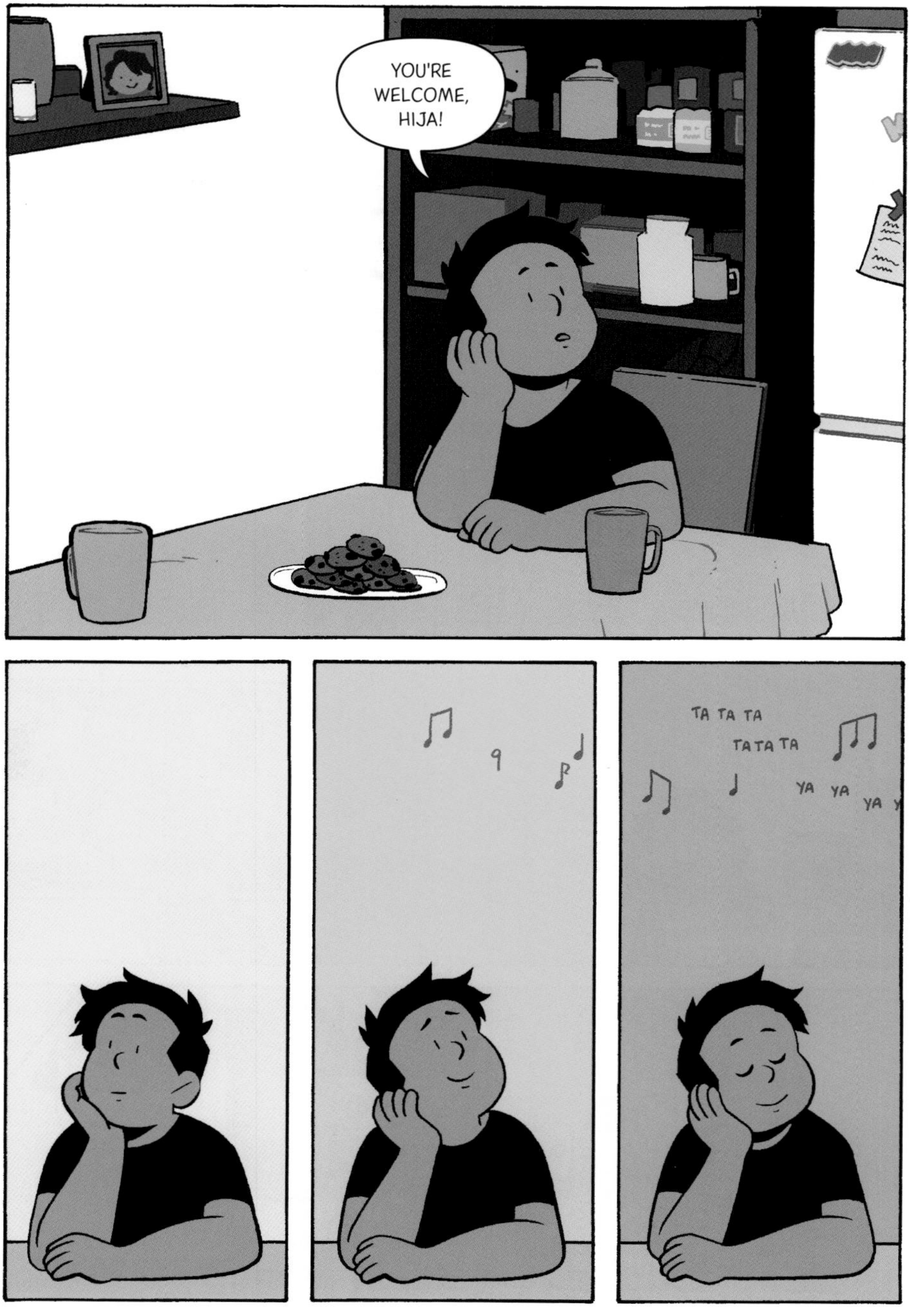
YOU'RE WELCOME, HIJA!
TA TA TA
TA TA TA
YA YA YA

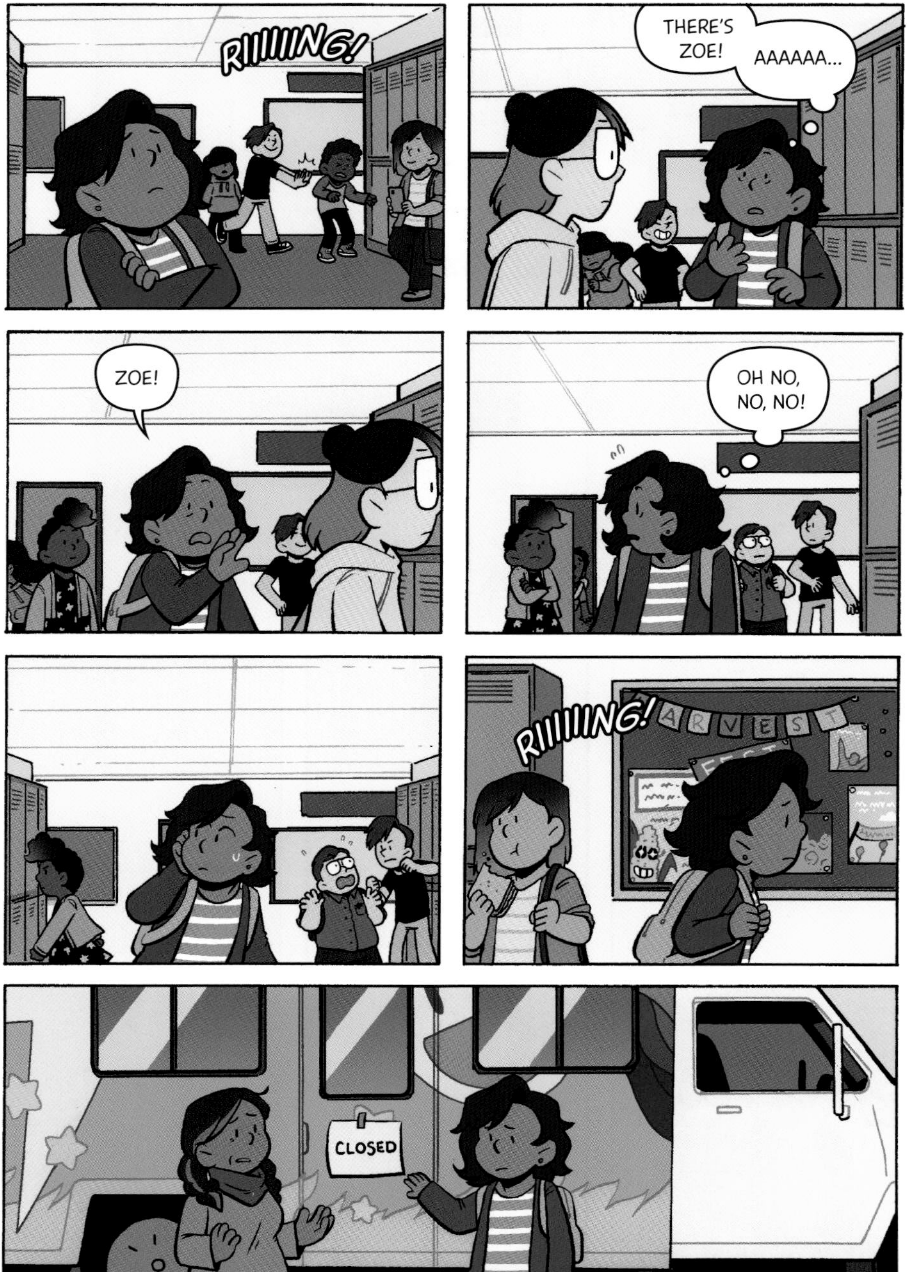
RIIIIIING!
THERE'S ZOE!
AAAAAA...
ZOE!
OH NO, NO, NO!
RIIIIIING!
ARVEST
CLOSED

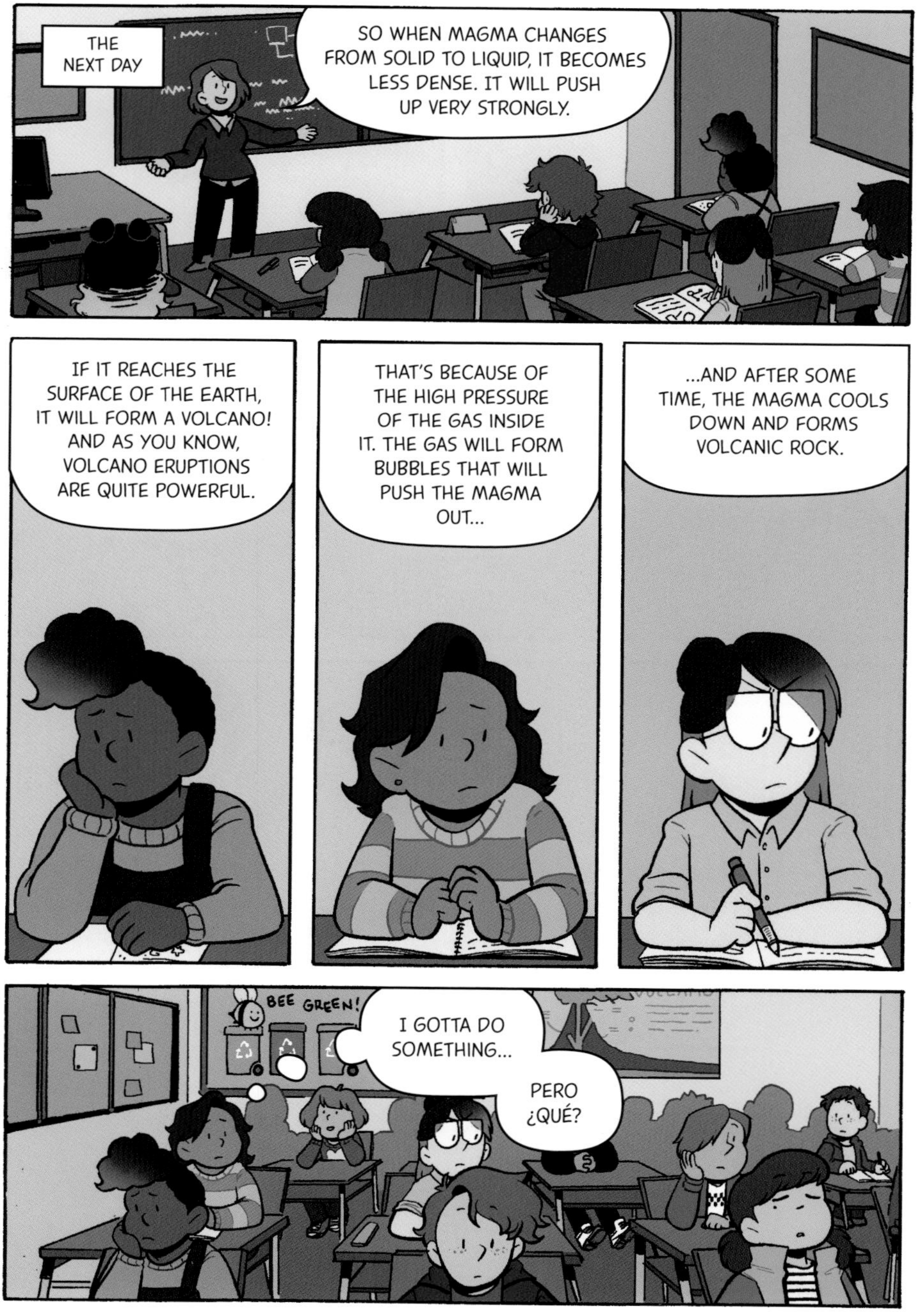
THE NEXT DAY
SO WHEN MAGMA CHANGES FROM SOLID TO LIQUID, IT BECOMES LESS DENSE. IT WILL PUSH UP VERY STRONGLY.
IF IT REACHES THE SURFACE OF THE EARTH, IT WILL FORM A VOLCANO! AND AS YOU KNOW, VOLCANO ERUPTIONS ARE QUITE POWERFUL.
THAT'S BECAUSE OF THE HIGH PRESSURE OF THE GAS INSIDE IT. THE GAS WILL FORM BUBBLES THAT WILL PUSH THE MAGMA OUT...
...AND AFTER SOME TIME, THE MAGMA COOLS DOWN AND FORMS VOLCANIC ROCK.
BEE GREEN!
I GOTTA DO SOMETHING...
PERO ¿QUÉ?

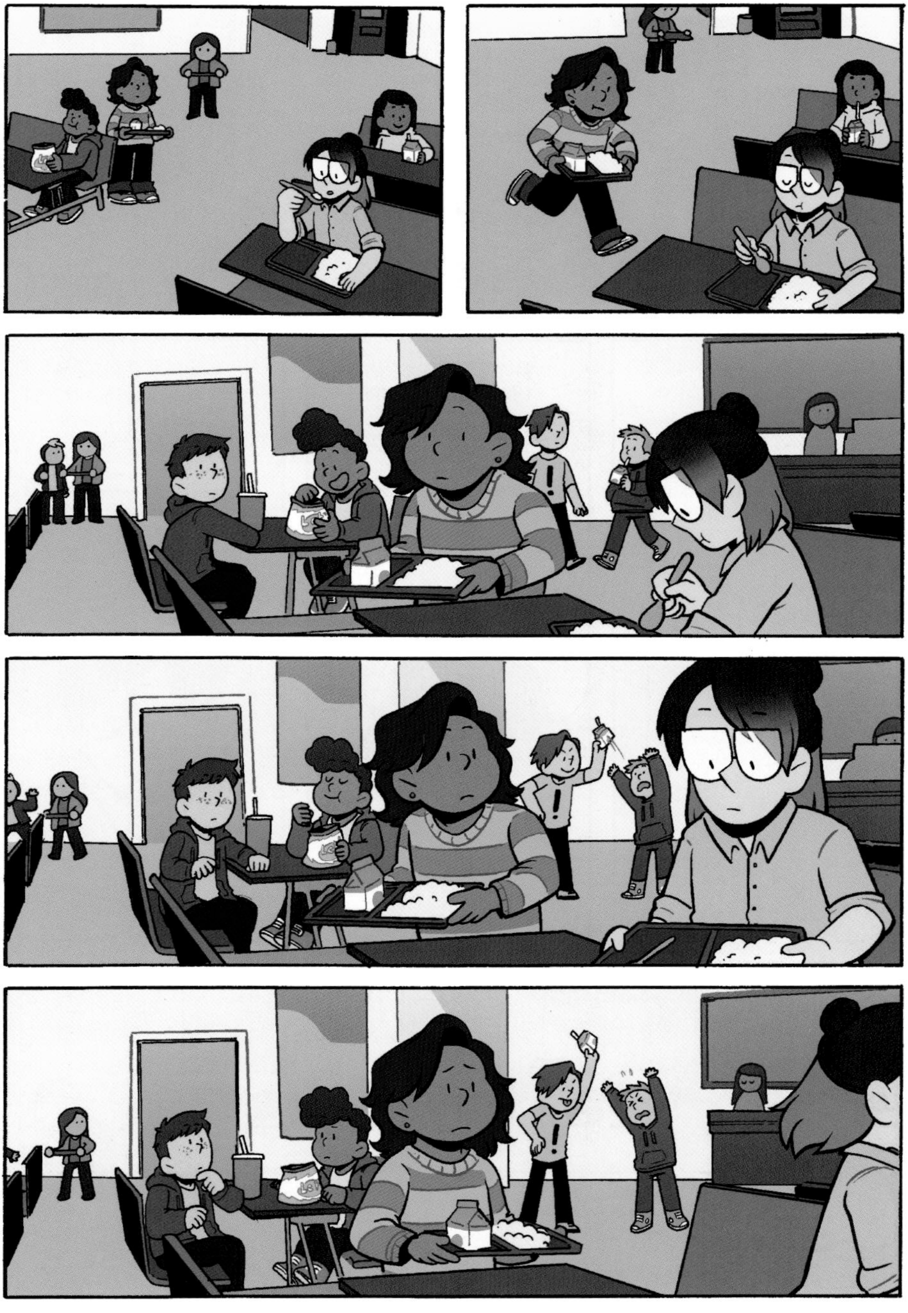

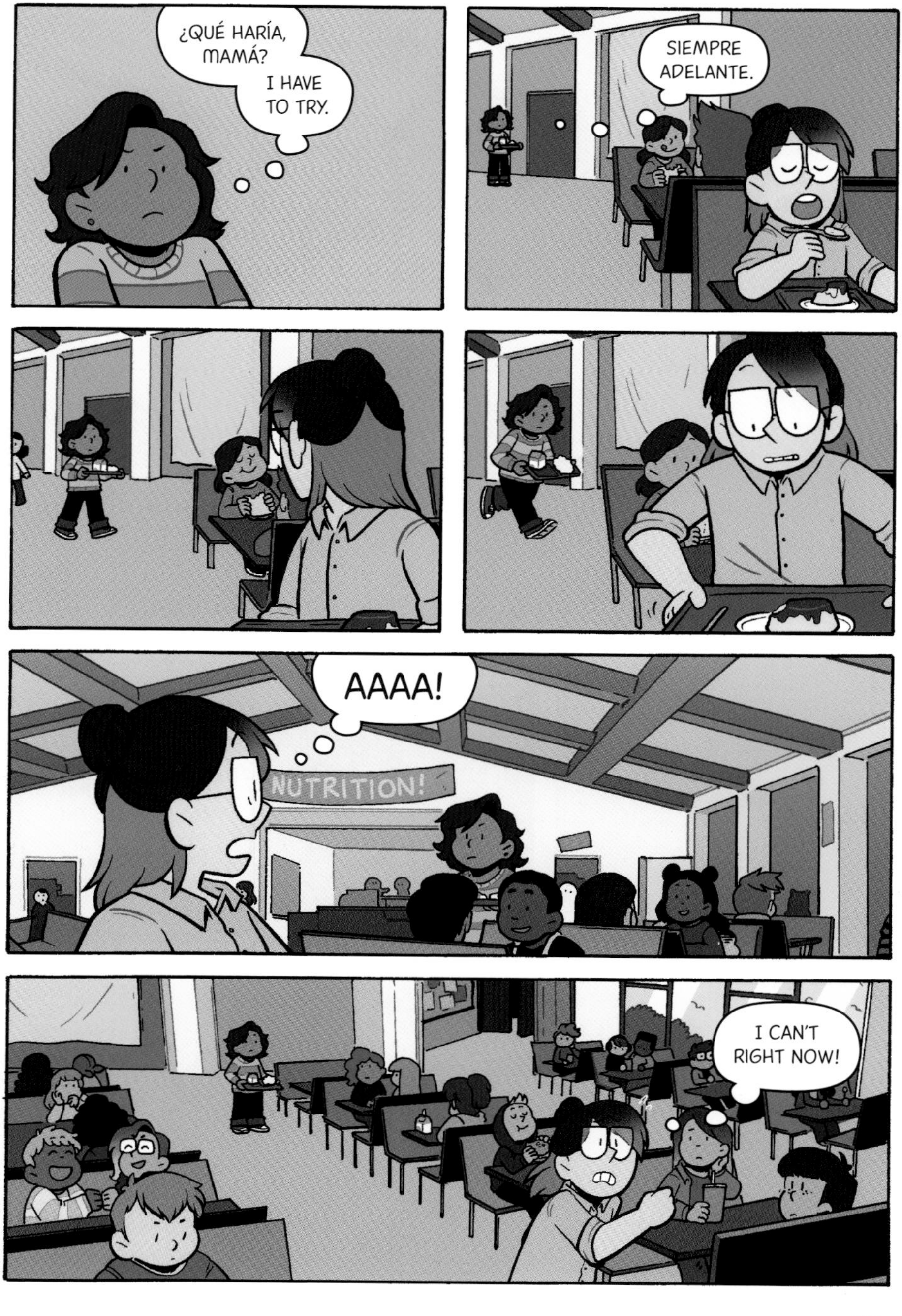
¿QUÉ HARÍA, MAMÁ?
I HAVE TO TRY.
SIEMPRE ADELANTE.
AAAA!
NUTRITION!
I CAN'T RIGHT NOW!

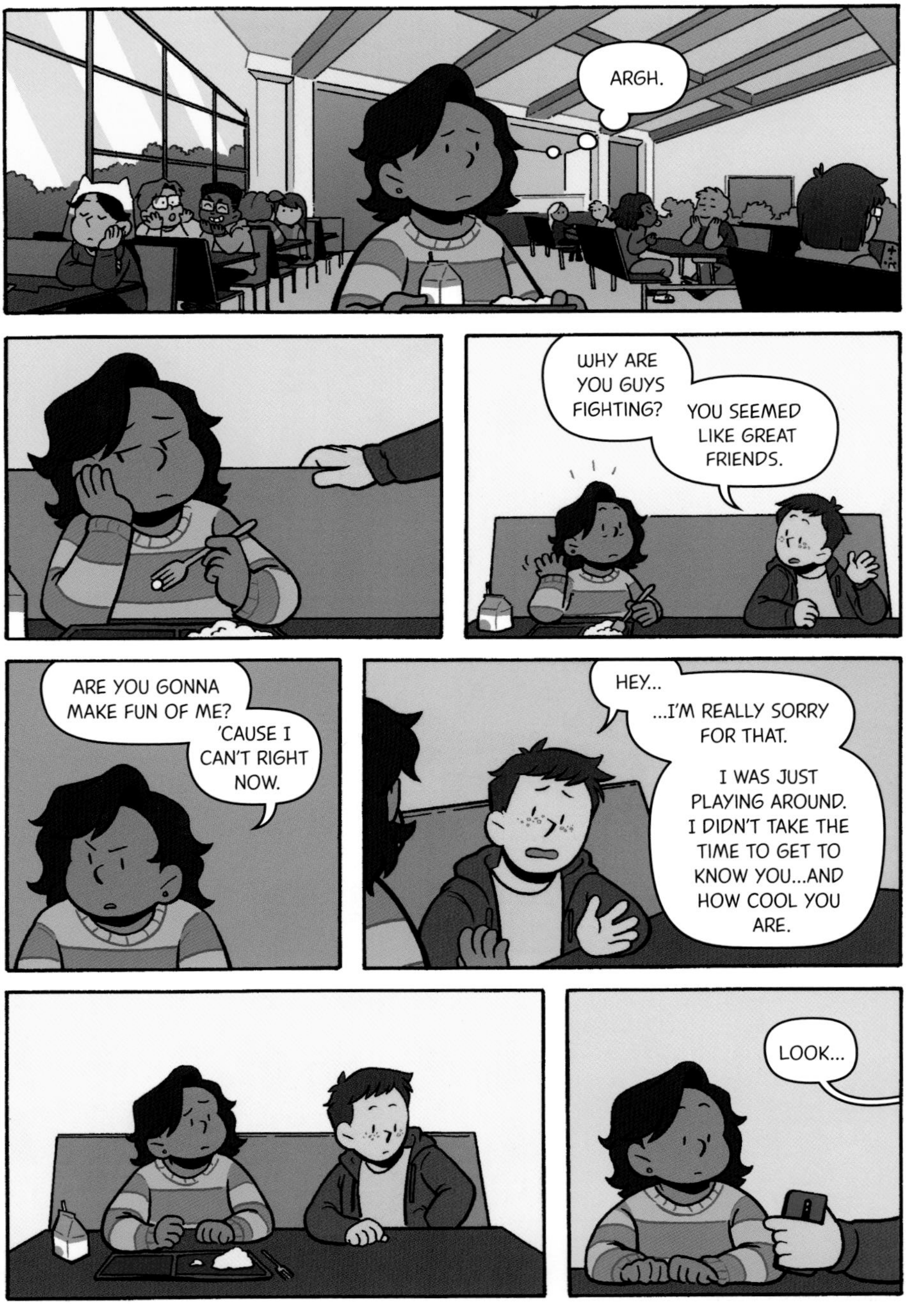
ARGH.
WHY ARE YOU GUYS FIGHTING?
YOU SEEMED LIKE GREAT FRIENDS.
ARE YOU GONNA MAKE FUN OF ME?
'CAUSE I CAN'T RIGHT NOW.
HEY...
...I'M REALLY SORRY FOR THAT.
I WAS JUST PLAYING AROUND. I DIDN'T TAKE THE TIME TO GET TO KNOW YOU...AND HOW COOL YOU ARE.
LOOK...

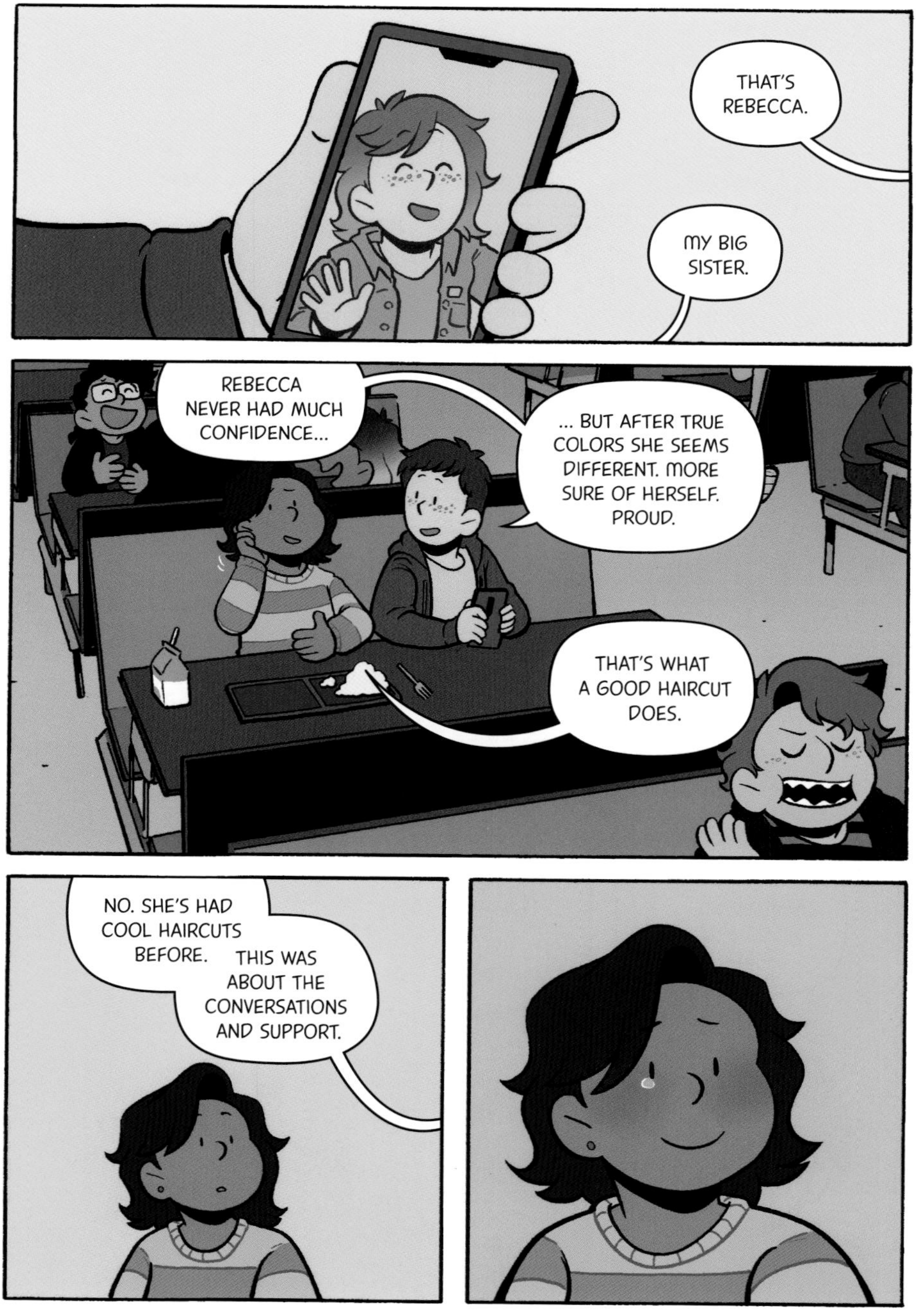
THAT'S REBECCA.
MY BIG SISTER.
REBECCA NEVER HAD MUCH CONFIDENCE...
... BUT AFTER TRUE COLORS SHE SEEMS DIFFERENT. MORE SURE OF HERSELF. PROUD.
THAT'S WHAT A GOOD HAIRCUT DOES.
NO. SHE'S HAD COOL HAIRCUTS BEFORE.
THIS WAS ABOUT THE CONVERSATIONS AND SUPPORT.

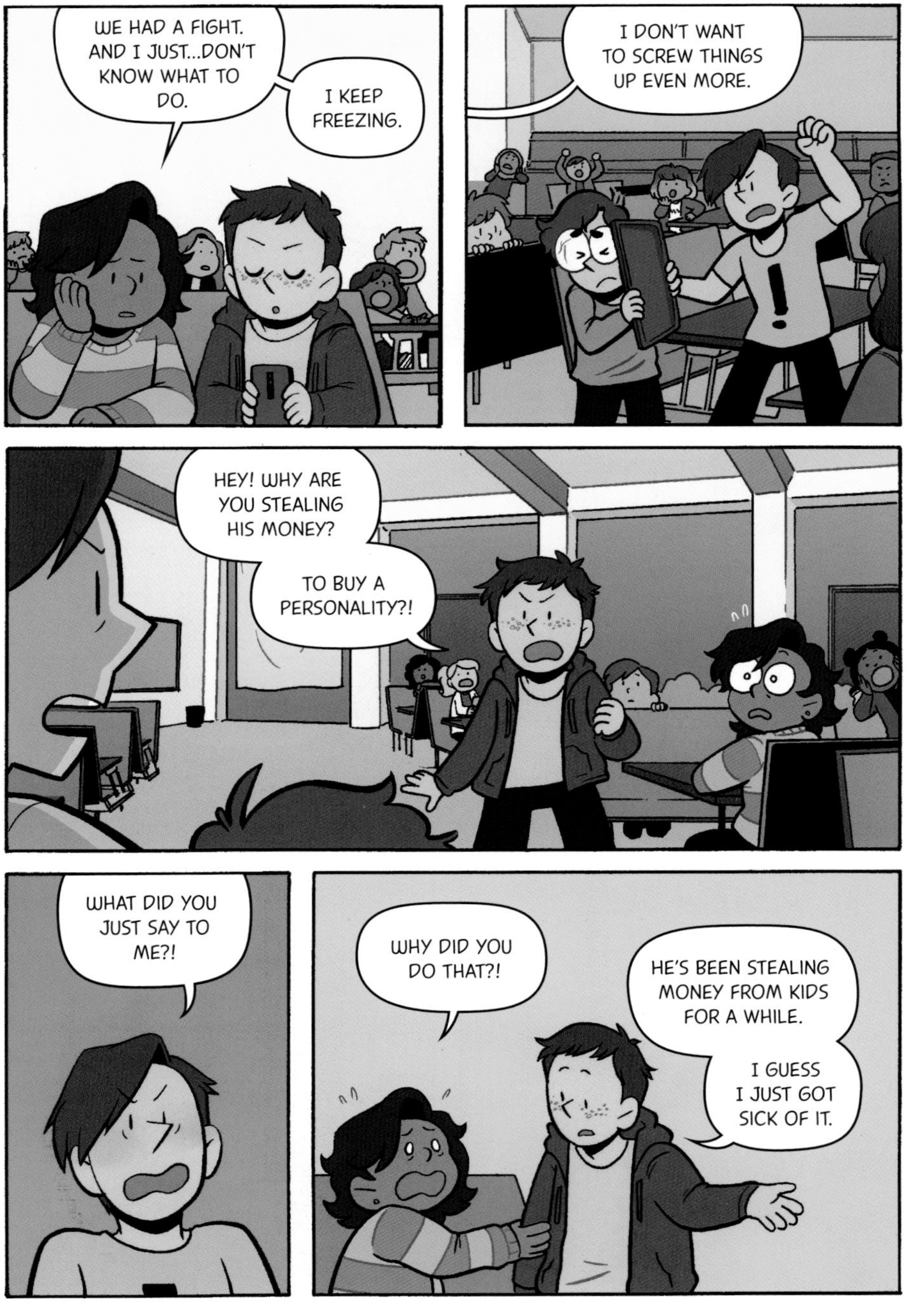
WE HAD A FIGHT. AND I JUST...DON'T KNOW WHAT TO DO.
I KEEP FREEZING.
I DON'T WANT TO SCREW THINGS UP EVEN MORE.
HEY! WHY ARE YOU STEALING HIS MONEY?
TO BUY A PERSONALITY?!
WHAT DID YOU JUST SAY TO ME?!
WHY DID YOU DO THAT?!
HE'S BEEN STEALING MONEY FROM KIDS FOR A WHILE.
I GUESS I JUST GOT SICK OF IT.

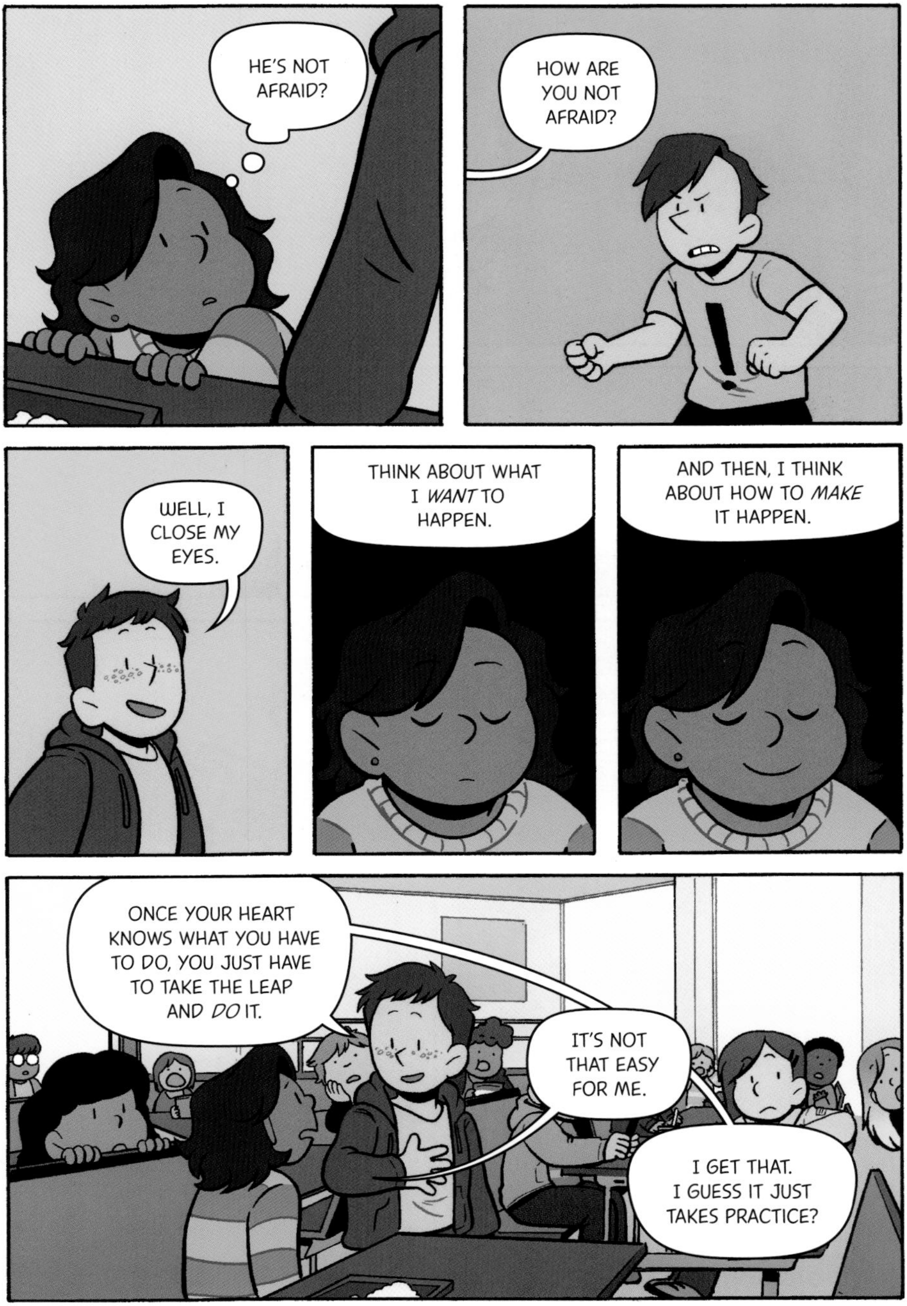
HE'S NOT AFRAID?
HOW ARE YOU NOT AFRAID?
WELL, I CLOSE MY EYES.
THINK ABOUT WHAT I *WANT* TO HAPPEN.
AND THEN, I THINK ABOUT HOW TO *MAKE* IT HAPPEN.
ONCE YOUR HEART KNOWS WHAT YOU HAVE TO DO, YOU JUST HAVE TO TAKE THE LEAP AND *DO* IT.
IT'S NOT THAT EASY FOR ME.
I GET THAT. I GUESS IT JUST TAKES PRACTICE?

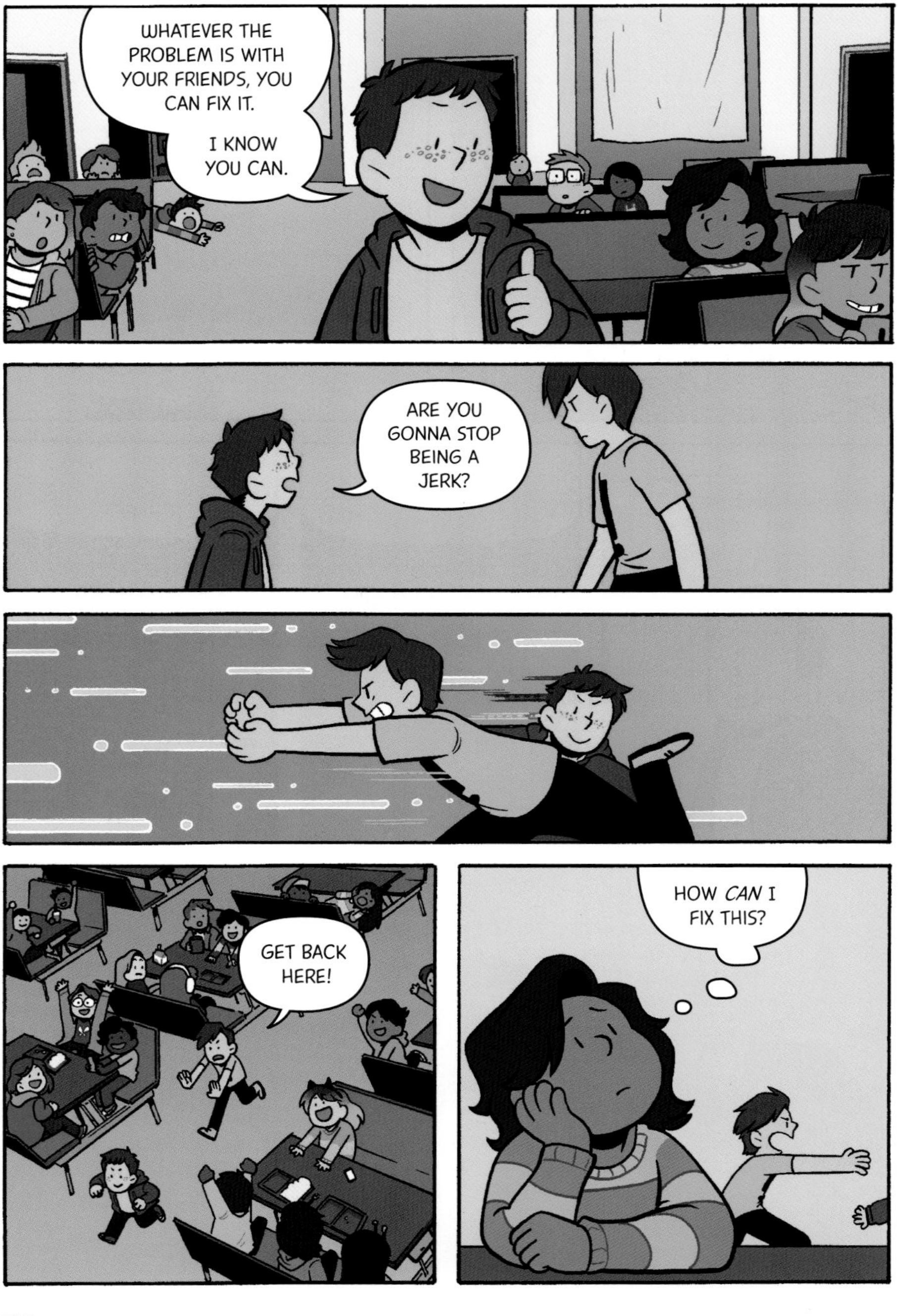
WHATEVER THE PROBLEM IS WITH YOUR FRIENDS, YOU CAN FIX IT.
I KNOW YOU CAN.
ARE YOU GONNA STOP BEING A JERK?
GET BACK HERE!
HOW *CAN* I FIX THIS?

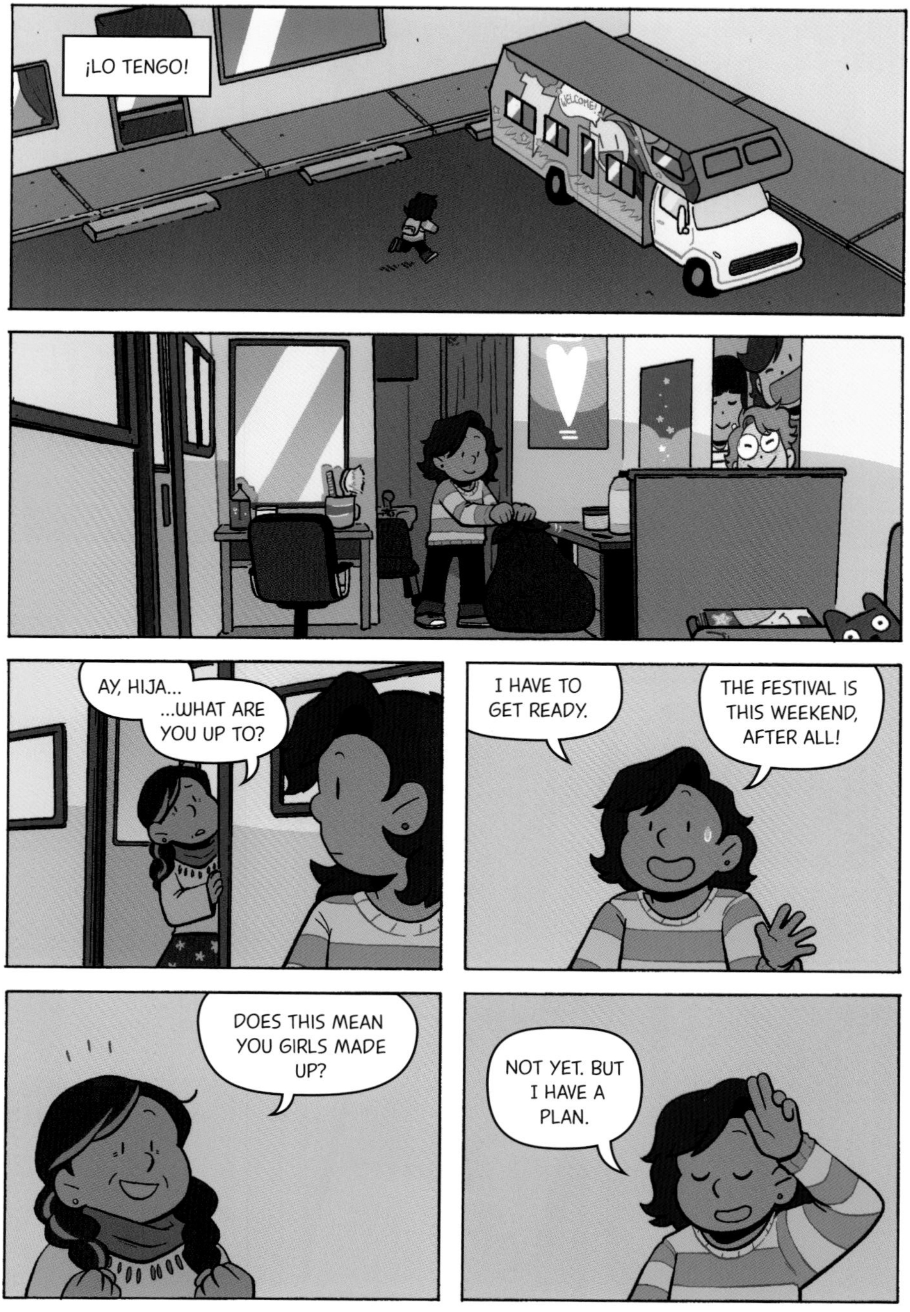
¡LO TENGO!
WELCOME!
AY, HIJA...
...WHAT ARE YOU UP TO?
I HAVE TO GET READY.
THE FESTIVAL IS THIS WEEKEND, AFTER ALL!
DOES THIS MEAN YOU GIRLS MADE UP?
NOT YET. BUT I HAVE A PLAN.

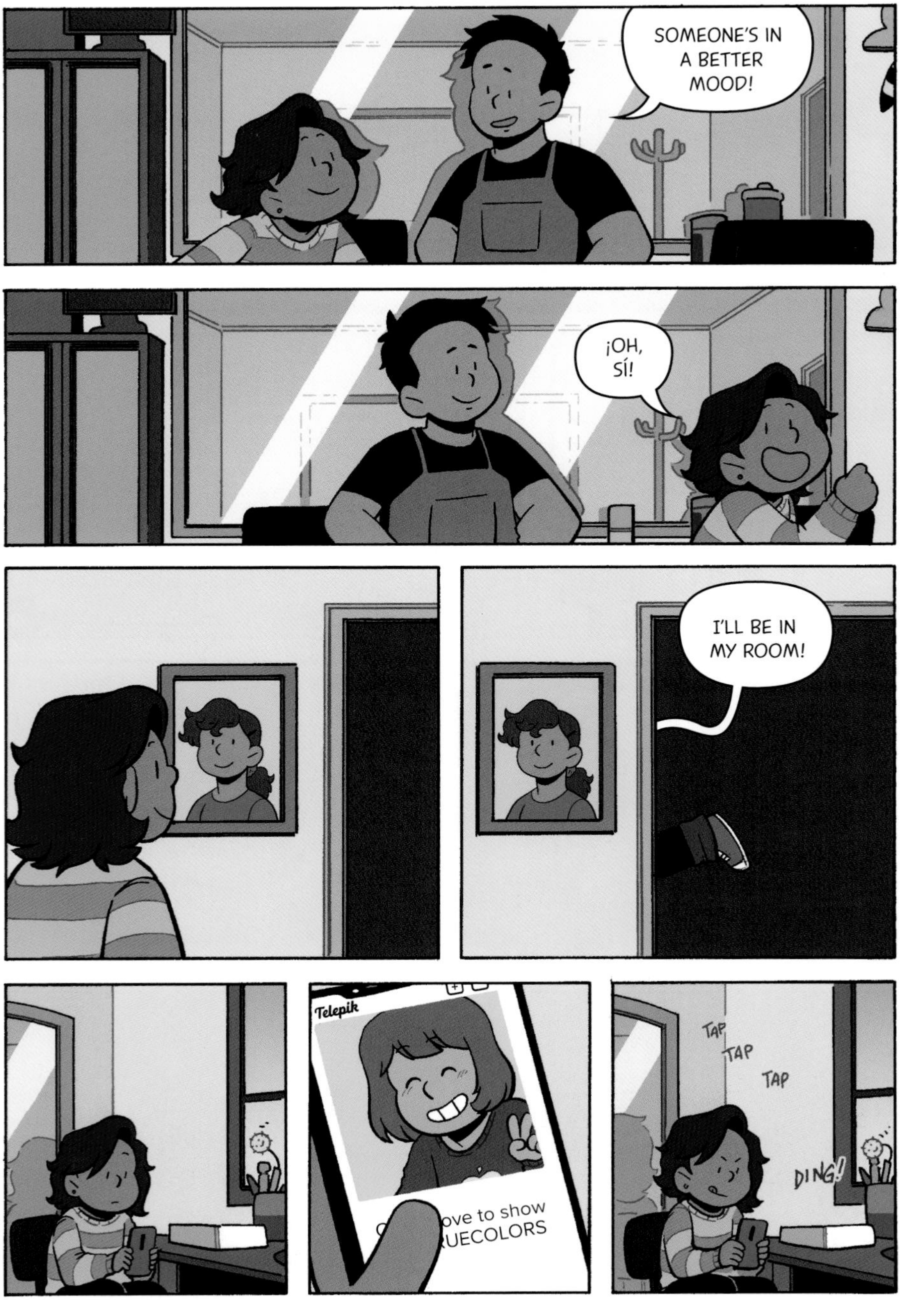
SOMEONE'S IN A BETTER MOOD!
¡OH, SÍ!
I'LL BE IN MY ROOM!
Telepik
ove to show
RUECOLORS
TAP
TAP
TAP
DING!

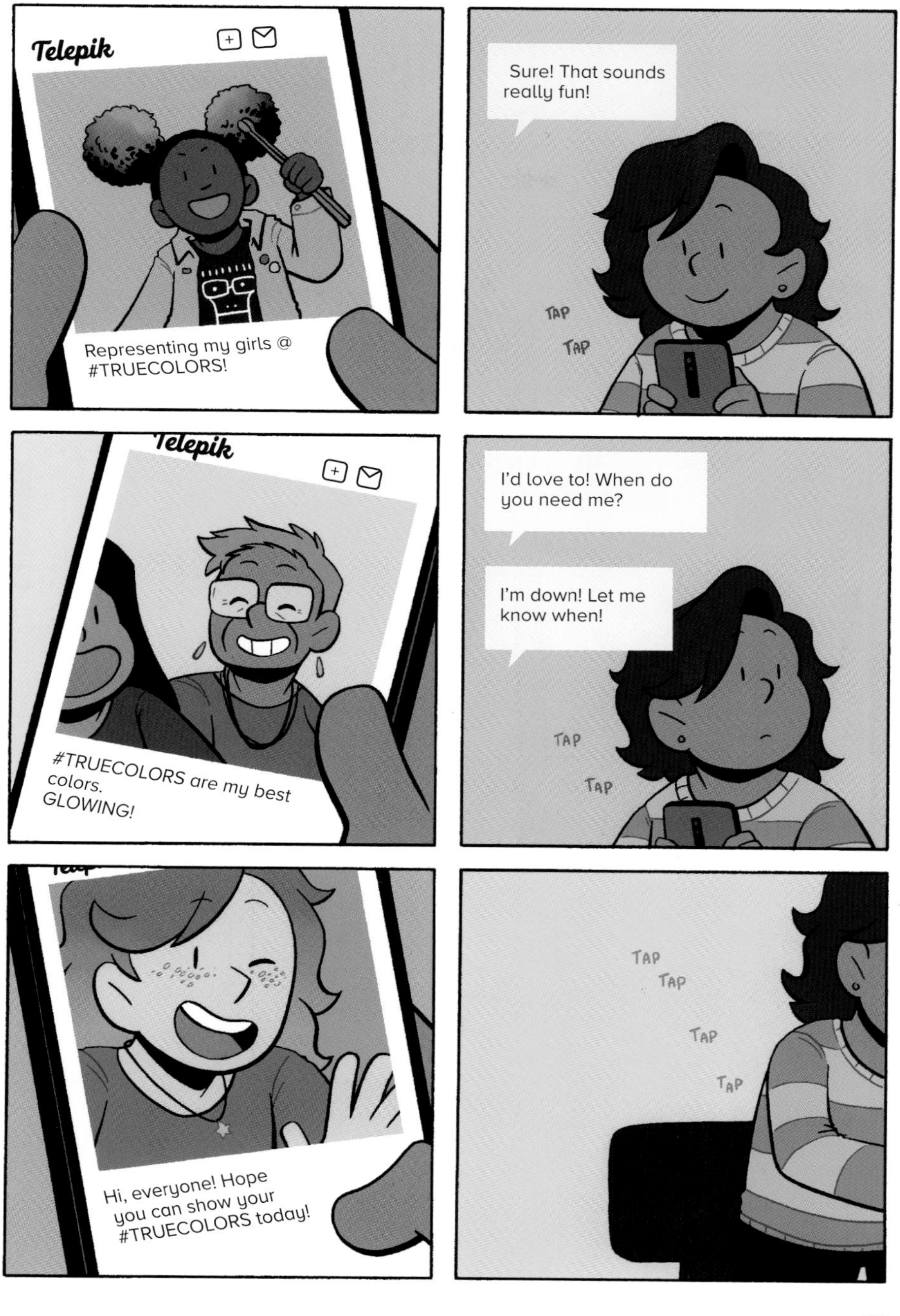
Telepik
Representing my girls @ #TRUECOLORS!
Sure! That sounds really fun!
TAP
TAP
Telepik
#TRUECOLORS are my best colors.
GLOWING!
I'd love to! When do you need me?
I'm down! Let me know when!
TAP
TAP
Hi, everyone! Hope you can show your #TRUECOLORS today!
TAP
TAP
TAP
TAP

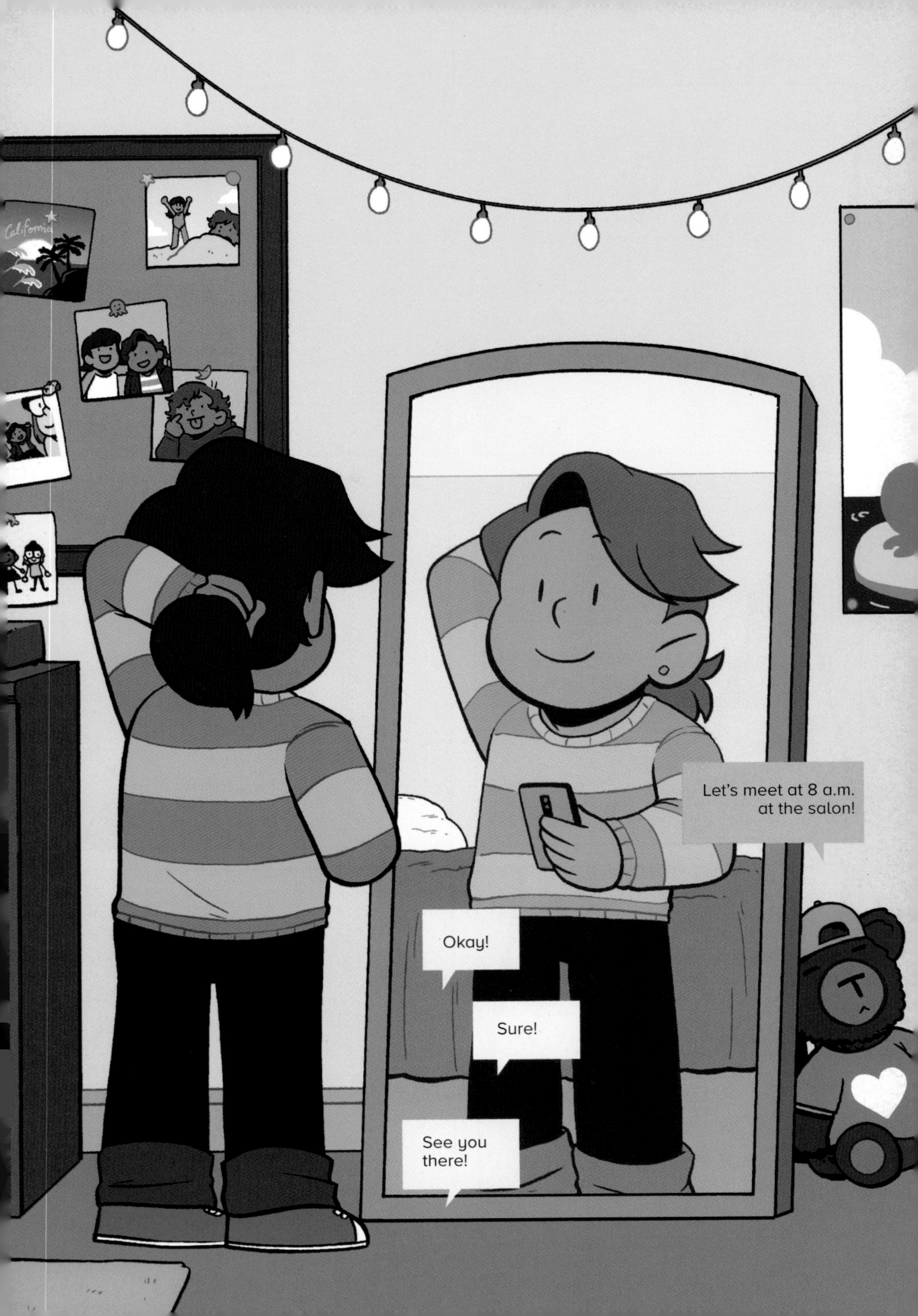

California
Let's meet at 8 a.m. at the salon!
Okay!
Sure!
See you there!

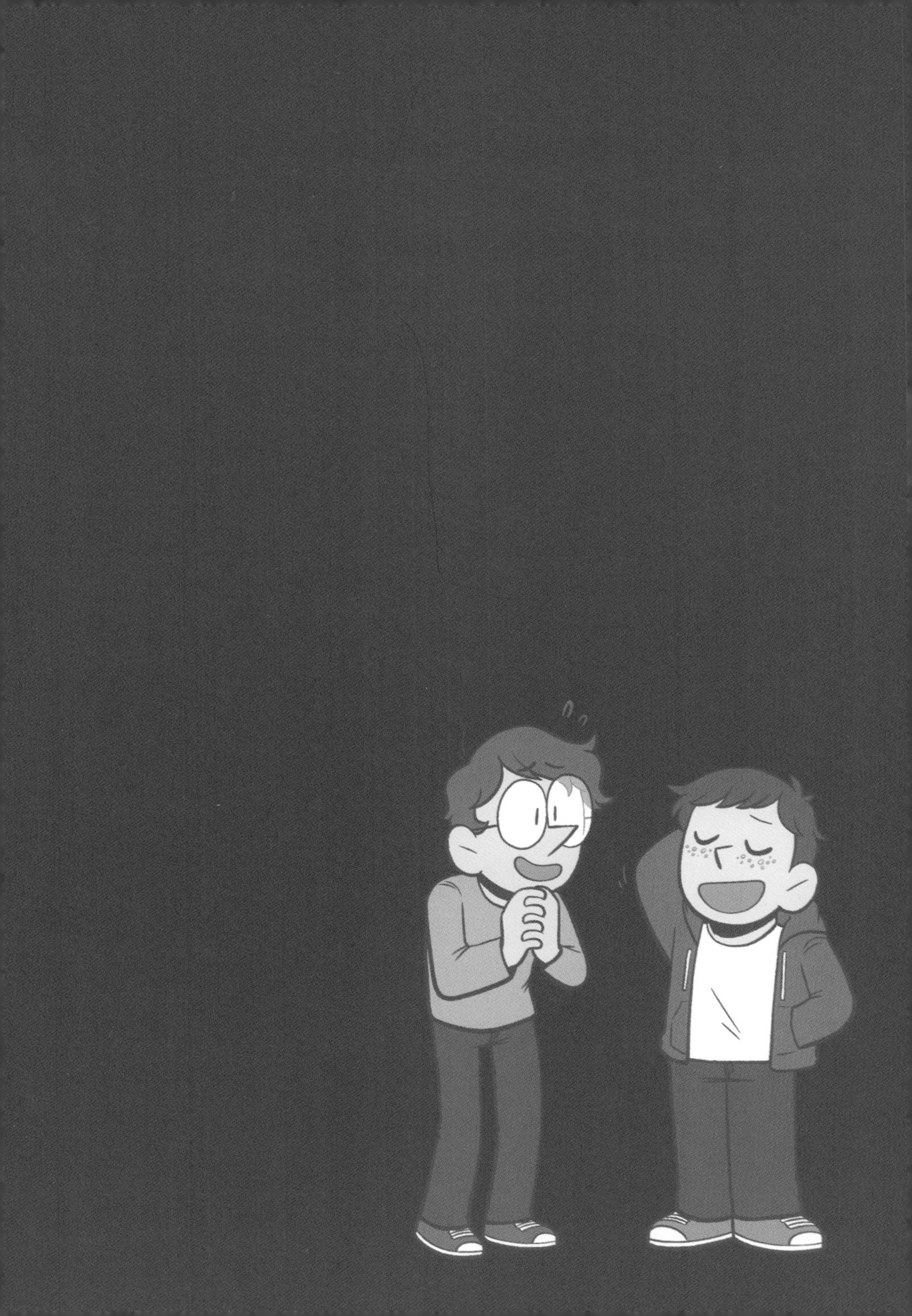

CHAPTER 6

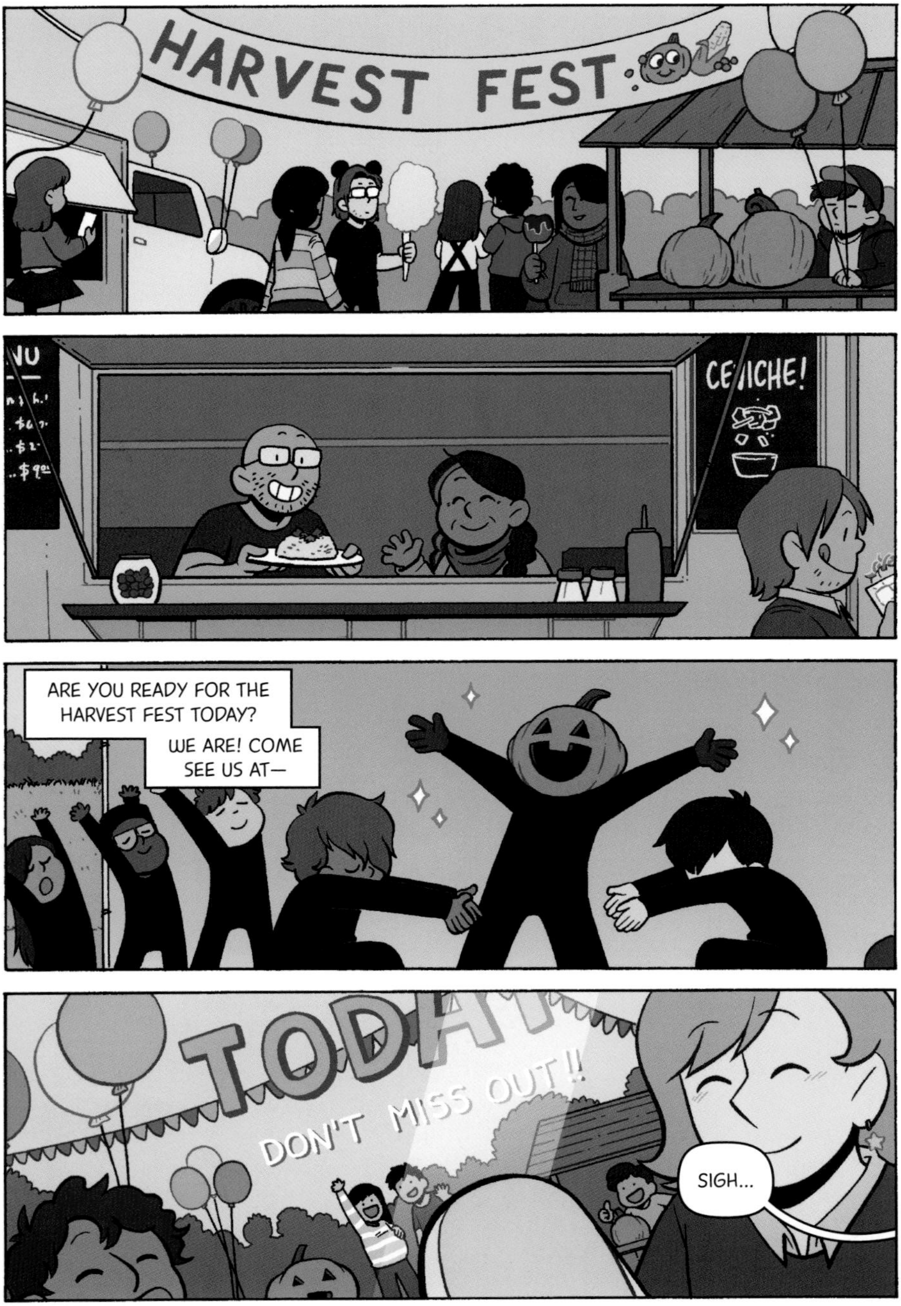

HARVEST FEST
CEVICHE!
ARE YOU READY FOR THE HARVEST FEST TODAY?
WE ARE! COME SEE US AT—
TODA
DON'T MISS OUT!!
SIGH...

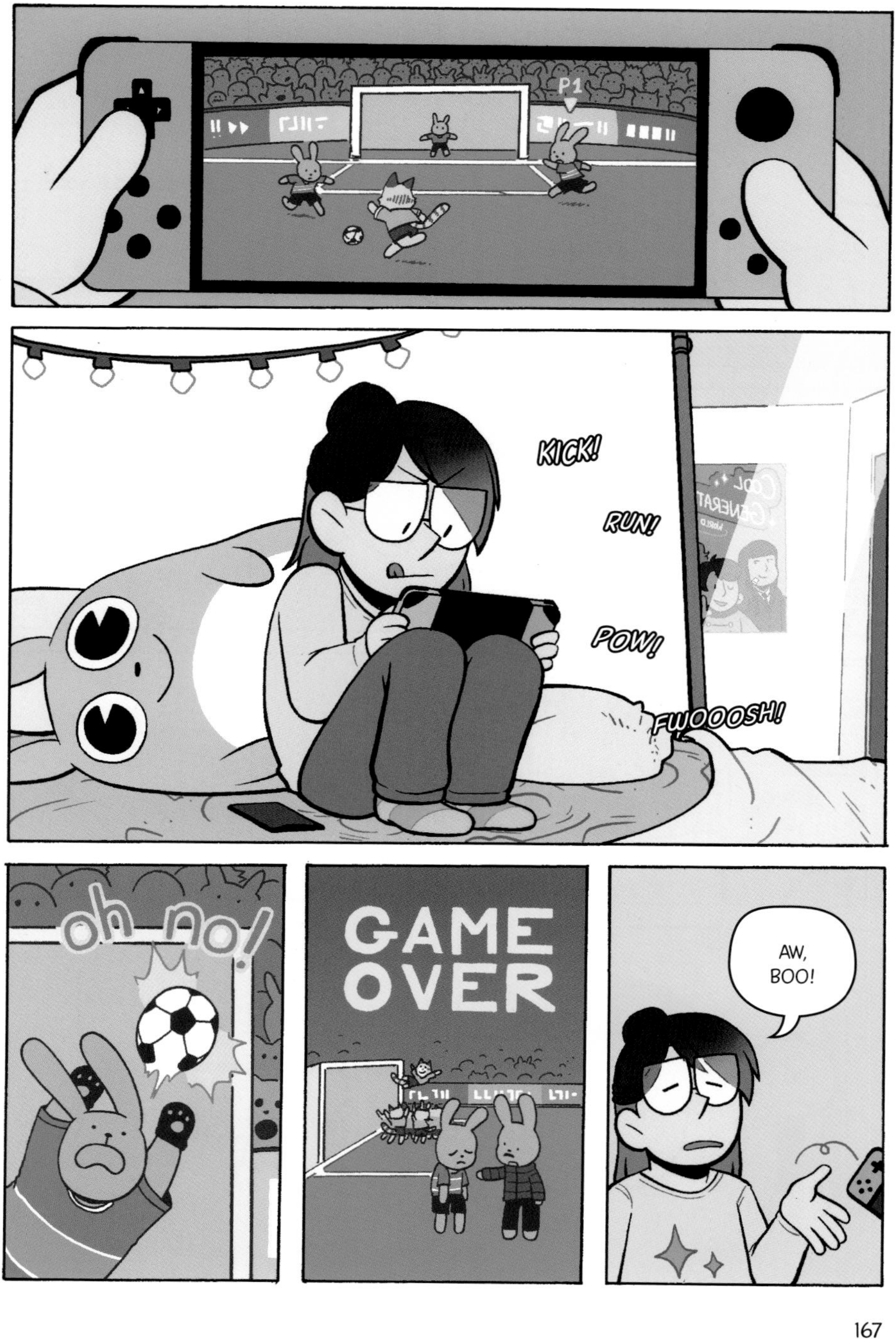
P1
KICK!
RUN!
POW!
FWOOOOSH!
oh no!
GAME OVER
AW, BOO!

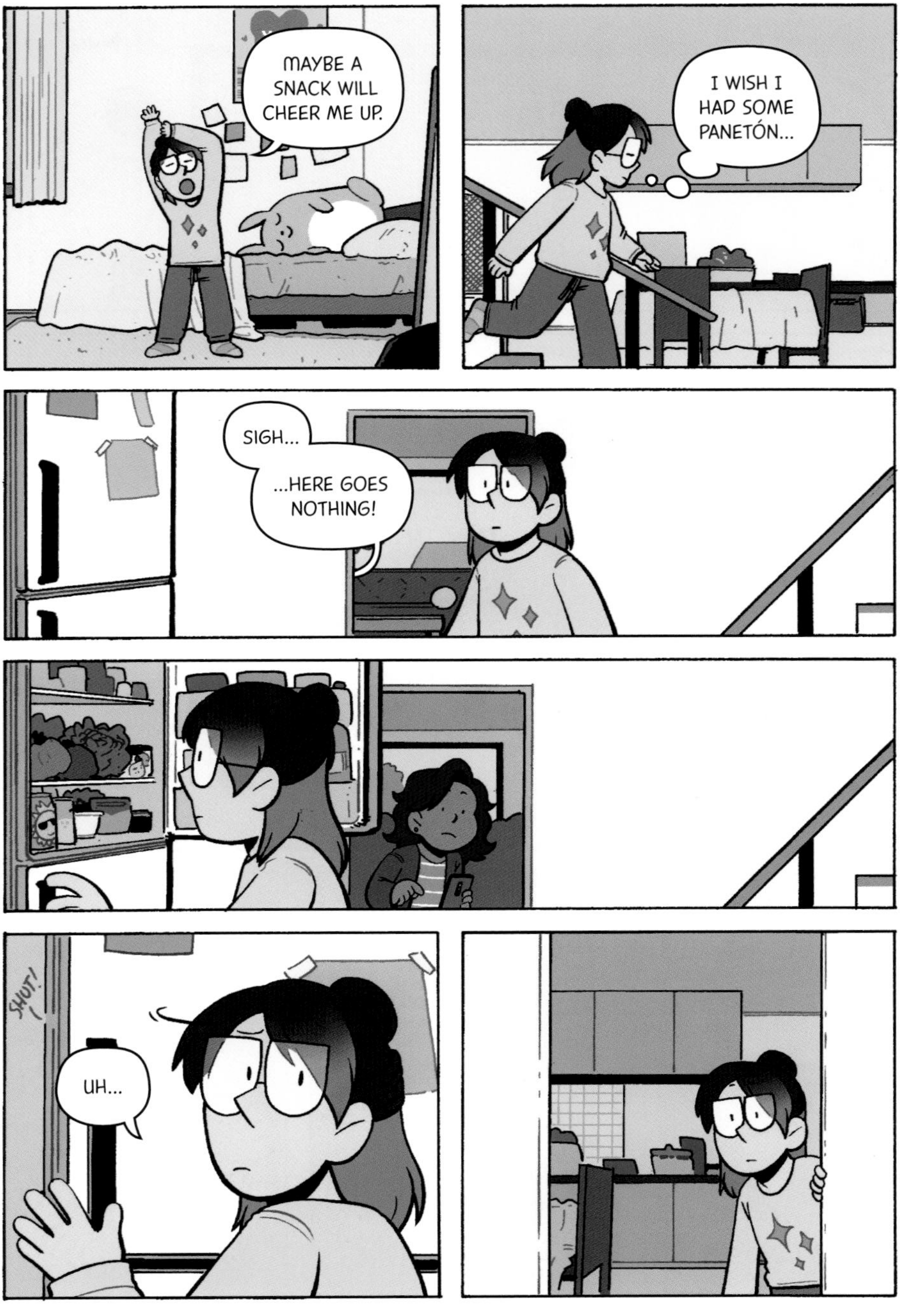
MAYBE A SNACK WILL CHEER ME UP.
I WISH I HAD SOME PANETÓN...
SIGH...
...HERE GOES NOTHING!
SHUT!
UH...

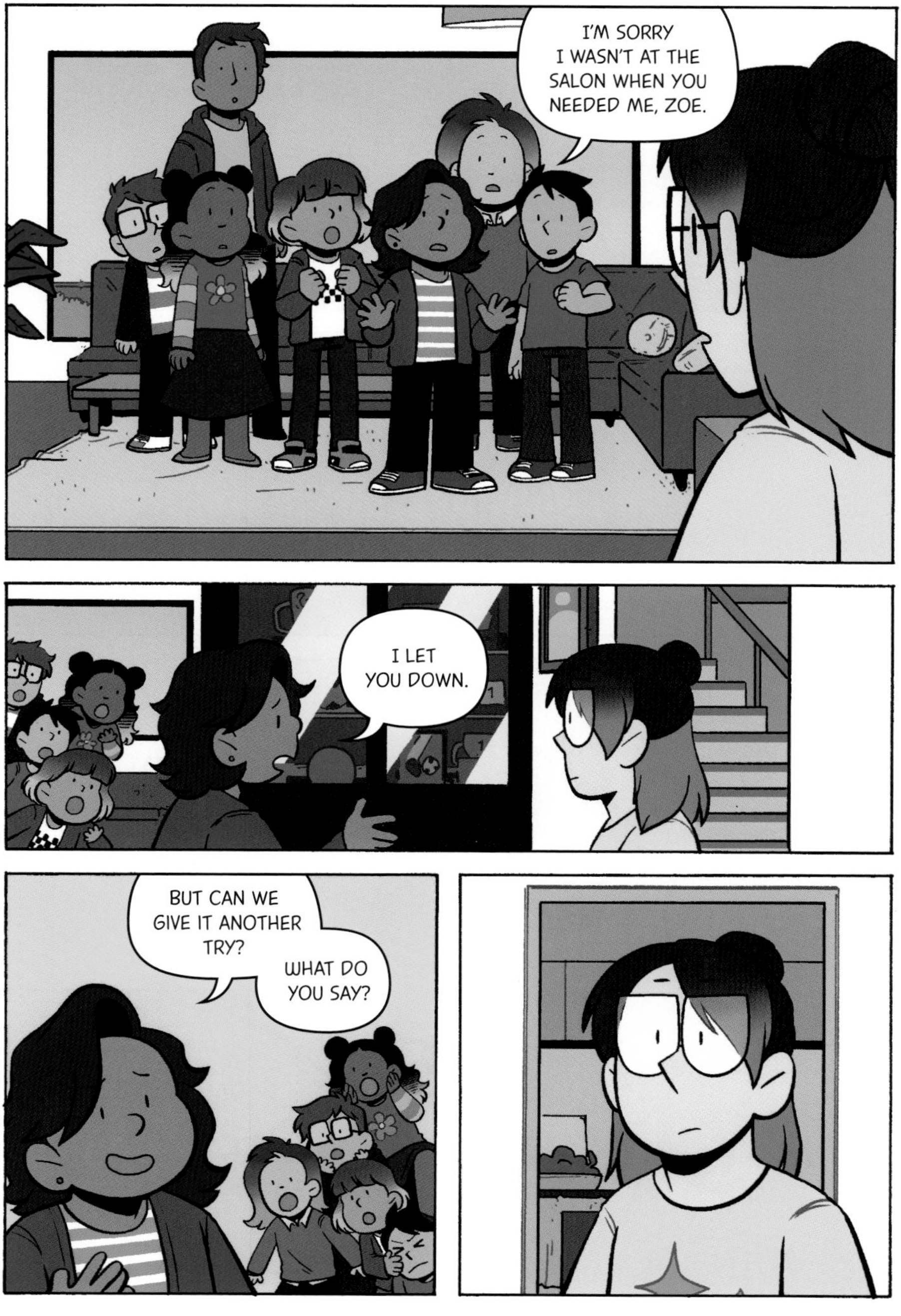
I'M SORRY I WASN'T AT THE SALON WHEN YOU NEEDED ME, ZOE.
I LET YOU DOWN.
BUT CAN WE GIVE IT ANOTHER TRY?
WHAT DO YOU SAY?

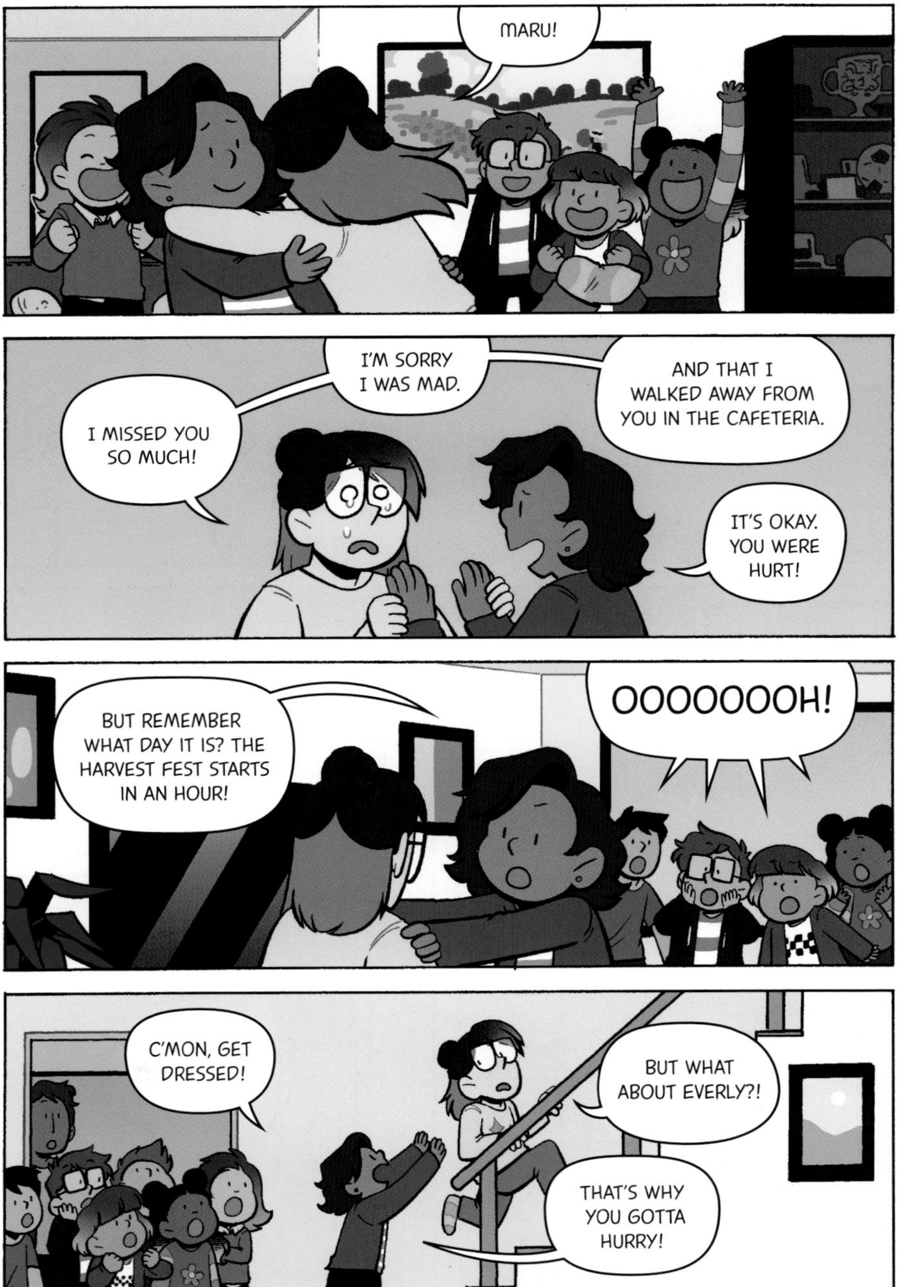
MARU!
I'M SORRY I WAS MAD.
I MISSED YOU SO MUCH!
AND THAT I WALKED AWAY FROM YOU IN THE CAFETERIA.
IT'S OKAY. YOU WERE HURT!
BUT REMEMBER WHAT DAY IT IS? THE HARVEST FEST STARTS IN AN HOUR!
OOOOOOOH!
C'MON, GET DRESSED!
BUT WHAT ABOUT EVERLY?!
THAT'S WHY YOU GOTTA HURRY!

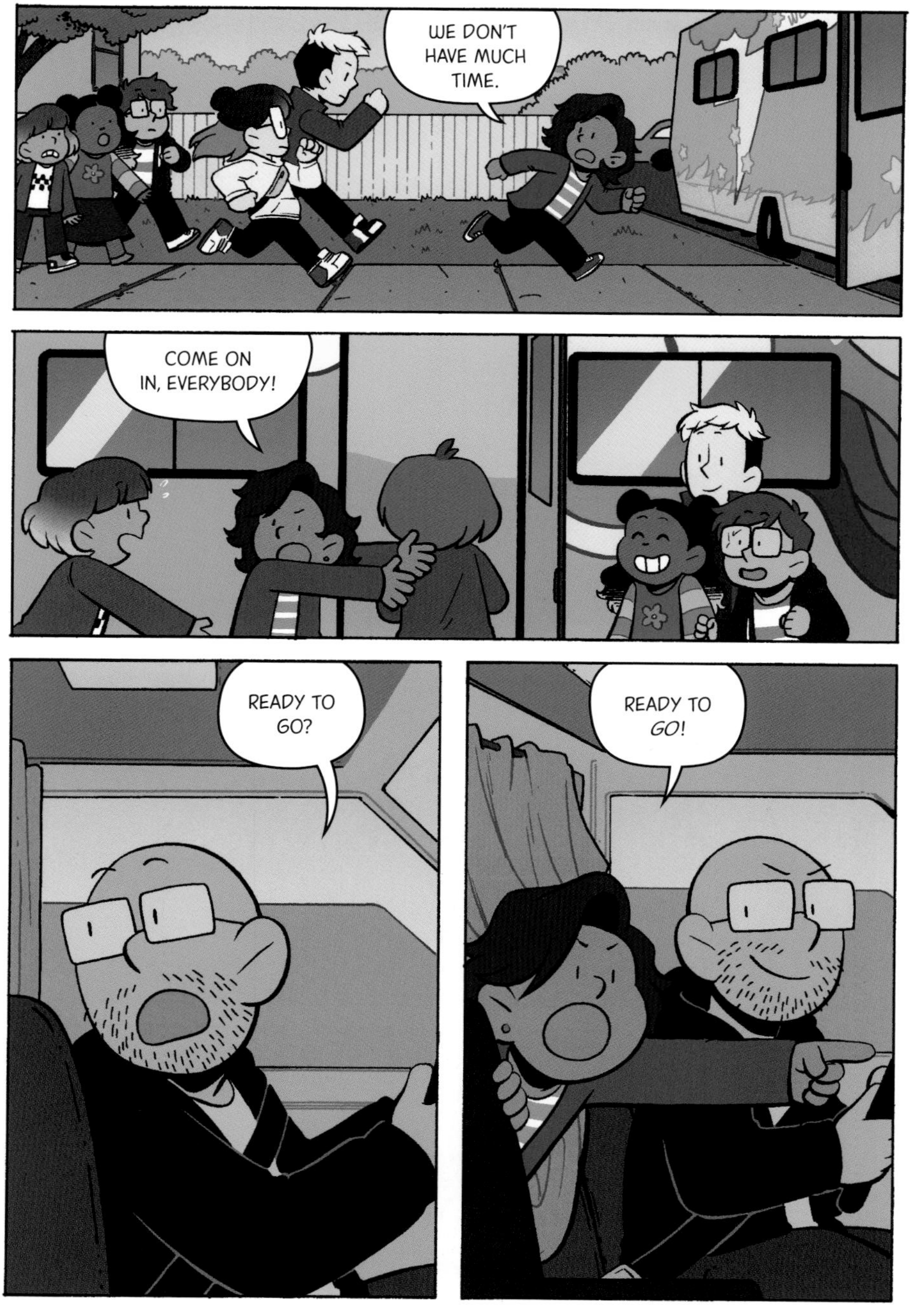
WE DON'T HAVE MUCH TIME.
COME ON IN, EVERYBODY!
READY TO GO?
READY TO *GO*!

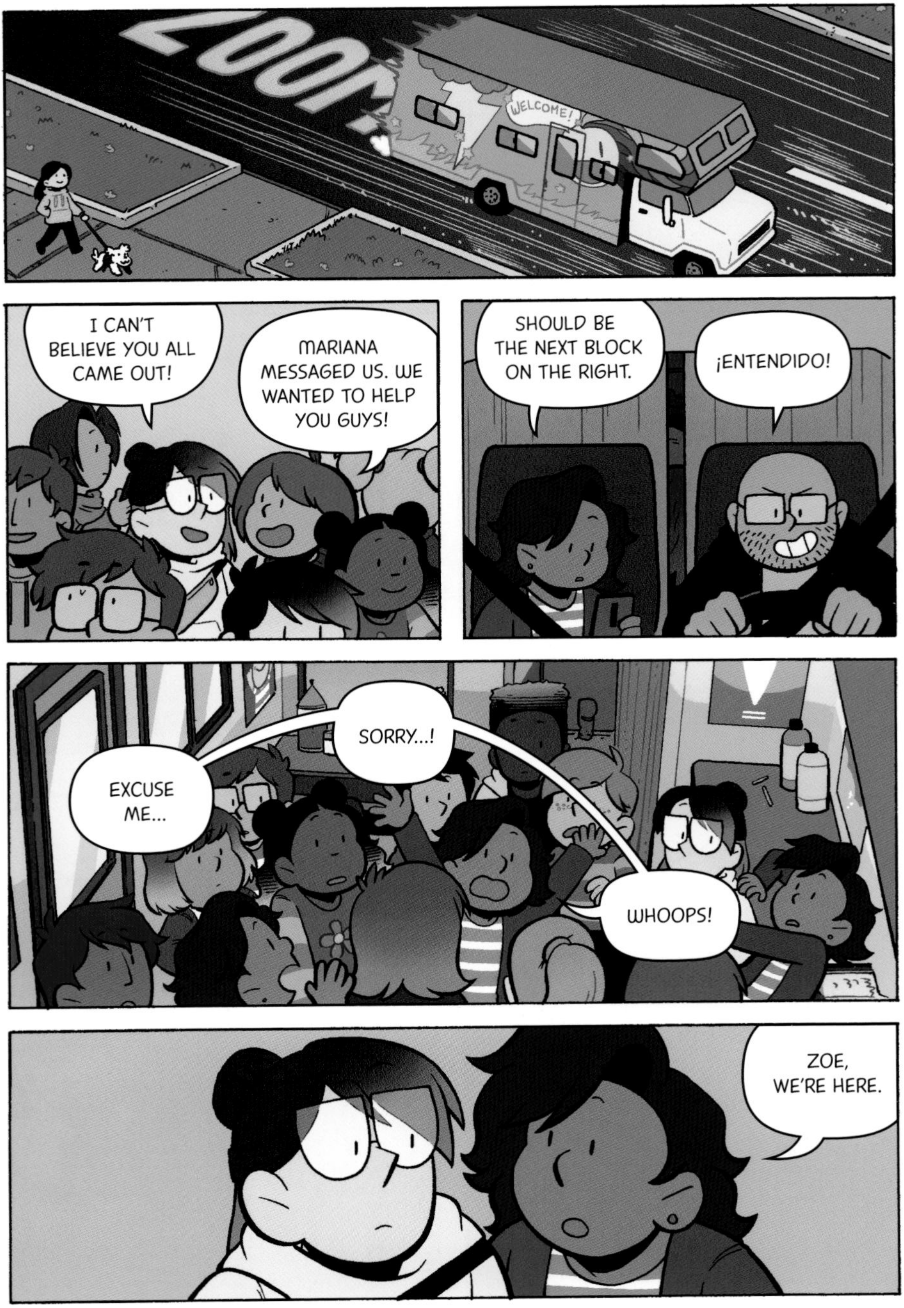
ZOOM
WELCOME!
I CAN'T BELIEVE YOU ALL CAME OUT!
MARIANA MESSAGED US. WE WANTED TO HELP YOU GUYS!
SHOULD BE THE NEXT BLOCK ON THE RIGHT.
¡ENTENDIDO!
EXCUSE ME...
SORRY...!
WHOOPS!
ZOE, WE'RE HERE.

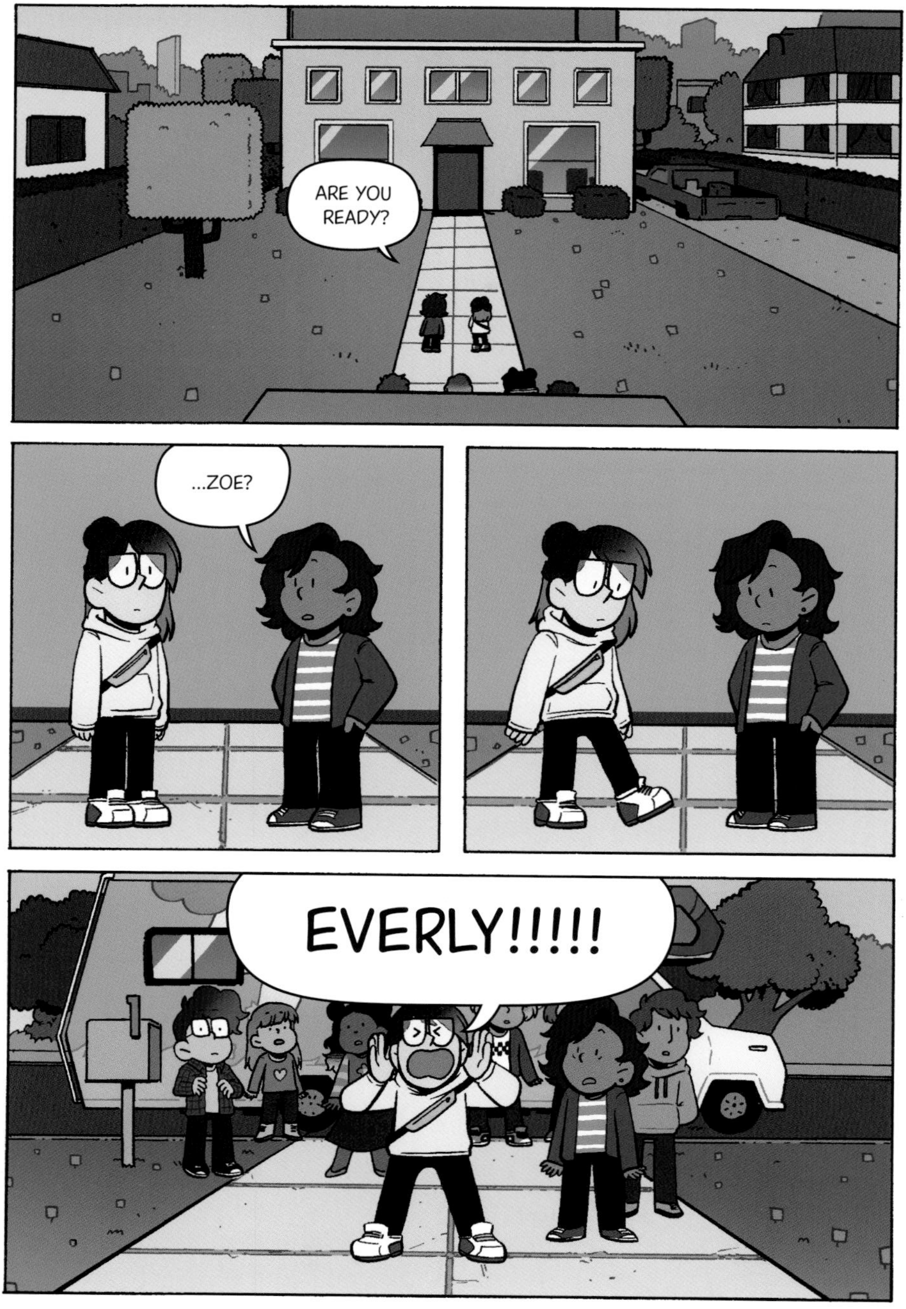
ARE YOU READY?
...ZOE?
EVERLY!!!!!

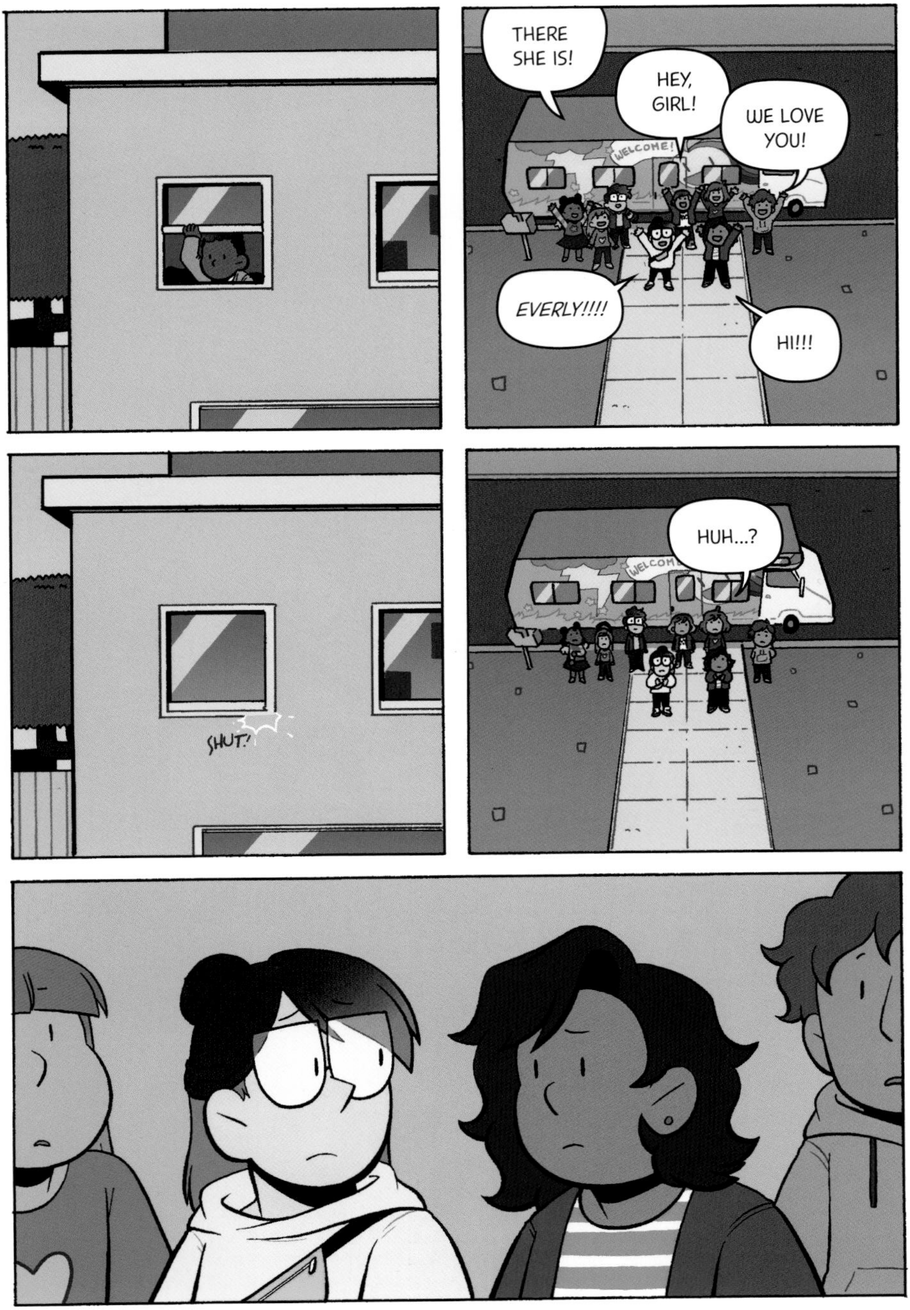
THERE SHE IS!
HEY, GIRL!
WE LOVE YOU!
EVERLY!!!!
HI!!!
SHUT!
HUH...?

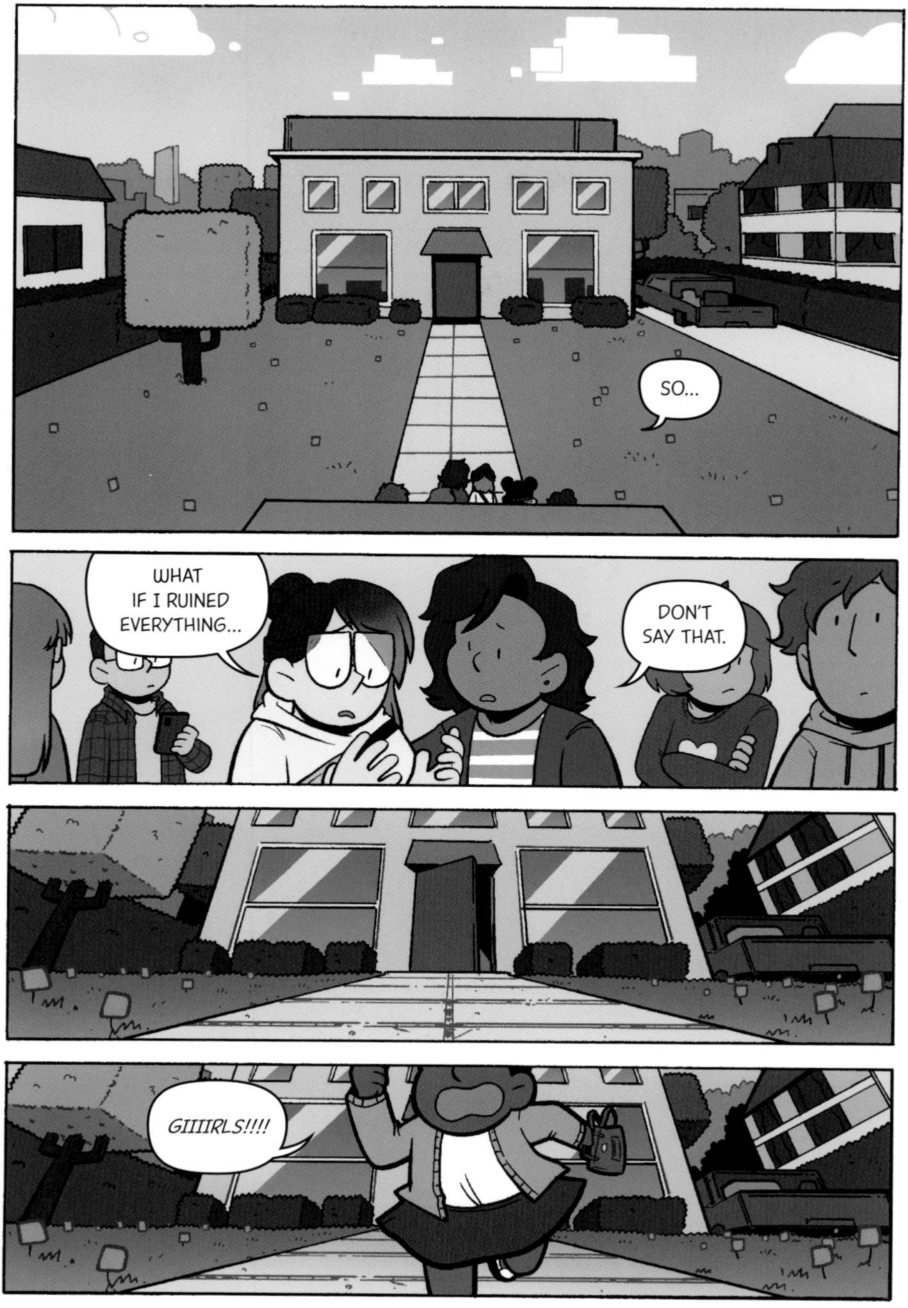
SO...
WHAT IF I RUINED EVERYTHING...
DON'T SAY THAT.
GIIIIRLS!!!!

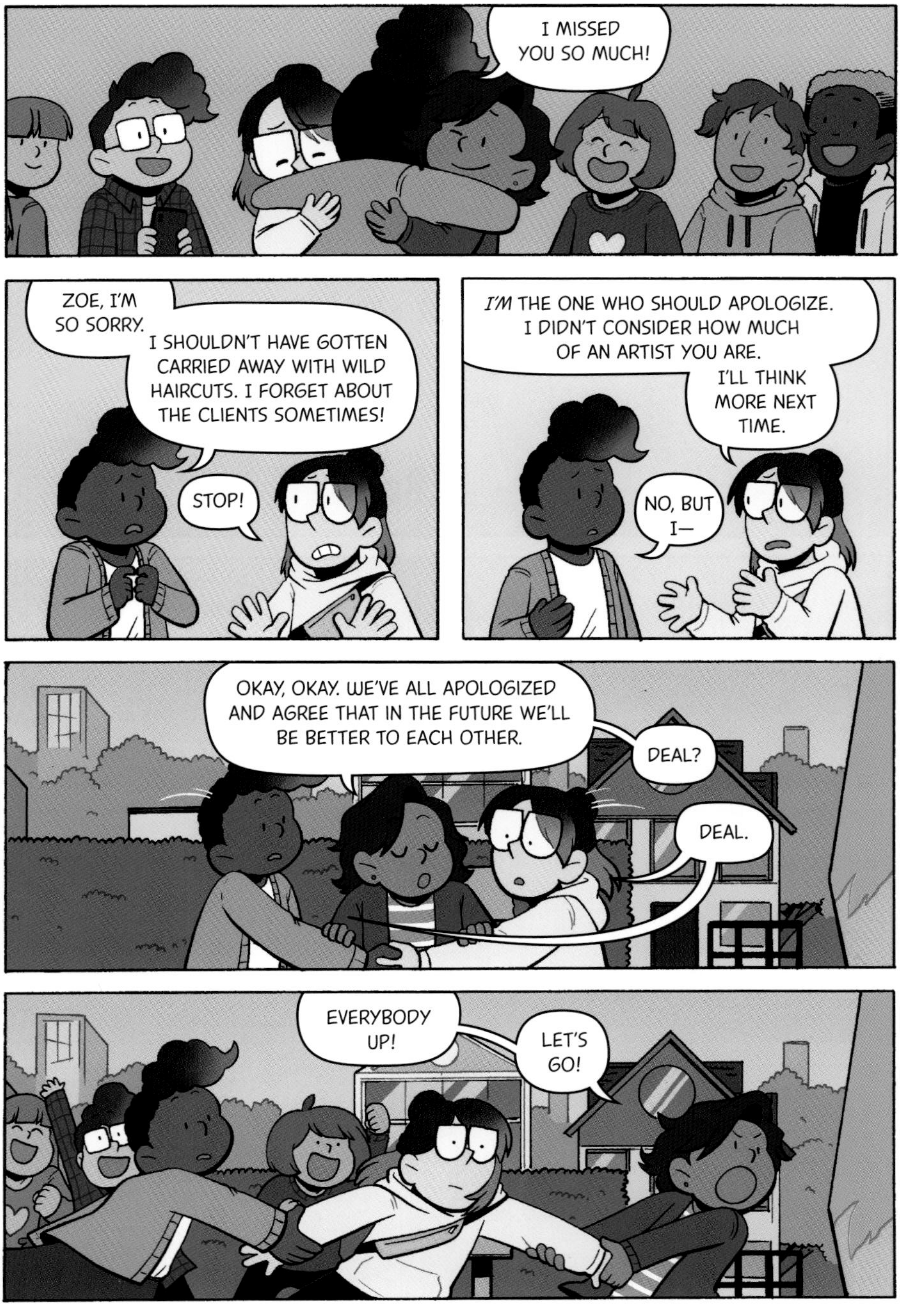
I MISSED YOU SO MUCH!
ZOE, I'M SO SORRY.
I SHOULDN'T HAVE GOTTEN CARRIED AWAY WITH WILD HAIRCUTS. I FORGET ABOUT THE CLIENTS SOMETIMES!
STOP!
I'M THE ONE WHO SHOULD APOLOGIZE. I DIDN'T CONSIDER HOW MUCH OF AN ARTIST YOU ARE.
NO, BUT I—
I'LL THINK MORE NEXT TIME.
OKAY, OKAY. WE'VE ALL APOLOGIZED AND AGREE THAT IN THE FUTURE WE'LL BE BETTER TO EACH OTHER.
DEAL?
DEAL.
EVERYBODY UP!
LET'S GO!

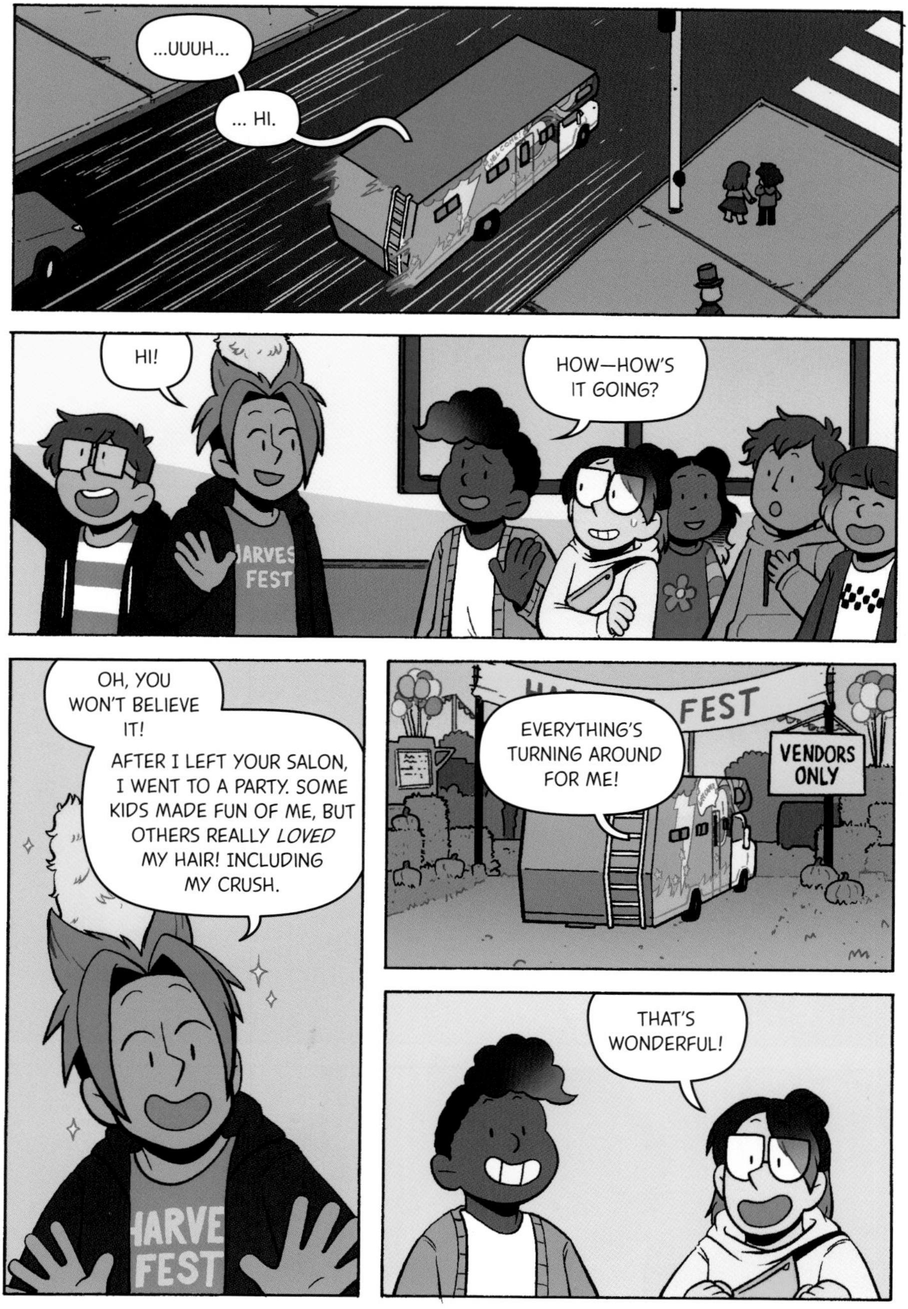
...UUUH...
... HI.
HI!
HOW—HOW'S IT GOING?
HARVEST FEST
OH, YOU WON'T BELIEVE IT!
AFTER I LEFT YOUR SALON, I WENT TO A PARTY. SOME KIDS MADE FUN OF ME, BUT OTHERS REALLY *LOVED* MY HAIR! INCLUDING MY CRUSH.
HARVEST FEST
EVERYTHING'S TURNING AROUND FOR ME!
VENDORS ONLY
THAT'S WONDERFUL!

WE'RE HERE, MARU.

SO WHAT'S NEXT?

INHALE

EXHALE

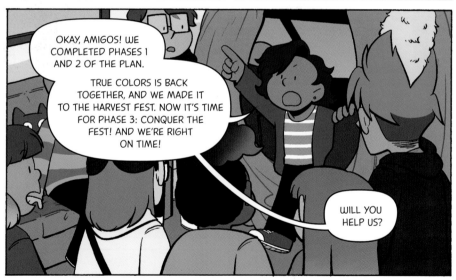

OKAY, AMIGOS! WE COMPLETED PHASES 1 AND 2 OF THE PLAN.

TRUE COLORS IS BACK TOGETHER, AND WE MADE IT TO THE HARVEST FEST. NOW IT'S TIME FOR PHASE 3: CONQUER THE FEST! AND WE'RE RIGHT ON TIME!

WILL YOU HELP US?

YEAAAH!

WOW...

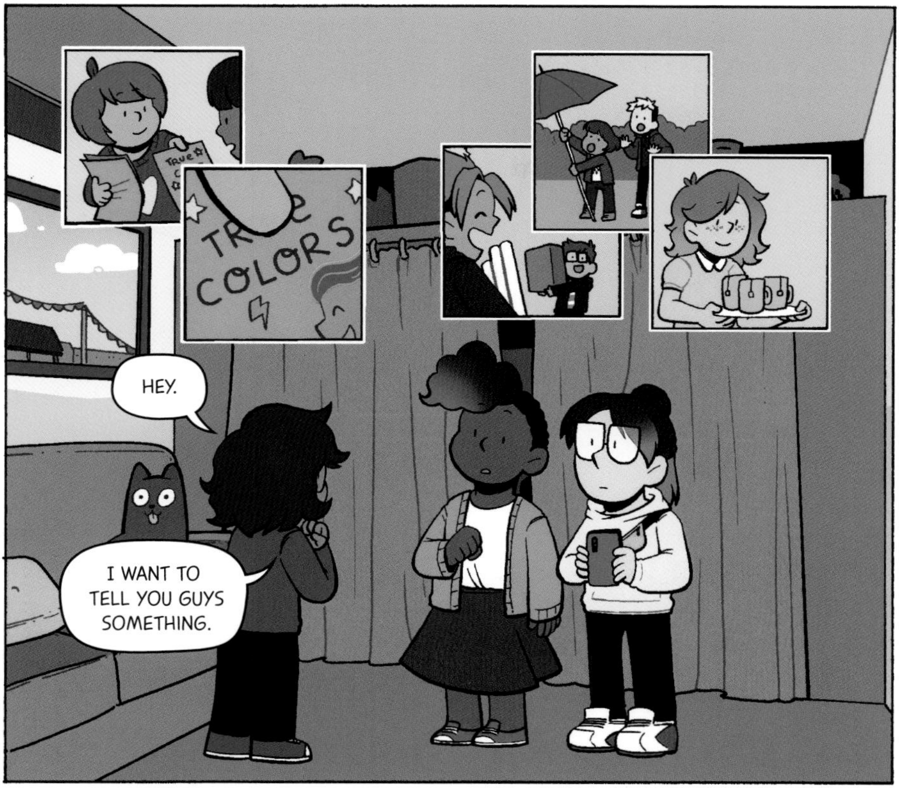
TRUE COLORS
TRUE COLORS
HEY.
I WANT TO TELL YOU GUYS SOMETHING.

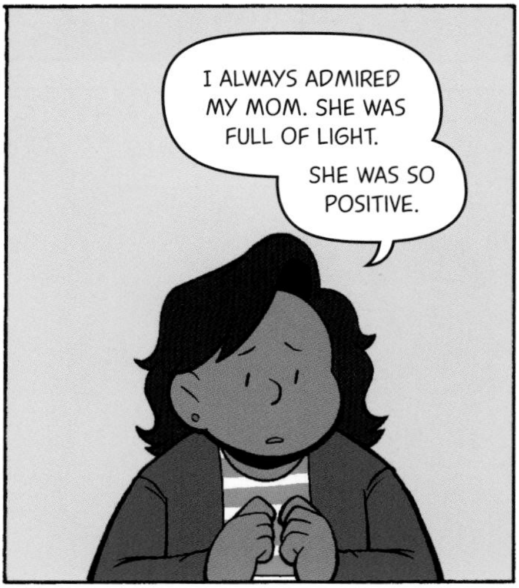
I ALWAYS ADMIRED MY MOM. SHE WAS FULL OF LIGHT.
SHE WAS SO POSITIVE.

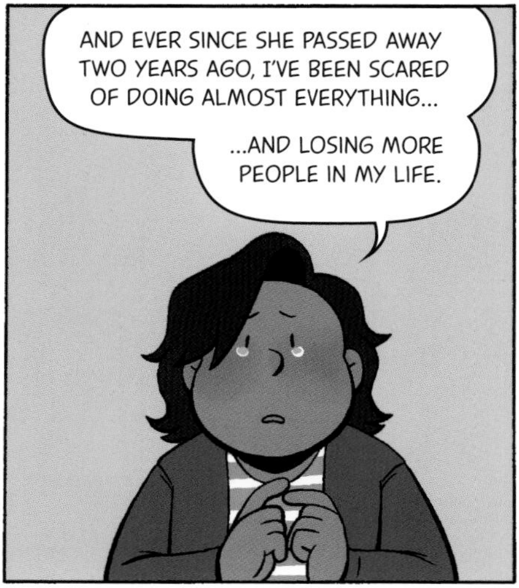
AND EVER SINCE SHE PASSED AWAY TWO YEARS AGO, I'VE BEEN SCARED OF DOING ALMOST EVERYTHING...
...AND LOSING MORE PEOPLE IN MY LIFE.

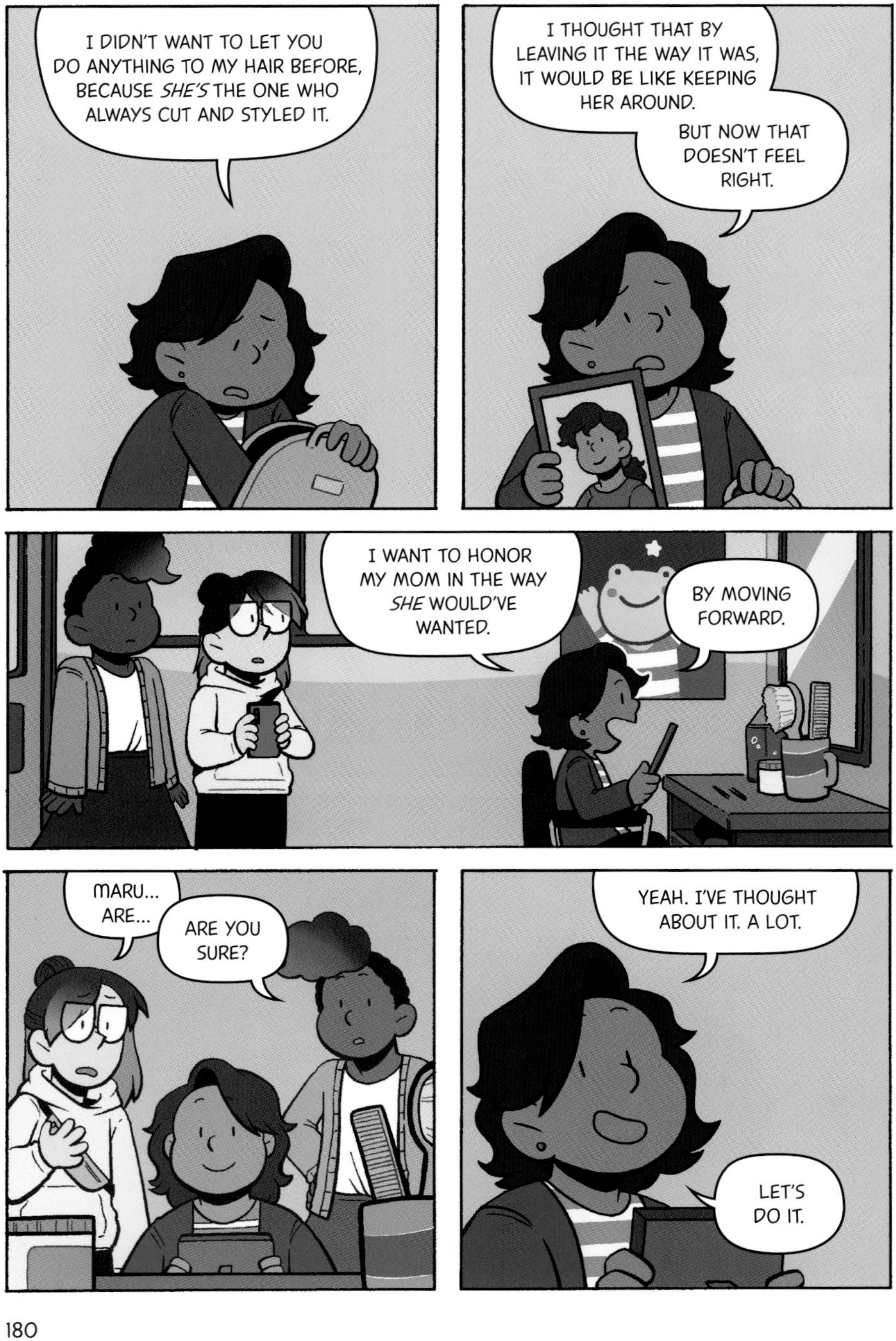
I DIDN'T WANT TO LET YOU DO ANYTHING TO MY HAIR BEFORE, BECAUSE *SHE'S* THE ONE WHO ALWAYS CUT AND STYLED IT.
I THOUGHT THAT BY LEAVING IT THE WAY IT WAS, IT WOULD BE LIKE KEEPING HER AROUND.
BUT NOW THAT DOESN'T FEEL RIGHT.
I WANT TO HONOR MY MOM IN THE WAY *SHE* WOULD'VE WANTED.
BY MOVING FORWARD.
MARU... ARE...
ARE YOU SURE?
YEAH. I'VE THOUGHT ABOUT IT. A LOT.
LET'S DO IT.

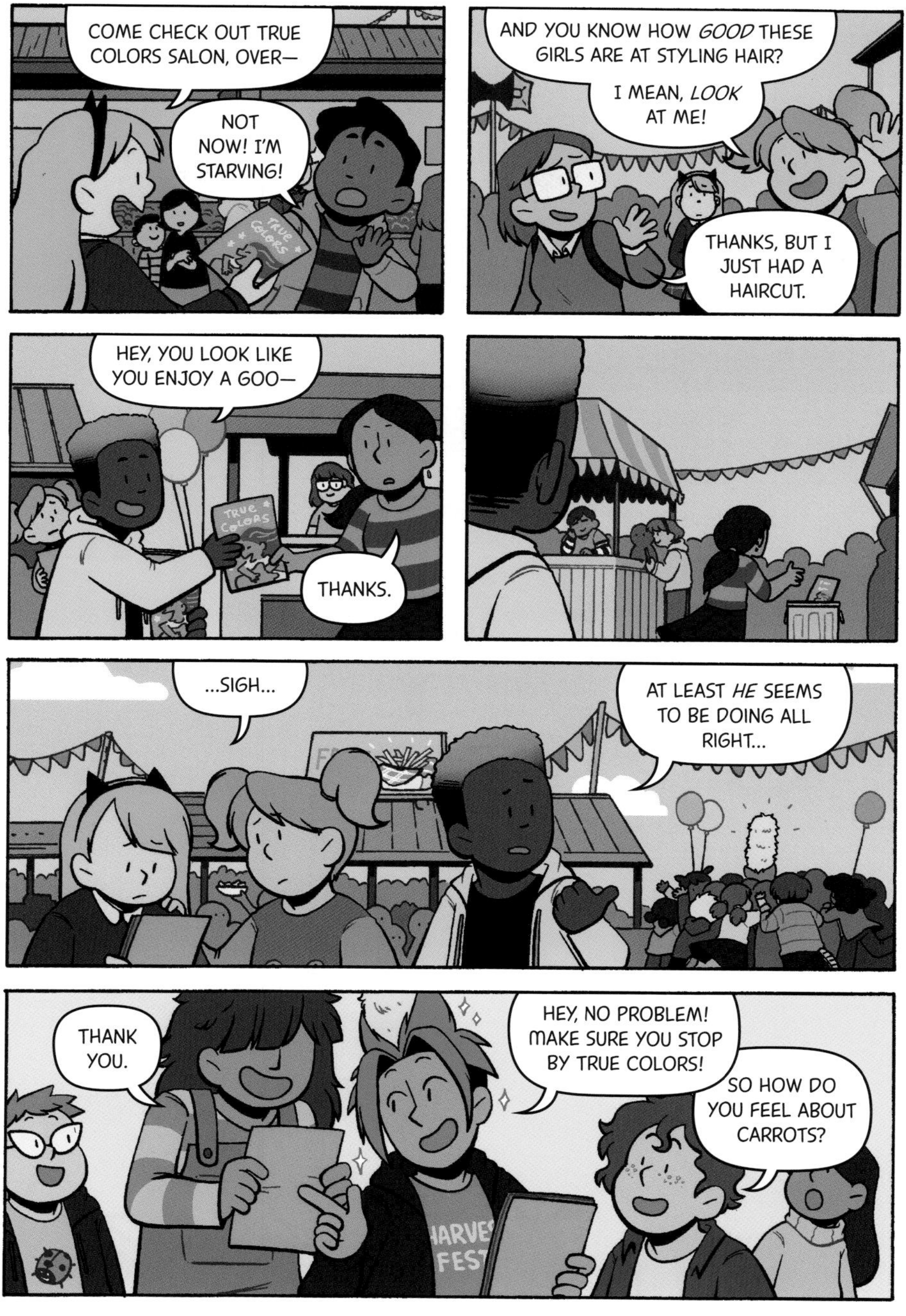
COME CHECK OUT TRUE COLORS SALON, OVER—
NOT NOW! I'M STARVING!
TRUE COLORS
AND YOU KNOW HOW *GOOD* THESE GIRLS ARE AT STYLING HAIR?
I MEAN, *LOOK* AT ME!
THANKS, BUT I JUST HAD A HAIRCUT.
HEY, YOU LOOK LIKE YOU ENJOY A GOO—
TRUE COLORS
THANKS.
...SIGH...
AT LEAST *HE* SEEMS TO BE DOING ALL RIGHT...
THANK YOU.
HEY, NO PROBLEM! MAKE SURE YOU STOP BY TRUE COLORS!
SO HOW DO YOU FEEL ABOUT CARROTS?

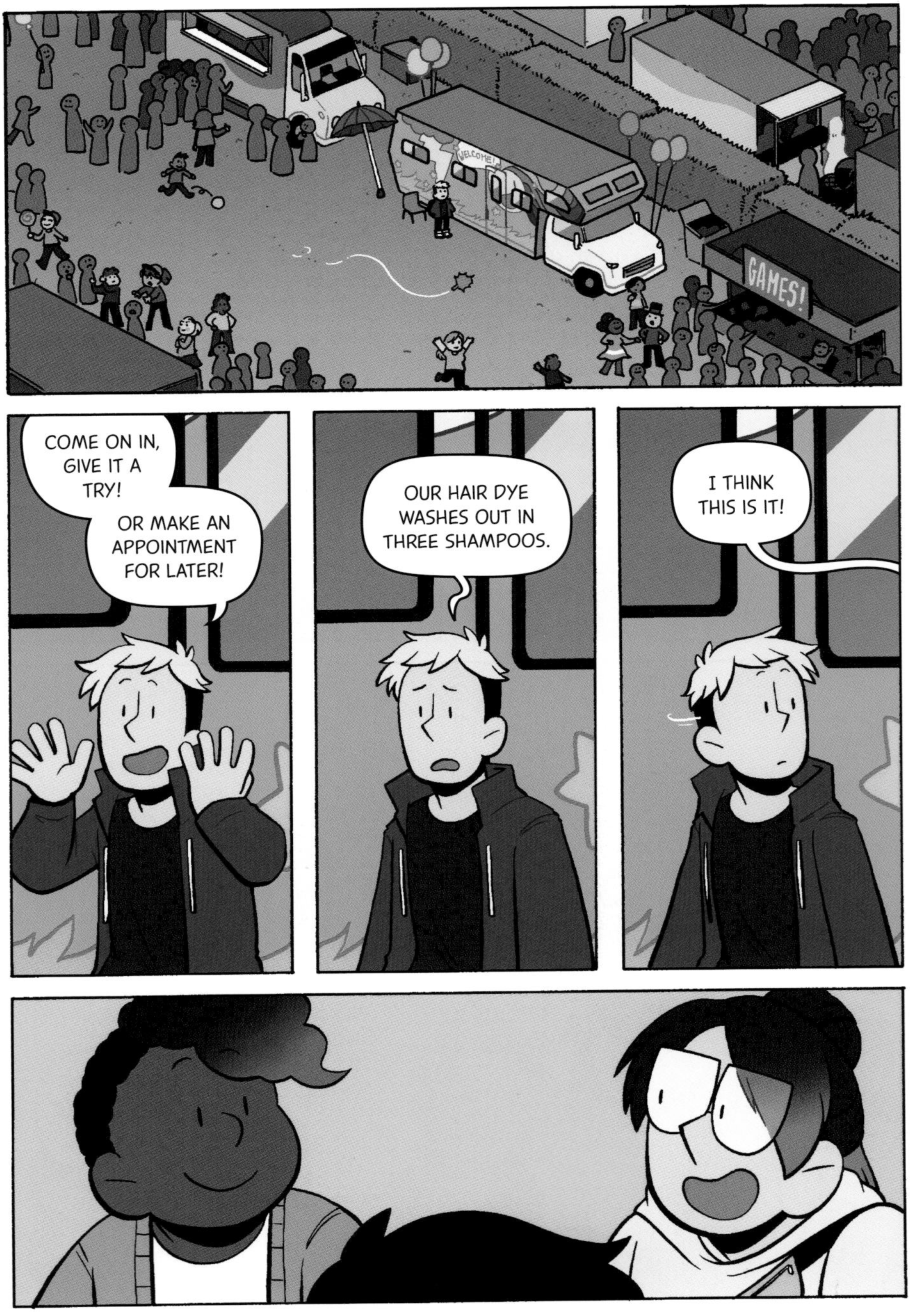
WELCOME!
GAMES!
COME ON IN, GIVE IT A TRY!
OR MAKE AN APPOINTMENT FOR LATER!
OUR HAIR DYE WASHES OUT IN THREE SHAMPOOS.
I THINK THIS IS IT!

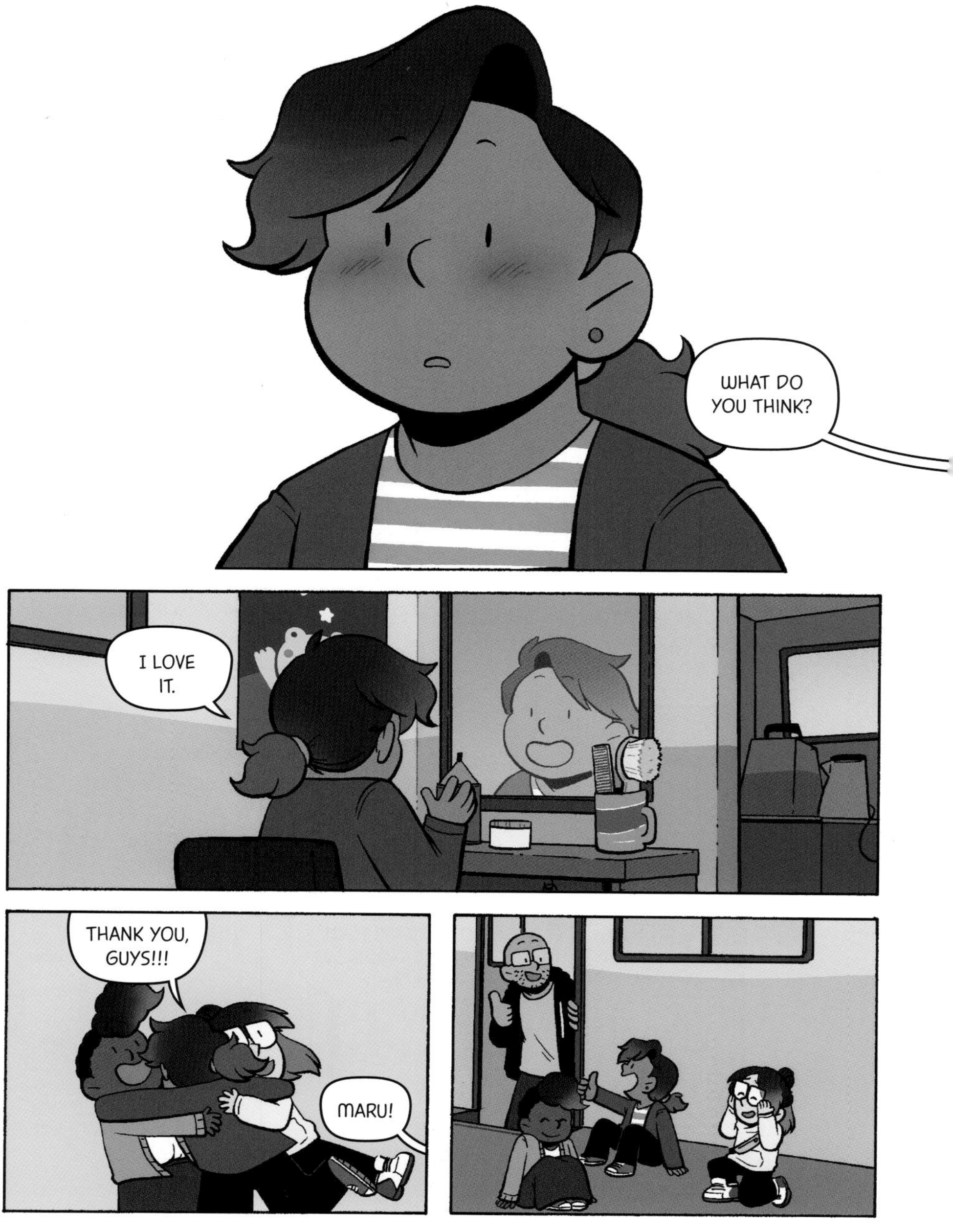
WHAT DO YOU THINK?
I LOVE IT.
THANK YOU, GUYS!!!
MARU!

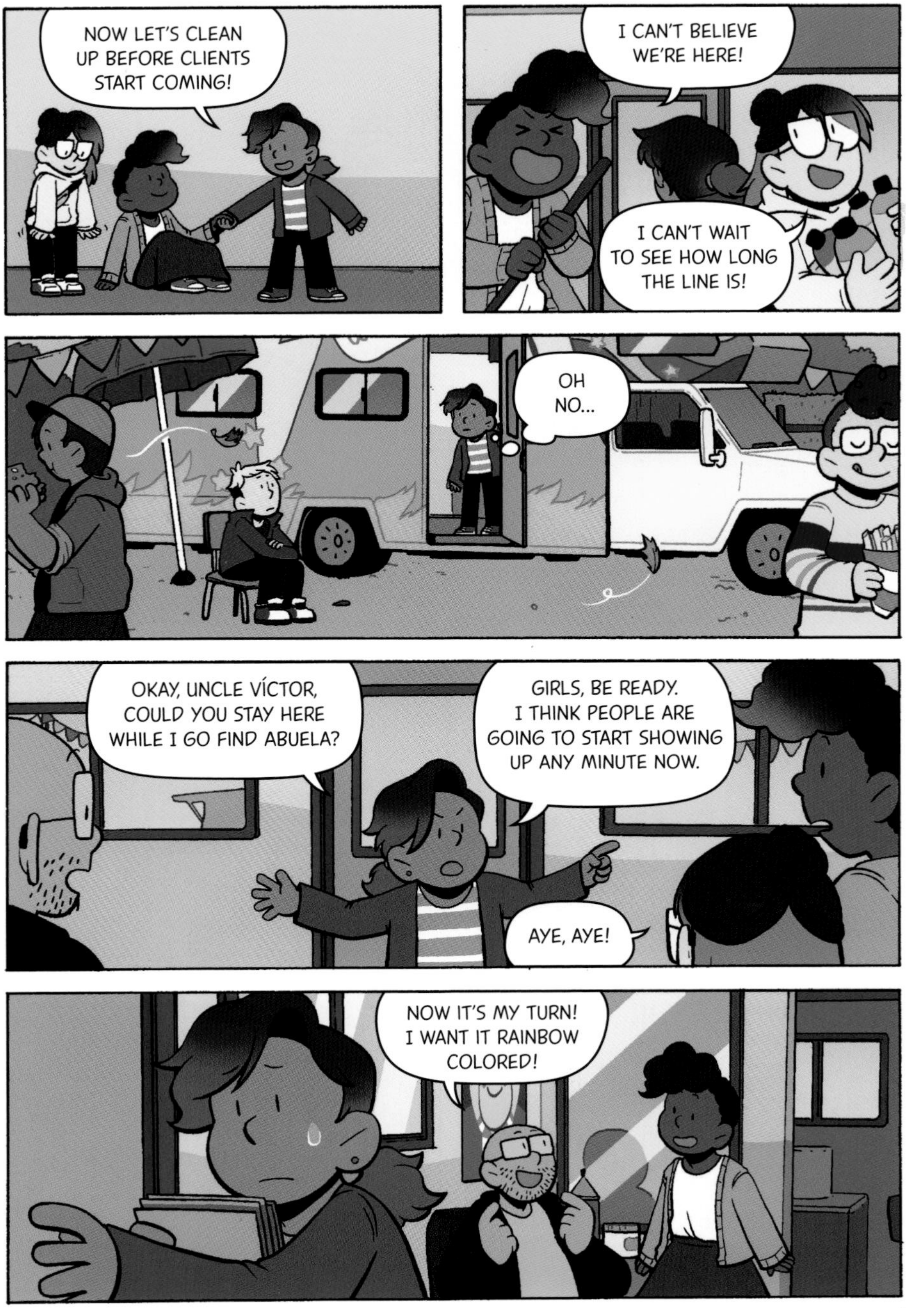
NOW LET'S CLEAN UP BEFORE CLIENTS START COMING!
I CAN'T BELIEVE WE'RE HERE!
I CAN'T WAIT TO SEE HOW LONG THE LINE IS!
OH NO...
OKAY, UNCLE VÍCTOR, COULD YOU STAY HERE WHILE I GO FIND ABUELA?
GIRLS, BE READY. I THINK PEOPLE ARE GOING TO START SHOWING UP ANY MINUTE NOW.
AYE, AYE!
NOW IT'S MY TURN! I WANT IT RAINBOW COLORED!

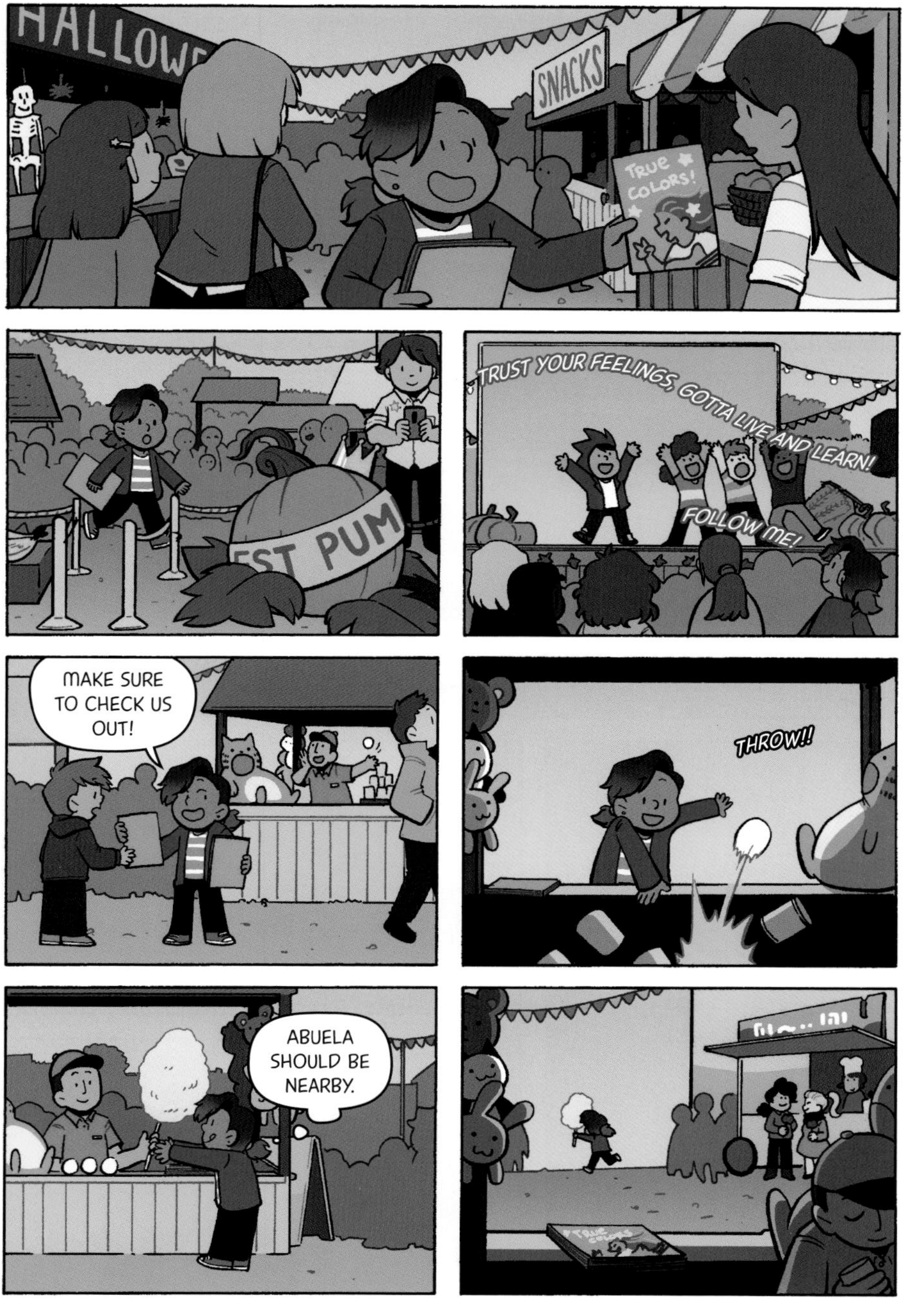
HALLOWE
SNACKS
TRUE COLORS!
EST PUM
TRUST YOUR FEELINGS, GOTTA LIVE AND LEARN!
FOLLOW ME!
MAKE SURE TO CHECK US OUT!
THROW!!
ABUELA SHOULD BE NEARBY.
TRUE COLORS

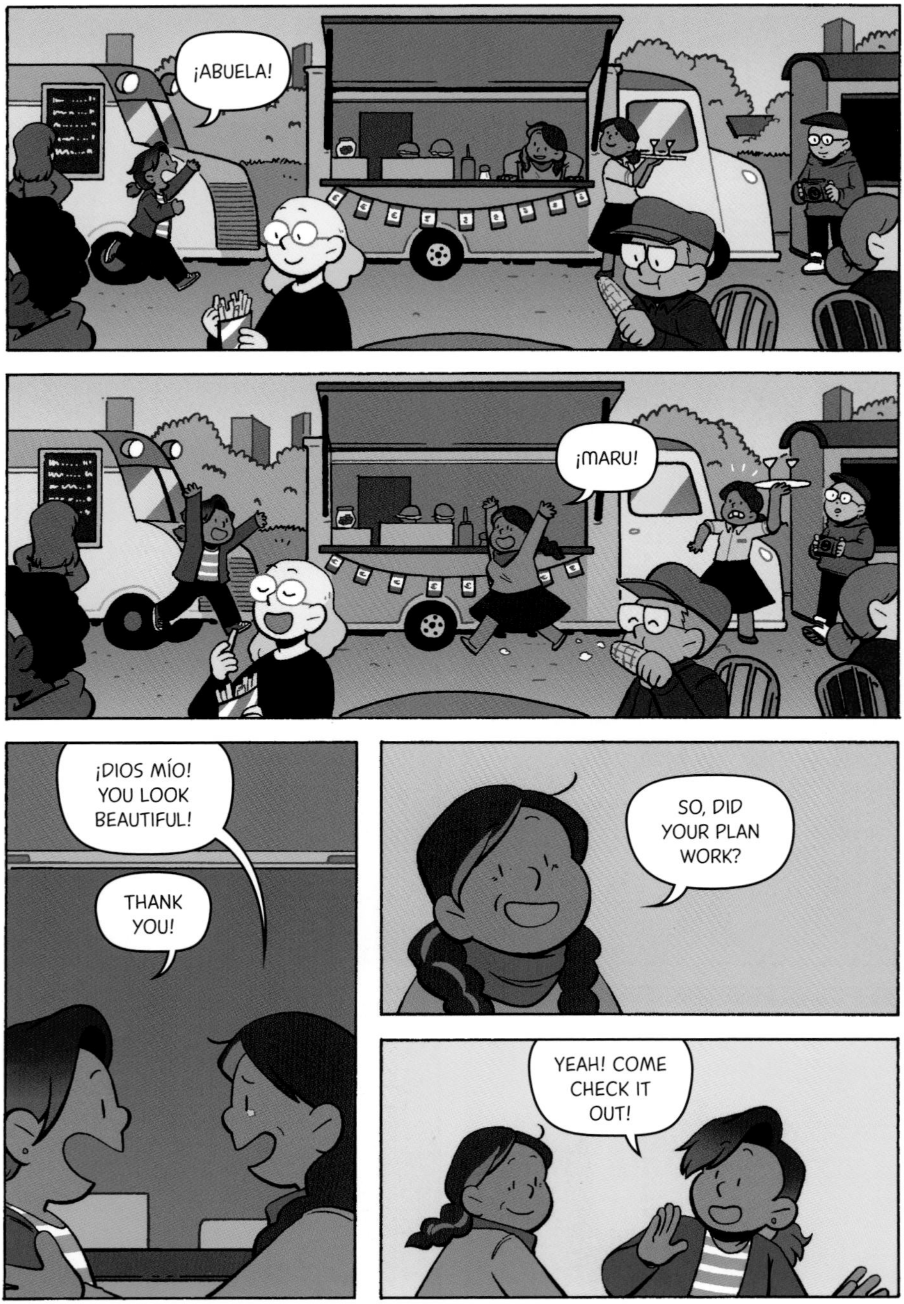
¡ABUELA!
¡MARU!
¡DIOS MÍO! YOU LOOK BEAUTIFUL!
THANK YOU!
SO, DID YOUR PLAN WORK?
YEAH! COME CHECK IT OUT!

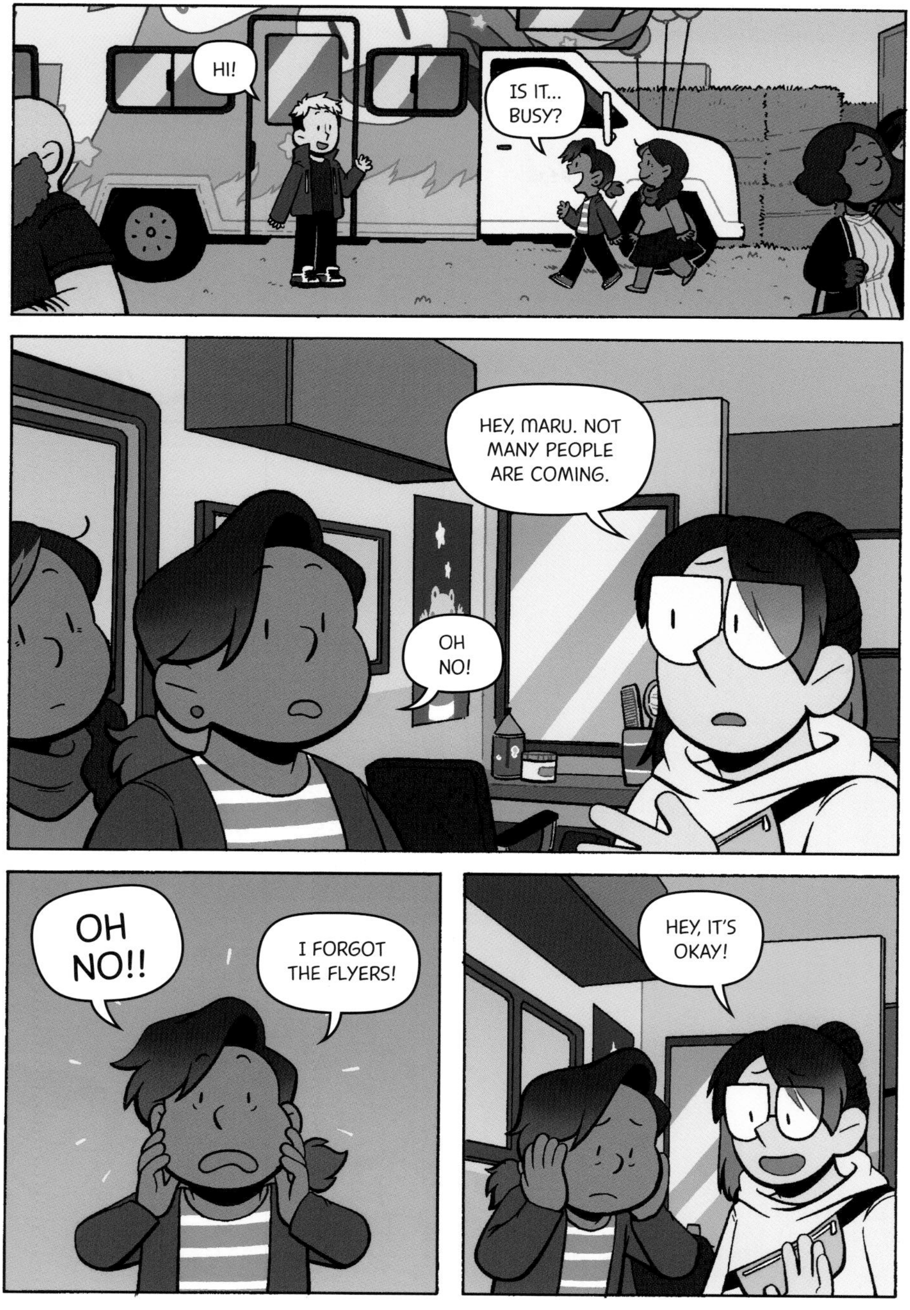
HI!
IS IT... BUSY?
HEY, MARU. NOT MANY PEOPLE ARE COMING.
OH NO!
OH NO!!
I FORGOT THE FLYERS!
HEY, IT'S OKAY!

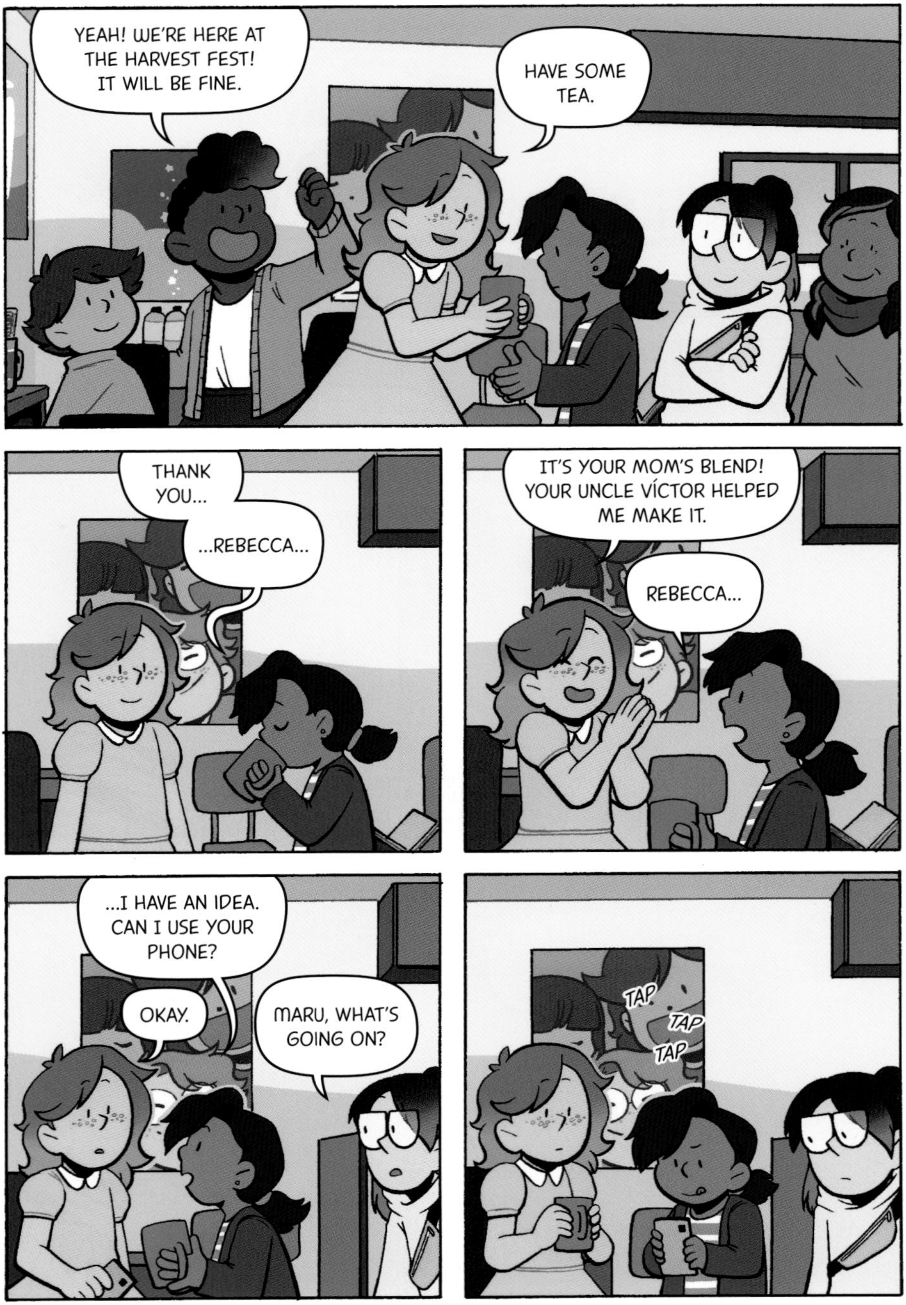
YEAH! WE'RE HERE AT THE HARVEST FEST! IT WILL BE FINE.
HAVE SOME TEA.
THANK YOU...
...REBECCA...
IT'S YOUR MOM'S BLEND! YOUR UNCLE VÍCTOR HELPED ME MAKE IT.
REBECCA...
...I HAVE AN IDEA. CAN I USE YOUR PHONE?
OKAY.
MARU, WHAT'S GOING ON?
TAP
TAP
TAP

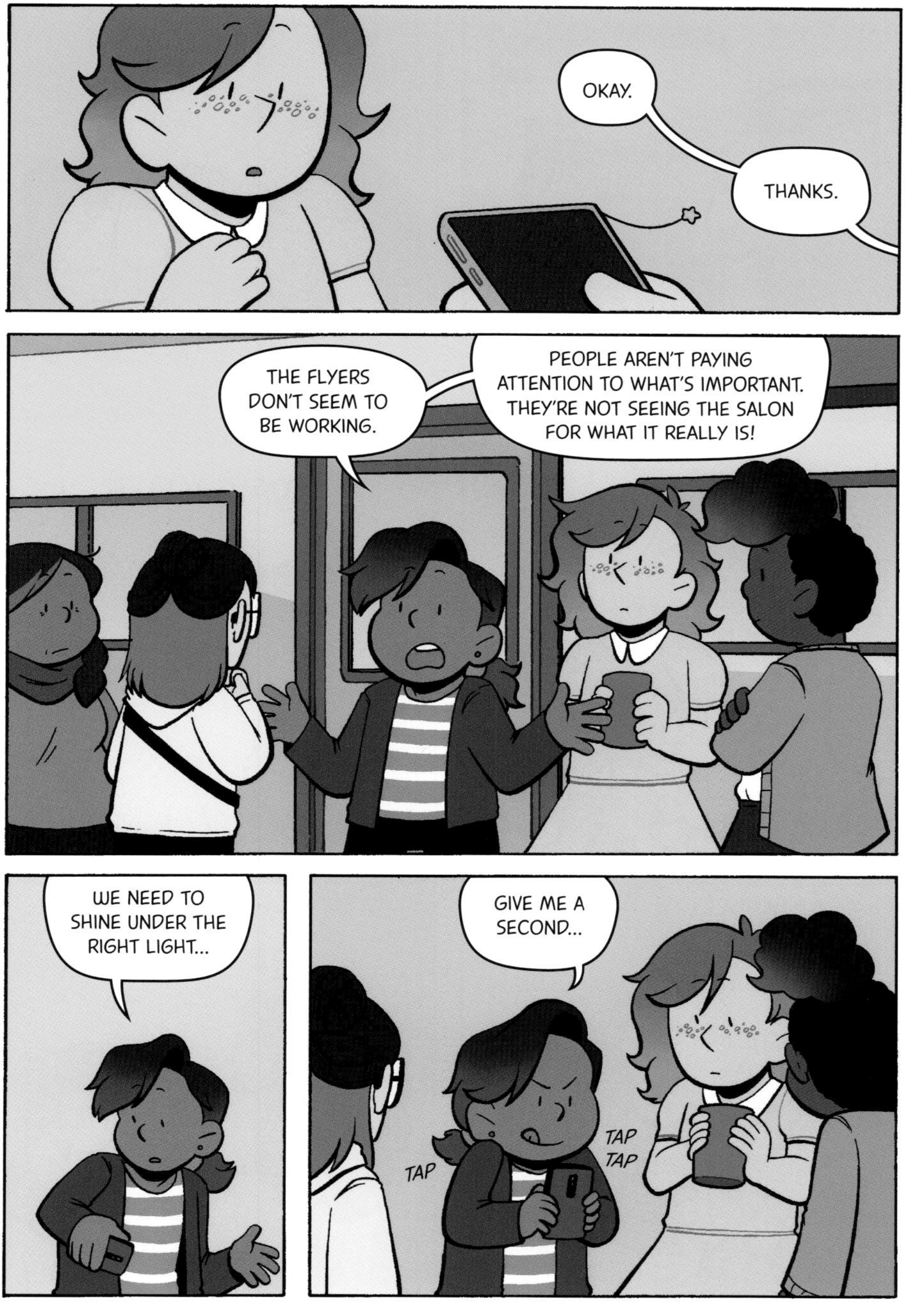
OKAY.
THANKS.
THE FLYERS DON'T SEEM TO BE WORKING.
PEOPLE AREN'T PAYING ATTENTION TO WHAT'S IMPORTANT. THEY'RE NOT SEEING THE SALON FOR WHAT IT REALLY IS!
WE NEED TO SHINE UNDER THE RIGHT LIGHT...
GIVE ME A SECOND...
TAP
TAP TAP

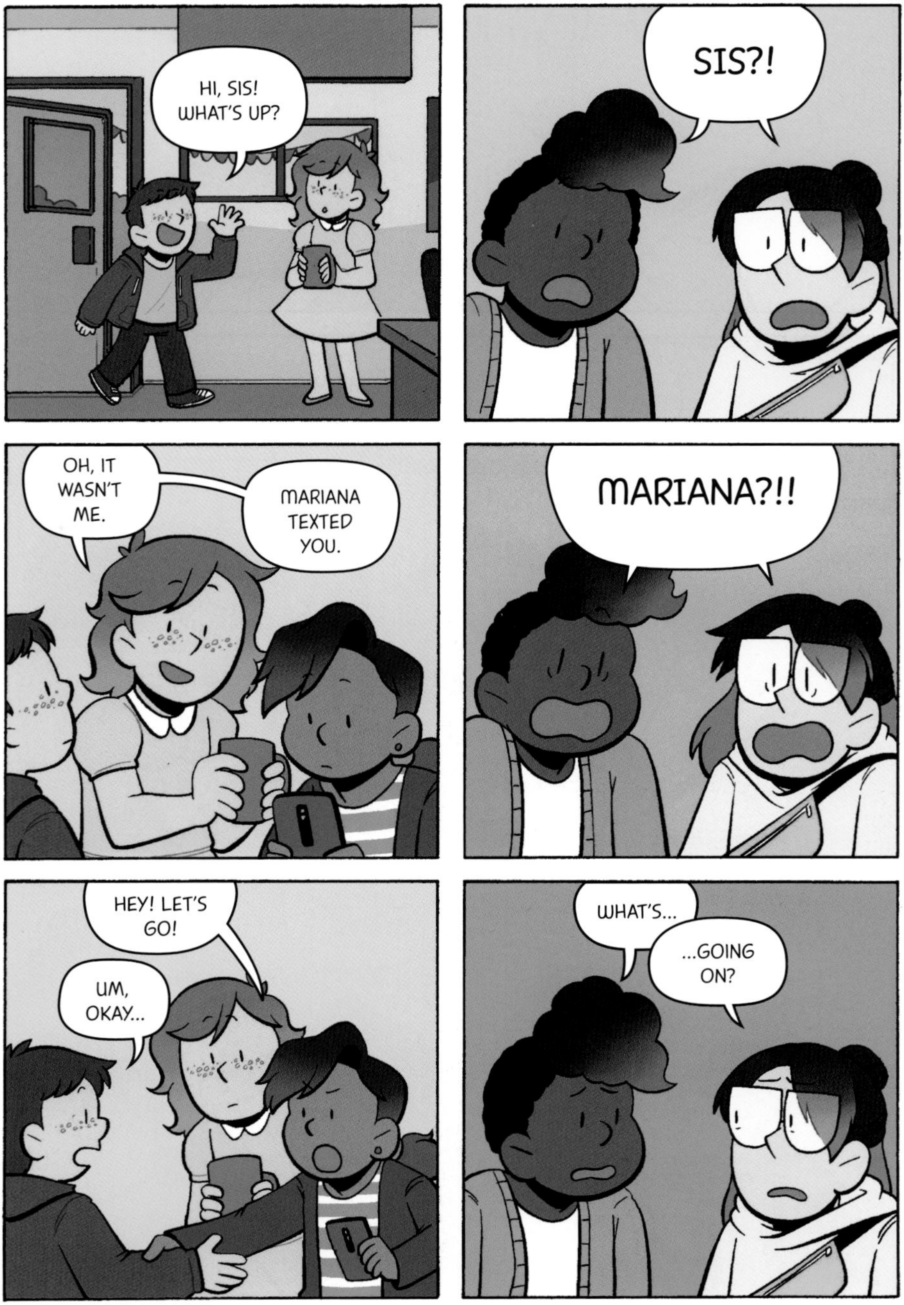
HI, SIS! WHAT'S UP?
SIS?!
OH, IT WASN'T ME.
MARIANA TEXTED YOU.
MARIANA?!!
HEY! LET'S GO!
UM, OKAY...
WHAT'S...
...GOING ON?

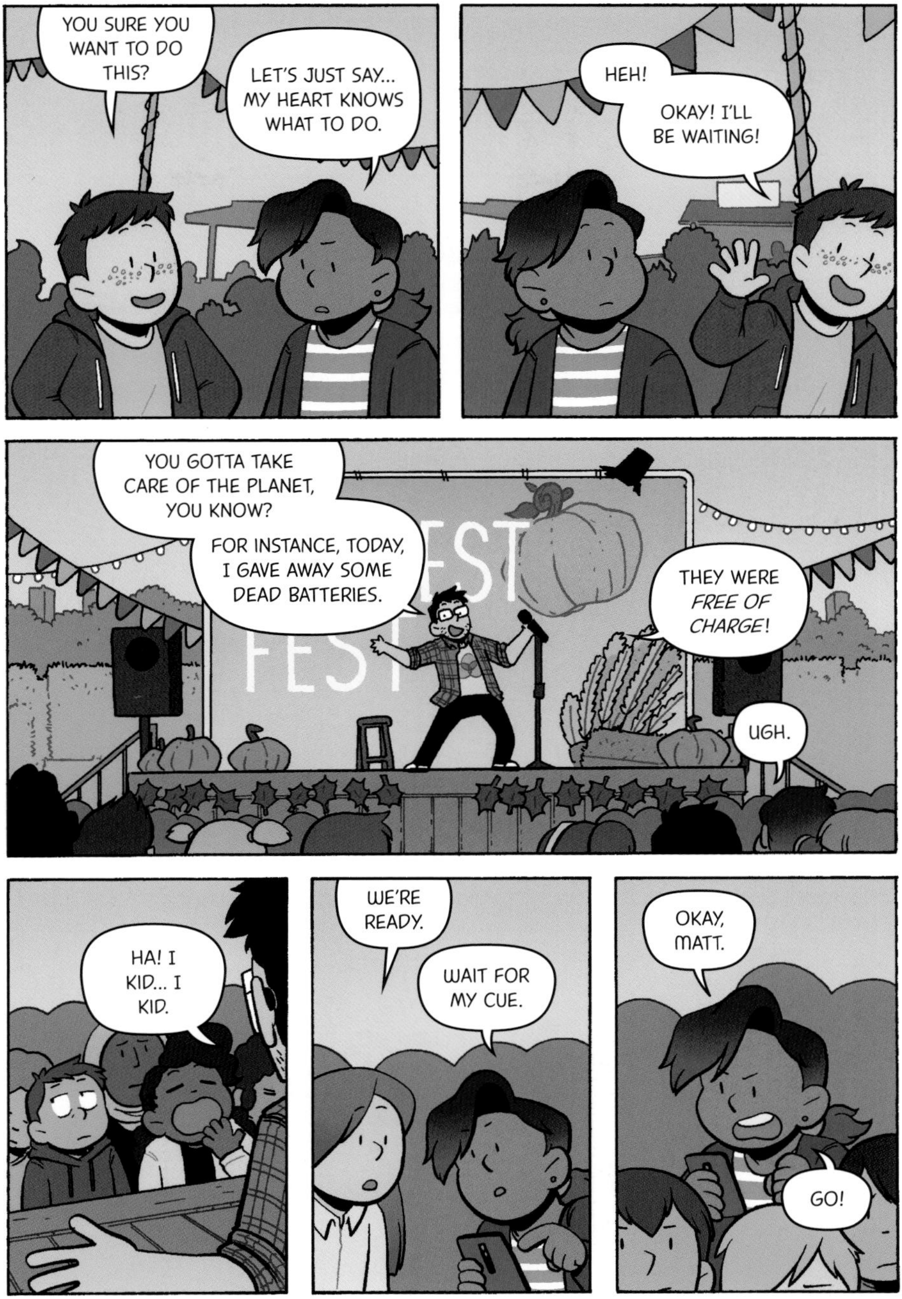
YOU SURE YOU WANT TO DO THIS?
LET'S JUST SAY... MY HEART KNOWS WHAT TO DO.
HEH!
OKAY! I'LL BE WAITING!
YOU GOTTA TAKE CARE OF THE PLANET, YOU KNOW?
FOR INSTANCE, TODAY, I GAVE AWAY SOME DEAD BATTERIES.
FEST
FEST
THEY WERE *FREE OF CHARGE*!
UGH.
HA! I KID... I KID.
WE'RE READY.
WAIT FOR MY CUE.
OKAY, MATT.
GO!

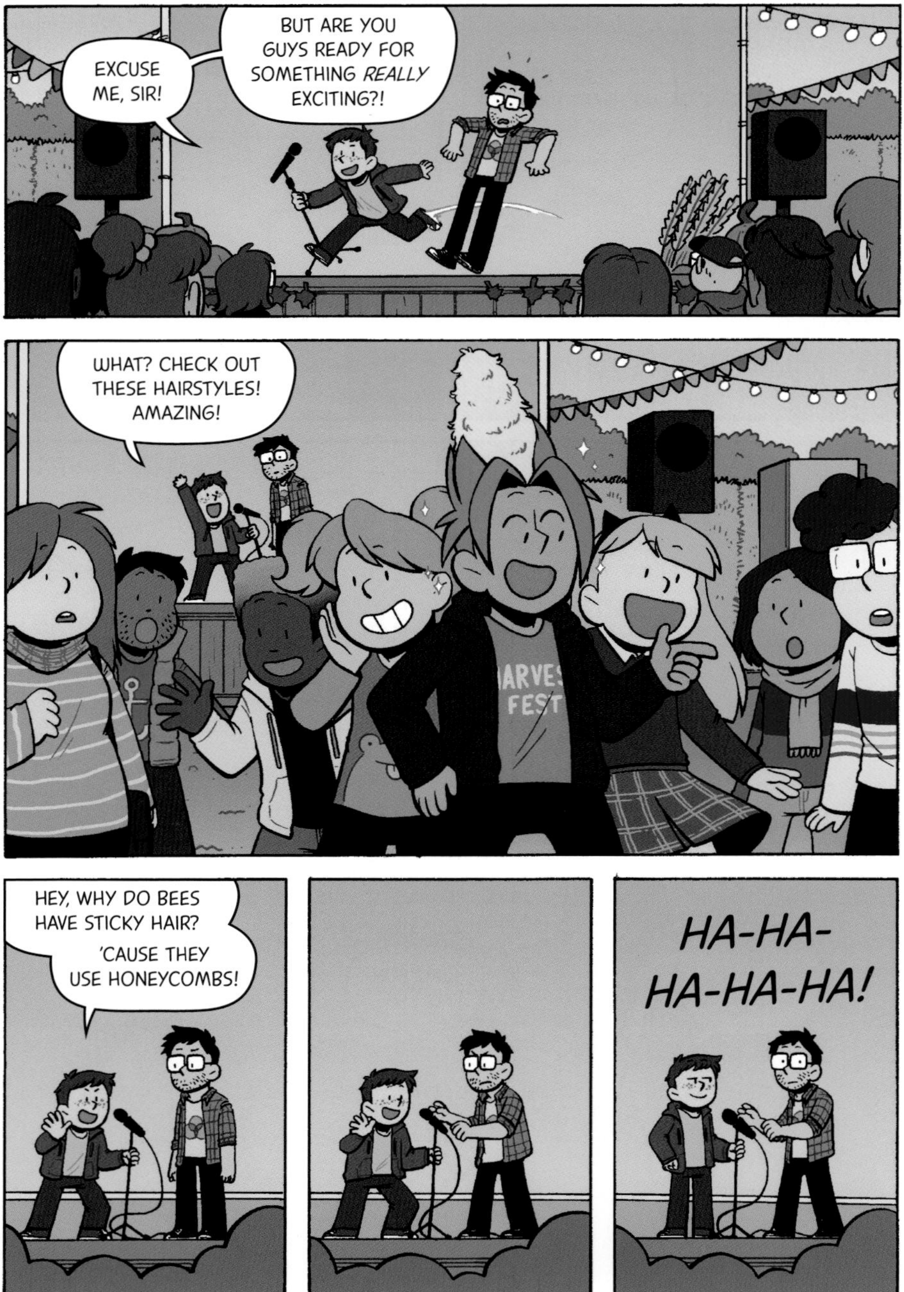
EXCUSE ME, SIR!
BUT ARE YOU GUYS READY FOR SOMETHING *REALLY* EXCITING?!
WHAT? CHECK OUT THESE HAIRSTYLES! AMAZING!
HEY, WHY DO BEES HAVE STICKY HAIR?
'CAUSE THEY USE HONEYCOMBS!
HA-HA-HA-HA-HA!

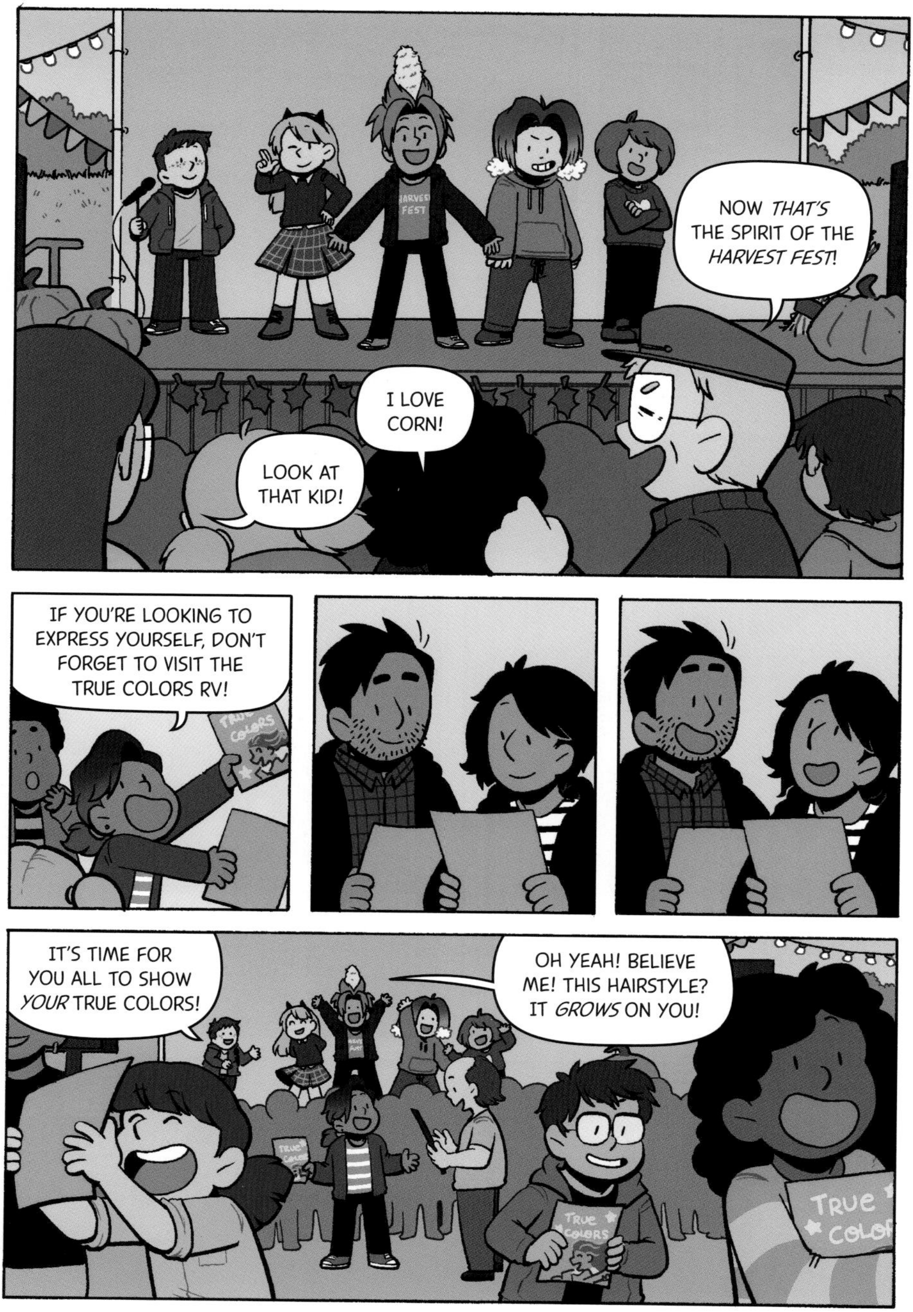

HARVEST FEST
NOW *THAT'S* THE SPIRIT OF THE *HARVEST FEST*!
I LOVE CORN!
LOOK AT THAT KID!
IF YOU'RE LOOKING TO EXPRESS YOURSELF, DON'T FORGET TO VISIT THE TRUE COLORS RV!
TRUE COLORS
IT'S TIME FOR YOU ALL TO SHOW *YOUR* TRUE COLORS!
OH YEAH! BELIEVE ME! THIS HAIRSTYLE? IT *GROWS* ON YOU!
TRUE COLORS
TRUE COLORS

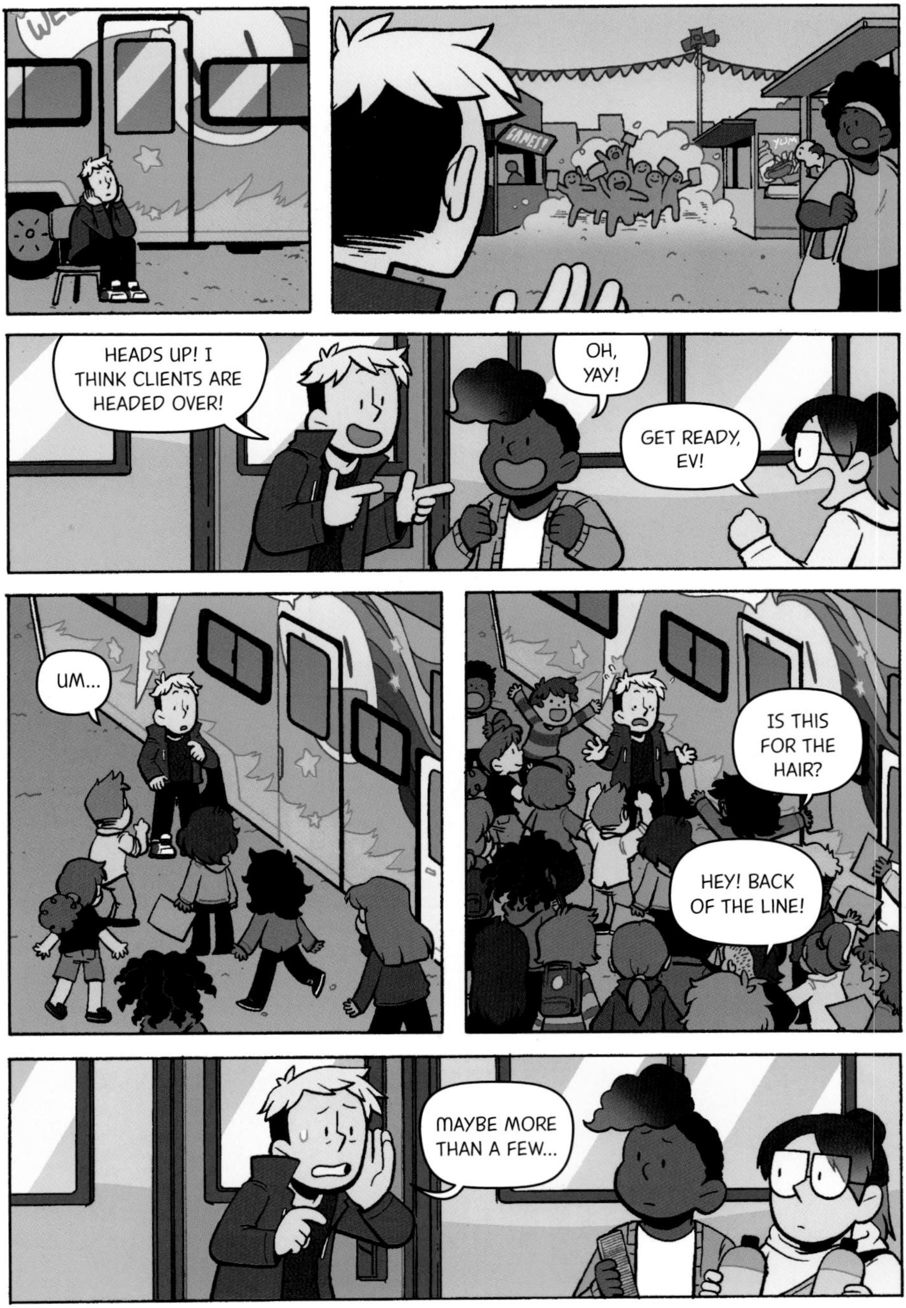
HEADS UP! I THINK CLIENTS ARE HEADED OVER!
OH, YAY!
GET READY, EV!
UM...
IS THIS FOR THE HAIR?
HEY! BACK OF THE LINE!
MAYBE MORE THAN A FEW...

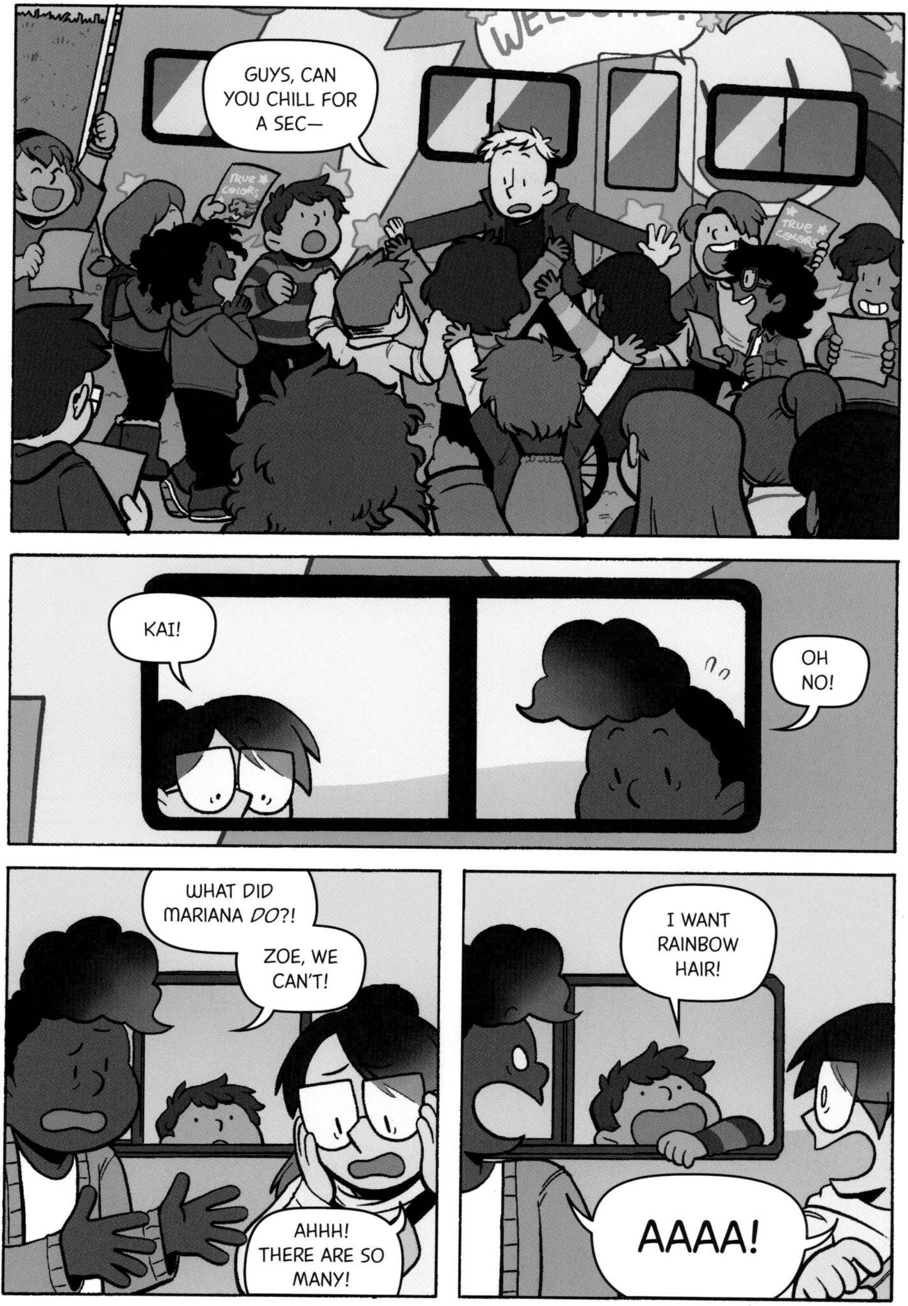
GUYS, CAN YOU CHILL FOR A SEC—
TRUE COLORS
KAI!
OH NO!
WHAT DID MARIANA *DO*?!
ZOE, WE CAN'T!
AHHH! THERE ARE SO MANY!
I WANT RAINBOW HAIR!
AAAA!

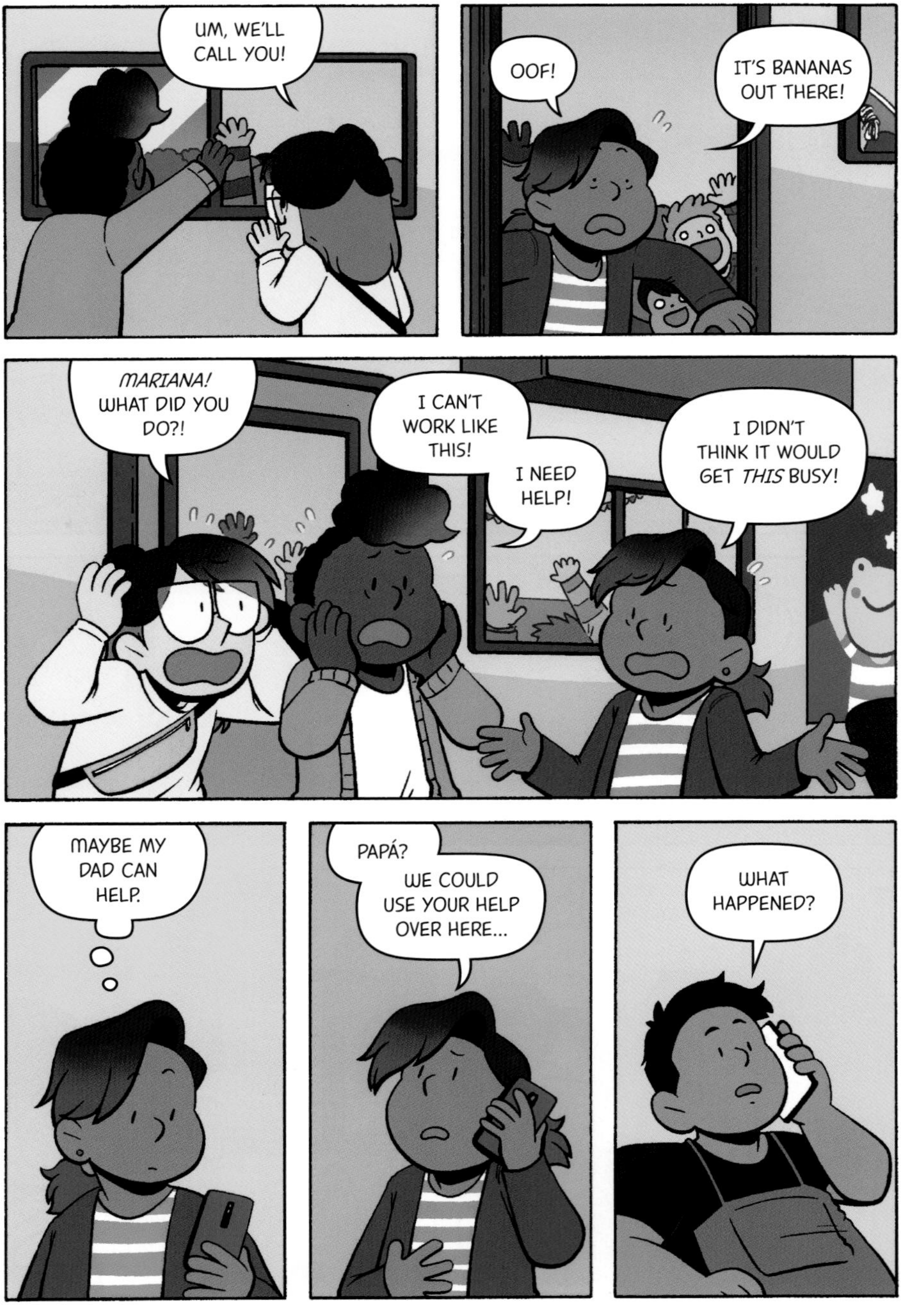
UM, WE'LL CALL YOU!
OOF!
IT'S BANANAS OUT THERE!
MARIANA! WHAT DID YOU DO?!
I CAN'T WORK LIKE THIS!
I NEED HELP!
I DIDN'T THINK IT WOULD GET *THIS* BUSY!
MAYBE MY DAD CAN HELP.
PAPÁ?
WE COULD USE YOUR HELP OVER HERE...
WHAT HAPPENED?

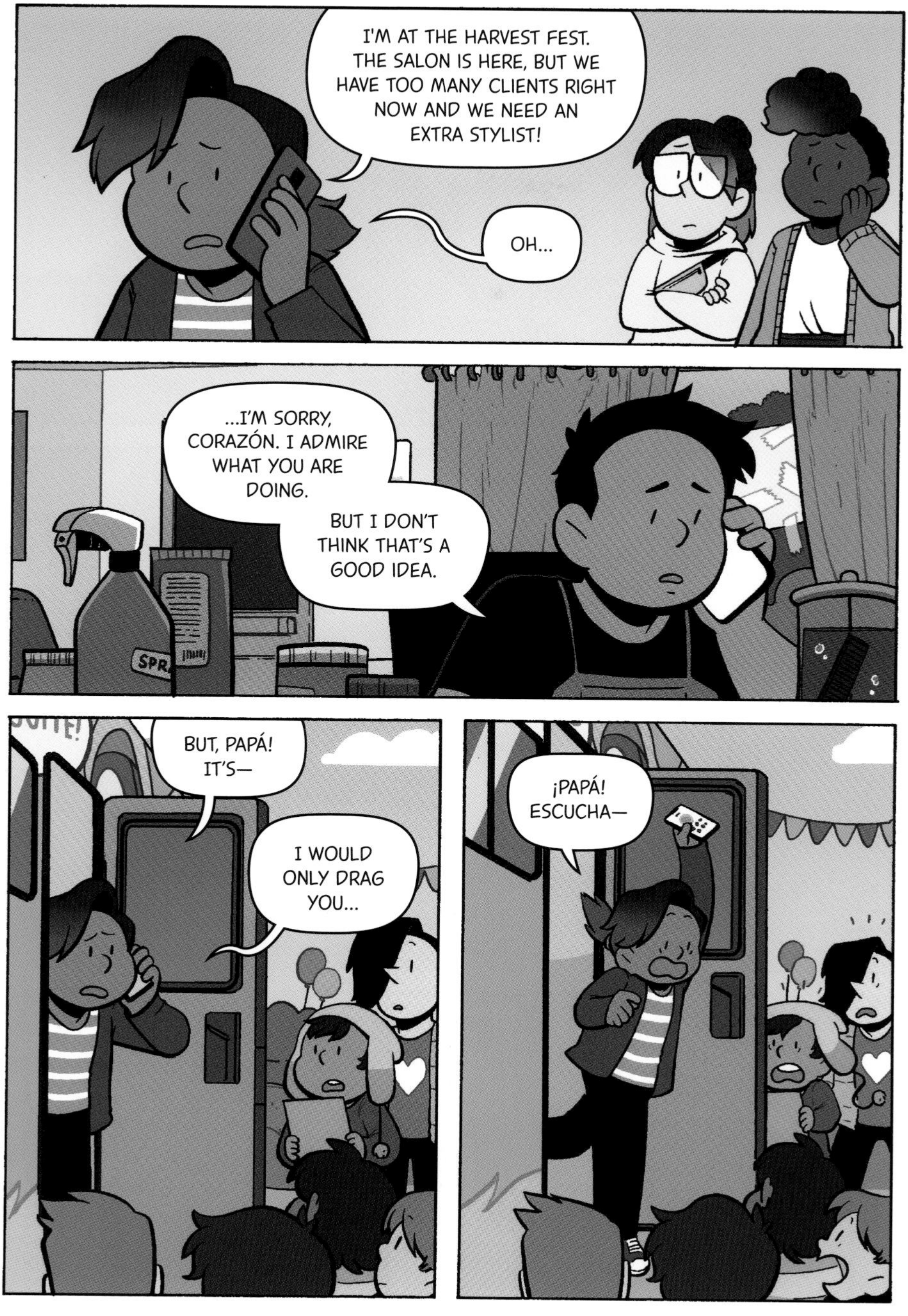
I'M AT THE HARVEST FEST. THE SALON IS HERE, BUT WE HAVE TOO MANY CLIENTS RIGHT NOW AND WE NEED AN EXTRA STYLIST!
OH...
...I'M SORRY, CORAZÓN. I ADMIRE WHAT YOU ARE DOING.
BUT I DON'T THINK THAT'S A GOOD IDEA.
SPRA
BUT, PAPÁ! IT'S—
I WOULD ONLY DRAG YOU...
¡PAPÁ! ESCUCHA—

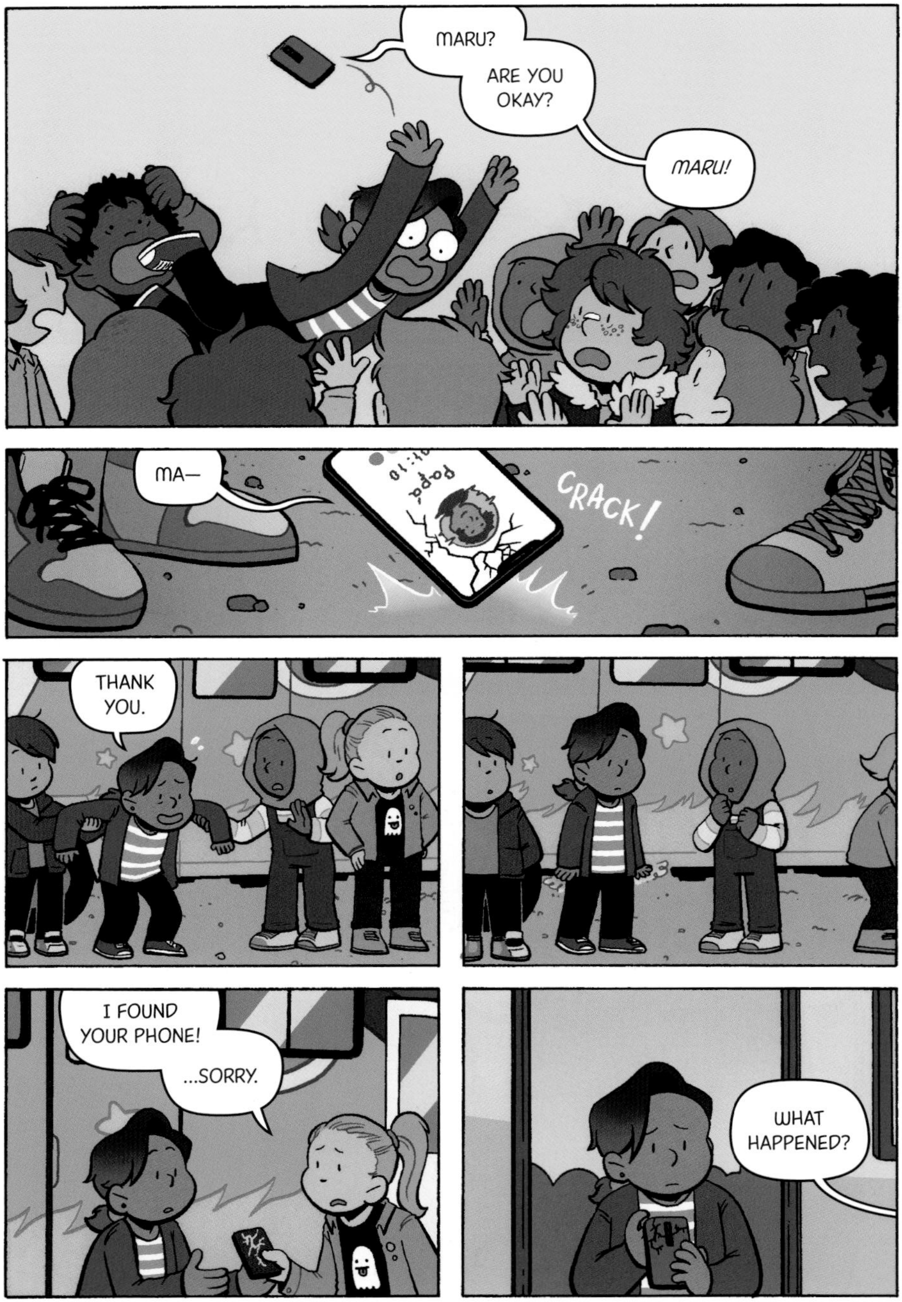
MARU?
ARE YOU OKAY?
MARU!
MA—
CRACK!
THANK YOU.
I FOUND YOUR PHONE!
...SORRY.
WHAT HAPPENED?

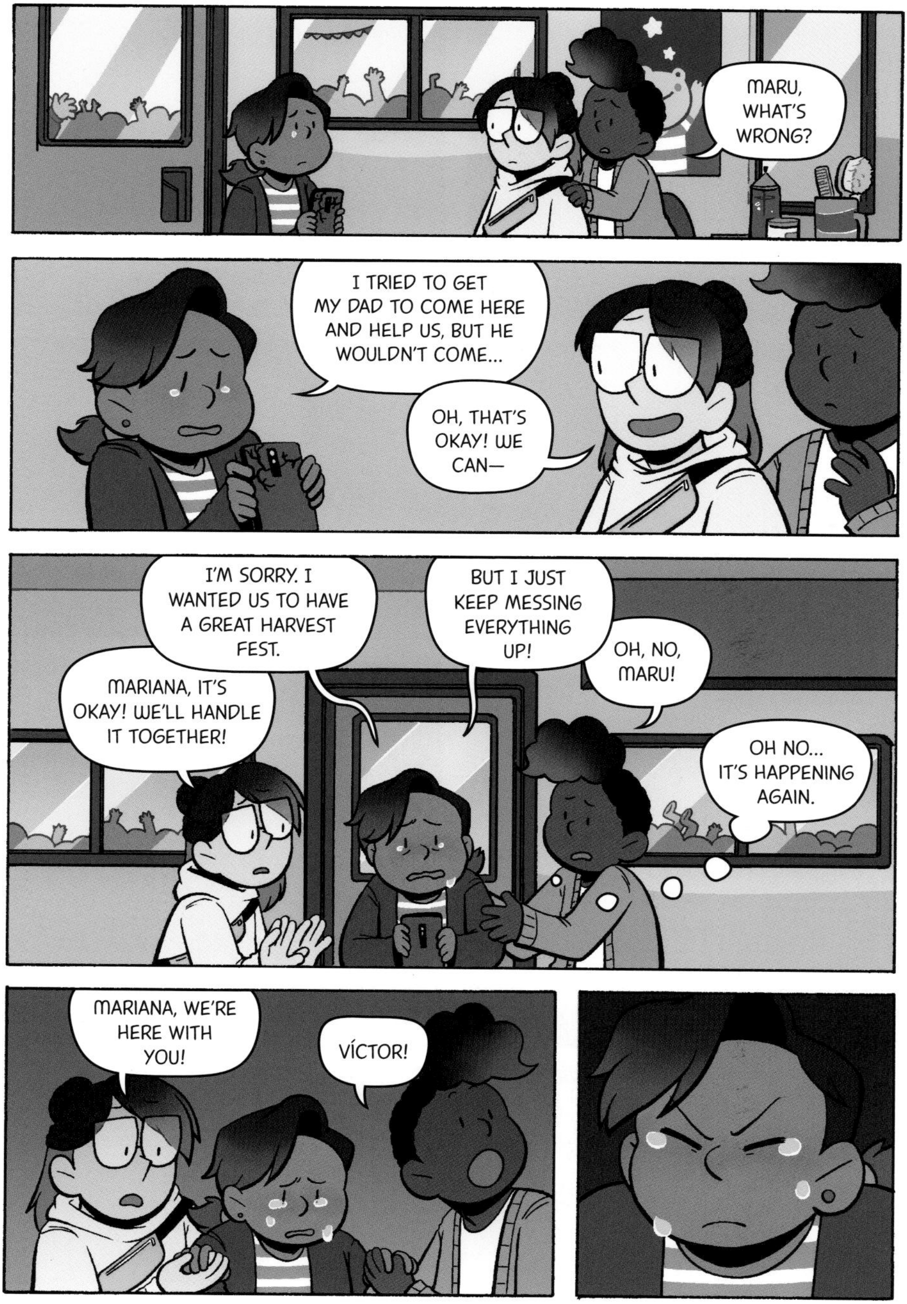
MARU, WHAT'S WRONG?
I TRIED TO GET MY DAD TO COME HERE AND HELP US, BUT HE WOULDN'T COME...
OH, THAT'S OKAY! WE CAN—
I'M SORRY. I WANTED US TO HAVE A GREAT HARVEST FEST.
MARIANA, IT'S OKAY! WE'LL HANDLE IT TOGETHER!
BUT I JUST KEEP MESSING EVERYTHING UP!
OH, NO, MARU!
OH NO... IT'S HAPPENING AGAIN.
MARIANA, WE'RE HERE WITH YOU!
VÍCTOR!

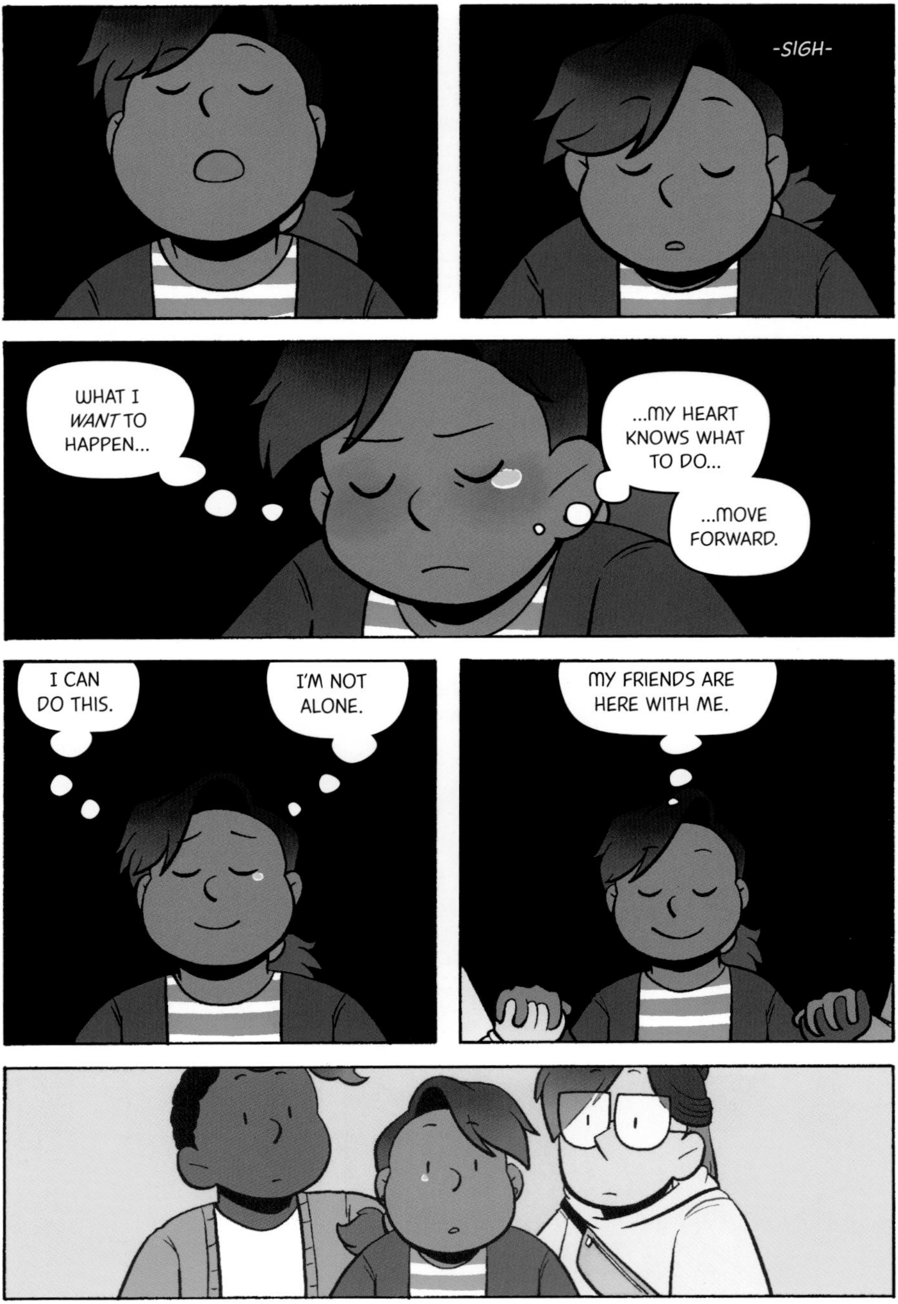
-SIGH-
WHAT I *WANT* TO HAPPEN...
...MY HEART KNOWS WHAT TO DO...
...MOVE FORWARD.
I CAN DO THIS.
I'M NOT ALONE.
MY FRIENDS ARE HERE WITH ME.

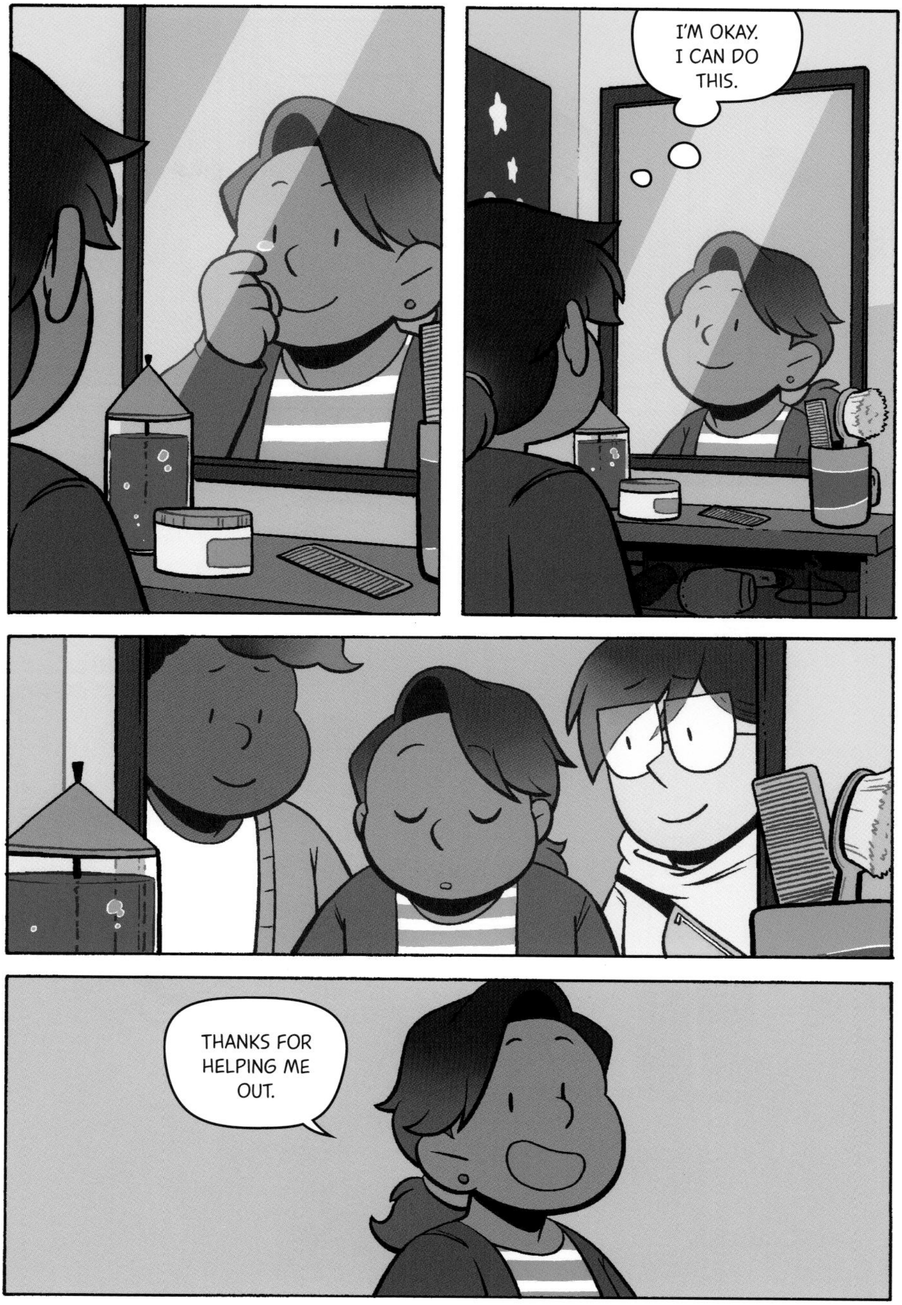
I'M OKAY. I CAN DO THIS.
THANKS FOR HELPING ME OUT.

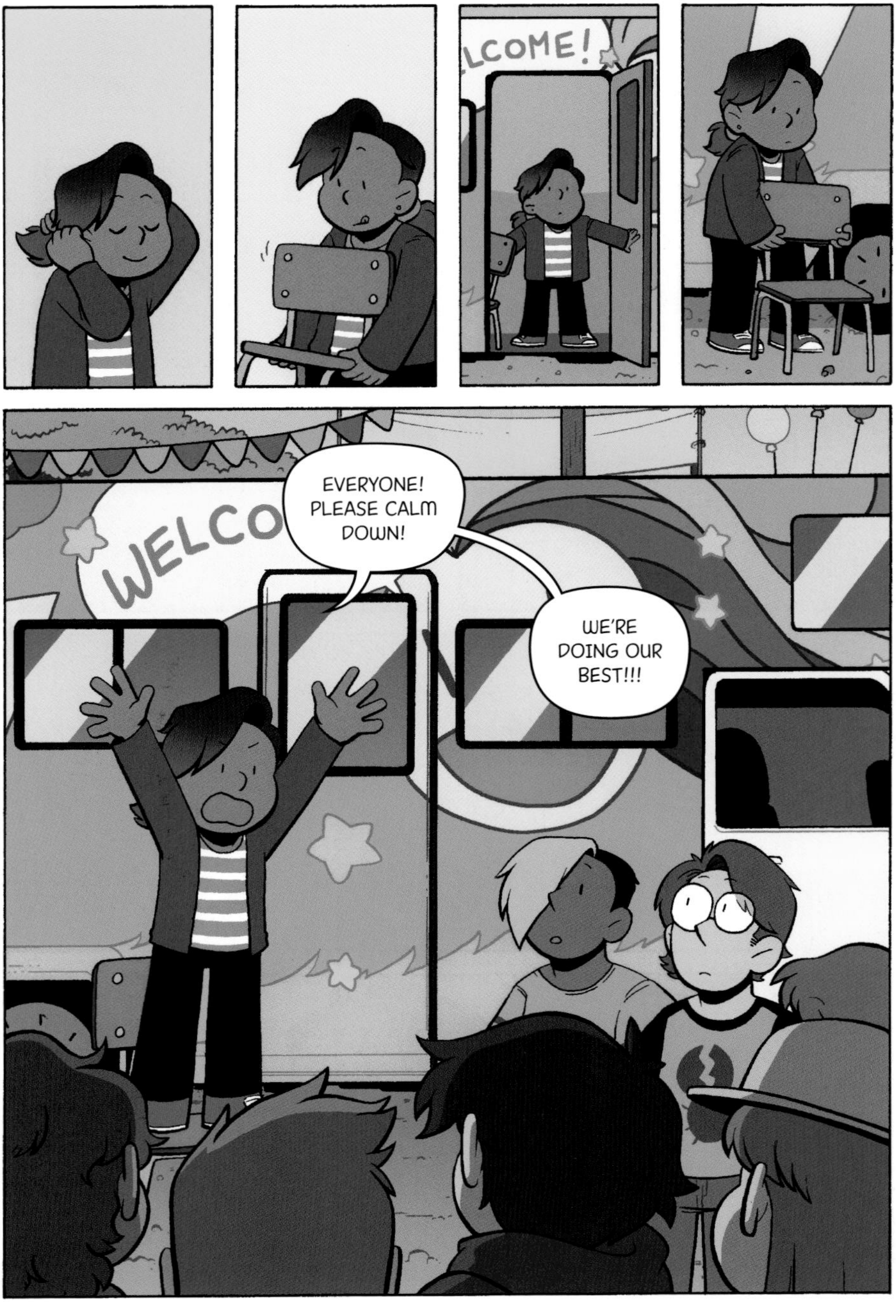

LCOME!
WELCO
EVERYONE! PLEASE CALM DOWN!
WE'RE DOING OUR BEST!!!

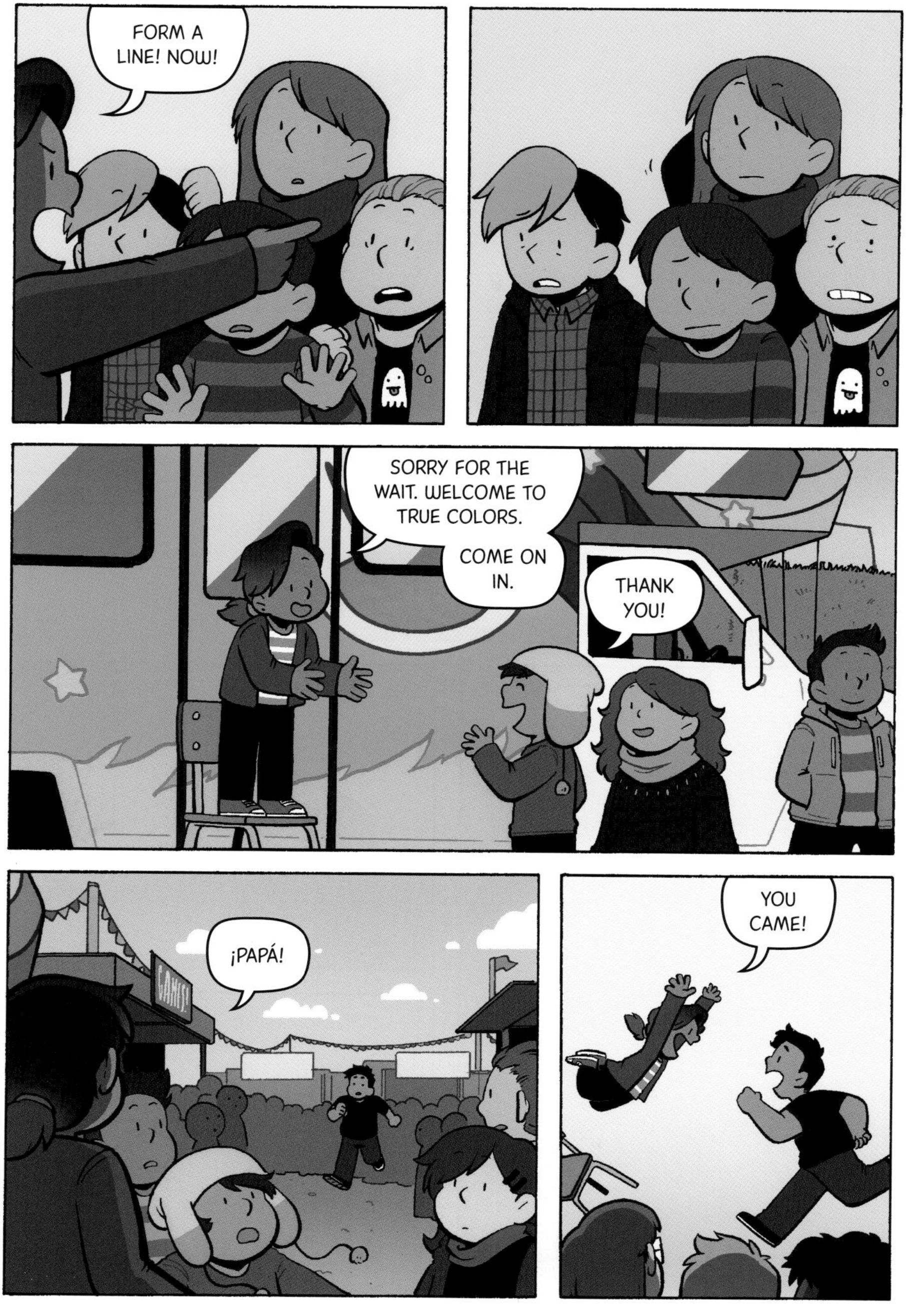
FORM A LINE! NOW!
SORRY FOR THE WAIT. WELCOME TO TRUE COLORS.
COME ON IN.
THANK YOU!
¡PAPÁ!
YOU CAME!
GAMES!

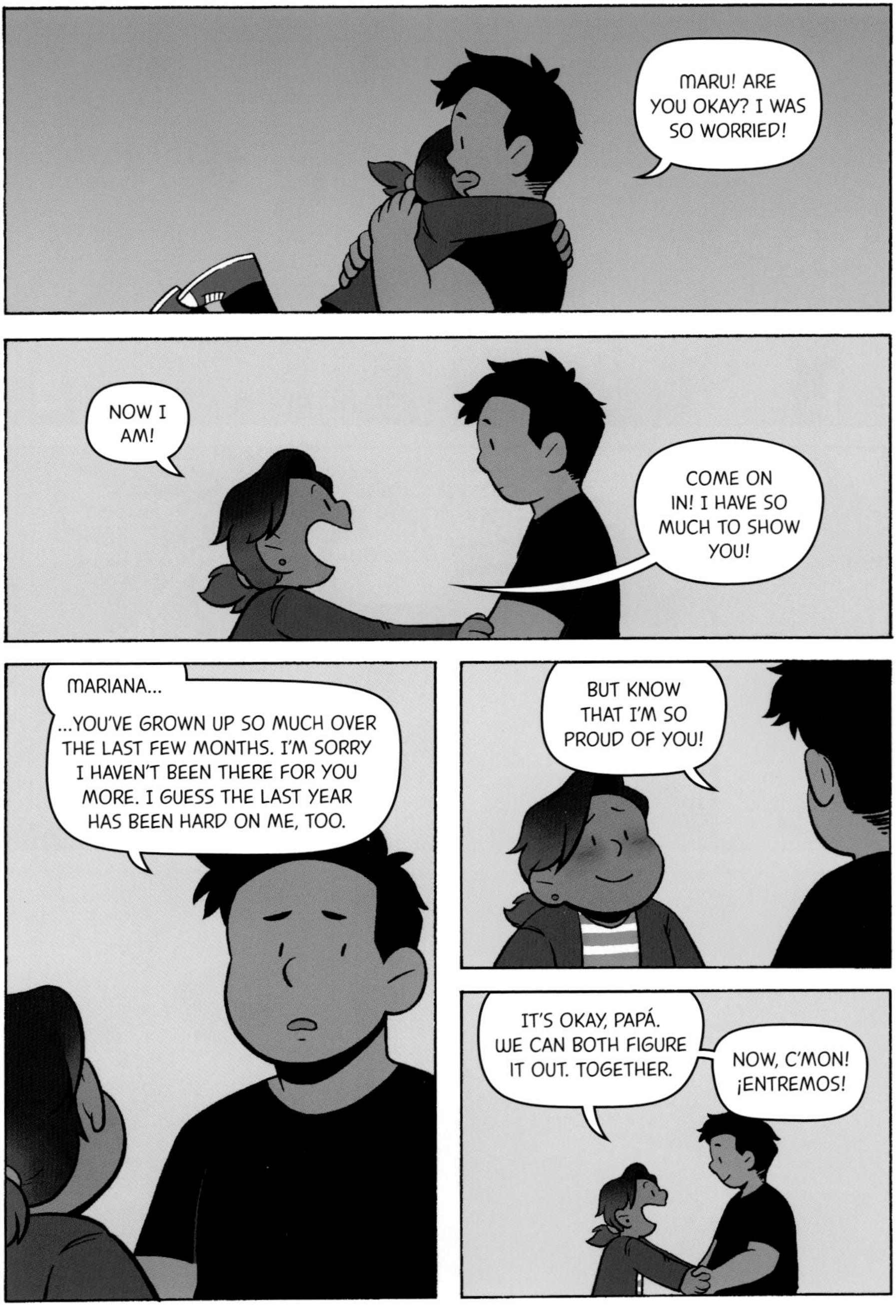
MARU! ARE YOU OKAY? I WAS SO WORRIED!
NOW I AM!
COME ON IN! I HAVE SO MUCH TO SHOW YOU!
MARIANA...
...YOU'VE GROWN UP SO MUCH OVER THE LAST FEW MONTHS. I'M SORRY I HAVEN'T BEEN THERE FOR YOU MORE. I GUESS THE LAST YEAR HAS BEEN HARD ON ME, TOO.
BUT KNOW THAT I'M SO PROUD OF YOU!
IT'S OKAY, PAPÁ. WE CAN BOTH FIGURE IT OUT. TOGETHER.
NOW, C'MON! ¡ENTREMOS!

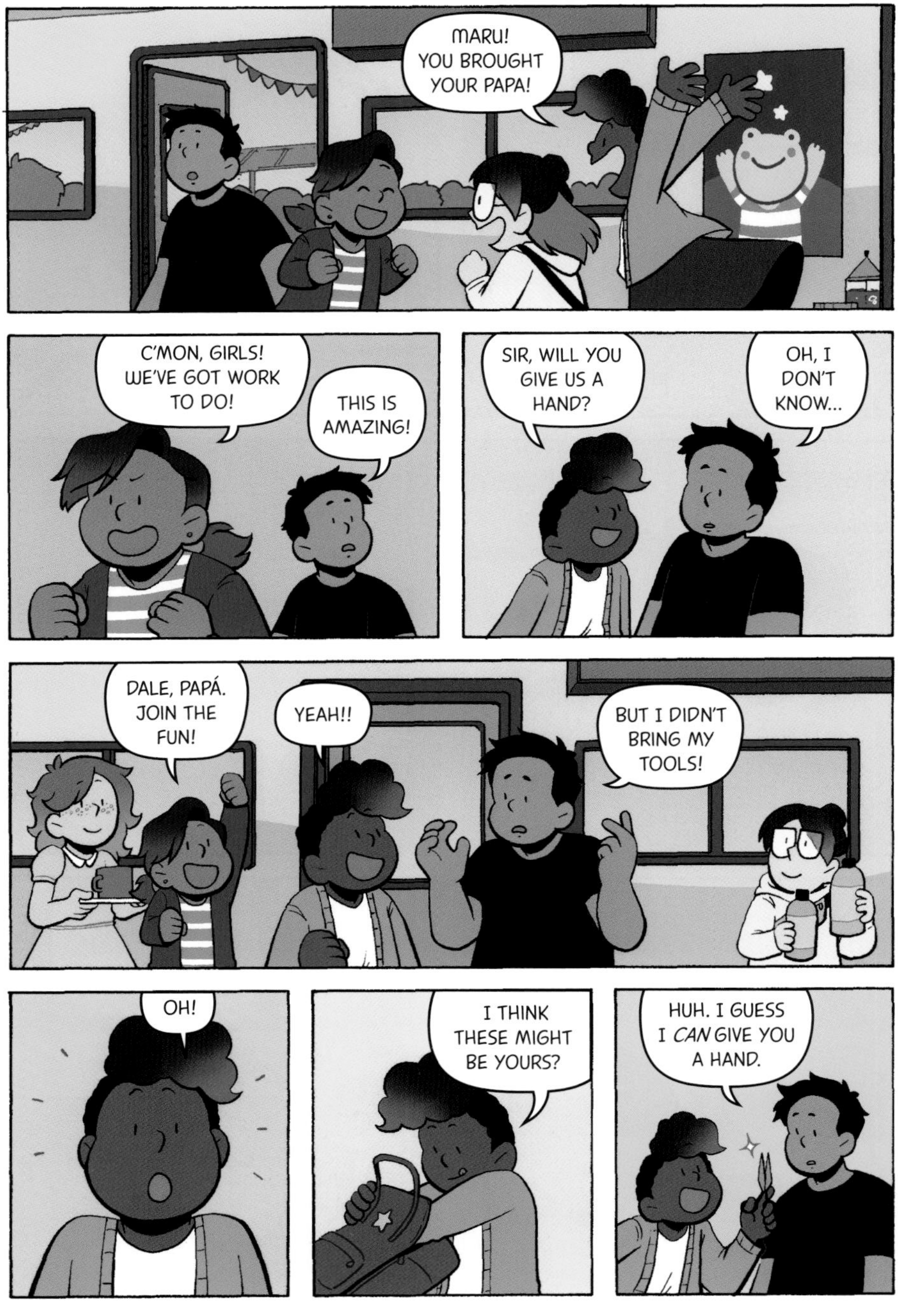
MARU! YOU BROUGHT YOUR PAPA!
C'MON, GIRLS! WE'VE GOT WORK TO DO!
THIS IS AMAZING!
SIR, WILL YOU GIVE US A HAND?
OH, I DON'T KNOW...
DALE, PAPÁ. JOIN THE FUN!
YEAH!!
BUT I DIDN'T BRING MY TOOLS!
OH!
I THINK THESE MIGHT BE YOURS?
HUH. I GUESS I *CAN* GIVE YOU A HAND.

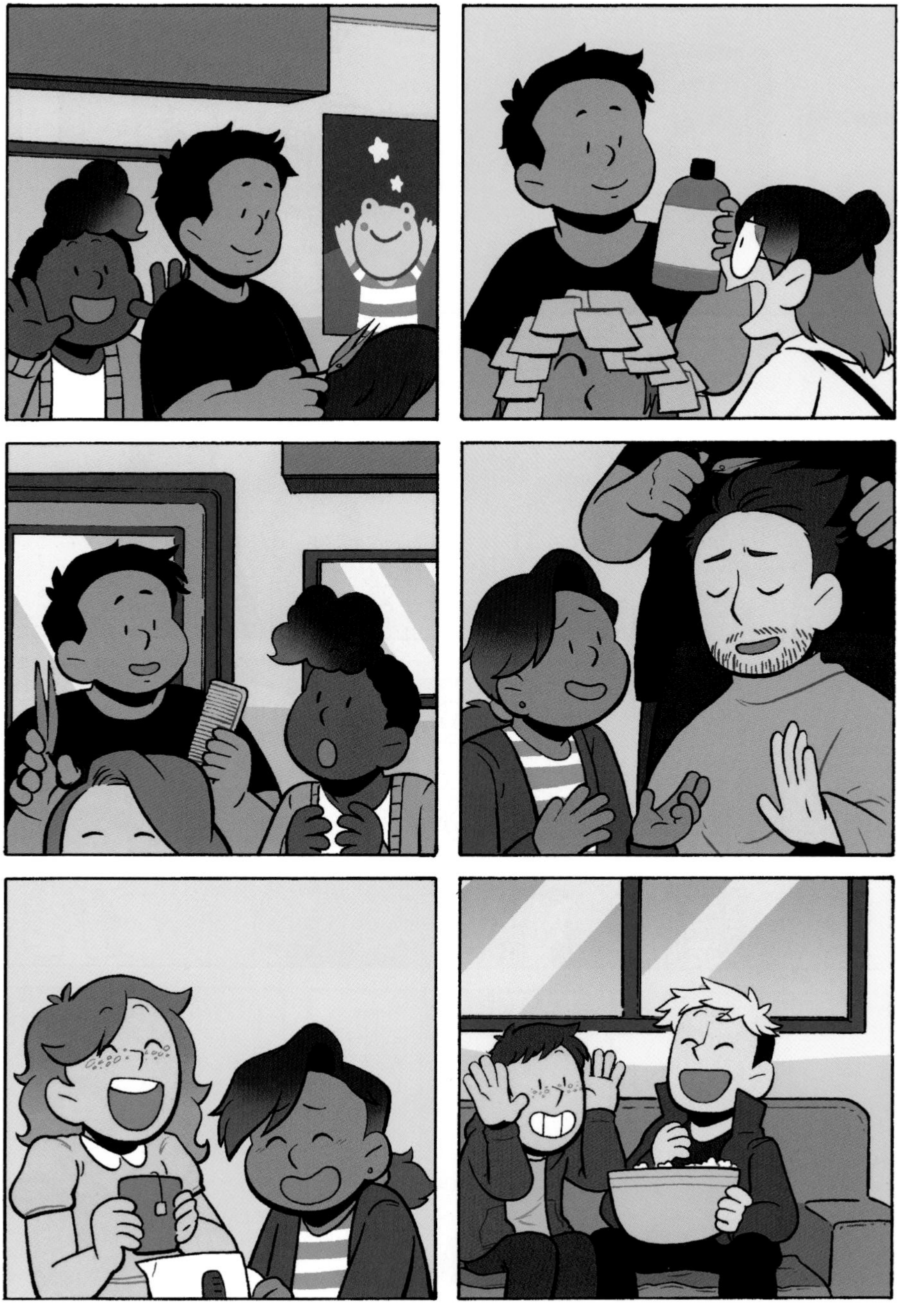

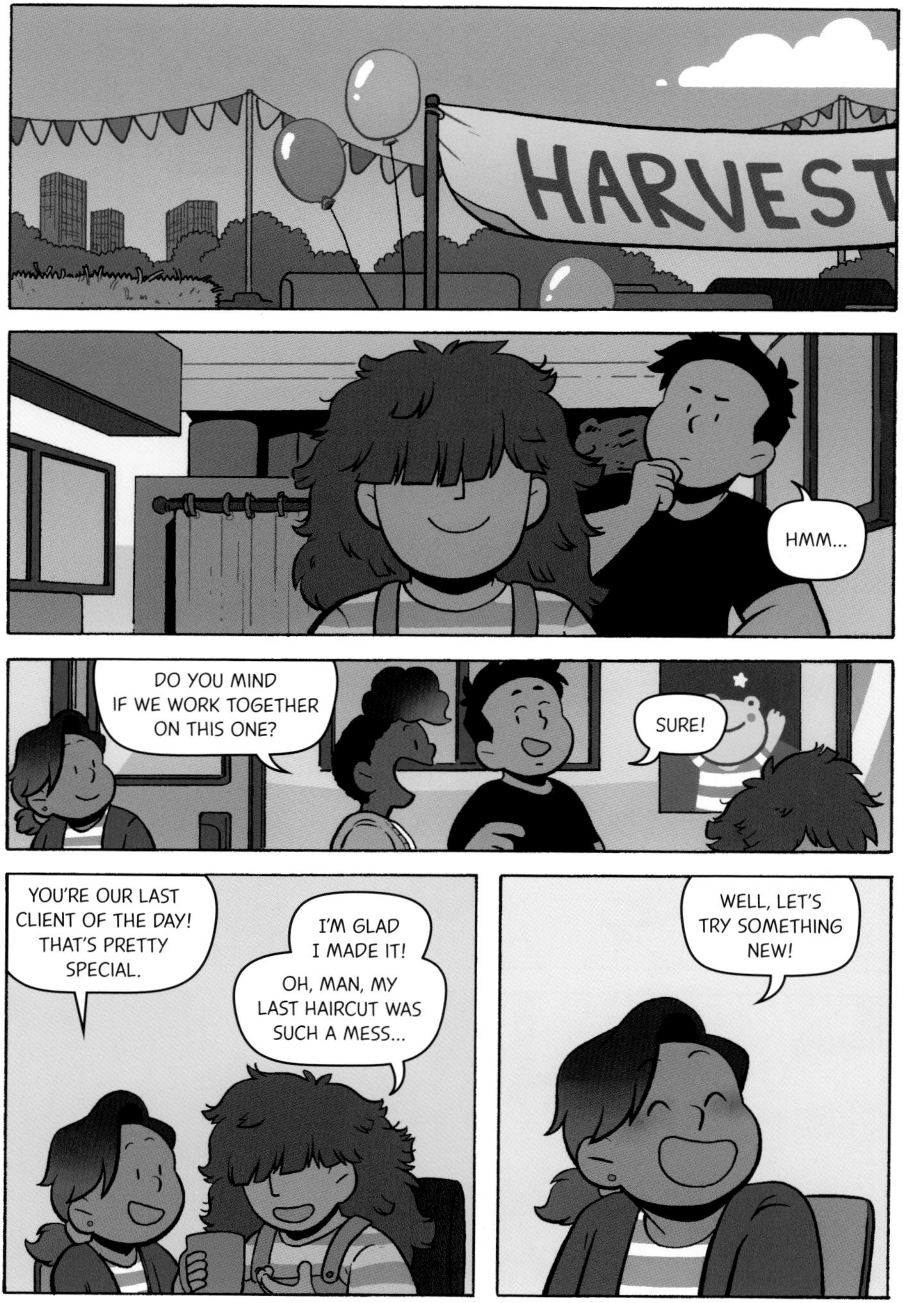
HARVEST
HMM...
DO YOU MIND IF WE WORK TOGETHER ON THIS ONE?
SURE!
YOU'RE OUR LAST CLIENT OF THE DAY! THAT'S PRETTY SPECIAL.
I'M GLAD I MADE IT!
OH, MAN, MY LAST HAIRCUT WAS SUCH A MESS...
WELL, LET'S TRY SOMETHING NEW!

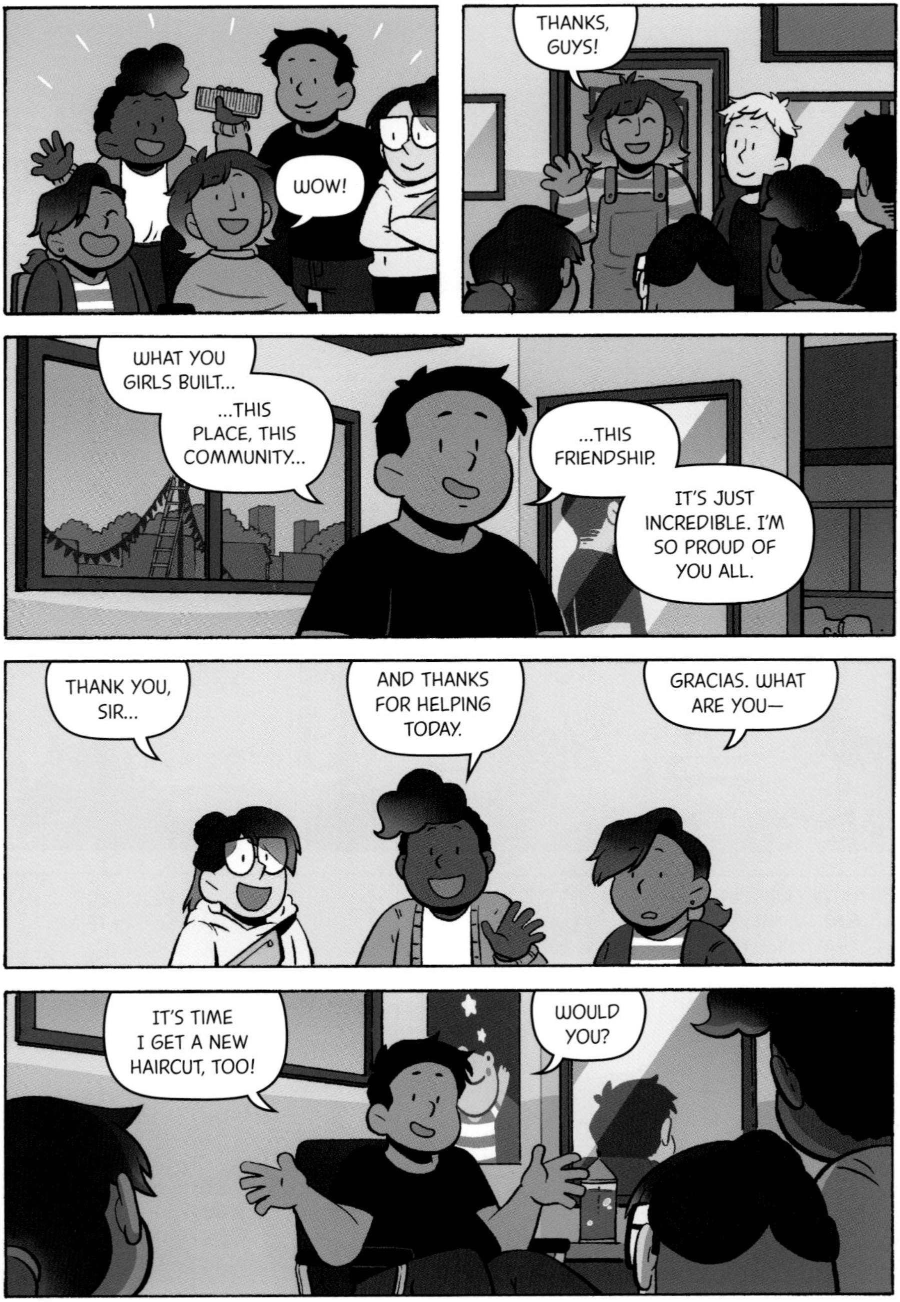
WOW!
THANKS, GUYS!
WHAT YOU GIRLS BUILT...
...THIS PLACE, THIS COMMUNITY...
...THIS FRIENDSHIP.
IT'S JUST INCREDIBLE. I'M SO PROUD OF YOU ALL.
THANK YOU, SIR...
AND THANKS FOR HELPING TODAY.
GRACIAS. WHAT ARE YOU—
IT'S TIME I GET A NEW HAIRCUT, TOO!
WOULD YOU?

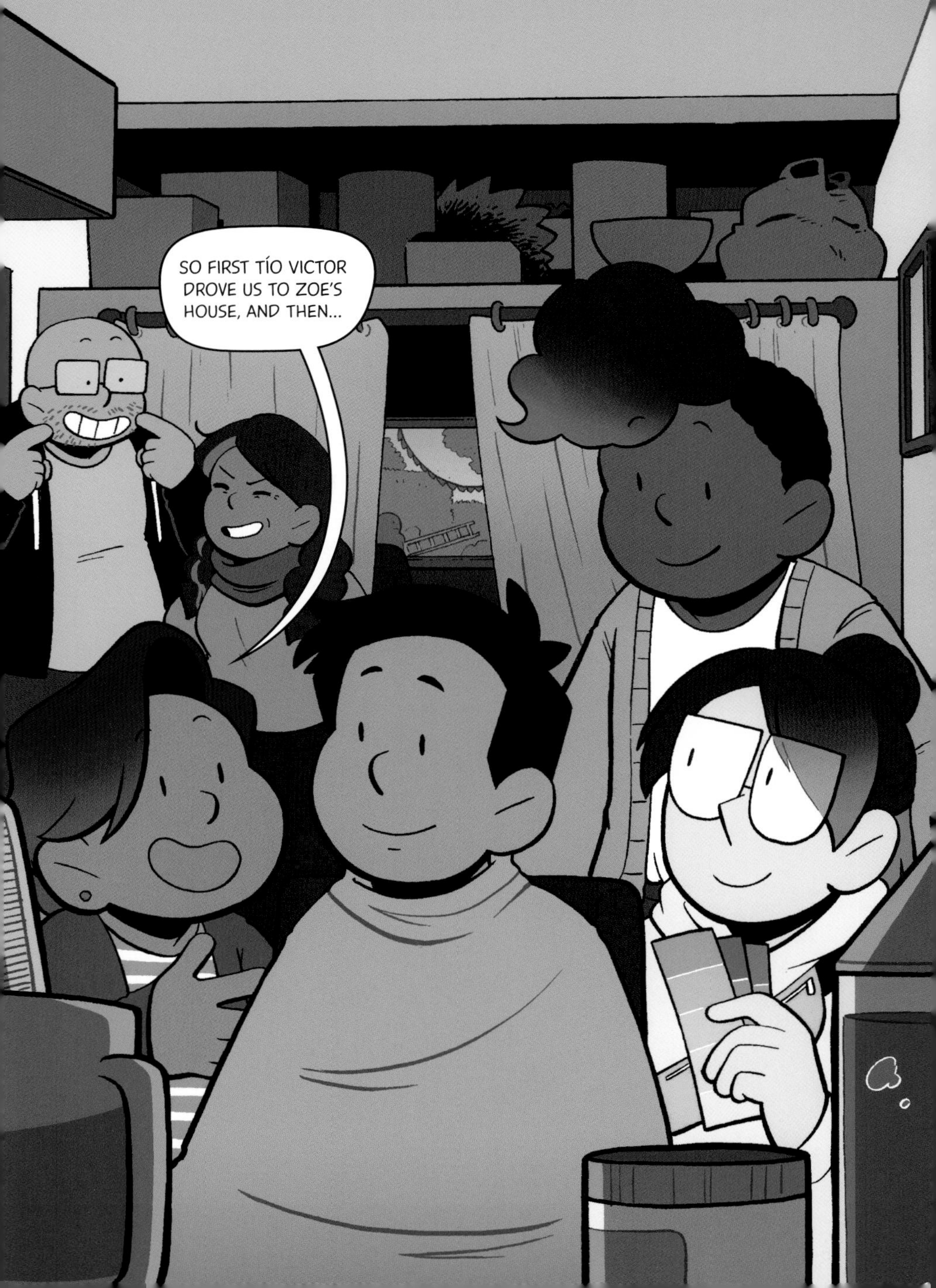
SO FIRST TÍO VICTOR DROVE US TO ZOE'S HOUSE, AND THEN...

EPILOGUE

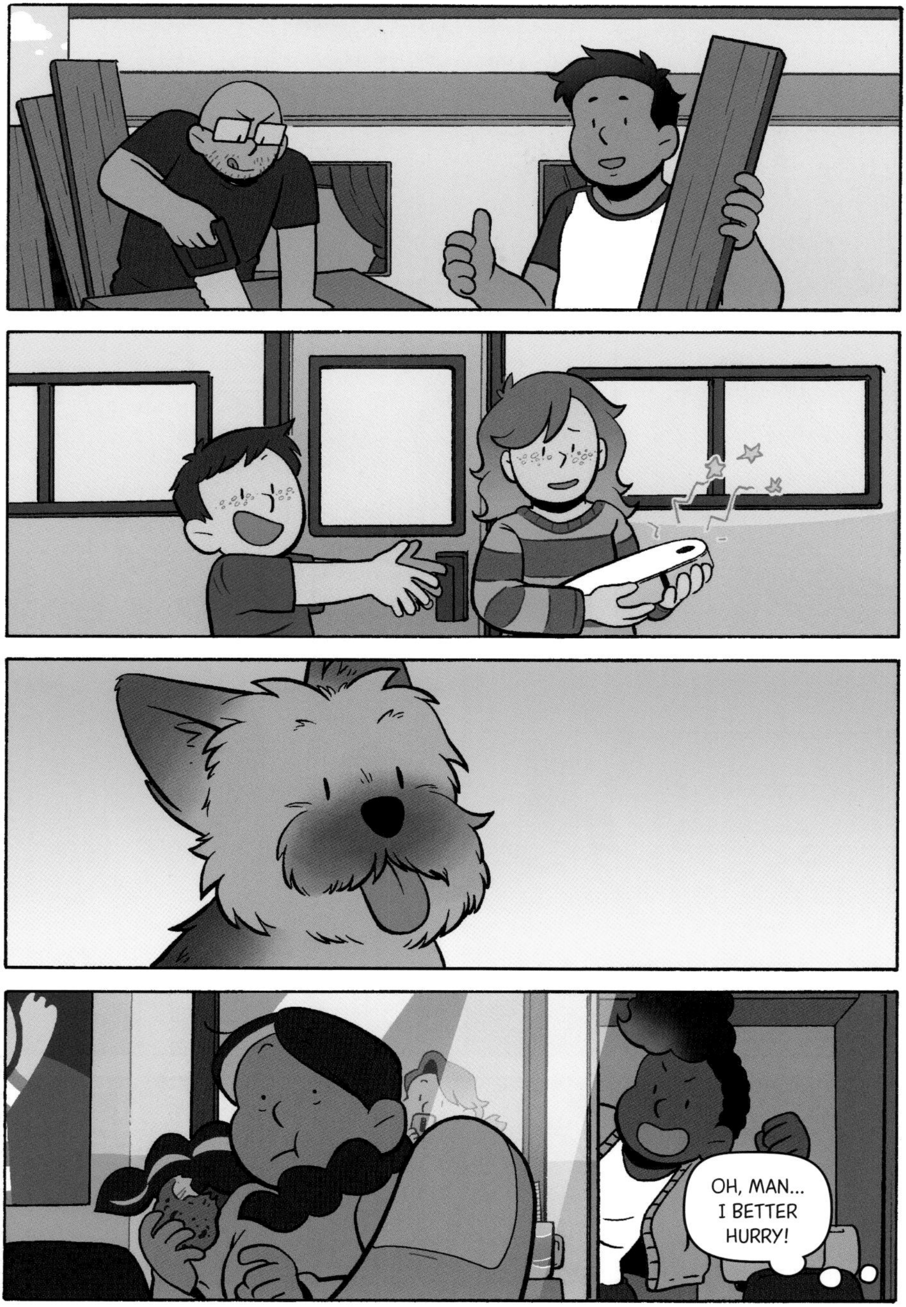
OH, MAN...
I BETTER
HURRY!

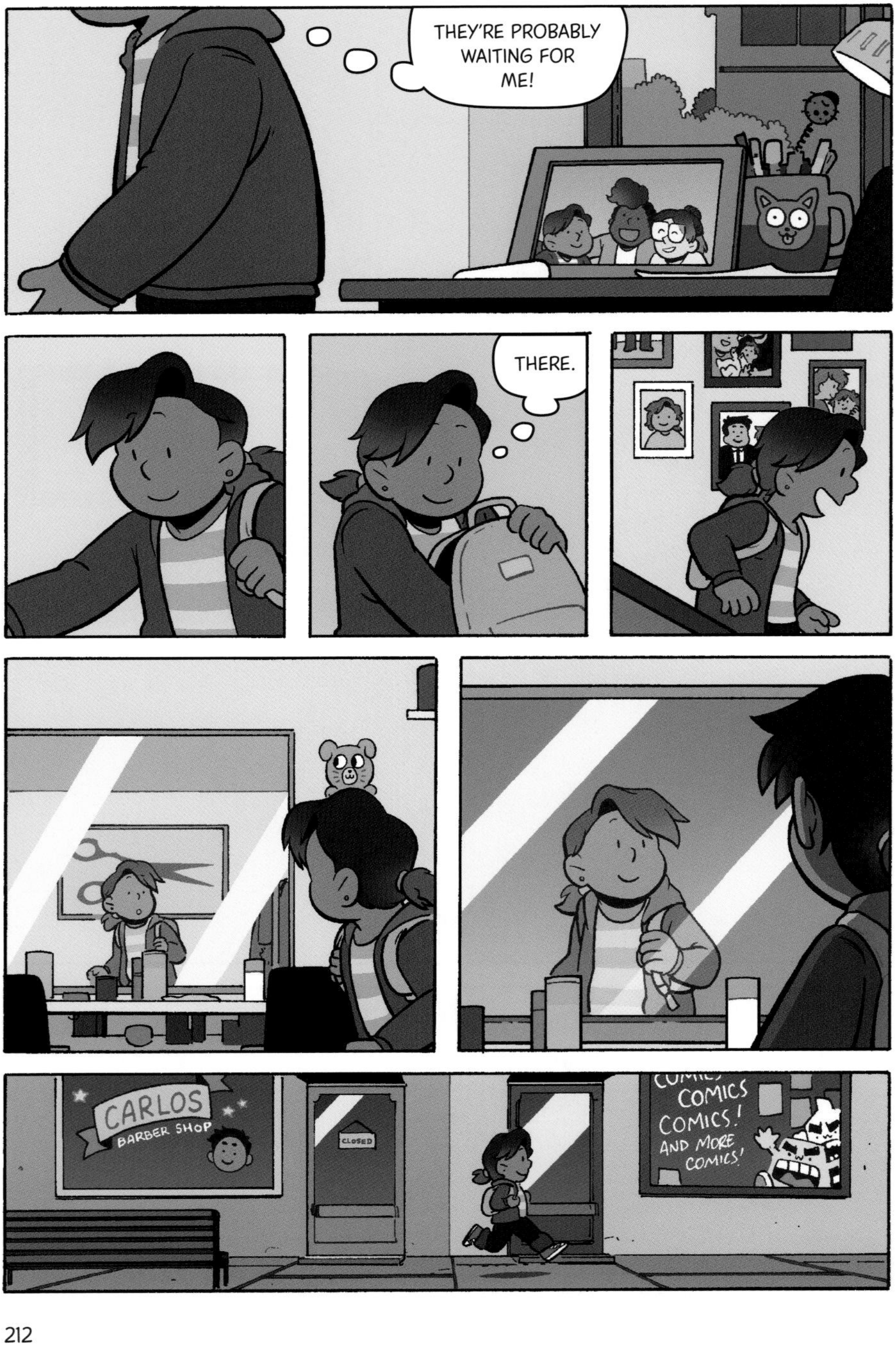
THEY'RE PROBABLY WAITING FOR ME!
THERE.
CARLOS
BARBER SHOP
CLOSED
COMICS
COMICS!
AND MORE COMICS!

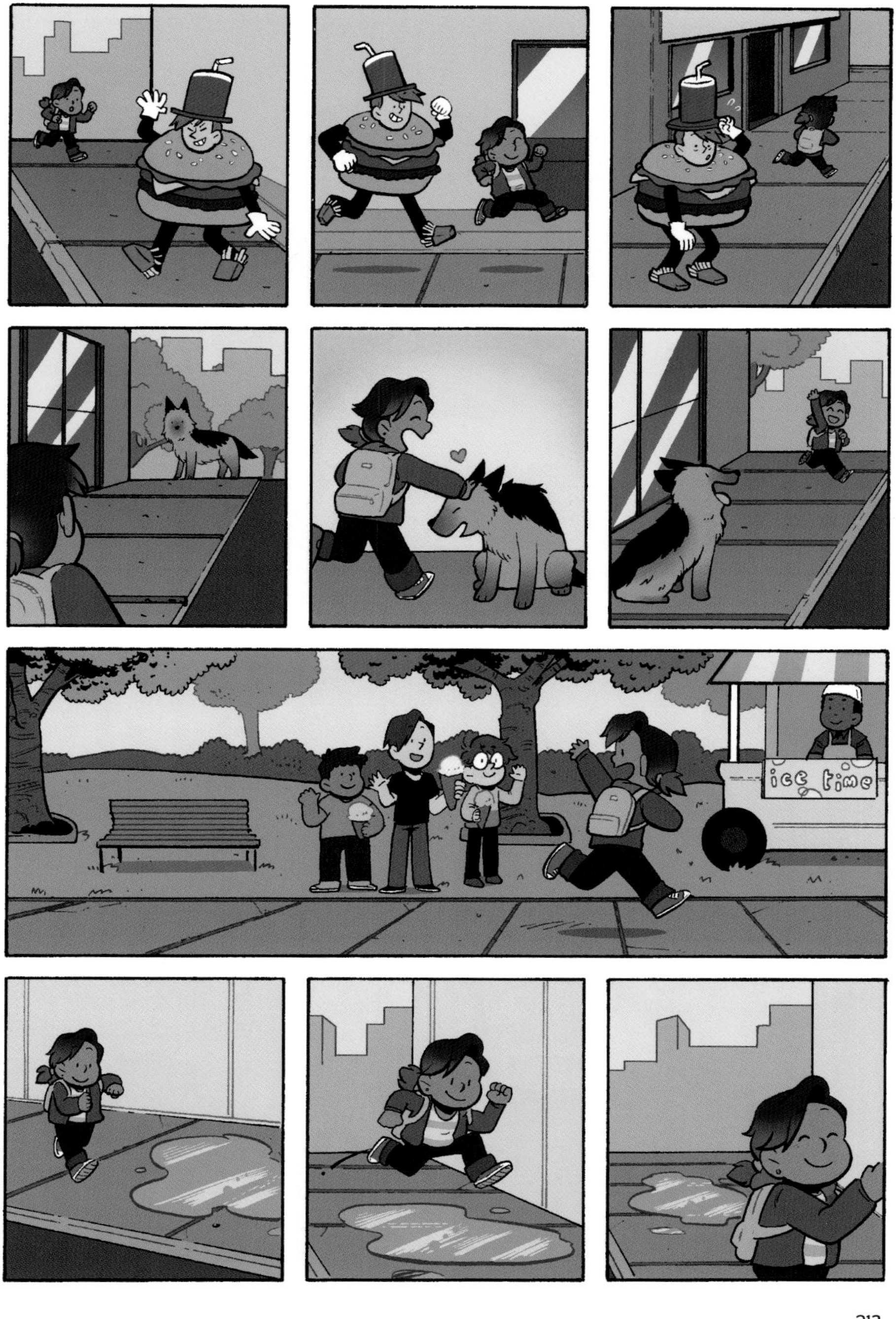
ice time

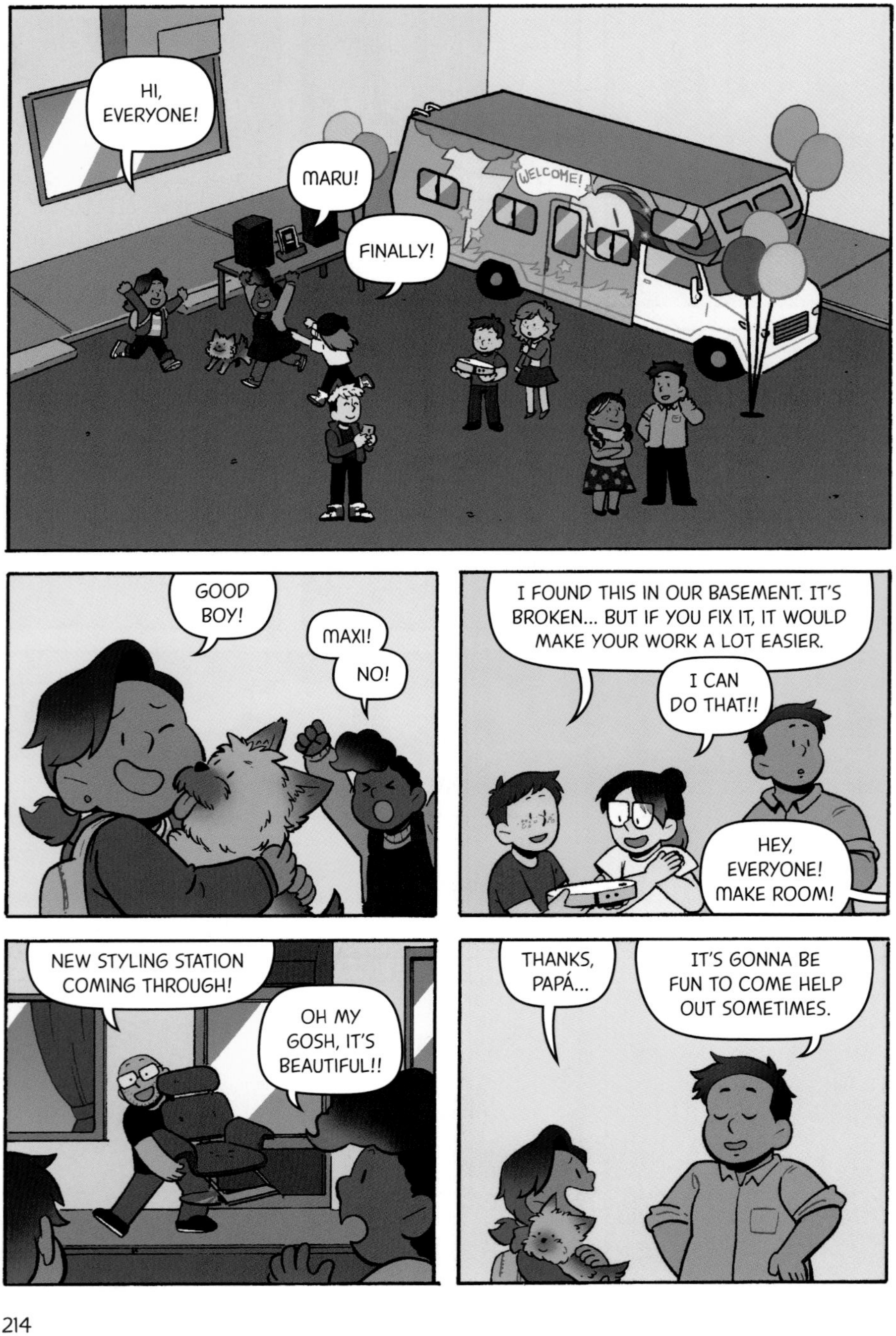
HI, EVERYONE!
MARU!
FINALLY!
WELCOME!
GOOD BOY!
MAXI!
NO!
I FOUND THIS IN OUR BASEMENT. IT'S BROKEN... BUT IF YOU FIX IT, IT WOULD MAKE YOUR WORK A LOT EASIER.
I CAN DO THAT!!
HEY, EVERYONE! MAKE ROOM!
NEW STYLING STATION COMING THROUGH!
OH MY GOSH, IT'S BEAUTIFUL!!
THANKS, PAPÁ...
IT'S GONNA BE FUN TO COME HELP OUT SOMETIMES.

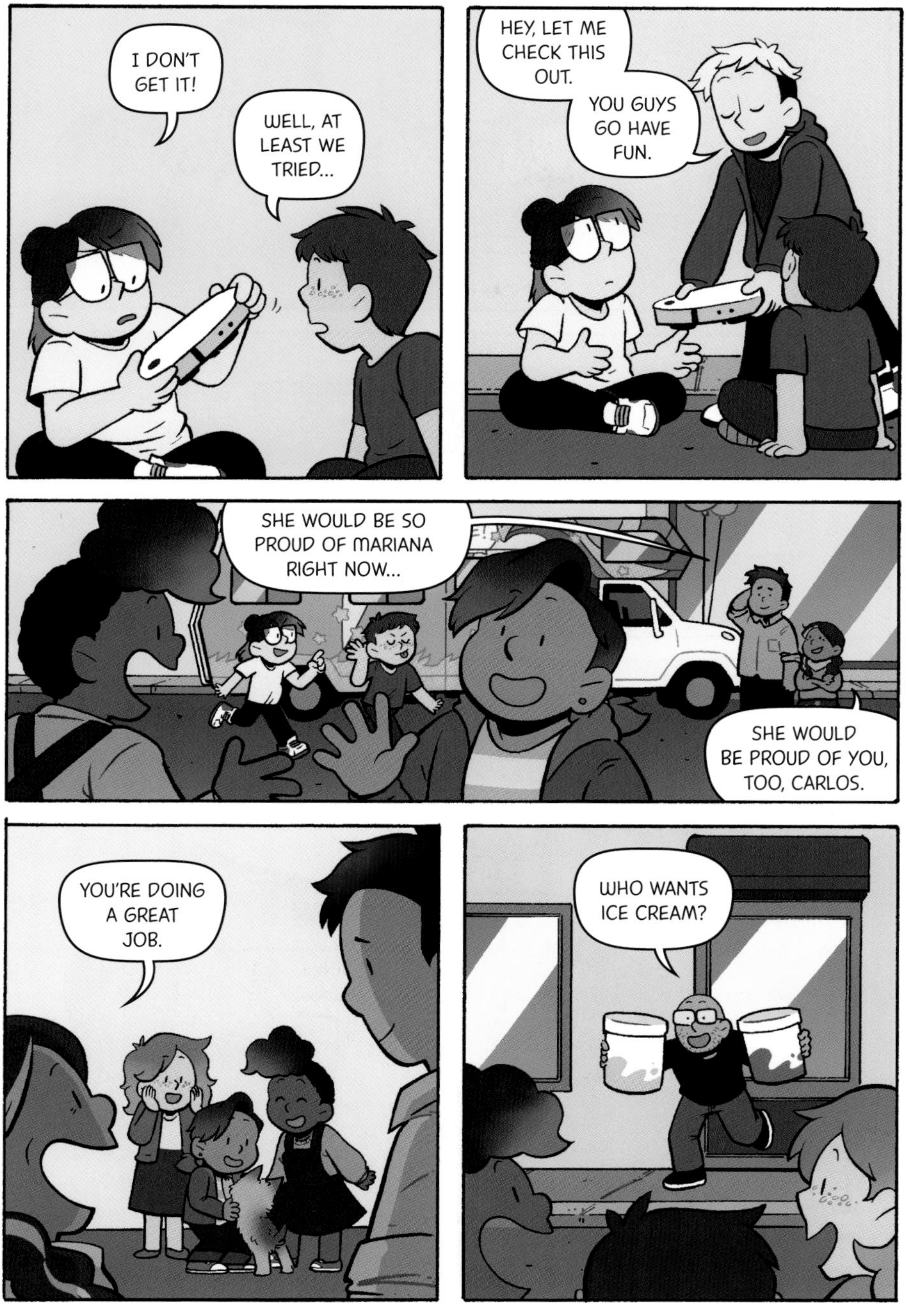

I DON'T GET IT!
WELL, AT LEAST WE TRIED...
HEY, LET ME CHECK THIS OUT.
YOU GUYS GO HAVE FUN.
SHE WOULD BE SO PROUD OF MARIANA RIGHT NOW...
SHE WOULD BE PROUD OF YOU, TOO, CARLOS.
YOU'RE DOING A GREAT JOB.
WHO WANTS ICE CREAM?

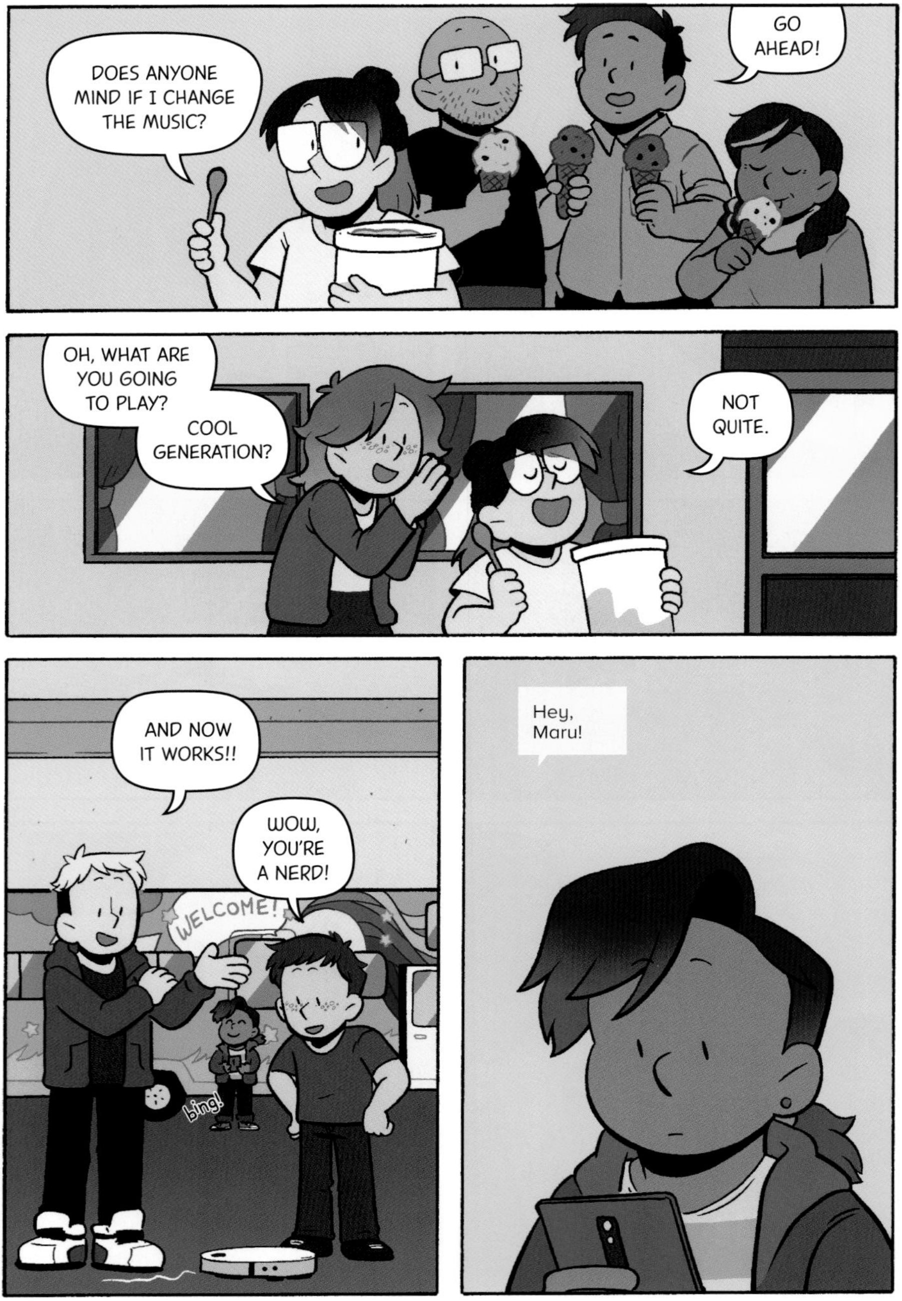
DOES ANYONE MIND IF I CHANGE THE MUSIC?
GO AHEAD!
OH, WHAT ARE YOU GOING TO PLAY?
COOL GENERATION?
NOT QUITE.
AND NOW IT WORKS!!
WOW, YOU'RE A NERD!
WELCOME!
bing!
Hey, Maru!

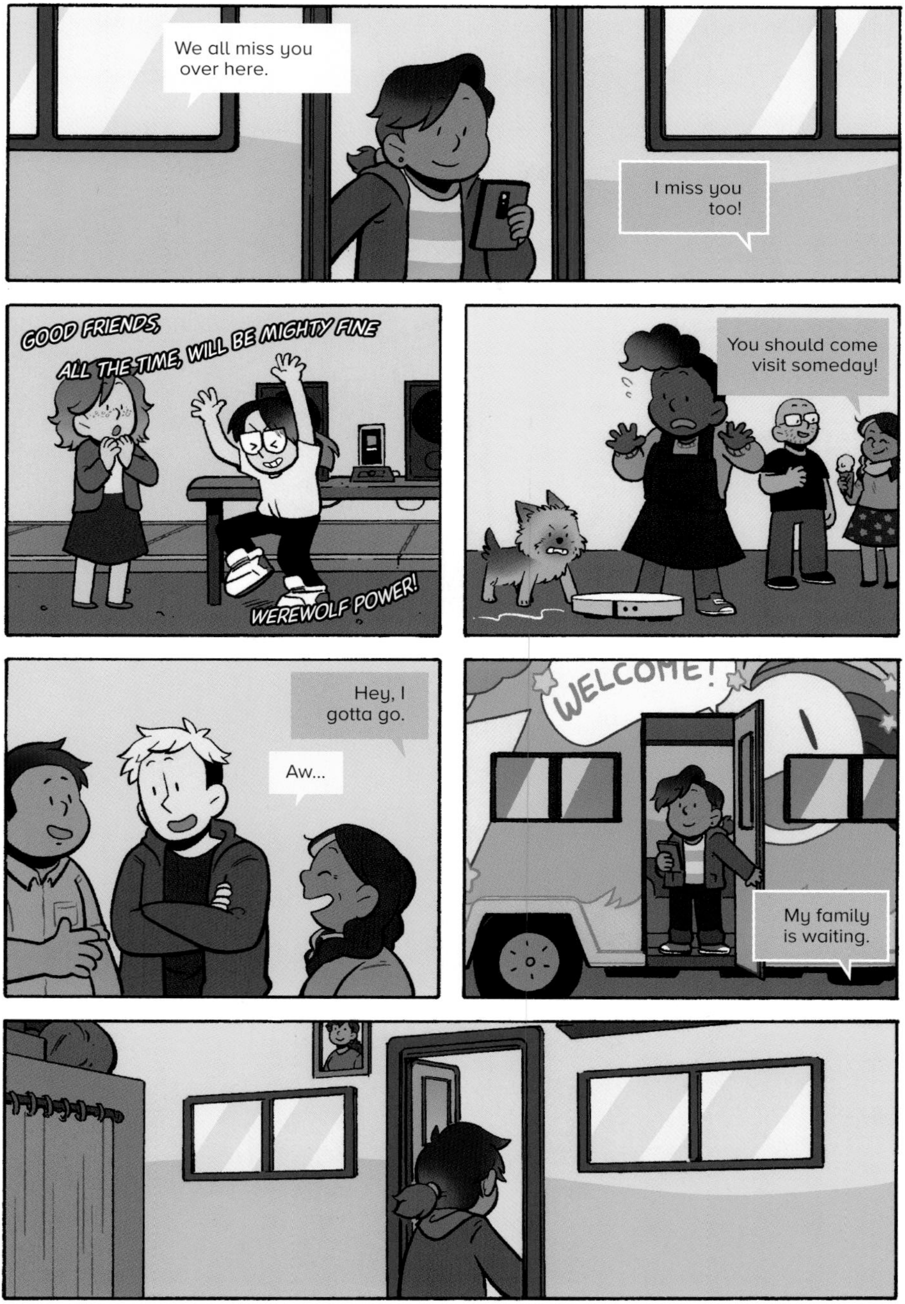
We all miss you over here.
I miss you too!
GOOD FRIENDS, ALL THE TIME, WILL BE MIGHTY FINE
WEREWOLF POWER!
You should come visit someday!
Hey, I gotta go.
Aw...
WELCOME!
My family is waiting.

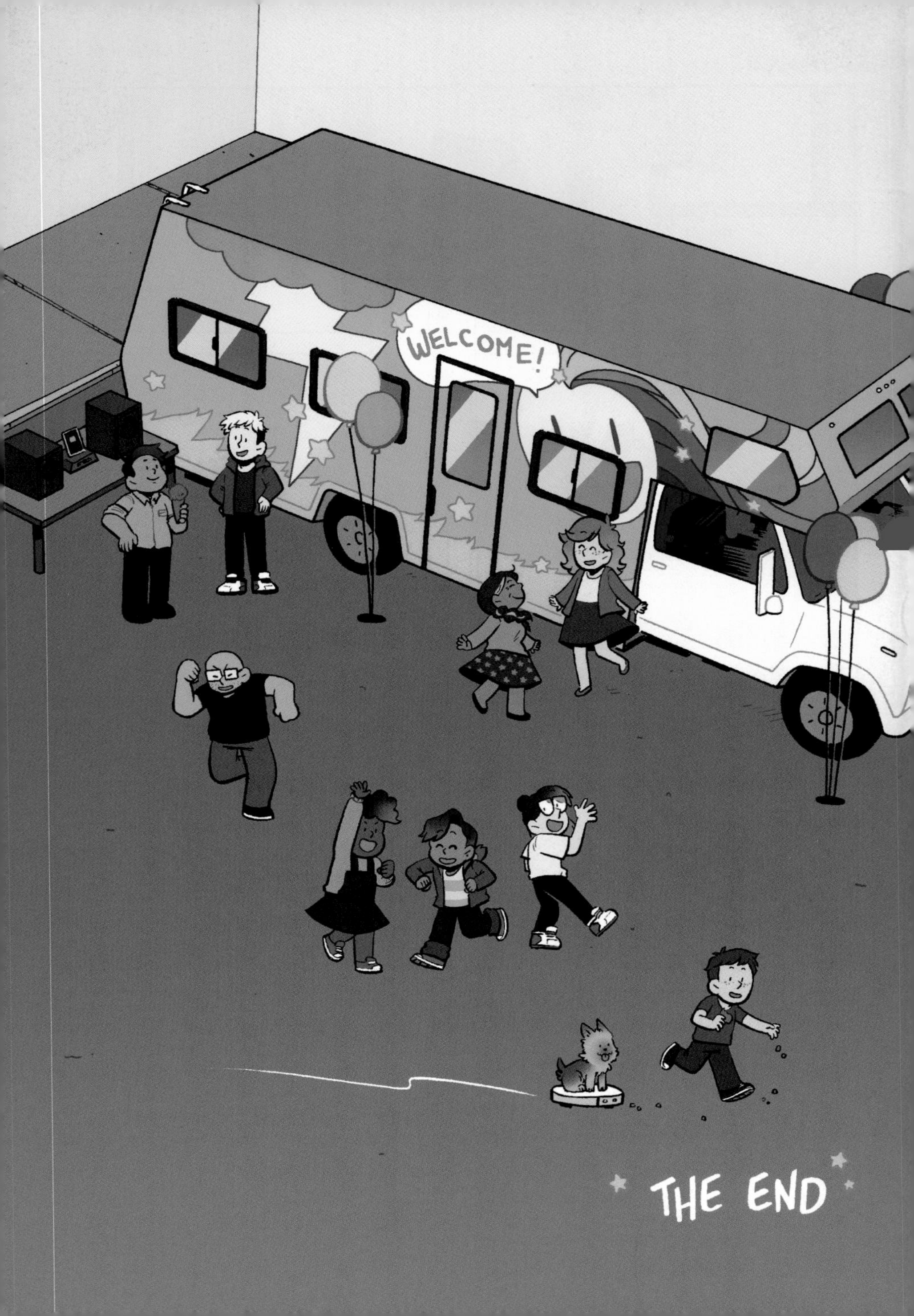
WELCOME!
THE END